W9-CKH-307

The Amish Clockmaker

The Amish Clockmaker

MINDY STARNS CLARK
SUSAN MEISSNER

HARVEST HOUSE PUBLISHERS
EUGENE, OREGON

Scripture quotations are taken from the King James Version of the Bible.

Cover by Garborg Design Works, Savage, Minnesota

Cover photos © Chris Garborg; Bigstock / DWStock

The authors are represented by MacGregor Literary, Inc.

This is a work of fiction. Names, characters, places, and incidents are products of the authors' imaginations or are used fictitiously. Any resemblance to actual persons, living or dead, is entirely coincidental.

The quote by William Andrews on page 7 is from an article titled "The Shadow Knows" by Dava Sobel, dated January 2007, and can be found at this link: www.smithsonianmag.com/science-nature/the-shadow-knows-142866936/#yjYbSu5vM7pkQQJc.99.

THE AMISH CLOCKMAKER
Copyright © 2015 by Mindy Starns Clark and Susan Meissner
Published by Harvest House Publishers
Eugene, Oregon 97402

ISBN 978-1-62953-338-4

Printed in the United States of America

In loving memory of
Mariette Smith,
1970 – 2013.
Precious friend,
sister in Christ,
fantastic mother,
adoring wife,
avid reader,
amazing woman,
missed beyond all measure.

Acknowledgments

Thanks so much to…

Everyone at Harvest House Publishers, in particular our wonderful editor and friend, Kim Moore.

Chip MacGregor, our literary agent, who brought about this collaboration.

John Clark, loving husband to Mindy and her number one story consultant/ idea man/ information resource.

Emily Clark, whose talent and dedication helped make this book a reality.

Rich Scannell, Ned Scannell, and Isaac and Lorraine Kauffman, for patiently answering our numerous questions.

The Riehl, Fisher, and Stoltzfus families of Lancaster County, for sharing your knowledge and your homes and businesses with us.

Lauren Clark and Tara Kenny, for being so helpful throughout the process.

To be a clockmaker is to work not just for yourself or your client, but also for someone else far in the future, someone who knows enough to judge your work and who will look at something you've made someday and—you hope—say, "That was done right."

William Andrewes, Curator
Harvard University Collection of
Historical Scientific Instruments

PART ONE
Matthew

One

Standing at the edge of the grassy lot, I squinted my eyes in the predawn darkness and envisioned the future. Construction hadn't even started yet, but I had pictured this place so many times in my mind that it was nearly real to me already, from the sweep of the roofline to the span of the side walls to the stretch of the covered walkway that would connect it to the barn. Once completed, the remodeled building wouldn't be fancy or showy, but it would be big—twice as big, in fact, as what we had now.

The expansion of Zook's Feed and Tack, my family's store, was set to begin in just two hours, not a minute too soon as far as I was concerned. My parents didn't exactly see it that way, but in the end it had been my decision. They would come around eventually—at least I hoped they would—but I didn't have time to wait. If I was going to save this company, I had to keep things moving forward. God had blessed us with some exciting opportunities, but taking advantage of them meant first doubling our space and our inventory.

God willing, we'd end up doubling our revenue as well.

Such a thought should have left me feeling excited and eager to get started. Instead, my emotions were mixed. On the one hand, I was thrilled to be breaking ground today and confident this expansion was the right move for us to take. On the other hand, I was frustrated with my father, with how he could not—*would* not—understand or embrace my vision. He and I had always gotten on so well, and he was a kind and godly man, but this situation had created a rift between us I feared we'd never be able to mend.

To make matters worse, a deep ache of loss had been rising up inside of me for days. That feeling came from the knowledge that my beloved grandfather—my kindred spirit in so many ways—wasn't here to share in this day with me. At least *Grossdaadi* had been in on the early planning, I told myself as I began walking across the dewy grass. He'd known and approved of my intentions before he died—and that was some consolation.

Then again, he had passed away more than three months ago, before the final plans were drawn up, before the crew was hired, before we were even certain we'd be able to pull this off. Now that it was finally happening, I missed him with an intensity that hadn't felt so piercing since the day of his funeral.

I came to a stop at the center of the scruffy, unused piece of land that stretched out beside and behind the current building and would be the site of today's construction. The last thing added to our property was a little cottage up by the house that had been put in a few years ago, when one of my older brothers was getting married. Amanda and I were living there now, but ultimately it would become my parents' home, their *daadi haus*, and Amanda and I would shift over to the main house.

This homestead sat on a hill, low at the front and higher at the back. Heading up our driveway, which ran along the right side of the property, one would encounter first the parking lot, then the tack store, the feed store, a horse barn, the main house, the cottage, and a small fenced-in field out back. At five acres total, this place wasn't big enough to call a farm, though we did own two horses and enough pastureland to keep them fed. Beyond that, we lived more like city folk than our friends and fellow church members, many of whom were farmers.

Standing now between the tack shop and the driveway next door, I glanced toward the eastern horizon and gauged the time. The sky had grown brighter in just the past few minutes, and I knew the sun would soon emerge above the trees. But there was still no one in sight at the moment, and the road that ran in front of the shop—the main thoroughfare of Ridgeview, Pennsylvania—was quiet and empty, several hours away from the busy commerce and congestion of the coming day.

Thus alone and unobserved, I lowered myself to my knees on the grass, removed my hat, bowed my head, and began to pray. My intention was to ask, yet again, that God's will, not mine, be done in this entire matter. But after a few minutes, I found my mind again returning to thoughts of *Grossdaadi*.

Taking a deep breath, I tried to still my thoughts and simply listen for the voice of God, so that His peace could flow through me. And though the frustration over the situation with my father did not abate, the grief over the loss of my grandfather did begin to lessen noticeably, almost as if the Lord's healing spirit was spreading a cooling salve over a painful burn.

Finally, my mind moved back into prayer, and I asked God for the safety and health of our workers over the coming days, not to mention the patience and good will of our customers. It wasn't going to be easy to get through this period of construction, I knew, but in the end it should be worth it, especially if Zook's became the number one source for feed and tack in all of Lancaster County, which was the idea.

Though only if that's Your plan, Lord. Show me how to see Your will clearly. Open doors You want me to go through and close those You do not.

Before a final "amen," I thanked Him for easing my sorrow and asked Him to soften my heart toward my father. *May I live in a way that honors* Daed*'s authority while also rescuing* Grossdaadi*'s legacy. Thank You for Your love and grace. Amen.*

Feeling much more at peace, I opened my eyes and got to my feet. As I was brushing wet grass from my knees, I heard a gentle, familiar voice behind me.

"Matthew?"

I turned to see my wife, Amanda, standing not too far away and gazing at me with a sweet smile.

"I thought I might find you here," she said softly, coming a few steps closer. "I'm not interrupting, am I?"

"Nope. All done," I replied, smoothing my unruly hair and then plopping my hat onto my head.

"I always love it when I catch you in prayer," she said, coming to a stop in front of me.

She tilted her head to look up at me, but as she studied my face, her smile began to fade. "You're not still thinking about what your *daed* said to you last night, are you?"

I shrugged and looked away. "I was praying about the expansion."

"Praying what, exactly? That God would convict you if this really is about 'your own personal ambitions'?" There was a mocking tone to her voice as she repeated the words my *daed* had said to me just last night. She'd found the whole conversation very upsetting, though she'd managed to hold her tongue until we were alone and she could vent in private.

I slid my thumbs under my suspenders. "*Daed* made some good points. Like how this whole project needs to be in God's hands. The expansion, the growth, the profit projections—all of that has to fit His plan, not mine. It doesn't hurt to be reminded."

"But you've known that—you've *done* that—all along, every step of the way. I can't imagine anyone following the Lord's leading more obediently than you have in this matter."

I closed my eyes, feeling something shift inside, a little piece that my father's words had broken in me last night being restored now by my wife's loving reassurance.

"Besides, your *daed* is the main reason you're having to do this expansion in the first place. I'm just glad you were able to come up with an idea to save the store before it was too late."

She tried to meet my eyes, but I looked away as she continued. "Matthew, you know very well that your father doesn't have the skills to manage this place, but you do. Your actions here aren't unwise or self-serving, no matter what he says. They're smart. You're just being a good steward of the family's business."

I slipped an arm about her shoulders and pulled her close before she could see the hint of tears her words brought to my eyes. I blinked the wetness away as I rested my chin on the top of her head, glad I was so much taller than she. As usual, she'd spoken to the exact issue weighing on my heart. The family discord over this expansion had been bothering me more than I'd been willing to admit.

"Your *daed* just needs a little time to adjust." Amanda wrapped her arms more tightly around my waist, and I could feel the amazing shape of her hard, round belly between us, the child that she would be bringing into the world in just two more months, God willing. "Once he sees so many new customers start pouring in, he'll come around."

"Maybe. Then again, maybe I should have—"

"Don't."

"But what if—"

"Shhh," she replied, pulling back to place a finger against my lips. "Matthew, look, I don't mean to sound disrespectful, really I don't. He may have nearly run this place into the ground, but just because your *daed* is bad at business doesn't mean he's a bad person. Quite the opposite, in fact. Harlan Zook is a good, good man. Faithful and patient and kind. As loving to me as my own father."

"*Ya*. He is."

She gazed up at me, her eyes pleading, her expression earnest. "But you know and I know that he did not belong at the helm of this company. Your grandfather knew it more than anyone—which is why he finally put you in charge. Once the profits start rolling in and your *daed* sees what a good move this was…" She reached for my arm and gave it a reassuring squeeze. "He'll be fine. I promise. Just tell me one thing."

"*Ya?*"

"Are there any questions in *your* mind about the necessity and wisdom of this expansion? Any doubts or concerns about it at all?"

I thought long and hard, and then I shook my head slowly from side to side. "I've never been more sure of a decision in my life."

She hesitated. "Never?"

It took me a moment to notice the teasing glint in her eye, and then I smiled.

"I'll try that again," I amended. "Except for the decision to marry you—"

"That's more like it." She grinned.

"—I've never been more sure of anything in my life." As the words came out of my mouth, I knew they were true. I was certain about this.

"There you go," she said with finality. "That's all that really matters, now isn't it?"

I gave her a nod and turned and looked out across the grassy area that would soon be full of men with stakes and mallets and framing squares. Standing there taking it in, a snip of a proverb came to mind, the one about a prudent wife being from the Lord.

I couldn't have agreed more.

Feeling much better, I shifted my gaze to a completely different construction site, the one right next door where a big, fancy resort hotel was slowly being put in. The place was still idle at this early hour, but the sun was fully up now, and its rays glinted off the shiny metal of the huge machinery there, trucks and tractors and backhoes that were lying dormant all about the property. By eight or nine the place would be crawling with activity as usual, the construction progressing in the typical *Englisch* manner. Meanwhile, we'd have our own kind of activity starting over here, though our methods would be decidedly more Amish.

"Are you hungry?" Amanda asked, gesturing toward the house.

I nodded, but just as she was about to turn and go, I grabbed her wrist, pulled her back toward me, and leaned down to bring my lips to hers.

She returned my kiss with enthusiasm. When we pulled apart, she gazed up at me.

"I love you, Matthew," she whispered. "And I believe in you. God will take care of everything, including your father."

I slipped a hand into hers, and together we walked toward the house, where I knew she would already have a warm breakfast on the stove. My stomach growled at the thought and I smiled, feeling much more at peace now than I had when first coming out here.

"What are these?" Amanda asked as we walked past a grouping of stakes I'd hammered into the ground the day before.

"They're markers for when the guys start putting in the foundation. They'll need to accommodate for some old footings."

"Footings?"

"For a post and pier."

Amanda came to a stop at the nearest stake and dropped my hand.

"A what and what?"

I smiled. "Post and pier. It's a type of foundation that uses concrete with wood beams and joists, supported by wood posts. The ones here are hidden down in the grass. They're quite old, as though they've been here forever."

Amanda knelt to study the ground next to the stake, seeing what I was talking about, footings that had been so overgrown for so long that she'd never even realized they were there. "Are there many of these things out here?" she asked.

"No, just the four. Which will be no problem as long as the men get them fully encased in the concrete. They already know about them. I just came out yesterday and marked the locations to make it easier for them to see exactly where the things are."

Amanda ran her hand over the concrete square, which was about a foot across and flush to the ground. "So are you saying there was a house out here at one time?"

I shrugged. "Too small to be a house. Maybe a toolshed or some other kind of farm building."

"What does the writing on it mean?"

"Writing?" I knelt down to get a closer look as she brushed away some grass clippings.

Sure enough, though the grooves had worn shallow over time, at the center of the square were some letters and numbers that someone had carved into the cement long ago:

MMCR
MK 1:35

"I don't know," I said, rising back to a standing position. "I never noticed it before. Must be some sort of notation for the builder."

Amanda glanced up at me from the ground, a twinkle in her eye. "That, or some secret message from the past."

I smiled. "Well, here's my message for the future. If this man doesn't get some biscuits and ham soon, he's going to end up one very hungry fellow."

I helped her to her feet, and with a smile of her own she said, "I'd better get you fed, then."

She took my hand and together we headed for home.

Two

The crew began arriving early. Coming down from the cottage after breakfast at quarter 'til eight, I spotted a small cluster of men waiting in the parking lot in front of the store. Amanda was right behind me, both of us loaded down with supplies.

We greeted the men—two relatives, three neighbors, and a few other fellow church members—with our thanks. I unlocked the door of the tack store and swung it open. Watching the men stream inside, I felt a surge of pure adrenaline.

Coming in behind them, I left the door unlocked but kept the "Closed" sign in place. I hated the loss of income from being shut down during the construction, but in the long run it would be worth it.

Amanda and I moved toward the register area, which offered a wide countertop for setting up the coffee and baked goods we'd brought along. I put down my load and started to help her with hers, but she shooed me away with a smile, preferring to take it from there herself.

Smiling in return, I moved off to one side and simply watched the bustle of activity before me. As Amanda laid out the treats and the men milled around, chatting among themselves and waiting to dig in, my mind returned to thoughts of my grandfather and how very much I wished he were here now.

Grossdaadi had been such a whiz at business, buying this place—house, barn, and store—back in the 1950s and turning what had been a dilapidated old clock shop into the shiny new Zook's Feed and Tack. Over the years it had become a solid company with a good reputation, a fixture of our town and indeed of Lancaster County.

Where things had gone wrong was when the time came for *Grossdaadi* to step down and let his only son—my father—take over the running of the business. That had always been the plan, despite the fact that *Daed* obviously hadn't inherited his father's gifts in this area. While the job required skills in sales, accounting, inventory control, and purchasing, *Daed* was far more suited to his position of leatherworker, which he'd held for years. Creative, artistic, and introspective, *Daed* could spend hours in his workshop at the back of the barn, turning out not just sturdy but beautiful, high-quality leather items for the tack shop. Put a grainer or a mace or a scoring iron in his hand and the man was a natural, but give him a calculator or a purchase order or an account book and he was completely lost.

Nevertheless, my grandfather handed over the reins when it could be put off no longer, and then for five long years my father ran this place, despite his lack of business skills, with my grandfather trying to help from the background and quietly suffering in silence as many aspects of the store began to decline. To put it bluntly, *Daed* nearly ran Zook's into the ground. Between his inability to delegate and manage time, his poor record-keeping, and his countless errors in judgment, the store took quite a few hits and profits plummeted.

That was why last December, just a month after Amanda and I were wed, Grandfather announced that *Daed* would no longer be in charge; I would. The decision itself hadn't been a huge surprise to anyone, as we all knew I seemed to have inherited my grandfather's knack for this kind of work, not to mention that I was the only one in the family who enjoyed it as much as he did. Neither of my older brothers had been interested, especially once they were grown and married and given other opportunities through their wives' families. I had always been the obvious choice.

The surprise of *Grossdaadi*'s announcement hadn't been about the "who" but the "when," given our respective ages. After all, *Daed* had just turned fifty-five, far too young to retire. And I was only twenty-four, barely old enough to take on such a huge responsibility.

Fortunately, rather than being hurt or angry by my grandfather's decision, my father had seemed almost relieved. He'd known how badly things were going—and he'd missed his prior position as the store's sole leatherworker. He returned to his workshop at the rear of the barn as I stepped into the manager position, and we had all quickly been able to find a new balance. The transition was achieved with a minimum of fuss, and life remained peaceful at home and at work, for the most part.

But that didn't mean the job of digging out from under the mess my father had created was an easy one. It had taken me several weeks just to figure out where we stood. After that, I'd spent many an evening with the books and many a morning on my knees, asking the good Lord for a miracle, for something that could save the business and bring us back into the black.

Then, as if in response to those prayers, two huge opportunities arose at once, both of which had the potential for providing us with a much larger customer base. First came the news that our biggest competitor, an *Englisch*-owned feed store about ten miles away called Waggoner's Animal Supply, would be going out of business at the end of the summer when the owner retired. That would leave a huge number of locals in need of a new source for their animal feed and tack. Second, construction finally began on what was to become a fancy new resort next door to our shop. It would be a good while before the hotel was up and rolling, but eventually it would bring a surge of tourist-heavy foot traffic, something we'd always tolerated but had never thought to take advantage of or encourage.

With these two developments staring me in the face, I found new hope. I dug in and began to research both opportunities, exploring how we might best attract and serve the customers from Waggoner's, especially if I could get that store's management to work in cooperation with us. I also looked into what types of merchandise we could add to our inventory that would fit within the parameters of a feed and tack store and yet appeal to the resort's *Englisch* tourists.

The tack portion of our store had always carried equipment and supplies for horses and other animals—everything from leather straps to cowbells to dog shampoo. But now it was time to start thinking bigger and broader about what we could offer. Amanda had been a big help with that, pointing out the number of Amish-made goods, such as quilted placemats or wooden toys, that featured animals in their designs. She believed we could add a line of such items to our stock and the tourists would snatch them up. We already carried Amish-made birdhouses, and those were a huge hit among the *Englisch*. If other Amish-made, animal-related items sold half as well as the birdhouses did, we'd be doing great. More than eight million visitors flocked annually to Lancaster County—that was twenty visitors a year per resident—so I knew the math regarding this expansion idea was on my side.

The biggest impediment I could see to our plan was the limited amount of space we had to work with. Waggoner's was wide and spacious and visually appealing, while Zook's was small and cramped and stuffed with goods from one end to the other. If we wanted to hang on to even a small portion of Waggoner's customers, then we had no choice but to grow—and fast. We had enough unused land beside and behind the store to make that feasible. And we had just enough cash reserves to afford the construction, as long as we moved on it immediately. But those reserves were dwindling weekly, so we had to act now or it would be too late.

All of my careful research and planning told me this would be a smart move, and when I presented the idea to my grandfather, he understood exactly what I was saying and approved one hundred percent. But then there was my father who, with his lack of business instincts, couldn't see the point no matter what proof I offered—even after I met with Mr. Waggoner and he and I agreed that if I would buy the bulk of his used fixtures and his non-returnable stock, he would promote our store to his customers via flyers and coupons and personal recommendation up until the day he closed. Being an *Englischer*, he also talked about putting the information into his online newsletter, sending out an e-blast to his mailing list, and utilizing social media, but I didn't know much about all that. What I did know was that he was a good and fair man, and that the solution I was offering him worked out beautifully for us both. Now that he didn't have to worry that his customers would be abandoned, he could thoroughly enjoy his retirement, and I could be fairly certain many of them would at least give us a try.

Even then my father still didn't agree. My *grossdaadi* passed away about the time I started taking measurements and drawing up plans for the expansion, but at least I'd already obtained his approval—not that it made any difference to *Daed*. From the moment my idea began to become a reality, he and I had been butting heads—and my mother, as a good wife, had taken her husband's side, even though I could tell she was ambivalent about it. Now the two of them stood united against me, terrified I was being foolhardy and would end up leaving us with no store at all and not a penny to our names. They kept harping on the fact that the construction costs would deplete all our reserves and make us dependent on the expanded store's success. My response was that if we kept doing things as we had been, those reserves would soon be gone anyway.

Bottom line, what they couldn't see was that there was nothing foolhardy about any of this. I'd been cautious and meticulous and diligent every step of the way, and now I was as sure as anyone in my position could be that this was the right move to make.

My thoughts were interrupted by the arrival of my little brother, Noah, who came dashing into the tack store with just a few minutes to spare, sweaty and breathless—no doubt from having rushed around getting ready and then running all the way down the drive to get here. I noticed *Daed* wasn't with him and was about to ask whether or not he'd be coming when I thought better of it. Either he would show up or not, and that was between him and me. There was no reason to drag Noah into the middle of it.

I gave my redheaded little brother a smile and a light punch to the shoulder before directing him toward the register, where he joined in with the happy throng and was soon juggling a giant muffin, a steaming cup of coffee, and a handful of paper napkins. The rest of the crew finished trickling in, and then we were ready to start.

My cousin Virgil, a skilled carpenter, was the foreman of the work crew and the one to lead us in prayer. There in the store, we all stood clustered together, heads bowed, eyes closed, each one speaking to God silently in his own way.

I prayed for safety and harmony and good weather, and I thanked the Lord again for this tremendous opportunity. I also asked Him to soften my father's heart in this matter and to guide me in reconciling with him. So strongly did I feel that God could and would do just that, I opened my eyes before the prayer time was over, half expecting to see my *daed* standing before me with outstretched arms.

He wasn't.

With a hearty "amen" from Virgil, the room sprang back to life. As the men began to get organized, I looked around and realized my father was still conspicuously absent. That thought bothered me more than I cared to admit.

Speaking over the chatter, Virgil began to address the group, and everyone quieted down as he explained the order of events and the various duties each person would be performing today. Most of these men were experienced in construction and didn't need much by way of instructions, but the expansion of an existing structure was a bit trickier than the erection of an entirely new one.

This building was in the shape of a large rectangle, the front two thirds containing the retail store and the back third containing an employees-only section that housed a small administrative area, an ancient bathroom, and lots of heavy-duty fixtures that dated back to the fifties, when this place used to be Raber and Son Clockmakers. Our plan was to expand in two directions—out and back—which meant relocating two of the building's four existing walls, not an easy task. Making matters even more complicated was the fact that those walls were currently lined with large, heavy shelving units from one end to the other.

Over the past few days we'd been able to empty those shelves, shifting their inventory to the barn to get it out of the way. Now we just needed to dismantle and remove the empty shelving units and cover up the remaining inventory with tarps to protect it from the dust and flying debris to come.

At the same time all of that was being done, the rest of the men would be outside getting a start on marking out the measurements and laying down the footings. We had a lot to do, but my hope was that by the end of this day the interior would have been dismantled and the footings and foundation poured.

Efficient and experienced, the men broke into groups and got down to work. My job was to help carry the dismantled shelves back to the barn. After my last trip, I remained there for a few minutes to make sure everything had been placed correctly. All was as it should be, with the older wooden shelves propped against the wall and the newer metal ones piled up under the eaves.

As I stepped outside, I couldn't help but glance over at the big resort hotel construction site next door, just now coming alive with activity for the day. It hadn't exactly been a picnic for us these past few months, living and working in such close proximity to so massive a project. Amanda complained about the dust that coated her clean laundry as soon as she put it out on the line. *Mamm* didn't like the coarse language and loud voices of the workers. *Daed* hated the sound of the machinery when it backed up, the piercing *beep-beep-beep* that went on all day long. My concern was for our current customers, who were also being inconvenienced by the noise and the dust, not to mention the frequent road congestion out front. We did what we could to minimize the aggravation, but we'd all be glad once it was over.

Unfortunately, that wasn't going to happen any time soon. Early in the planning stages for the expansion, I'd initiated a conversation with the foreman at the site—a brusque, muscular fellow in his early forties named Kenny

McKendrick—who had told me they were doing the work in two phases, with the first phase scheduled to be completed in about a year and a half. At that point they would open for business while moving on to the second phase, one that did not involve the main structure and would take an additional year or so.

Startled, I told him I couldn't imagine any construction project taking more than a few months, but he acted as if it were no big deal. With a laugh, he'd added that his last job—on a bigger, even fancier resort—had ended up taking five years.

I supposed that shouldn't have surprised me, given the lack of a work ethic we had observed among the crew. Often it seemed that for every one man laboring diligently over there, two or three more were standing around doing nothing. Part of me wondered if all that fancy machinery had made them forget how to roll up their sleeves and get their hands dirty.

Peering over at the site now from where I stood at the barn door, I spotted a case in point, a small cluster of workers hovering near a cement mixer, apparently doing nothing more strenuous than watching it turn. Behind them, movement caught my eye, and I realized it was Kenny, marching across the packed earth toward them, barking out orders as he went.

At that same moment, a handful of my own crew members emerged from the tack store's back door, loaded down with the equipment they would need—surveying tools, wooden stakes, mallets, and other implements—to get started on the footings and foundation. The men fanned out across the grass and got right down to business. I was expected inside the tack shop, however, so I headed there, ready for the next step.

I went in through the back, and it wasn't until I'd crossed the room and emerged into the front part of the store that I realized my father was there. I froze.

Apparently, he'd decided to show up after all.

Three

I hesitated near the doorway as I watched *Daed* interacting with Amanda and several of the men up front. I couldn't hear what they were saying, but judging by their postures and expressions, nothing contentious seemed to be going on. In fact, my father said something that made my wife throw her head back and laugh.

When I stepped forward, the movement caught his attention. With a tentative smile—one that looked very much like an olive branch—he turned and began heading in my direction. I met him halfway, out of earshot of everyone else. We both came to a stop and then just stood there, face-to-face. *Daed* reached out his hand without a word, and I responded in kind. With a firm grip on both sides, our eyes locked as we shook.

"Funny thing, this morning's Bible passage," he said in a low voice as his hand dropped back to his side.

"*Ya?*"

"*Ya*. It was about the three servants who were given talents by their master. They were supposed to invest them, but one got scared and buried his in the ground instead. When the master returned, he scolded that servant, saying something along the lines of you can't reap if you don't sow and you can't gather if you don't straw." With a shrug, he added, "I know I'm the bury-it-in-the-ground type, son, but maybe God wants you to sow and straw."

"Thank you, *Daed*," I replied, my voice gruff with emotion. "That means more to me than you can imagine."

We shook hands a second time, and after that I felt about a thousand pounds lighter.

He wandered back to Amanda to help spread more tarps over the inventory, and I returned to my next task, that of demolition. Together with Noah and my brother-in-law Andy, we took apart the old bathroom, piece by piece, and hauled it all away, including the sink and toilet. Then we donned masks, took up sledgehammers, and began knocking down the interior bathroom walls.

We were just starting to make some progress when I noticed one of the workers waving from the back door.

"*Ya?*" I asked, stepping away from the mess. I pulled the mask from my face and wiped the sweat off my brow with the back of my arm.

"We have a problem out here," he said, gesturing for me to come.

I couldn't imagine why I might be needed, but the urgency in his voice told me I should hurry. I set the mallet over to the side and told the other two I'd be back in a minute.

I went out the door and followed the guy toward the side of the building. As I came around the corner, I was surprised to see that the workers were just standing there, watching and listening as Kenny, the foreman from next door, stood in the middle of our construction area, yelling at Virgil.

On the ground around them were the stakes that had already been laid for the foundation, poking up out of the ground at intervals and connected by strings. As I moved closer, Kenny saw me coming and broke off mid-sentence. Then he began yelling at me instead.

"What do you think you're doing here?" he shouted.

"Expanding the feed store," I replied, coming to a stop in front of him. "I told you about it that day we talked. Why? What's the problem?"

After all the inconvenience we'd put up with from the construction next door, I couldn't believe he was going to harass us about our project now. At least I had all the right permits, which I'd be happy to show him once he calmed down.

"Yeah, I remember what you said, but you never told me you were going to build right here."

I stared at him for a long moment, trying to understand what was happening. "What's wrong with right here?"

He let out an angry growl and said, "It's not your property."

"What do you mean? Of course it is."

He shook his head emphatically. "No, it's not. Our hotel group is in negotiations to buy this land."

"Negotiations? With whom? This tack shop is ours. It's been in my family for three generations!"

He shook his head, a scornful expression crossing his face. "I'm not talking about the tack shop. I'm just talking about the land right here, beside the store." He gestured toward the ground all around us, explaining that the parcel in question ran two hundred and fifty feet from front to back and one hundred and seventy-five feet from side to side. "It's only an acre, but it's important that we acquire it."

"Listen, I don't know where you're getting your information, but this entire place—including the piece of land we're standing on—belongs to my family. To my parents, Harlan and Erma Zook. And it's not for sale."

Kenny hesitated, his brow furrowing. "Zook? No, that's not the owner's name. It's something else. I can't remember right now, but I'm sure it's in the paperwork."

"In the paperwork," I repeated, totally lost. What on earth was he talking about? "Listen Kenny, I assure you that my grandfather purchased this homestead almost sixty years ago. I can show you the deed. His name was Isaac Zook."

"Deed or not, my records tell me otherwise," Kenny replied, crossing his arms over his barrel-shaped chest. "You're going to have to cease and desist on your expansion until this is straightened out. You can direct your questions to our lawyer."

Cease and desist? Was he crazy? I glanced over at Virgil, who seemed as startled and confused as I was. Then I turned back toward the store where, judging by the muffled booms, Noah and Andy were still hard at work, smashing the bathroom walls to bits.

Kenny shifted in place and cleared his throat. "Do I need to contact the authorities to make you stop?"

Authorities? Like, the police? I shook my head in disbelief. "This is ridiculous. Wait here. I can straighten this whole thing out."

Turning my back on the man, I went inside the shop in search of *Daed*. I found him in the main area with Amanda and told him that the foreman from next door was outside, telling me that we had to stop our expansion because this wasn't our property.

"He said what?" Amanda asked.

"I need to show him the deed. I'm hoping that'll clear things up."

Daed said, "It had better."

"I assume it's in the box with all the important papers?"

With a nod from my father, I ran all the way to the main house at the top of the hill. I took the porch steps two at a time, relieved when I spotted *Mamm* at the clothesline out back. I really didn't want to explain anything right now.

Inside, I went straight to the living room and then to the old wooden breakfront where the family's important documents had always been kept. The lower cabinet held a fireproof metal box, so I knelt down and pulled it out, set it on the floor, and quickly began sifting through its contents—birth certificates, marriage licenses, and so on. I found the deed near the bottom in a manila file folder with several other property-related papers, including a survey map of the area.

Perfect. I grabbed the whole file, shoved the box back into the cabinet, and headed back out. By the time I reached the bottom of the hill, *Daed*, Amanda, Noah, and Andy had joined the other workers outside.

"Here's everything you need," I said as I handed Kenny the file. "Proof this land is ours. See for yourself."

He scanned the papers quickly and quietly, his frown setting even more deeply on his face. Around us, the only sounds I could hear were the whispers and murmurs of the workers. Suddenly, I found myself wishing that we could settle this matter in private, away from an audience. I turned my attention to Kenny, who seemed to be growing more confused the longer he studied the deed and survey map.

"Come with me," he grunted. He handed the papers back, turned sharply in the direction of his construction site, and began walking.

I told the crew to take a break till we returned, and then *Daed*, Amanda, and I followed Kenny across our grassy lot, over the paved driveway next door, and onto the packed dirt of the site. Halfway there, as we rounded a giant backhoe, I saw where we were headed, a small trailer on the far edge of the property.

Daed and I removed our hats as we stepped inside a room that was serving as an on-site office. Kenny sat at a metal desk, pulled out a drawer, and began rifling through a thick row of hanging file folders.

He found the document he sought and pulled it out. "Take a look at this."

I took the page from him and studied it, *Daed* and Amanda flanking me to get a look as well.

It was identical to the map I'd produced with one critical difference. This map was missing a small portion of our homestead, a long, narrow rectangle that ran between the tack store and our westernmost property line. The rectangle on this page marked the space as being separate from rest of our property, and in its center was the numeral "23."

Kenny scratched his head. "I don't know what to say. All I've been told is that we're planning to buy that portion of land to use in Phase II of our development project."

"But it's not a separate portion," *Daed* explained. "Our map clearly shows that it's part of our farm."

"And my map shows that it isn't. Look, I'm just as confused as you. Like I said, you're gonna have to talk to our lawyer. In the meantime, you can't do any more work over there until this matter gets cleared up. Understand?"

"What I understand," I replied, anger pulsing through my veins, "is that this whole thing is ridiculous. Zooks have been living on that land for the past sixty years—and will still be living here sixty years from now. Including lot twenty-three, which we have every intention of expanding on."

Leaning back in his chair, Kenny offered an exaggerated shrug. "Hey, go ahead. Build all you want. But in the end, when I'm proven right, you're just going to have to take it all back down."

"Proven right?" I demanded. "Are you kidding me?"

Sitting forward again, he slid open the desk drawer, rifled through its contents, and pulled out a business card that he handed over. "Like I said, talk to the lawyer. I hope he can straighten out this ownership issue nice and quick."

"There *is* no ownership issue!" I shouted in a voice that reverberated around the trailer's metal walls. At my side, *Daed* let out a soft grunt, which was his way of telling me to calm down. I took a deep breath and blew it out. "*We're* the owners," I continued at a lower volume. "It says so on our deed. Wherever this map of yours came from, it's obviously old and out of date."

"Sorry," he said, taking the page back from me and setting it on the desk, "but this map came from the city clerk's office within the last year or two. It was acquired when Starbrite was scouting properties for a hotel."

"Starbrite?" I asked, the name sounding vaguely familiar.

"The resort's management group, Starbrite International. Anyway, the people there liked this spot but wanted a little more acreage, so they looked into purchasing the various neighboring properties—including yours, I imagine. Though obviously you declined to sell."

I nodded, realizing now why the name sounded familiar. I remembered when the hotel people made an offer for our homestead. *Daed* had very clearly turned them down, though we'd been surprised to learn that our next door neighbors had not. Instead, they had chosen to sell and move away. Since then, not only had we missed them as friends and fellow church members, we'd also been suffering from the fact that their land could have separated our homestead from the new resort. By selling out, our former neighbors had left us with no buffer at all—except, of course, for the portion of our own property we were debating about now.

"Anyway," Kenny continued, "we were able to acquire enough of the neighboring properties to proceed as planned. The only step we lack is the acquisition of lot twenty-three as well. But that is in the works."

I narrowed my eyes. "You said you're in negotiations to buy it now?"

Kenny cleared his throat, looking hot under the collar all of a sudden. "Yeah. Well, sort of. There have been some…issues."

"Issues?"

"Yeah. With locating the owner."

"That's because we *are* the owners. And we've already turned you down."

"Hold on," Kenny added as he shuffled through his papers again, looking for something else. *Daed* glanced at me and then piped up.

"Records or not," he said to Kenny in a calm, even tone, "my father bought this entire place from a woman named Lucille Raber in 1956. She's passed on now, but I'm sure one of her children—"

Kenny looked up. "Raber?"

Daed nodded. "Lucille Raber." He pointed to her name at the top of our deed, the one I'd brought down from the house. Kenny looked at it and then up at me.

"That's it. That's the name I was trying to think of, the owner of lot twenty-three. Raber. But not Lucille. It's a man."

He flipped through a few more pages, pulled one out, and handed it to me. "Here you go, right here. According to county records, lots twenty-four and twenty-five belong to a Zook, but the parcel in question, lot twenty-three, belongs to a Raber. *Clayton* Raber."

Clayton Raber?

I sucked in my breath. How could that be? I looked over at *Daed,* who seemed just as startled—and worried—as I.

"All right," I said. "We'll look into it, then."

Kenny's scowl softened. "And you'll cease and desist with your expansion in the meantime?"

"*Ya,*" *Daed* and I agreed simultaneously. We turned to go.

"We'll be in contact with your lawyer," I told Kenny over my shoulder as I took Amanda's arm and guided her down the steps of the trailer.

Then we began making our way back across the construction site as fast as we could.

"What's going on?" Amanda asked, trying to keep up. "What's wrong? Who's Clayton Raber?"

Daed and I exchanged another look, and then I leaned close to her ear.

"He's the Amish man who used to live here, the old clockmaker," I whispered. "The one people say murdered his wife."

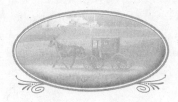

FOUR

I first learned about Clayton Raber's past from twin brothers who used to live up the road. I was about seven or eight. We were playing in my yard one evening after we had all finished our chores, and when I invited them inside for some of my mom's pie, they refused. When I asked why, they looked at one another and then back at me.

"That's where the murderer used to live," one of them said.

They then proceeded to tell me the story—or as much of it as they had overheard. The rest I gathered on my own after talking to my parents later that night. Legend had it the clockmaker known as Clayton Raber was a bitter man prone to fits of temper. He'd been the victim of a childhood accident that had left him with various injuries, including a badly mangled leg that had healed poorly and made it difficult for him to walk, as well as a disfiguring scar on his face. He also had a troubled marriage, and when his wife died under suspicious conditions, Clayton was charged with killing her. He was only twenty-seven. Everyone knew he'd done it, they said, but for some reason all charges were eventually dropped and he was released from jail. He later left the community—and the Amish church—in disgrace, and no one ever saw him again.

Up to that point I had known only that a family by the name of Raber once lived in my house and that they'd had a clock shop in what was presently my grandfather's tack and feed store. But even after my friends told me the story, which I'd found startling and more than a little intriguing, I still didn't understand why it scared them so. My house was warm and safe, its wooden floors worn soft by generations of running, skipping, and playing. What did some silly rumor from the past have to do with anything now? Those twin brothers may have thought of Clayton Raber as a murderer, but to me he'd always just been the guy who grew up in the bedroom that had eventually become mine.

And I loved that room, especially when my older brother moved out and I had it all to myself. My favorite part was the window seat, where I used to sit and read for hours as a boy, just as Clayton Raber had probably done years before when it had been his room. A wide strip of molding ran vertically along the wall beside the window seat, and I used to gaze at it often, at the markings that covered the length of it.

The reason it held such fascination for me was because those markings charted Clayton's height as he'd grown. Someone had measured him at various ages and sliced little horizontal lines into the wood. Beside each one—which started at about four feet high and ran all the way up to nearly six feet—was a date and his initials.

Though the dates had all been carved by the same feminine hand, it seemed as if Clayton had added in the initials himself. Down low, the first few *CR*s were childish looking and barely legible, but each one became less so as he worked his way up the wall through time. When he measured in at about the height of an eight or nine year old boy, his letters had become for the most part neat and straight. By the time he'd reached his full height, they were downright elegant, carved by the hand of a teenager who was on his way to becoming a clockmaker and talented woodworker.

For some reason, the sight of those measurements and dates and initials on that strip of molding had always pleased me, though I was never sure why. I supposed it made me feel connected somehow to the house, and to the boy who had once lived there. Learning those new facts from the neighborhood children about Clayton's wife and the murder charge and everything had not changed my feelings about my room nor repelled me from my home—quite the opposite, in fact. In bed that night, I didn't lie there thinking about murder or death or jail or any of that stuff. Instead, I trained my eyes on the beautifully carved initials near the top of that growth chart and told myself that if the police let the guy go, then he must have been innocent and that was that.

I hadn't thought about Clayton in years, but now my life was once again intersecting with his in a new way. Whatever happened from here, I told myself as we neared the group waiting for us on the lawn, I could only pray it wouldn't hinder any more of my carefully laid plans for the expansion.

Everyone's eyes were wide with curiosity as we drew close. Not wanting to broadcast to the whole group what we'd learned, I pulled Virgil aside and told him we had a problem with the paperwork and I would have to see a lawyer before we could keep going with the construction.

"Send the workers home for today," I added. "I imagine we'll be able to start back first thing tomorrow morning, but I'll get in touch with you as soon as I know for sure."

"Okay," Virgil replied with a worried frown. "I'll be waiting to hear from you."

We returned to the crew, and I thanked them for their work thus far and apologized for the mix-up. Virgil took it from there, addressing the men as Amanda and I went inside, my mind spinning. I was embarrassed to have to send these guys home so soon, and more than a little frustrated. How was I going to get my business up and running again with a delay like this? If the foundation wasn't poured today, then it would be like dominoes tumbling down the line, ruining the project's entire time frame. My window of opportunity with the work crew would be gone and I would lose them to other jobs. Once that happened, who knew how long it would be before we were back on track?

First things first, I told myself as I took a deep breath and tried to calm down. I waited for the men to leave and then used the phone in the shop to contact Jim Purcell, the lawyer on the business card. When I was finally put through to him, he said he'd been expecting my call.

"I just heard from Kenny McKendrick over at the Ridgeview site, and he told me about the situation." The man's voice sounded cool yet melodic, his tone the kind one might use to soothe a worried child into going to sleep—or to trick a jittery cow into entering a slaughterhouse. I asked him what all of the confusion was about.

"It's complicated. Any chance you could come into my office and we could talk here? I have some time now—well, I can make time, I mean. This is important."

I asked where he was located, and when he said Lancaster City, I told him that meant I'd have to hire a car and driver but that I would make my way out there as soon as I could, which would probably be in an hour or two.

"Fine. Just get here as soon as you can, Mr. Zook."

He hung up without a goodbye. Returning the phone to its base, I looked over to see *Daed* and Amanda standing beside me, waiting to hear the details of what the lawyer said. I relayed our conversation in full, and then Amanda offered to arrange for a car and driver.

We traded places by the phone, and while she called around, *Daed* and I neatened the shop and put things away as best we could. Finally, the three of us locked up and left, agreeing to meet in front of the store in half an hour, when our driver would arrive.

As we walked up the hill together, I knew what *Daed* was thinking, that maybe this holdup was a sign from God that the expansion wasn't supposed to happen. To my relief, however, he never said a word except for a quick, "See you in a bit" as we parted. Now that he and I had made our peace, I guessed the last thing either of us wanted was to start arguing again.

Once Amanda and I were inside our cottage, I pulled off my dusty work shirt and walked into the bathroom to clean up from my morning's activities before returning to the bedroom to change into clean clothes.

"All right," she said, coming to stand in the doorway. "I can't wait any longer. You have to tell me. Who is Clayton Raber? And what is all this about him killing his wife?"

She sat on a side of the bed, watching me expectantly.

"It's a sad tale," I said. "One I don't like to think about much."

"Why? What happened?"

I looked over at my wife. This was her home now too, and she deserved to know what had gone on here all those years ago. So I gave her as much of the story as I knew.

Her expression was somber but curious. She reached toward the hat I had placed on the bed and took it in her hands. She turned it slowly, fingering the tightly woven straw as she processed what I had said.

"But you don't believe he did it, do you? How come?"

Her eyes searched my face. My wife had the uncanny talent of seeing beyond my words and straight into my heart.

Truth was, I had learned in subsequent years that no one really knew why the police had changed their minds about Clayton and let him go, though most assumed it was simply from a lack of evidence. Still, local folks had been convinced that the man had committed the murder just the same. I, on the other hand, had always held the opposite opinion, that the reason there was no evidence was because Clayton hadn't done it.

"It's hard to explain. I've always felt a kind of connection with him even after I heard the story. Somehow, I had trouble believing it was true—then *and* now."

"Why?"

I had to think for a moment. It had been a while since I'd sifted through any thoughts about Clayton Raber. "Well, I grew up in the same room he did, so I always felt kind of a bond with him. Plus there's this thing on the wall…" My voice drifted off as I realized how silly it might sound to tell her about Clayton's old growth chart and how it had always made me feel connected with him in some strange way. "You'd have to see it, I guess."

"What? What is it?" Her eyes were wide with interest.

I shrugged, feeling embarrassed, and told her I would show her later.

She frowned in mock displeasure as she handed me my hat. I fit it onto my head, gathered the last few things I needed, and followed her to the kitchen. She grabbed a paper bag from the counter—sandwiches she had made for me while I'd freshened up—and we continued on outside. When we reached the end of the driveway, we sat on the bench in front of the store and I ate my lunch as we waited for the hired car to arrive. *Daed* joined us just as the vehicle was turning into the parking lot.

As my father stood and greeted the driver, I crumpled the wax paper that had been around my sandwiches and handed it to Amanda.

"Say a prayer for us," I told her.

"I will."

I got into the car and settled into my seat next to *Daed*. As we drove off, my mind again returned to the clockmaker, this stranger whose life had somehow intersected with mine even though he moved away from Ridgeview more than thirty years before I was born.

Where had he gone when he fled Lancaster County? Was he still alive now? And *had* he really killed his wife and gotten away with it?

As the scenery flew past, I put away such questions, praying that once we met with the lawyer, none of it would matter anyway.

When we reached the address on Mr. Purcell's card, I decided it had to be one of the biggest, fanciest buildings in Lancaster City. The entire third floor belonged to the law office, and we stepped out of the elevator doors into a reception area that had marble floors, big oak furniture, and elegant decor.

Even the people who worked there were fancy. The woman at the front desk had on a suit that looked more like something a person might wear in New York City than around here.

As soon as I gave her our names, she brought us through the main doors and down a hallway lined with offices. When we approached the end, she knocked on a door with the nameplate "James T. Purcell" on it. The door swung open, and there stood the lawyer I had spoken with earlier. I was expecting someone equally as fancy as the surrounding building and the receptionist, but this guy looked like a short, unkempt Santa Claus.

He welcomed us with a shake and a smile. His was a corner office, and as we stepped inside my eyes went to the big windows that looked out over downtown Lancaster. The view was nice, and it even included the tip of the county courthouse up the street.

Mr. Purcell took his place behind a beautiful mahogany desk and then gestured toward a pair of plush chairs across from it. "Please. Have a seat."

Once we were settled, I pulled out our documents from the manila file and handed them over.

As he took them from me, he began to give us a little background on Starbrite Management Group, saying they were based in California and had been in business for more than twenty years. He explained that the company had its own in-house legal counsel, but that his firm had been hired to handle local matters such as this one. "I made some calls after we spoke this morning," he added, "and I think I have a pretty good feel for what's going on here."

"I'm glad someone does," *Daed* quipped, causing the lawyer to smile.

I wasn't smiling. "What's going on," I said, "is that we're being taken advantage of by your client."

"I know it looks that way," he said as he handed back the papers. "And I do want to assure you that this situation is in no way your fault." He removed his reading glasses and placed them on the desk in front of him. "But the bottom line, Mr. Zook, is that you have a bad title. The homestead was sold to your family by a Mrs. Lucille Raber, but as it turns out, a portion of it wasn't hers to sell. The piece of land in question had been given away by her husband before he died to their only son, Clayton. And because that son wasn't a party to the sale, you folks never got legal title to his parcel."

Daed and I looked at each other and then back at the lawyer again.

"Her thinking she could sell it to you along with the rest was probably just a mistake," he concluded. "But, as it turns out, an important one."

Daed leaned forward in his chair. "Well, if it's a mistake, we should be able to fix it."

"I'm afraid it's not that simple, Mr. Zook. The only way to fix it is to get the current owner to sign it over to you—assuming that's something he would even want to do."

"Why wouldn't he?" I asked, my tone sounding more irritated than I had intended. I tried for a calmer tone. "It's not like he's using it. And surely he would see that his mother just made an error."

The lawyer shrugged. "Yes, true. I imagine he'd take that into consideration. But, once he learns about this, he's going to have a big decision on his hands."

I mulled over his words. Something about them made me uneasy. "What are you trying to say, Mr. Purcell?"

He fiddled with the glasses on the desk. "My client wants that land, Mr. Zook. They fully intend to pursue the purchase and acquire it for themselves, if possible. It's needed for Phase II of the resort."

He gestured toward the far side of the room, and I realized he wanted us to see a small creation that resembled an elaborate doll house sitting on top of a table. *Daed* and I stood and walked over to it to get a better look.

"That's a model of the resort in miniature," the lawyer explained. "As you can see, phase one includes the basic hotel and banquet facility, with an indoor pool and a restaurant. Once that's complete, they'll open for business while moving on to phase two, which will add an outdoor pool, an indoor/outdoor sports bar, four tennis courts, and a small spa facility."

We stared at the tableau in front of us, dumbfounded. It was all very impressive, but spilling over onto the land of lot twenty-three was the edge of a large pool and the indoor/outdoor sports bar, which would end up next to the tack shop.

"Look how close that bar is to our building," I said to *Daed* as I pointed toward the tiny structure. "We'll practically be sitting *in* the restaurant area."

Sick at heart, we stared at it a moment longer and then returned to our seats.

"Let's not exaggerate," the lawyer told us as we again sat facing him. "Zoning requires a twenty-foot setback from the property line. And of course they'll use plenty of landscaping to delineate the borders."

"As if that'll make any difference," I said. "Landscaping or not, how would *you* like to live twenty feet from an outdoor pool and sports bar?"

I closed my eyes and pinched the bridge of my nose. I had visited a sports bar or two during my *rumspringa*, and though that had been a while ago, I could still remember what they had been like. Drunk fans screaming at television screens, fighting with each other, driving home while intoxicated. The memory made me feel exhausted. And deaf.

Daed found his words before I could. "But the land is *ours*. My father paid for it. Deed or not, that was the buyer's intent—and the seller's—at the time of the sale. That has to count for something. Even if a mistake was made back then, we just need to correct the documentation."

The lawyer studied *Daed* for a moment. "I'm sorry, Mr. Zook. It may work like that in your world but not out here. A person's intention isn't enough, even when it comes from an honest man like yourself."

I began to gather my things, taking the lawyer's last words as the beginning of his dismissal. But then *Daed* spoke again, asking if we had any recourse at all.

"Sure. Title insurance. Maybe a quitclaim deed. But I don't see either one of those..." His voice trailed off, as if that answered the question.

But *Daed* wasn't ready to be ushered out just yet. "Title insurance?" he persisted in a calm, respectful tone.

Mr. Purcell glanced at his watch, as if to say our time was up. "Yes, that's something your father should have purchased when he first took hold of the property, though I doubt that he did."

Daed shook his head. "He wouldn't have. It's not the Amish way."

"Well, there you go, then."

Daed nodded thoughtfully. "And the other? A 'quitclaim deed'? What is that?"

The man began to squirm, eager to be done with us and probably wishing he'd never answered my father's question about recourse at all.

"Basically, it's a document that says 'I give up any rights to my land,' and so on. If you could get Clayton Raber to sign one of those, then the lot would legally be yours and there's nothing anyone could do about it."

"So we'll try that then," *Daed* said, optimism growing on his face.

The lawyer grunted. "You're welcome to give it a shot, Mr. Zook, but you need to understand something. Starbrite's pockets are very deep. I assure you, whatever offer you make, my client will be able to outbid you."

Daed glanced at me and then returned his attention to the lawyer. "Perhaps Mr. Raber will choose to honor his mother's intentions and sign the land over to us without any payment at all."

"Yeah, well, even if he did—which I doubt—that's assuming you could find the guy in the first place. Which you won't, at least not before we do."

"How do you know Clayton Raber hasn't passed away by now?" I asked. "He left here an awfully long time ago."

"That's a fair question," Mr. Purcell replied with a nod. "All I can tell you is that thus far, we've turned up absolutely no proof of death—no death certificate, no hospital records, no obituary, nothing. If he'd died before now, there would likely be at least some sort of record left behind. So the assumption at this point is that he's still alive."

"How about his siblings? Are any of them still living?"

He hesitated before answering. "One sister, quite old. Our investigators talked to her, but she doesn't know where her brother is."

I wasn't surprised. Word had always had it that once Clayton left, he was never heard from again.

"And this quitclaim deed thing that you mentioned, do we have to see a lawyer for that?"

He waved a hand, as if to brush off the question. "Not necessarily. It's a standard form, I'm sure they're available online." He seemed to realize what he'd said after the words were out of his mouth. "Or…you know. Maybe at the clerk of court's office or something."

I didn't bother telling him that even the Amish could google if needed, as long as they did it on a computer outside of the home.

"But, frankly, I wouldn't waste my time if I were you," he added, placing both hands on the desk. "My client is going to track this man down first, and once they do, they intend to make him a *very* good offer on that land. It'll be a done deal before you folks have half a chance to do anything."

Daed fixed his eyes on the man. "So they're still going to proceed with this matter and try to buy the land out from under us, even though it was clearly an oversight? A simple mistake?"

The lawyer looked from *Daed* to me and back to *Daed* again. "What can I say? It's just an acre, but it's a very crucial acre to their plans."

"Well, it's an acre they're not going to get," I insisted. "We'll track the man down and explain what happened. If he has even a speck of decency, he'll make this right and sign the land over to us as his mother intended."

Mr. Purcell hesitated, and then he stood and came around to the front of the desk. "Look," he said, for the first time seeming genuinely sorry for us. "Starbrite has trained investigators, computers, legal databases at their fingertips, you name it. There's no way you folks can compete with that. They'll probably find him within another week, and then it'll be a done deal. I'm sorry, but that's just the way it is. Everyone leaves a digital trail. Even the Amish."

"Ex-Amish," *Daed* clarified. "Clayton Raber broke away from the church years ago."

"Whatever. I'm just saying, with all of our technology and resources, I'm afraid we have a far better shot at finding him than you do." His eyes were surprisingly apologetic.

We both rose, and he reached out to shake our hands. *Daed* took his willingly, like the forgiving man he was, and after a moment's pause I followed suit. Though I was grateful to this lawyer for sharing with us as much as he had, I was still deeply frustrated. As we turned to go, one thought began to burn inside of me.

If this was a race to the finish, then I had to get to Clayton Raber first. But how?

FIVE

Daed and I rode home from the lawyer's office in silence, the steady hum of the car's engine the only sound. We sat in the back together, and at one point I stole a glance at his face, but he was staring straight ahead, his expression unreadable. What was he thinking? Had he let the lawyer's doubts sneak into his own mind? Was he regretting the olive branch he'd so graciously offered me this morning?

He and I were probably thinking the same thing, that without this land we wouldn't be able to expand. He was probably happy about that, but I knew the truth. If we didn't expand we would end up having to go out of business. We had to have that land, which meant we had to find Clayton Raber.

But could we find him before Starbrite did? The lawyer's words rolled around in my head like an ungreased wheel, and I wondered if their fancy technology and resources did indeed give them advantages we couldn't overcome. I voiced this concern to *Daed*, though I was wary of what his response might be.

After a moment of thought, he spoke. "You know, we have resources those people with their investigators and fancy computers would never think to use."

I looked at him, curious, as he continued.

"The Amish community has a lot of its own tools, some of them entirely unavailable to the *Englisch*."

"Like what?" I asked. I hadn't expected optimism.

He turned and looked at me. "The Amish grapevine, for starters. Church directories. Genealogy books. Local lore. That sort of thing."

I smiled. Of course. We had our own databases right at our fingertips. The information didn't need to be stored on a computer. It was already stored in the hearts, minds, and memories of every Amish person we knew. It was already inscribed in the pages of dozens of directories and family histories. We just needed to know where to look and whom to ask. Suddenly, I felt a surge of appreciation at how solidly my father was now supporting me.

"You think we'll be able to find Clayton before they do?"

He nodded. "God willing, I think we have a chance."

When we reached home, he and I agreed we would touch base at supper tonight when dining together in the main house. He had some tasks to finish around the farm, he said, and I told him I'd be spending the rest of the afternoon with the Amish directories, trying to track down Clayton's relatives still living in the region.

We parted in the driveway, and as I headed off toward the cottage, it struck me suddenly how supportive *Daed* was being through all of this. The thought surprised me, though it shouldn't have. He always stood by his word. What he had said this morning about not burying the talents really had indicated the end of his doubting. He'd made up his mind to be on board, and now on board he was. With a rush of gratitude, I thought how very blessed and humbled I was to have such a good and decent man as my father.

Amanda was at the cottage when I got there, so I brought her up to speed on the visit with the lawyer as I grabbed some things I needed from the bookshelf in the living room. Then I spent the next hours down at the shop in the emptiness and quiet, sitting at the counter and poring over my resources, making phone calls, and leaving messages.

Thanks to *Daed*'s advice, I started my search for Clayton Raber with the Amish directory for Lancaster County, a huge, heavy book that included names, addresses, histories, and more of all the Old Order Amish families in the region. As one who had broken away from the church, Clayton himself wouldn't be in there, but the book should have the names and contact information for many of his family members.

Because my family and I lived in Clayton's house—and, therefore,

Clayton's old district—I had always assumed we attended church with the same families he had, or at least with later generations of the same families. But now I realized that wasn't the case, thanks to the Amish policy on the uniformity of districts.

Within an affiliation, Amish churches were organized geographically, with each individual congregation, or district, limited by size. Once a district had more than thirty or forty families, it had to split into two separate districts. That way, families could continue to meet in homes, maintain an intimate sense of worship, and prevent any one group from growing larger or more powerful than any other.

The system worked well, but it sure was making more trouble for me now. Since 1955, the Rabers' district had split several times—which meant I had to trace things out through every single split, just to be sure I had the right branches of the family. Making my task even more complicated was the fact that Clayton had six sisters—Katrina, Pauline, Dorothy, Libby, Joan, and Maisie—but no brothers, so a lot of different surnames were also involved.

It took hours to sort it all out, but by tracing the line of the Rabers' church with the family names and genealogies, I was able to narrow things down to the crucial people who were apparently still around, the ones I wanted to contact first. I jotted the names down line by line until I'd written on almost three sheets of paper—an end result that was both encouraging and daunting.

I briefly considered going back and repeating the entire process for the family of Clayton's late wife as well, tracing it out to find any remaining family members. But my understanding was they had moved away from the area decades ago, and I doubted any of them would have kept tabs on the man anyway. I decided not to go that route for now. Besides, even if I did find someone, I couldn't imagine them wanting to hear from me about such a dark part of their family's history.

Instead, I returned my attention to the information I already had. Flipping to a fresh sheet, I calculated what the current ages of Clayton and his sisters would be. If Clayton had been in his late twenties when he moved away from here, he would now be in his late eighties. That meant the youngest of his sisters would be in her early nineties—and they only got older from there.

The lawyer had said there was just one surviving sibling left. By cross-referencing several of my sources, I tried to figure out which one it might be, but I wasn't sure. My best guess was Joan. One listing showed her date of birth, so I did the math and saw that she was ninety-four now. At that age, she would be living with one of her children.

But how to know which one? I was trying to think of some way to figure that out when one of our neighbors came to mind, an old Amish man named Ben Sauder. Ben knew everyone and everything that happened around here. Chances were, he'd know which sister was still alive and where she lived now.

I decided I'd start my search with him first thing tomorrow. I'd walk over to his home, which was only a few blocks away, and pick the man's brain.

Whichever sister it was, with her in her nineties, I could only hope her memory was still intact—and that she would be willing to tell more to me than she had to the *Englisch* investigators.

I closed the pad and looked around the empty shop, and a pang of regret and sadness shot through me. Maybe this was God's way of answering my prayer for doors to be closed where He didn't want me to go. I closed my eyes and leaned my head against the desk.

Is that what this is, God? A closed door? Or just a bump in the road that means nothing beyond what it seems?

I opened my eyes again, distracted from my prayer by another pressing issue. Should we keep the store closed or reopen it until this issue was solved one way or the other? I locked up and headed for home, my mind burdened by questions.

I began carefully considering the reality of our situation. Because of the expansion, we'd already been planning for the shop to be closed, but now that we knew what we were in for, I had to admit that this whole thing might take longer than expected—if it was ever going to happen at all. We couldn't afford to keep the store closed for too long and should probably go ahead and open back up right away—at least until the matter was settled one way or the other. Then again, I needed my time free so that I could spend it searching for Clayton Raber, not working in the store.

I decided to give myself one day, tomorrow, to gather information. If after that things weren't looking promising, I would open back up for business on Friday.

I entered the cottage and saw that it was empty, which meant Amanda was at the main house helping with dinner. I put my notes away, washed my face and hands, and walked over to my parents' place across the drive. When I came through the door, the scents of baking bread and sugared ham greeted me.

"You're just in time, Matthew," I heard my wife call from the kitchen. "Supper's almost ready."

I followed her voice to the warmth of the next room, where she stood with her mitted hands in the oven, her plump tummy bulging out from beneath her apron.

"Let me get that," I said, moving quickly to her side.

"I have it." From the oven's depths she pulled out a juicy, steaming ham and placed it on the top of the stove.

Mamm was setting the table, her back to us, so I seized the opportunity to wrap my arms around Amanda's ever-growing waist.

"Not in front of your mother," she whispered with a giggle, "and not while I'm trying to cook!"

She let me give her a peck on the cheek before shooing me away. Smiling, I walked back to the door and hung up my hat. *Daed* came inside at that moment, hung up his hat as well, and then headed to the sink to wash his hands. I made my way to the table and sat.

I couldn't help but smile even more as I took in the spread of food in front of me: mashed potatoes topped with melting squares of butter, fresh green beans from the garden, fried okra cut into crispy circles, and a bowl of chopped strawberries, blackberries, and peaches drenched with cream.

Noah showed up at the last minute and tried to slip into his seat unnoticed, but *Mamm* made him wash his hands. He returned just as *Daed* sat and then led us all in a silent grace.

After a hearty "amen," my father asked me if I'd made any progress with the directories. I sighed and told him it had taken the rest of the afternoon, but at least I had a list of names to start with first thing in the morning. I spooned some beans onto my plate and passed the dish along.

"I still can't believe that land really doesn't belong to us," Amanda said, shaking her head from side to side.

I cut a piece of ham with my knife. "I know. According to the lawyer, it was never ours to buy in the first place."

"What?" Noah asked, looking up from the decimated pile of mashed potatoes he'd been focused on. Judging by his incredulous expression, I realized no one had updated him since our visit with the lawyer.

I looked at *Daed* again, but he was studying his plate, so I answered Noah's question, giving him the details in a nutshell and explaining that our only option now was to hunt down Clayton as soon as possible and convince him to sign the lot over to us.

"What happens if you can't find him in time?" Noah asked, his eyes wide.

I just shrugged and looked away, unable to say the truth aloud. If we couldn't find him in time, we might as well say goodbye to our business for good.

Later, before we left for the night, I brought Amanda up to my old childhood bedroom and showed her the strip of molding near the window seat where Clayton Raber's height had been charted over the years as he was growing up here.

Like me, she seemed most drawn to the last few markings at the top, where Clayton had carved into the wood with delicate and artistic lettering. She reached out and ran a finger over some of the initials, and after a moment I began to do the same. In a way, they were as familiar to me as the lines on my hand or the hills outside the window.

I realized she had withdrawn her hand, and when I looked over at her, it was to see that she was watching me. With a gentle smile, she thanked me for showing this to her. Gazing into her eyes, I had a feeling my wife understood what I was wanting her to know, that this had been my introduction to Clayton Raber, to the man everyone else thought was a murderer. I didn't understand it, but somehow I just knew that the person who had carved his initials here all those years ago could not have grown up to become the monster most folks thought he was.

Later, back at home, I tried to sleep but couldn't. My mind was racing. What if I wasn't able to find Clayton? And even if I did, who was to say he would be receptive to what I had to tell him? The uncertainties gnawed at my stomach. I looked over at Amanda, whose chest rose and fell with her steady breathing. We were going to be parents soon. How would I ever be able to provide for the two of them if I couldn't keep the shop open? The Amish community would be there to support us financially in a time of crisis, of course, but that was no solution for the long term. I still had to make a living.

More than anything, I wished *Grossdaadi* were here. Would he have known what to do, how to handle this situation? Or would even he, with all his business intelligence and experience, have been as stumped as I was now?

Six

The next morning, I sat down with a map of Lancaster County and the list of people I wanted to contact and began geographically organizing, from closest to farthest, the ones I'd decided to see in person. When I was finished, I added one more name at the top of the list, Ben Sauder, the neighbor down the street who always knew the goings-on of everyone around here.

I headed out just before nine and was at his house in minutes. He and his wife lived just a few blocks away on a small homestead that had been in his family for a century. Their setup was similar to ours in terms of size and layout, with a store and a small parking lot at the bottom of the hill, out front, and their house and barn at the top of the hill, out back. In their case, the family store was a woodworking shop, where Ben had labored for decades building custom cabinets.

Nowadays, that shop was in the capable hands of his children and grandchildren, and he spent most of his time puttering around the homestead or helping with the grandkids or shooting the breeze with the other old guys at the coffee shop down the street. I parked my buggy near the house, and as I climbed down I spotted Ben in his vegetable garden, trimming back some aggressive watermelon vines. Even in his seventies, he was still very much involved with the upkeep of his home. The yard and gardens were immaculate and beautifully trimmed and cared for.

"Matthew Zook!" he said, when he saw me walking toward him. "What brings you here? Could you smell my wife's homemade biscuits from all the way over at your place?"

I smiled, pausing to inhale. "Nope, but you're right. Something sure does smell good." I came to a stop at the fence. "Actually, I'm here because I need help with something and I thought you might be a good place to start."

His interest was immediately piqued. "Oh?"

"Guess you could say I need to talk to the guy who knows everything about everyone."

Beaming, he set his hoe against a fence pole. "Well, then. Come on up to the porch and let's have a chat."

With a nod I turned and continued along the walk as he made his way through the garden. We met at the house and ascended the three stairs to the wide porch together. As we did, Ben's wife, Sue Ann, appeared on the other side of the screen door, greeted me warmly, and offered me a cup of coffee.

"You might bring the boy a biscuit as well," Ben told her. "That's the real reason he's here, you know."

She chuckled. "Of course. Cream and sugar in your coffee, Matthew?" she asked as she started to walk away.

"Just black, please. Thanks."

Ben settled into the first in a row of rocking chairs that lined the porch. I chose the one next to his and sat as well.

"So I hear you've big plans for the tack store," he said, his tone clearly indicating he'd not only heard about those plans but had discussed them at length with his friends at the coffee shop. I shouldn't have been surprised. It had to be big news around here when something that hadn't changed in sixty years was about to undergo a metamorphosis, even it if was just an old tack shop getting a much-needed expansion and facelift.

Before I could reply, he added, "I also hear you've run into a bit of a problem."

Of course he knew all about that too. He'd probably been pumping people for information since he'd first gotten wind of the scene that had taken place yesterday morning, outside, amid the construction.

"Well, seeing as how you already know everything, maybe you can answer my biggest question, which is how to find Clayton Raber."

Ben let out a low whistle. "Clayton Raber? The clockmaker? Why on earth would you need to know that?"

How to quickly explain?

"There was a small problem with the deed back when his mother sold their homestead to my grandfather, and I need Clayton's signature on a legal document now in order to straighten it out."

"His *signature*? I can't imagine he's still..."

"Alive?"

He nodded.

"Actually, from what I've been told, there's a good chance that he is. I just don't know where."

Ben considered that for a moment. "Well, wherever he's living now, he must be pushing ninety, at least. My, my. You have your work cut out for you, son, finding a man no one's heard from in more than half a century. Folks said your big ruckus over there had something to do with a property dispute, but I didn't realize—"

Sue Ann emerged from the door at that moment, carrying a tray. I jumped up and retrieved a nearby side table, inhaling the scents of coffee and fresh-baked biscuits as I retook my seat and she placed the tray in front of us.

The biscuits she had made were warm, fluffy, and golden brown. I chose one and gently pulled it open, releasing the steam from inside.

"May I ask how well you knew the Rabers back then?" I asked, using a knife to slather on some butter. "I assume pretty well, since they were in your same church district."

He shrugged, blowing at his hot coffee before taking a sip. "Fairly well. They were a part of the community, but Clayton was an odd sort. He kept to himself more than most."

"I understand he was handicapped as a result of a childhood accident?"

"Had a bad leg and a hot temper to go with it. He married a woman who didn't love him and ended up killing her and getting away with it." As soon as the words were out of his mouth, he must have realized how they sounded, because he quickly added, "Or so people have always said."

Surprised at his words, I let them sit between us for a long moment, focusing my attention on adding jelly to my biscuit, setting down the knife, and taking a bite. I wasn't here for gossip. I needed facts. And even though Ben was a busybody, he didn't usually go around repeating rumors.

"Sorry," he said finally, looking appropriately sheepish. "I was just twelve when she died. Guess I gobbled up what everybody said back then and took it all as truth."

I nodded, appreciating his admission. "Do you remember that time at all?"

"*Ya*, I remember a lot of it. Her death. His arrest. His release from jail. His break with the church. It was all very dramatic and the only thing anyone talked about for weeks and weeks."

"How sad for everyone involved. Any idea where he might have gone once he left here?"

"Not a clue. I don't think anyone ever knew. It was like he disappeared off the face of the earth."

"What do you recall about his break from the church?" I took another bite of biscuit and followed it with a sip of coffee.

"He was excommunicated, I remember that." Ben squinted, as if trying to peer back through time. "Seems like the excommunication came first, and then he left town. As far as I know, he never tried to come back."

"What were the grounds for the discipline?"

Ben set his mug on the tray. "To be honest, Matthew, I'm not sure. At the time I assumed he was renounced from the fellowship because he wouldn't confess to having murdered his wife. But looking back now, I realize that sounds kind of bizarre. There was no proof that he killed her, just speculation—albeit *lots* of speculation."

"So you say."

"Now that I think about it, the discipline was probably because he stopped coming to church, stopped being a part of the fellowship completely. He attended one Sunday service soon after he got out of jail, but just that once— and then never again."

I leaned forward in my chair. "Really."

"*Ya.* I remember it well. We expected him to show up, you know, because he'd been released and the charges were dropped. We boys tried to scare the girls, telling them the wife-killer was coming. They were convinced he was going to commit some sort of violent act in the middle of the service—and, of course, all the boys were kind of hoping he'd try so we could take him down in front of all the girls."

Ben chuckled, but then his smile faded into a mix of sadness and chagrin. "Poor Clayton," he said, almost surprised, as if those were two words he'd never considered putting together before. "If he really didn't do it, then that must have been awful. Imagine, getting cleared by the *Englisch* authorities only to be found guilty in the court of Amish opinion."

Truer words were never spoken.

Shifting in my seat, I reached into my pocket and pulled out the list I'd made of people relevant to my search. Though it helped to understand the situation as fully as I could—and I was finding these details fascinating—I'd come here for a very specific reason, to ask about Clayton's whereabouts and his surviving relatives.

Unfolding the page, I held it out toward Ben and asked if he knew which of Clayton's sisters was still alive. "The lawyer said they have all passed away except one. My guess is that would be Joan. She married a Glick?"

Ben nodded, taking the page from me. "*Ya*, Joan Raber Glick. She's still alive, but the lawyer's right. The other sisters have all passed." Looking down at the list, he scanned it for a moment before pointing at one of the entries. "Joan lives with her youngest daughter, Becky. Nice family. Becky and her husband have a goat farm just north of Leacock."

He handed back the page, pointing again toward the name, which was Rebecca Helmuth, followed by an address in a nearby town. Looking down at it, I could feel my spirits lift. At last I was on the right track.

"Thank you so much, Ben. I think I'm going to head over there right now to see if they can tell me how to get in touch with Clayton."

The man nodded, but his expression seemed hesitant. "Don't get your hopes up, son. Joan is ninety-five if she's a day, and her health and memory are failing. Or so I hear."

I folded the paper and slid it back into my pocket, confident that all would go well regardless. "That's okay. Even if Joan herself can't tell me where Clayton ended up, maybe her daughter can."

Ben's forehead creased even further.

"What?" I asked, my hands already on the arms of the rocking chair, ready to push myself up and get going.

He shrugged. "I know this is important and you have to do what you have to do. But just remember that Clayton left a lot of pain and sadness in his wake. Most folks I know would be glad if they never heard his name spoken again."

I hesitated, sobered by the thought. Ben was right. To me, this was about tracking down a property owner for help in settling a boundary dispute. To Clayton's family members, it was another matter altogether.

"Thanks, Ben. I'll keep that in mind."

I stood to go and he followed suit, but I could tell there was something else he wanted to say.

"Clayton Raber wasn't a happy man, Matthew," he finally blurted out. "Everybody knew it."

I thought for a moment. "But that doesn't make him a bad man," I replied evenly. "It doesn't make him a murderer."

Our eyes met, and as Ben and I shook hands and I thanked him for his help, I could see he was still struggling with that notion. After a lifetime of assuming Clayton was guilty, it couldn't be easy to accept that perhaps he might have been innocent after all.

Then again, I realized as I turned to go, the same could be said for me. All these years I'd sided with Clayton, believing in his innocence. But for all I knew, the man was guilty.

For all I knew, he really had murdered his wife and gotten away with it.

Half an hour later, I pulled into the Helmuth place, a carefully maintained goat farm set off East Newport Road. Three or four family dwellings were located on the farmstead, and I saw a collection of family buggies both inside a shed and outside. Clothes on the line included dresses and pants of all sizes. I was pretty sure at least four generations of Helmuths lived here. As I pulled up to the main house, a young woman about my age emerged from the door with a baby on her hip. She greeted me as I hooked my reins on the hitching rail.

"Afternoon," I said. "My name's Matthew Zook. May I speak with Becky Helmuth?"

The woman turned toward the screen door she had just come out of.

"*Grossmammi*, someone is here to see you." Then she turned back to me. "You here about the ad for kids?"

I smiled, thinking for a moment what Amanda would say if I came home with some baby goats. "No."

I was wondering how much I was going to have to tell the young woman when the screen door opened and an older woman with silvery hair under her *kapp* stepped out. She had a dish towel in her hands, wore eyeglasses, and looked to be in her seventies.

"Can I help you?" she asked as she dried her hands.

"Becky Helmuth?"

"*Ya.*"

I came closer to the front step and told her who I was and where I was from. My last name, common enough in Lancaster County, still gave her pause.

"Your family owns the tack and feed in Ridgeview?" she said, cocking her head to the side as she studied me.

"*Ya*. Going on sixty years now."

Her hesitation allowed me to ask my next question.

"I was wondering if you might know how I could get in touch with Clayton Raber."

The towel froze in her hands. "Young man," she responded, and I could tell by her rough tone that I had offended her somehow. "No one around here has seen my *onkel* in decades!"

I thought about apologizing for the interruption and excusing myself before causing more insult, but I realized I was already committed. And I needed this information a lot—more than I needed to observe good manners. I plunged onward. "Well, could I perhaps speak with your mother, Joan Glick? I understand she lives here?"

Becky wordlessly handed the towel to her granddaughter. She moved closer and stood so that she towered over me from the porch. "Absolutely not." Her tone was protective. Authoritative.

"I mean no disrespect," I continued. "It's just that there's an issue with a land deed and I—"

"I don't care what issue brought you here. I told you no one has seen my *onkel* in sixty years. And you're not going to speak to my mother about him."

As our eyes met and held, I thought of Ben's warning and realized he'd been right about folks not wanting to hear Clayton's name. If everyone else on my list reacted to this extreme, I was in for a difficult quest indeed.

I wanted to object, to persist, to *insist*. But I knew that would only push me further from my goal. Instead, I simply thanked her, apologizing for the intrusion. She remained where she was as I returned to the buggy, and when I looked back at the house from the end of the drive, I saw that she was still standing there, watching me, her posture stiff and tense. I would try again tomorrow maybe, after I had time to come up with a new approach.

In the meantime, once I had driven off of their property, I pulled over and checked my list. Next up was Becky's first cousin once removed, a man who lived about a mile from here. I put the list away and started up again, allowing the steady *clip-clop* of the horse's hooves to calm my nerves.

I could only hope this guy would be a little more forthcoming.

SEVEN

Warren Yoder was the grandson of Clayton's sister Maisie. As I found the home and turned into the driveway, I allowed myself to feel a small flash of optimism. Maybe, at last, I'd get some answers.

A man responded to my knock at the door. He was tall and broad shouldered, with brown hair and broadfall trousers stained green at the knees.

"Hi," I started, "I'm looking for Warren Yoder. I'm Matthew Zook from Ridgeview."

"Warren Yoder? That's me," he replied with a broad smile. He opened the screen door and gestured for me to come inside.

Things started out well enough. After neighborly pleasantries I stated my reason for coming and my predicament. I was politely shown the door.

Warren Yoder had no idea where Clayton Raber was.

Warren Yoder didn't care where Clayton Raber was.

Warren Yoder didn't want to discuss Clayton Raber at all.

I got back into my buggy, disheartened. I pulled out my list of names, took a pen, and drew a black line through *Warren Yoder*.

With a click of the tongue and snap of the reins, my horse and I were off again, heading in the direction of Bird-in-Hand, a town about five miles away, where the next two people on my list would perhaps be a bit more helpful.

My first stop was a bit of a surprise. At the next address, where I had expected to find cornfields or dairy cows or a tobacco farm, instead I came upon a sea-monster-themed miniature golf course. I stood beside the buggy in the gravel parking lot and looked around, hoping to spot someone older and in charge who might be able to tell me more about the home that had been here before and where the family was living now. But all I saw were teenagers dressed in matching shirts and glinting name tags, handing out colorful golf clubs or ice cream cones from a stand.

I was about to climb back into the buggy when I heard a squeal. I looked up to find a little boy pointing at me, his eyes wide and smiling. He was standing on the green of the hole nearest to where I was parked, waiting for his turn to knock a golf ball through the open mouth of a sea serpent. He wore a straw hat, the cheap imitation kind they sold in *Englisch* gift shops around Lancaster County, and he was jumping up and down.

"Mom! Mom! Mom! Look, there's another one! See? That man has the same hat as me!" He pointed more vigorously in my direction until his mother saw what he was doing and shushed him, embarrassed. I waved at them both and smiled, taking my hat off and holding it up toward the little boy in a sign of solidarity. He squealed again and jumped some more until it was his turn to putt, at which point he turned his attention back to the game.

At the next house, there were no buggies or signs of activity outside, and no one came to the door when I knocked. I knocked again, louder this time, and as I waited for a response, I noticed someone in the yard next door, an older Amish woman hanging laundry. I moved down the steps, walked over to the fence that divided the properties, and called out to her, asking if she knew when her neighbors would be returning.

"Never, I expect."

"Excuse me?"

"As of right now, no one lives there."

"Oh," I said, unsure if she was playing with me or just being factual.

Then she cracked a broad smile, straightened the glasses on her nose, and leaned in my direction. "If you ask me, it's obvious it's been abandoned by the terrible state of the front yard. The wife died last fall, and her widower moved up near Hershey way to live with his youngest daughter—much to his eldest daughter's relief." She snickered and looked at me as if I would know what she meant. "In any case, no one's been around to water the flowers, and the house looks just awful. I've done what I can, but I'm not in a position to care for two houses and two yards, now am I?"

I hesitated, not even sure how to reply. I'd met this kind of woman before. She was the gossiping type—the sort to latch on to any bit of news and exploit it at the expense of other people's reputations. I didn't want to humor her now, but she wouldn't stop talking long enough for me to excuse myself and go.

"Anyway," she continued, "rumor has it his grandson may move in soon if he ever marries the girl he's been courting. But who's to say? They're not exactly my idea of a perfect match, but at least it would be a step up from his mother's cooking—God bless her."

She chuckled again, and I took the opportunity to get a word in edgewise. "Do you by any chance know how I might contact the homeowner?"

The woman's eyes narrowed. "What for?"

"I'm just trying to track someone down, a relative of these people. A man who used to live in Ridgeview."

"Can't help you there," she said as she pinned another shirt to the line. "But I'm originally from Leola. Maybe I know the person you're looking for. What's the name?"

It struck me that if anyone might know the whereabouts of someone once involved in a scandal, it would be a busybody like her. I placed my hands on the fence and said the two words that apparently no one wanted to hear.

"Clayton Raber."

The woman hesitated for a moment, as if her brain had to process my words. Then she gasped, nearly dropping the pair of pants she was holding.

"The clockmaker who killed his young wife? Why on earth would you be looking for information about him?"

"Never mind," I said with a sigh. "It's a long story."

Suddenly overwhelmed with irritation and frustration, I managed to thank her for her willingness to help and then made my way back to the buggy as quickly as I could. I slipped into the driver's seat, glad to be free from such a difficult woman but devastated that Bird-in-Hand had been a complete bust.

The rest of the day went much the same. I worked down my list, visiting all of the houses on it that were within buggy-driving range. In each case, Clayton's relatives either wouldn't speak to me or had no information to give.

I once again pulled out my list and scanned it carefully, making sure I hadn't missed anyone. At this point, every single name was either crossed out or scribbled over with notes, even though I knew nothing more than I had when first starting out this morning.

There was just one stop left to make, but not to a relative of Clayton's. I needed to run by and speak to Virgil, the foreman of my expansion project, and give him an update on where things stood.

Fifteen minutes later I was in his workshop, bringing him up to speed. Turning the hat I held in my hands in a slow circle, I explained about the meeting with the lawyer and my daylong search for information on Clayton Raber. He listened sympathetically, assuring me that the crew would be as flexible as they could.

"But there are limits, Matthew. The problem is that we have a lot of projects pending. Some of them are time sensitive and can't be put off for long."

Moving to the day planner on his desk, he flipped through the schedule and offered a solution. He said he had one project that would take just about a week to complete and that he could put his men on that.

"That would have us coming back to you a week from Monday—which is eleven days from now. Do you think your situation will be figured out by then?"

I appreciated his flexibility and willingness to help me out, but I hesitated before answering. What if I settled this matter in a day or two? Then I'd have to wait a whole week to get rolling again.

My stomach sank as I thought about the list of scratched-off names sitting in the front seat of my buggy. What if tracking down Clayton took even longer than eleven days? Then I'd lose my window of opportunity, and who knew when they could come and finish the extension? We were fighting the calendar in another way as well, because autumn was just around the corner and the footings and the foundation all had to be poured and given ample time to cure prior to the first frost.

"Okay," I agreed, telling myself to take this one day at a time. "Let's start up again a week from Monday."

We shook hands and he walked with me to my buggy.

"Matthew?" he said as I hauled myself into the seat. His brow was knitted in concern. "If it turns out you can't track Clayton down, let me know as soon as you can, all right?" He cleared his throat. "'Cause either we start a week from Monday or we'll have to rethink the whole thing and slot it in for the spring instead."

I nodded, my stomach churning with frustration and disappointment and despair. "I'll find him," I said. Then I cracked the reins and began to roll down the driveway.

I have to.

By the time I reached home, the sun had already set and supper had long been finished. I walked through the door of our small house and slipped off my shoes, my mind exhausted from the frustrating and fruitless day. I hung my hat on the peg by the door and dropped into my favorite chair. The warmth of the summer evening and my weariness pulled my eyes closed. When they opened again, Amanda was sitting across from me, a cup of hot tea in one hand and a plate of food in the other.

"Hi, sleepyhead," she said, humor in her voice.

"How long was I out?"

"Only about ten minutes. I heard you come in the door and came to heat your dinner for you, but by the time I got here, you were already sawing logs." She leaned forward and handed me the cup and plate. I placed them on the table beside my chair and then took her hands in mine.

"Thank you," I said, looking in her eyes. "This is just what I needed after a long, long day."

Her smile faded as her face filled with concern. "Tell me everything."

And so, between bites of roast beef and carrots, I recalled my day to my beautiful wife, the burden of each failure feeling that much lighter with her to share the load.

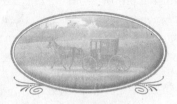

EIGHT

The next morning at the store, I took Noah around to the last aisle and explained that we wouldn't be returning the row of shelves to the walls and restocking them just yet. Instead, I needed him to rope off the area and make it inaccessible to customers for now. As he did that, Amanda and *Daed* went about removing all of the tarps from the other shelves and displays, and I grabbed a marker and some paper to write out a few signs apologizing for the mess and offering a "construction discount" of ten percent off everything.

We'd been spreading the word for several weeks that the store was going to be closed because of the construction, so I expected business to be slow. My intention was to help open up and then duck out, slipping over to the library to use the computer there and do some research.

But instead of a quiet day, the store quickly became swamped. I realized I wouldn't be able to leave for a long while, not until after the rush was done. All morning long, the bells hanging from the door handle chimed as people flooded in and out—and in again. We were used to being busy, especially in the mornings, but this steady of a stream was unusual for a Friday.

The urge to move my search forward grew even stronger when I realized that most of the customers weren't looking for horse feed or new reins. They were looking for gossip.

I spent some time in the part of the store that was closed, using the tall, empty shelves to sort out stock that had become mixed up in the shuffle of construction day. I couldn't see the customers from there as I worked, but I could hear them.

"I'm sorry about your shop," one man said. "It's too bad the hotel next door is kicking you off your property and building a second hotel."

"Oh, boy," I heard Amanda reply, forcing her voice to be light and friendly. "Sounds like the rumor mill is working overtime on that one."

The next customer asked if we offered guided tours "of the murderer's house and the farm that had been mysteriously willed to him by his father." The accent sounded *Englisch*. When I peeked my head around the corner, I saw a group of young men in jeans and T-shirts standing at the register. I walked over to relieve Amanda from the situation, asking them if they needed help finding anything. They pelted me with questions about Clayton Raber, but when I offered no exciting answers, they left.

I was about to return to my work area when, yet again, the bells rang. Two Amish men walked through, one younger and one older. I was prepared to tell them we wanted no part of their curiosity or rumors, but I could see by the knowledgeable way they looked around the store that they were here to shop, not gossip. Finally, some actual customers.

"Excuse me," the younger man said. "Where is your leather strapping?" He motioned to the older man beside him, explaining that he and his grandfather had a buggy shop down near Strasburg. "We've always bought our supplies at Waggoner's since it's so close, but now that he's retiring, he suggested we look here."

Deeply pleased at this development, I was about to respond when I heard Amanda gasp. I turned around quickly to see if she was okay, but when I looked at her, she was smiling. She walked past me and up to the two men.

"What a nice surprise seeing you in here!" she exclaimed. She shook both of their hands warmly, as if they were old friends. Turning to me, she said, "This is my husband, Matthew." I stepped forward and shook both of their hands. "Matthew, this is Joel and Tyler Miller."

The tone of her voice indicated I should know who they were. *Miller.* I recognized the last name but couldn't remember why.

Tyler must have seen the confusion on my face because he paused to explain. "We're related to the blacksmith Jake Miller. I'm his nephew—though we grew up more like brothers—and this is his father."

Miller. Now I remembered. Fumbling over my words, I welcomed them to the store, shook their hands again, and excused myself, retreating to the closed aisle as fast as was polite. I was more familiar with the name "Jake Miller" than I wanted to be. Amanda had courted him. She had been courting him, in fact, at the same time she was falling in love with me.

Whether these two men knew the whole story or not, I could still feel the heat in my face as I considered what Jake Miller must surely think of me, the "other man" who stole his girlfriend away. Then again, by doing so, I had freed him up to be available for the true love of his life. Obviously, things had worked out well for both of us in the end.

Working back behind the shelves, I couldn't really hear Tyler and Amanda's conversation at the register. But then she brought him to the section of the store with the leather straps, which was right on the other side of the aisle where I stood. Through no fault of my own, I was privy to their entire conversation.

At first they just talked about the merchandise and the kinds of products the Millers would be buying here from now on. But then their voices grew silent for a moment.

"How's Jake?" Amanda asked after the lull.

"He's doing well. He and Priscilla just had their first child a few weeks ago, a boy. They named him Daniel, after her late father. Mother and son are healthy."

"That's wonderful," Amanda said with sincerity.

"Jake misses his family and friends here, of course, not to mention his mother's cooking. But otherwise he's happily married and enjoying Indiana. His blacksmith shop there has grown so much, in fact, that this past spring he hired his first employee, a second blacksmith, to work along with him."

Amanda expressed her happiness and asked another question, but I was no longer listening. Relief had washed over me. I'd harbored such guilt about the whole matter, and seeing Joel and Tyler had reawakened that fear. But now that I knew Jake really had ended up with the right woman after all—as had I—I could forgive myself and let it go.

My mind was pulled from my thoughts when I heard Tyler say my name.

"Matthew looked sort of…uncomfortable about us being here. It's not going to be a problem for him, is it? That you used to date Jake?"

I cringed. Had I really been that obvious?

I heard her laugh. "No, Tyler. He's not uncomfortable. He's preoccupied." To my relief, she proceeded to inform him of the current situation with the expansion, the tension with Starbrite, and trying to locate Clayton Raber. I'd grown weary of the day's gossip, but this time around, the explanation was just the thing that was needed to reinforce Amanda's response.

Tyler was quiet for a moment once she was done. I could hear him picking up and putting down various leather straps. "You know, maybe Matthew should talk to someone in the police department to find out if they have an address for wherever Clayton moved to after he left here. That's where I'd start."

My eyes widened at the thought. It was a good idea, one I would try as soon as things slowed down a bit and I could leave.

"I found what I needed. Are you ready to check out, Tyler?" asked an older voice. Joel must have joined Amanda and Tyler in the next aisle.

"Yep, I'm ready. We were just talking. *Daadi*, have you ever heard of a man named Clayton Raber?"

"The clockmaker?"

"*Ya*. Amanda says he used to live here. This was his clock shop."

"Oh." Joel was quiet for a moment as he seemed to process this.

"Did you ever meet him?" Tyler asked.

"No," Joel replied, and then he cleared his throat. "Gosh. I was just a little thing when he lived around here, maybe four or five at the most when he moved away. Though now that you mention it, I do have a connection with the man. *We* have a connection with him, actually, in a sense. You know how we give free safety inspections on any buggy, even ones that didn't come from our shop?"

"*Ya*," Tyler said. "I did one of those yesterday for a guy who was buying a used spring wagon from a friend."

"Well, the reason we offer that service is because of something that happened to Clayton when he was a child. His father had bought an old market wagon from a neighbor, and it had a faulty axle—though neither one of them realized it at the time. One day when Clayton and his parents were out, the axle snapped and he was terribly injured. My father didn't know the family, but when he heard about the poor little Amish boy who had been so hurt and nearly lost a leg, he made a decision. From then on, he would provide free safety inspections on any buggy because he knew accidents like that one could be prevented with just a simple check by a person who knew what he was doing."

The volume of their voices lessened as they walked across the shop to the register, though I was glad I'd caught at least part of their conversation.

It was nice to hear that at least one good thing had come out of Clayton's tragic childhood accident, free safety inspections at one of the best buggy shops around.

I managed to get out of the store by noon, and after a quick lunch at home, I went to the police department. Two miles up the main road from home, I pulled in to see a long multicolored building painted in strips of blue, orange, and tan with a series of red garage doors. It was oddly colorful for a municipal building, and its cheery exterior gave me hope that it might contain what I needed inside.

The officer manning the desk asked what he could help me with, so I told him I was looking for information from an old case, one that had happened in the county in the fifties.

"You're going to need to fill out an information request form."

"I really just want the address of one of the people involved, if that information is even in there."

"Like I said, you'll have to file an official request."

"Can you at least tell me if it's going to be worth the trouble?" I asked. "It's kind of a long shot that the address would even be on there, isn't it?"

"Sorry, but that's not something I can look up here," he said, gesturing toward the computer. "Our digital records only go back to the late seventies."

"So how do I get that information?" I asked, trying to keep the frustration from my voice.

He looked at me blankly. "File an information request."

I pinched the bridge of my nose. "How long will that take to process?"

"If it gets cleared, you should have what you need in about five days."

Five days? Starbrite could have tracked down Clayton by then. But what else could I do?

"All right. I assume there's paperwork I need to fill out?"

"There is."

"May I have it?"

"We don't keep that here, sir. You'll need to go to the clerk of court's office in Lancaster."

I sighed. That would require hiring a car—and missing another day of work at the shop.

"You might be able to do it on the Internet," a policewoman offered from a nearby desk.

Deciding that was my best bet, I thanked them both and left for the nearest library, which was in Leola. Once there, I signed up for a computer, waited my turn, and then filed the request form online. Sure enough, it said I would receive the results in approximately five days. Why had I even bothered?

Hoping to redeem the trip, I moved on to another task. Still online, I googled "quitclaim deed" and then looked through the list of options until I found what I needed to create such a document for myself, just as the lawyer had suggested. Fortunately, a template was provided, and it wasn't long before I felt confident in what I was doing. Step by step, I pulled the deed together, filling in every blank except the price, as I knew that depended on Clayton and what we ended up working out once I found him and explained what had happened.

When I had finished creating the deed, the site instructed me to print it and have it signed in the presence of a notary public. After that, I was to take the notarized deed to the country records office to get it recorded, which would require a filing fee. Then all that would be left was to wait for the original deed to be mailed back to me.

Satisfied, I printed out the completed page and paid for it at the front desk. *Maybe I'm jumping the gun,* I thought as I returned to the computer, *but I want to be prepared for when I finally track down Clayton.*

I still had time to spare before my hour on the computer was up, so I decided to go into some old newspaper archives and read whatever reports I could find from back in 1955 about the death of Clayton's wife, his subsequent arrest, and his later release. Unfortunately, that was easier said than done. I knew the Lancaster paper, the *Intelligencer Journal*, had been around for a long time, so I started there. As it turned out, the paper had actually been in existence since the late 1700s—but their online archives only went as far back as 1989.

The Philadelphia papers weren't much better, the oldest archives dating from 1978. Frustrated, I tried casting the nets a little wider, searching papers in New York City and Washington, DC. I didn't know if the story had been big enough to merit coverage outside the Lancaster/Philly area, but given the unusual Amish element, I knew there was a chance. And though I was able to find some archives that went back that far, none of them included anything about it.

After a good fifteen minutes of poking around, I'd come up with only one thing, a single, brief mention in a now-defunct newspaper out of Baltimore I'd never heard of. It wasn't even an article about the incident, just a photograph and a snarky caption. The picture, taken from behind, showed a man in Amish clothing being led toward a police car by two uniformed officers. The wording underneath said simply: *So much for nonviolence: Lancaster County Amish man taken into custody, charged with killing his wife.*

There were no other details, no other related articles before or after, no mention whatsoever of the Amish man's name. I couldn't even know for sure that it was Clayton, though I didn't doubt it. The date fit, not to mention such an occurrence was incredibly rare—especially back in the fifties, when there were only about ten Old Order Amish communities in all of Pennsylvania.

Otherwise, my newspaper search was a wash—at least for today. If necessary, I knew I could go into Lancaster to the main library, where they probably had all the old newspapers on microfilm, but looking through that would take a lot of time and trouble, so I decided to hold off for now.

Before giving up the computer, I still had one last avenue to try, an idea Amanda had suggested last night: the membership rosters of the various clockmaker associations around the country. I thought such a search might be difficult, but it ended up being the easiest task I'd tackled all day. A few simple Google searches gave me access to a number of clockmaking groups, which I found encouraging. Unfortunately, they didn't pan out. Though I eagerly scanned every roster I could find, I saw neither a "Clayton" nor a "Raber" among them. By the time I was finished, my eyes were tired and my heart was heavy.

Once I left the library, I headed back to the Helmuth homestead. I'd made up my mind to try to speak with Joan again, to insist they help me out and give me some answers. But when the first of their pastures came into view, I pulled over, out of sight of the house. I studied the farm from where I sat. Long shadows of the animals played against the ground in the last rays of the day's light. Lamplight flickered in the kitchen window. The family might be sitting together, reading from the Bible, enjoying a piece of pie or strawberries-and-cream for dessert. Something told me not to go back there yet, that I needed something else—something new—that would get me through the door. Something that would persuade Becky to let me see her mother and then convince Joan to trust me enough to share any information she might have on the whereabouts of her brother that could aid in my search.

Dejected, I looked out across the rolling farmland one last time and then started up again. As I made my way home, I wondered if this was a hopeless cause. I wished again that my *grossdaadi* were around to advise me. I thought about my prayer that God would close any doors He didn't want me to go through. Maybe this really was one of those closed doors, and I should accept it as a sign to give up entirely. At this point, I just didn't know any more. All I knew for sure was that I was angry, hungry, exhausted, and hopeless.

Too bad our construction was on hold, I thought, because in that moment I would have loved nothing more than to take all of my frustrations out on the walls of the old clock-shop-turned-tack-store, busting them down with a vengeance.

Nine

I made it back in time to help Amanda close up the shop. As we worked, I spoke little, my mind preoccupied with the disappointing day. She must have noticed my silence, because as soon as she flipped the sign on the door, she came over to where I stood and placed her hand on my shoulder.

"Want to talk about it?"

The sweetness of her voice and sincere care in it drew me out of my thoughts. "I'm just frustrated." I rubbed my temples with my fingers. "It'll be okay."

"Well, this isn't going to make you feel any better," she replied, and then she reached under the counter and pulled out the spiral notebook in which we logged the store's phone messages. As she began relaying the returned phone calls that had come in for me today, I found myself growing so agitated that I picked up the broom and began sweeping the floor. From what I could tell, every single person on my list of out-of-town Raber relatives that I'd left a message for had called me back, but not a one had any answers to offer.

"At least that rules out the farther-away people," she said, trying to lift my spirits.

I swept the debris from the floor into a dustpan and bent over to pick it up, my stomach churning. With those people scratched off my list, there was no one else to approach, no more tactics left to try.

If only I could get in to see Joan Raber Glick. I just knew with her being Clayton's only surviving sibling that she had to have some kind of information that could point me in the right direction.

"Since when do Amish refuse to help other Amish?" I asked as I banged the dust from the pan into the trash bin. "We are always there for one another."

Amanda let me rant, perhaps sensing I needed to get the frustration and worry out of my system. When I was finished, she didn't even try to say anything to cheer me up, for which I was grateful. She must have caught on to how dire our situation was growing and knew that mere words would not encourage me now.

After she finished closing out the register, we carried the money to the back room to put it in the safe.

"What's that?" she asked, looking toward the area that had been partially dismantled when we'd broken down the old bathroom on Wednesday. Glancing over, I realized she was talking about an ancient coal hamper that our work had uncovered. Unused for I didn't know how many decades, it had been built into the far wall of the original structure and later covered over with plaster.

"Do you know?" she prodded, stepping toward it to get a closer look.

"*Ya,* that's an old coal bin," I explained as I finished locking away the cash. "Which means this building must have used coal heat at some point in the past."

Located at about knee level, the bin's metal door was flush to the wall and had been designed to work in tandem with a similar door on the exterior, where the coal would have been dumped into it from the outside. That door was long gone and bricked over, but this one had been made accessible again the other day when we'd broken away some of the wall's plaster. Amanda leaned down to study it now, and then she gripped the handle and gave it a tug.

"I wouldn't do that if I were you," I said in warning. "You might end up in a cloud of coal dust."

But it was too late. She'd pulled it open and was already peering inside.

"No dust," she said, her voiced echoing against the metal of the bin. "It's perfectly clean, as a matter of fact. But come look, Matthew. There's something else in here."

Skeptical, I joined her and peered down into the hamper. Sure enough, there was something at the back, wrapped in what looked like blue cloth. I reached into the hamper and pulled the bundle gently from its tomb-like niche, hoping it wouldn't disintegrate at my touch. But the space felt cool and dry, and I was able to easily lift the item from its hiding place. The cloth was soft to the touch, with hand-stitching around the edges, though whatever it encased seemed heavy and hard. I laid the package on a nearby table. Together, Amanda and I peeled back the corners of the blanket.

Inside was a clock, an intricately carved but very dusty mantel clock. For a moment, we just stared at it. It sat on an equally finely carved pedestal, and even though the cabinet was discolored and covered in dust and cobwebs, and the glass over the face of the clock was cloudy, I could see that it had been beautiful and quite fancy in its day.

It was definitely not an Amish clock, but I had a pretty good idea which Amish man had made it.

For a long moment, Amanda and I stood in silence, taking in this unexpected sight.

"Why in the world was a thing this beautiful shoved into a coal bin?" she asked.

My thoughts exactly. "I don't know. Maybe Clayton or his father used the old bin for storage once the shop converted over to another source of heat."

Amanda took the clock and studied it more closely, looked in the bin again, and said, "I don't think it was put there for storage. I think someone was using the coal bin as a hiding place, someone who didn't want this clock to be found."

She handed it back, and I carried the clock over to the desk, set it down, and began to examine it in a better light. I brushed away the dust and webs and turned it over. On the bottom were the initials *CR* and the Scripture reference *Ecc 3:1.*

CR. I'd recognize that lettering style anywhere.

I turned the clock back over and ran my finger along a delicate carved vine. The craftsmanship was extraordinary.

"You know what this is, don't you?" I whispered, my heart suddenly pounding in my chest. "It's my ticket to convincing Becky Helmuth into letting me talk to Joan. If I show up there with this clock, Becky will have to let me in."

I looked down at the clock and traced my fingers over the initials. How many times had I run my hands over them in my childhood room, wondering about the boy who had dug the letters into the soft wood decades before?

As I studied this work of art in my arms, I felt, once again, connected to its creator—a connection I had known my entire life. Was I sympathetic toward a misunderstood outcast or a cold-blooded murderer?

While that thought chilled me to the bone, it had no bearing on my current situation. I just needed to find Clayton and get his signature, not learn every detail of his life.

Yet now that I stood looking down at this clock, new questions began to flood my mind, ones that, in this moment, felt even more pressing than his whereabouts. Why was it hidden in the bin? Had he really killed his wife? And why did everyone around him seem to think he was guilty?

Most importantly, what *really* happened all those years ago?

PART TWO
Clayton

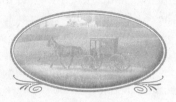

TEN

Lancaster County, Pennsylvania
1955

The two Amish men sat at opposite ends of the long wooden worktable inside Raber and Son Clockmakers shop. Clayton, the son, was busy filing the rough spaces between the teeth on a gearwheel the size of a dinner plate. His father, Simon, silver-bearded and pale, was repairing a sticking pendulum. They were quiet as they worked, each man concentrating on his own task. Occasionally, Clayton's *daed* would ask him to fetch something, so the younger man would rise from his stool without a word to attend to his father's request, limping to the parts bin or the tool rack and back again. It wasn't Simon's way to have others wait on him, especially not his physically impaired son, but after his recent diagnosis of heart failure, the man's activities had been strictly limited.

The doctor in Ridgeview had not minced words about it, saying no more barn chores, no more hitching up the buggy, and no more long hours at the shop. Instead, he'd given Simon two options: either complete bed rest, as was the norm with heart patients, or something called "armchair treatment," which he explained was a new, more active approach, one that was just catching on in the medical community.

"Lie in a bed or a sit in a chair? Those are my choices?" Simon had asked.

"Well, only if you want your heart to keep beating," the doctor had responded drily.

He was trying to make difficult news light, but everyone knew Simon would never allow himself to be that inactive—and that it would be only a matter of time even if he did. Limiting his activity would not heal his failing heart, but it might lengthen the span of his life. The doctor had not speculated on how long he could expect to live, and they had not asked. A man's days were numbered by God alone. Still, Simon agreed to follow the doctor's orders—for about three days, when he'd finally had enough of that and insisted on going down the hill to the clock shop.

"The doctor told me I could spend the day in an armchair," he said when challenged by his entire family. "So what difference does it make whether I'm in that chair in the living room, staring at the walls, or in a chair in the clock shop, doing something useful with my hands? I'm going stir-crazy here."

They had given in, reluctantly, and then set about making it happen. Clayton managed to rig up a sort of ad hoc wheelchair, which allowed him to ferry his dad from the house to the clock shop and back again each day—no easy task with a bad leg and a long, sloping driveway. They lived in Ridgeview, Pennsylvania, on a five-acre parcel of land that held a clock shop out in front at the bottom of the hill and several other structures—house, barn, and chicken coop—farther back, at the top. Thanks to the steep angle of the gravel driveway, Clayton had to struggle to keep the chair from going downhill too fast in the mornings and use all his might to push it back up the hill in the afternoons.

Making matters worse, it was obvious that Simon didn't like having Clayton do all the physical work, especially when it took twice as long to do it. His father didn't say so, but Clayton could see the frustration in the man's eyes every time he needed something from the house and Clayton had to hobble up to the homestead behind the shop, a process that was slow and tedious. That frustration was evident tenfold when it came to the barn chores, as Clayton had to leave the store extra early each day so he could get them all done before dark.

"I don't mind," he had said the first day he did the chores alone and also ferried his father back and forth to the shop.

"I know *you* don't," *Daed* had replied. "But I don't like just sitting here watching you—" he hesitated for a moment—"do what I used to do."

Clayton knew what his father had been about to say, that he didn't like watching him struggle. Both of his parents had always accepted what had happened when Clayton was five and a disastrous buggy accident had left him with a scarred face and a mangled leg. They trusted that God had allowed the accident to happen, and as Clayton grew up, they had taught him to see it that way as well. The maimed little boy aged into a quiet, aloof child who couldn't play the games the other boys could and often chose to be by himself instead. His self-imposed isolation continued once he was grown. He couldn't chase down a loose cow, carry around a sixty-pound bag of feed, or do much at barn raisings besides sit and saw planks. It took him minutes to climb the ladder to the hayloft instead of seconds. So why even try to keep up with the other young men?

Clayton had never attracted much attention from the women, either. Thanks to the impaired leg and the facial scar, he knew he wasn't husband material and that he would likely never marry. He had come to accept that as his fate.

Then again, that was when he'd pictured his future playing out much like his present, living with his parents in the house and working in the shop alongside his father for decades to come. Now that the doctor had diagnosed *Daed* with heart failure, however, Clayton's vision of his own life had been rocked to its core. He couldn't bear the thought of losing his father, but lose him he would, and probably soon. According to the doctor, Simon's heart was slowly winding down, like a clock whose key was lost and no replacement would do.

Raber and Son Clockmakers shop sat at the very end of the row of stores that made up Ridgeview's main shopping district. Housed in a simple white rectangular building, Clayton's father had erected it twenty-seven years earlier, the same year Simon and Lucille, who already had six daughters by then, were finally blessed with a son. Inside the shop was a showroom area for displaying and selling the clocks the two men made—beautifully decorated grandfather, mantel, and wall clocks that the *Englisch* were fond of, not to mention sturdy but far plainer timekeepers for their Amish clientele.

Beyond the sales floor, separated by a tall counter, was a large work area that included the broad table where they spent most of their time. They often used a pair of kerosene lamps to help them see the intricacies of their work, but those lamps sat unlit now thanks to the late afternoon March sun, which poured into the room from the wide windows at the front of the store.

Gas-powered table and scroll saws rested at the rear of the work area, crowded by shelves of clocks in varying stages of completion. A curtained doorway led to a back room with the store's will-call section for repaired clocks that were waiting for pickup, along with a small office area made up of a single desk and file cabinet. That room also held shelves filled with assorted parts and supplies, as well as a small bathroom.

Just as Clayton handed his father the item he'd requested and returned to his place at the table, various clocks surrounding them began to chime three thirty. That meant Clayton would be laying down his tools soon to take care of the horses and other livestock up at the homestead. Clayton and his parents were the only ones living at the house these days, as they had for the past four years, ever since Joan, the youngest of his six sisters, married one of the Glick boys and moved to her husband's family's place closer to Lancaster City. Clayton's other sisters, also married, were scattered about the county, busy keeping house and raising thirty-five children—and counting—among them.

Clayton didn't mind how quiet the house was now with just him and his parents living there. He had grown used to the peacefulness of it. Any need he had for socializing was met by visits with his large, extended family and through fellowship with the Amish community. But his closest childhood friends had long ago wed and were busy with their wives and children. And because Clayton accepted the fact that God's will for him was more than likely not to marry at all, he had learned to nurture his affection for a quiet home life instead.

"All right, then," his *daed* said, breaking the silence. "This one's now in working order. You want to take it on back?"

"Sure." Clayton swung his good leg around and rose slowly from his stool. He shuffled over to his father.

Daed laid the wall clock carefully in Clayton's hands. Though it functioned just fine now, the pendulum was still. Its owners would set the clock and wind it after getting it home.

"Careful," *Daed* said as Clayton turned and took a tenuous step.

"I got it." Clayton knew his father's eyes were on him as he limped toward the back room with someone else's heirloom in his hands.

Before he reached the curtain and the shelves that lay beyond, he heard the sound of a car pulling into their tiny gravel parking lot outside. He paused and turned to look through the front windows.

"*Englischers,*" *Daed* said.

A few seconds of silence passed as they watched a man, two women, and three children climb out of the big red automobile.

"Want me to handle them and put this back later?" Clayton started to set the clock down on the worktable.

"No, I can do it. Take that on back. I'll be fine."

Clayton nodded with relief. He hated the thought of *Daed* having to move around to help these people, but he hated even more dealing with folks he didn't know and therefore weren't used to the scar on his face and his pronounced limp.

Clayton pulled open the doorway's quilted curtain. The brass rings grated merrily across the metal rod as if happy to be of use, even as he closed the curtain again behind him. In four steps he was at the shelf for finished repairs, where he gently set down the clock. From the other side of the fabric barrier he heard the front door open, the little bells on the handle clanging against the frame. *Daed* greeted the people as they came inside, and they responded warmly, their voices carrying a hint of a Maryland accent, probably Baltimore. Giggling children were immediately admonished by what sounded like the older woman—their grandmother, perhaps?—not to touch anything.

Daed asked if he could help them and the man said they were looking for a clock to hang on a bedroom wall. Clayton tuned them out when the younger woman jumped in to describe the size of the space and type of decor. He hoped they wouldn't stay long, as he wanted to get back to the task he'd been doing at the worktable before the interruption.

As the minutes dragged on, however, he realized this wasn't just a quick tourist stop, which meant he had a decision to make. He didn't want his father's energy to be taxed—though so far, it sounded as though he was handling things just fine from his chair at the worktable. And Clayton knew the man would call out to him if anything physical was required.

But Clayton also really wanted to finish sanding all of the gearwheels before having to call it a day and go on his chores. But that, too, would mean shuffling out there in front of an audience, something he'd rather avoid. He decided to stay behind the curtain and tend to a few things there until either *Daed* called for him or the *Englischers* were gone, perhaps using this opportunity to make sure all was fully stocked and supplied.

Clayton looked toward the desk, where they kept their records and parts catalogs, glanced at their covers, and then he turned to the back wall where long strips of wood—stored in bins and stacked in planks—waited to be made into gearwheels and cases and clock cabinets. Clayton noted the plentiful supplies before turning to the wall opposite the desk to the parts section. From one of the middle shelves he pulled out a box of wood screws, gazed at its contents, and pushed it back.

This was pointless. He had already inventoried their parts supply just last week. Nothing was needed from any of the catalogs. He turned again to the will-call area, where clocks that had been repaired waited for their owners to return for them. Beyond the curtain he could hear his father still talking with the *Englisch* family, and one of the children was whining about how long it was taking. Clayton couldn't agree more.

He pulled opened the front of a mahogany wall clock that was lying on the shelf, took a handkerchief from his pocket, and began rubbing at the glass, even though he had already cleaned it the day before when he'd repaired the thing and put it there. One of the other children was now asking *Daed* what made an Amish clock different from a "regular" clock. Clayton imagined himself telling the child that the Amish were given three extra hours a day, so naturally their clocks had more numbers on them. He smiled at his own private joke—until he caught his reflection in the glass. Taking in his mirror image, the smile faded away, and the unspoken joke with it.

Clayton didn't need a reflection to tell him what he already knew, that his face was hideously marred by the scar he'd acquired in the same accident that had ruined his leg as a boy. Running nearly the width of his face just below his eyebrows, the injury had not affected his eyesight, for which he would always be thankful. But it had damaged some of the muscles in his forehead, and though the lines of it had faded somewhat over time, its effect on Clayton's appearance remained unchanged. Faded or not, something about the scar made him look as if he wore a perpetual scowl. Even when he smiled or laughed, the brows stayed tilted downward at the center, making him seem angry—an effect reinforced by his gruff exterior and occasional flare of temper.

His family had always insisted his facial scarring wasn't that big of a deal, that he was a fine-looking man regardless. He didn't believe them. That scar was all he could see when he glanced in a mirror, and he knew it was what others saw as well. As far as he was concerned, it made him seem like a monster—especially in combination with the bum leg.

Trying not to think about all of that now, Clayton closed the clock, stuffed the handkerchief back in his pocket, and stepped away from the shelves. As he did, he noticed faint movement outside the small window nearby. The neighbors' daughter, Miriam Beiler, was strolling slowly along the pasture fence that separated their two properties. She was unaccompanied, but even from a distance Clayton could see that her mouth was moving. That meant she was singing again, probably an *Englisch* tune from the radio her parents had made no secret that they wished she wouldn't listen to so much.

The reason for hiding out in the back office faded from his mind as Clayton stared at the figure in the white *kapp* and lilac-hued dress. Norman and Abigail Beiler's youngest daughter, newly twenty-one, often walked around humming songs from the world beyond Lancaster County. There was much about the auburn-haired Miriam that fascinated Clayton, not the least of which was her odd way of entertaining herself when she was alone. She was also known for being headstrong and opinionated, for unabashedly letting her beautiful singing voice carry across the fields, for resisting various other constraints of Amish life.

But what fascinated Clayton most about Miriam was that she hadn't stared at his leg nor been repelled by his face the first time they met, when she and her parents moved into the house next door five years before. She was the only person in his entire life, in fact, who had treated him as though his disability made him intriguing rather than troubling.

Not only had she not shown one bit of surprise or dismay upon seeing him for the first time, she'd actually told him, just a few weeks later, how she thought the leg and the scar made him seem "mysterious and interesting." He still blushed whenever he thought of that day. If he closed his eyes, he could see her taking in the sight of his scar up close, could still feel her fingertips gently touching his brow.

It happened on a sunny summer evening, when Clayton was twenty-two and Miriam just sixteen—though he hadn't realized her age at the time because she looked and acted so much older. Clayton's family kept chickens out behind the house, and he'd been standing in the chicken yard, sprinkling out feed for the hens when she came over from next door, stood at the fence, and watched him work. She announced that she was bored with "ordinary life," as she called it, something he would come to learn was not an uncommon state for her.

She offered to keep him company as he tended the chickens, and they chatted easily until he'd finished and put the bucket and rake away. Once he let himself out of the gate, latched it shut, and turned toward her to bid her goodbye, he was startled to see that she was staring at his leg—with not a hint of embarrassment on her face at having been caught doing so.

"How did you get all that, anyway?" she asked, gesturing toward his leg and then his face. She hadn't asked what had happened to him or what had he done, but rather how did he *get* it, as if it was something one might choose to acquire.

"A buggy accident a very long time ago," Clayton answered, which was his usual eight-word reply to those who did not know why he wore a permanent scowl or limped so badly.

He expected her to change the subject, or say she had to go, or fumble for comforting words like "sorry" or "that's too bad," as most people did. Instead, she simply waved for him to come closer. He didn't know what she wanted, but he felt certain she was teasing him somehow—and that made him angry.

"Come here," she said, motioning more insistently this time.

Confused, he allowed himself to look into her eyes—and that's when he realized she was sincere, her expression merely curious. She seemed in no way repelled or disgusted or disturbed. Tentatively, he limped toward her. To his astonishment, when he came to a stop in front of her, she raised up one hand and began running her fingers lightly along his scar.

Clayton swallowed hard, his heart pounding. There was nothing indecent or inappropriate about such an action, yet her touch felt more intimate to him than anything he had ever experienced in his life. His face burning with heat, he told himself to step away, that this wasn't right, that someone could be watching them at this very moment and misunderstand. But he was unable to move. It was as if his feet had taken root in the ground.

Finally, she lowered her hand to her side. "Tell me more," she said.

Clayton let out a breath that he hadn't even realized he'd been holding. "You really want me to?"

"Of course." She smiled. "But wait."

Miriam looked around, spotted a row of hay bales near the barn, and went over to them. She sat and then patted the bale next to hers, motioning for Clayton to join her. She pulled her legs up under her and tucked her dress around her shins.

When he hesitated, she said, "Stories are best told sitting down."

Stories. As if the events that had led to Clayton's crippling were meaningful, a plot point in an overarching adventure story, one in which he was the hero.

"All right." Almost oblivious to the pain that was his constant companion, Clayton limped the distance between them, breathing heavily as he lowered himself onto the hay bale beside hers. Then he was quiet for a moment. It had been so long since he'd told this story to anyone that he wasn't even sure where to start.

"I was five," he said at last, clearing his throat. "It was a Saturday afternoon, and my parents and I were on our way home from the farm supply store in New Holland."

He glanced at her. She gave him an encouraging nod, so he continued, his voice growing stronger as he spoke. "We always took the family buggy wherever we went, but that day my *daed* was planning to buy a new water tank, so we'd had to go in our rickety old market wagon instead."

Clayton hesitated, not sure how to proceed. Never before had anyone shown such compassionate interest in his story. He fumbled through his memories, trying to think of the best way to explain.

"He'd bought the wagon on the cheap from a neighbor who was moving away," he said, backtracking just a bit. "He got it just to use around here, solely as a farm vehicle." Clayton smiled. "I mean, you wouldn't exactly call this a farm—even if we do have some chickens and a milk cow—but this place is big enough to need a wagon now and then."

Miriam nodded, thoroughly engrossed in his tale as he continued.

"At the store, we loaded the big tank onto the wagon and headed for home. My parents sat up front, side by side, on the driving bench, and I sat in back." He felt his cheeks warm as he added, "I was supposed to stay in the seat, but after a while I climbed up on top of the tank and straddled it, pretending it was a horse and I was riding it home."

Miriam chuckled. "I can just picture it. Then what happened?"

Clayton rubbed his neck. It was strange recollecting the events of the accident in such detail. It all felt so far away, like it was a different lifetime. And yet he could still remember quite clearly the woodsy smell of the air, the cold hardness of the metal tank beneath him, the *clip-clop* sound of the horse as it struggled to cart the heavy load home.

"We'd just reached the upward slope of the bridge when the wagon's front right axle gave out—I remember the loud *thwack!* as it snapped—releasing the wheel and sending it careening off into the ravine."

Clayton closed his eyes, remembering his sudden shock at the buggy crashing down to one side, ripping loose some of the straps from the horse and causing her to twist and tumble. He remembered the sensation of flying through the air, followed by the strike of hard ground and then something heavy on top of him, crushing his leg, something liquid in his eyes, making it hard for him to see.

"All three of us were thrown from the wagon when it crashed. My parents landed on grass and just ended up with some cuts and bruises. But the wagon fell on me so I didn't fare as well. Oh, and the poor horse had to be put down."

"Your parents got you to a hospital?" Miriam whispered in a shaky voice.

"Some cars came along pretty soon after, so there were people around to help. They managed to get me to the emergency room, where the doctors sewed up my face and did what they could with my leg—though for a while there, it looked like I might lose it. I ended up staying for two weeks, and then they sent me home."

Clayton looked down at the useless limb, once so normal and now just a painful souvenir of his journey on a faulty wagon with a bad axle.

"And that's the story," he said. "Sorry you asked?"

Miriam shook her head, dabbing at glistening tears at the corner of her eyes. "Thank you for telling me."

He nodded, unable to resist turning his face to meet her eyes. When he did, he saw that she was gazing right back at him, taking in the scar at his brow and then reaching up once more to touch it softly with her delicate fingers.

"It looks like it still hurts," she said. "Does it?"

He took in a breath, unsure how to answer. Yes, the injury *did* still hurt, but not so much in the physical sense. It hurt inside. It hurt to know that his life had been so inextricably altered in the snap of a single axle. It hurt that no woman could ever love a broken man like him—not even Miriam. She might be different from the other girls in the district, but she was beautiful, far too beautiful for the likes of him. No question, someday she would end up winning the affection of a handsome, able-bodied Amish suitor, one who could offer her everything that Clayton could not.

Even now, five years after that particular conversation, he could still feel the pain of that realization. Standing at the window in the back room, gazing out at her as he continued to wait for the customers to leave, he had to admit that she'd only grown more beautiful with time. And though no one had snatched her up for marriage just yet, it would no doubt happen soon.

Suddenly, almost as if she could sense Clayton staring at her through the glass of the clock shop, Miriam looked up from her odd reverie. Startled, he backed clumsily away from the window, hoping to duck out of sight—and ended up nearly toppling over a small boy who was standing right behind him.

Clayton grabbed for the shelving unit to keep from toppling onto the child, nearly knocking over an antique anniversary clock and its glass dome. As he struggled to steady himself, the gasping, wide-eyed boy took a step backward, tripped over a trash can, and fell onto his bottom.

A quick mix of embarrassment and anger roiled up from within Clayton as the child gaped at him from the floor, taking in his scarred brow and comically awkward movements. It was a look Clayton had seen plenty of times, whenever he was out in town among strangers or in the shop with new customers. He had once heard an *Englisch* teen joke to another that he shuffled around like Frankenstein's monster—and from the look in this kid's eyes, he was thinking the very same thing.

After a momentary pause, Clayton extended his hand to help the boy to his feet. "You're not supposed to be back here," he said, nervousness making him sound perturbed.

The child reached for the curtain behind him as he got to his feet but grabbed only at air.

"You need to go back to your parents." Clayton took a few lurching steps forward and reached for the curtain to pull it aside for him.

The boy apparently assumed Clayton was instead grasping for him, and he let out a wail as he lunged for the curtain and nearly pulled it off its rungs. He swept past it and emerged on the other side, out of Clayton's view.

"Theodore!" From the other side of the swaying fabric, Clayton heard one of the women call out the boy's name. "What's wrong with you? What were you doing back there?"

"There's a weird man in that room! He tried to grab me!"

Clayton felt a blade of shame slice through him, a familiar cut.

"What on earth are you talking about?" the male voice demanded.

"There's a weird man back there!" the boy said again, less fearful, more insistent this time.

"He's my son," *Daed* said. "He's not weird; but he was just injured as a child. That's all. Clayton, come on out."

That's all. Instead of doing as his father asked, Clayton backed up against the wall, away from the curtain, and tipped his head back on the window glass.

"Oh," the woman replied, pity replacing her earlier concern. "That's too bad."

"He tried to grab me!" the boy said again.

One of the other children, a girl, whined that she wanted to go back to the hotel.

"I'm sure he did not try to grab you, son," *Daed* replied. "Clayton!"

Seconds of silence.

Clayton finally limped toward the curtain, pulled it aside, and stood in the doorway facing six sets of *Englisch* eyes. "The child startled me," he said. "He fell. I was only trying to help him to his feet. He shouldn't have been back here."

"Clayton," *Daed* said, frowning slightly.

More seconds of awkward silence.

"No. He's right. Theodore shouldn't have been back there," the younger woman finally said, gentle and sincere but with finality in her tone. They would be leaving without buying anything, Clayton was sure of that. "Well, then," she continued. "Thanks for showing us your clocks. They're very lovely."

"I was only trying to help the boy to his feet," Clayton repeated.

"Of course you were. Thanks." The man moved toward the front door and the others followed him. The family stepped outside.

Clayton and his father watched through the glass as the car doors were opened and shut and the people drove away.

"He shouldn't have been in the back room. I didn't see that boy. I nearly fell over him and brought down a clock," Clayton said defensively.

Daed took a minute to respond. "It's all right. They weren't going to buy anything, son. I think they were just looking. Why don't you go on up to the barn and start on the chores."

When Clayton hesitated, his father smiled gently at him. "Don't worry about it. Just keep in mind what I'm always telling you. That even though something is true, you don't need to say it. You were right that he shouldn't have been back there, but you didn't have to speak so harshly. You didn't have to say it at all."

From his position in the doorway, Clayton was half in the shop and half in the back room. He turned his head to view the pasture on the other side of the window. Miriam was no longer in sight.

His father was at the curtain now, standing right beside him. "Did you hear me?"

"*Ya*. I heard you." Clayton made no move to leave the shop.

Daed was silent for several seconds. "Go on, then. Get the chores done so that you can get me back to the house before the sun goes down. Don't forget that Joan and Maisie and their families are coming over for supper tonight."

At the sound of his sisters' names, Clayton turned to face his father. He knew what this was about, but he didn't want any part of it.

"Why do you insist on talking about this stuff?" Clayton asked, his heart heavy.

"We have to plan for the inevitable. You'll need some help around here when I'm gone, son."

"I can handle things."

His father shook his head. "The shop and the animals and the house are too much for one person."

"I have *Mamm*."

"You'll need more than just her. And you know her asthma makes it hard for her to help with the barn chores."

Clayton wanted to reply that he most certainly did not need more help than just *Mamm*. But he knew his *daed* had been thinking about this for a while, ever since his diagnosis of heart failure. Now it seemed he'd come up with a solution, one that involved the whole family. One that Clayton didn't want to hear.

"Do we *have* to do this?" he murmured, already picturing the peaceful silence of the evening being shattered by the chaos and noise of Maisie's and Joan's combined brood of eleven children.

But *Daed* had started to walk away and hadn't heard him.

Clayton limped to the back door of the shop, reached for his straw hat on the peg, and stepped outside into the chilly March afternoon.

ELEVEN

Clayton hobbled up the dirt path from shop to homestead with his hands in his pockets, pondering how to convince *Daed* he didn't need Maisie or Joan at the shop once the man's weak heart finally stopped beating. It wasn't that Clayton didn't get along with his older sisters—he got along fine with all six of them—but he just didn't like the ceaseless chatter when they were around, the constant fixing and straightening, the hovering over him as though he were still a wounded child, and the endless interfering, no matter how well-intentioned.

He didn't want that kind of attention once *Daed* was gone. It would be hard enough getting used to working alone in the shop without Maisie and Joan smothering him with far too much consideration. Clayton had been working in his father's shop since he was a child. *Daed* had taught him everything he knew about making clocks, and while they didn't say much to each other during the hours they were there, he had always felt a keen sense of camaraderie with his father no sister could replace. Nor could *Mamm*.

He was willing to concede he might need help with the barn chores, but not in the shop—and especially not Maisie, with her overpowering ways and need to correct everything he did. That was *not* going to happen. Maisie was tolerable only in small doses.

As Clayton trudged up the hill, he decided he would calmly listen to whatever plan *Daed* had come up with. He would give the appearance of thoughtfully considering it. He'd thank his father for thinking ahead. He'd thank his sisters for coming out for supper. But when the day came when *Daed* was gone, the shop would be *his* to run. He would do so alone, and if it turned out to be too much for him, *he* would be the one to decide who could come in and share the workload with him.

There was only one problem with that plan, and the thought of it made him sigh. If he manned the shop by himself, he would have no choice but to take down the curtain. It had been his idea to begin with, placed there so that when out-of-towners came he could stay out of sight and save them the distress of having to look at him—not to mention save himself from having to put up with their questions and stares.

As he pictured yanking the old quilt off its rings, Clayton knew that if he chose to work alone, he could no longer hide from others. He'd just have to make more of an attempt to be pleasant and cordial when someone he didn't know came into the shop or when little kids didn't stay where they were supposed to or when curiosity got the best of people and they simply had to know why he shuffled around like that. And yes, maybe he would need some help in the shop on Saturdays, especially during the busier summer months. Perhaps one of his quieter nephews, one of the ones just out of eighth grade, such as Maisie's Titus or Joan's Obed, would like to learn the clockmaking trade, or at least to earn a few dollars helping to wait on customers.

Clayton entered the barn feeling good about his plan of action. He didn't like thinking about life without *Daed* in it, but for the first time since his father's diagnosis, Clayton felt that he had a handle on what would befall the family in the foreseeable future.

He breathed in the earthy scents of hay and animals, relishing the quiet solitude. After feeding the pair of pigs they were raising for butchering in the fall and shoveling out the chicken coop, Clayton grabbed two lead ropes and walked out to the small pasture between the houses where Miriam had been earlier. Their horses, two Standardbreds Clayton's mother had long ago named Winnie and Snowflake, needed to be brought in from the field out behind the house. He looked up at the Beiler home as he attached the lead rope to Winnie's nose halter, and then he just as quickly turned his head away when he realized he had done so.

Clayton led their horses to their stalls, fed and watered them, and then turned his attention to the newest addition to the barn, a sweet-tempered

Jersey who was due to give birth in the coming weeks. He had just finished raking out Rosie's pen and was about to lay down fresh straw when he heard a voice behind him.

"Will you let me know when Rosie starts to calve?"

Startled, Clayton whipped his head around. Miriam was standing with her arms crossed nonchalantly over the rail, almost as if she had been there for hours. She and her family didn't have any livestock at their place other than buggy horses, so she often came to the barn at chore time. But that's when *Daed* was usually here too, and the two of them could hear her singing all the way toward them.

"Miriam! When did you come in?" Clayton glanced toward the door, knowing they shouldn't be in here alone together for too long, as it might reflect poorly on her.

"You will, won't you?" she said, bypassing Clayton's question. Her brows were knit together in careful thought. She was beautiful as always, and Clayton had to look away from her.

"Uh. *Ya.* I guess." Moving as quickly as he could, Clayton tossed out new straw for Rosie and then slipped from the pen, latched it shut, and put the pitchfork away. "She might calve while we're all asleep, though," he added as he headed for the door. "That happens more often than not."

"Well, tell me when it gets close, then," Miriam replied, falling into step behind him, "and maybe I'll come down here and sleep on the hay next to her so I won't miss it."

"Miss it?"

"Newborn calves. They're adorable."

Clayton laughed nervously, partly because it was a crazy notion, and partly because Miriam was the sort of person to attempt such a feat. The thought of her curled up in Rosie's pen all night, just a stone's throw from the house, made his heart pound. "I don't believe your parents would think that was a great idea," he said, peeking at her from beneath the brim of his hat.

"You're right." She sighed in frustration, the sun's long rays surrounding her shiny auburn hair, neatly bound in its twisted bun and partially covered by her crisp white *kapp*. "I don't know why they're always so critical of everything I do."

Clayton waited a moment to see if she expected him to respond. It wasn't exactly a question, even though he knew the answer. It was because Miriam didn't fit the mold. She was her own person, one who marched to the beat of her own drum, and that was about as un-Amish a thing as anybody could be. As a child, she'd gotten away with far more than most. But now that she was grown, the time for being unconventional was over. Clayton knew that Miriam's parents were eager for their daughter to wrestle down her more individualistic tendencies, join the church, and submit to authority and community.

"They're not just critical," she continued. "They're meddlesome too."

Finished with the chores, Clayton should have been making his way back down to the shop to help *Daed* close up and then wheel him back to the house. But Miriam was making no move to return home herself. If he said he needed to get back to the shop, she'd end their conversation.

And he didn't want it to end.

Clayton glanced toward the horizon. Judging by the angle of the sun, he decided he could spare another fifteen more minutes or so before his *daed* would start wondering where he was. Until then, he would remain here with Miriam, using the time to do some pruning as they chatted.

"Meddlesome?" he asked as he walked over to a nearby sapling, Miriam following close behind.

She let out a laugh, one without mirth. "To put it mildly."

"But they're your parents, Miriam. It's been their job to train you up in the way you should go."

"Even now that I'm in my twenties? Even when it comes to choosing a mate?" Her voice was coated with challenge.

Clayton felt an odd lurch in his stomach. Choosing a mate? Was Miriam considering marriage? With his bare hand, he snapped a dying branch from the tiny trunk with such force that the wood made a loud *crack* and splintered. He swallowed hard and glanced at her, afraid she may have noticed his change in temperament, but she seemed oblivious. He turned his attention back to the tree, trying to keep his eyes on the task at hand. "I didn't realize you were being courted," he managed to mutter.

"I'm not."

The relief he felt almost made him exhale aloud.

She pulled some browning leaves from one of the branches and continued. "They've been harassing me to find a husband. Settle down. Start a family. All that stuff."

"All that stuff," Clayton echoed again, feeling an odd mix of elation and dismay—elation that she wasn't yet involved with anyone, dismay that it was only a matter of time.

"Like tonight, for example. Would you believe they've invited someone to dinner—as a date for me? Some older man from another district who apparently needs a wife and thinks I might fill the bill. I can't believe their nerve—of them for asking him to come, and of him for coming. Since when do Amish parents meddle in their children's love lives? It's ridiculous. How embarrassing!"

Clayton wanted to say something in response, but hearing her confide in him about a potential suitor made the words in his head disappear. She was right. Among the Amish, when it came to marriage and dating decisions, parents rarely were involved. Instead, once their children reached the age of sixteen or seventeen, they would look the other way, at least somewhat, allowing such choices to be worked out in private. Parents might offer a word of advice here and there, but sometimes they wouldn't even be aware of a serious relationship until their children informed them that they were engaged.

"I'm sure they think they're acting in your best interests."

"Don't kid yourself, Clayton. This is about *their* best interests, not mine. They seem to think that because I'm not being courted by anyone and I've quit another job, I simply must get married by tomorrow or they'll be stuck with me forever."

"You've quit another job?" He tore a twig from the tree, wanting very much to be done with the topic of dating entirely.

Her shoulders slumped. "I hated working at the furniture store. It was so boring. It smelled like sawdust and varnish, and everyone was always so serious. And they didn't allow singing. Not even humming."

"Oh." A tiny thought began to percolate at the back of Clayton's mind. "So you're looking for another job, then?"

She turned to him and smiled triumphantly. "Actually, I already have a lead on a new job. Cleaning house for an *Englisch* couple in Lancaster. They want an Amish woman because they say we know how to keep a house. They're tired of *Englisch* girls who only do a job halfway."

"Oh?"

"My friend Kate told me about it. You know Kate, right? She's had the job herself for only a few weeks, but now she and her husband have decided to move down to Quarryville, so she has to quit. She told them she knew someone else who might be interested, and now they want to talk to me."

"You said the job's in Lancaster?"

She nodded. "According to Kate, the people have a big house, lots of money, and no children. She's a career woman, so she doesn't have much time to fool with housework and stuff. Kate's job has been to clean up after them, do their laundry, dust and mop, shine the silver, and have dinner waiting on the stove for when they come home. She says when they arrive, they just collapse in front of their television and eat. They have a television, Clayton!"

"Oh."

"I've never seen one myself. You probably haven't either, but Kate says it's really something. She says you can't imagine all the different kinds of shows there are. Kate's favorite is called *Secret Storm*, and it comes on every day. It's a drama, but she says there are also comedies. Shows where people play games and win money. Shows just for children, with puppets and stuff. There are even shows where all the people do is sing."

"Really?" Clayton said, only half listening.

"Yes, really. Can you imagine? How fun."

Miriam went on, but Clayton hardly heard a word she said. Instead, his mind was consumed with asking her the question that had been somersaulting in his brain for the past few minutes, ever since she told him she'd quit her latest job. Now that she was available, would she consider working for him? At the clock shop?

If she did, he wouldn't need Maisie or Joan or anyone else pestering him about trying to man the store all by himself. Between him and *Mamm* and Miriam, everything would be covered.

But the thought of even framing such a question made his face grow warm. He cleared his throat to chase the nervousness away. "Do you think you will like cleaning up after people and cooking for them?"

"Well, it sure beats breathing in sawdust all day. And I can sing whenever I want to. There won't be anybody there. Of course, my parents aren't too happy about it. They said they don't want me in an *Englisch* house, just singing all the time or watching television. As if I'd have time for that with all of the cleaning and cooking to be done."

Clayton snapped off one last tiny limb and prayed for the courage to ask Miriam if perhaps she would like to work in the clock shop instead. In fact, if she started soon, they could train her on all the facets of the business while *Daed* was still around. Besides handling the customers, she could also take on the bookkeeping and other administrative functions, freeing Clayton to focus almost exclusively on clockmaking and repairs.

Then again, there was the matter of propriety, he realized, as it wouldn't do for an unmarried man and woman to spend their days together inside the same small building, alone except for the occasional customer or two. But there had to be some solution for that, even if it meant one of his nephews working there with them, as he'd been thinking about before, and serving as a chaperone of sorts.

"I just feel like I need a break from life here," she continued before he could speak. "I need to see something different. I need a change. Do you ever feel that way, Clayton? Like you just wish you could do something new. Something not Amish?"

Clayton coughed back his shock. "Not Amish?"

"I just want to see something pretty every day. I want to be surrounded by pretty things. Not for forever. Just for a little while."

"You…you mean fancy things?"

"Yes, okay. Fancy things. I want to see photographs of the ocean and feel lace on my skin and smell perfume and watch the sun glint off stained glass. And I want to sing in the rain and dance on tiptoe and wear a sparkly bow in my hair and paint with watercolors. I want to hear someone play a cello and have my nails done and go to the theater to see a play or a symphony."

Clayton had never heard Miriam talk this way. It was almost as if she had forgotten she was speaking to one already baptized into the church. Her eyes had a faraway look, and it suddenly struck him that he needed to speak with her about all of this—as a Christian brother, if nothing else. Because if this was how she really felt, then taking a position in a fancy *Englisch* house was only going to make things worse. This new job, if she ended up getting it, would carry her even further away from the Amish principles with which she'd been raised. He was trying to decide how to phrase his objections when she shot him an astute glance.

"I know what you're thinking, Clayton, but please don't say anything. You're the only one who doesn't have a fit when I talk this way. I just need some place where I can spit it out like this, just the honest, gut-level truth."

He hesitated and then nodded. If she already knew, what would be the point in speaking his admonishments out loud?

"I'm sure that after a while I'll want to come home and marry and live an Amish life, but right now, I feel like I'm going to burst. I just want something *different* to happen. Church member or not, I know you know what I mean."

His mind returned to the thought of her working at the clock shop, and it was on the tip of his tongue to ask her about it when they heard footsteps approaching.

They both turned their heads as Clayton's petite *mamm* stepped around tree. She smiled cordially at their neighbor, but Clayton detected a shimmer of apprehension.

"You're wanted at home, Miriam," she said. "Apparently you have company coming and you need to get ready."

Miriam turned away, a flash of irritation crossing her features as she did.

"*Danke*," she said, as she started to walk off. "Bye, Clayton."

"See you," he called after her, feeling as unfinished as a sentence interrupted after the first word. *If only* Mamm *had come along just a few minutes later!*

Miriam strode across the wide grassy field between their houses. Clayton watched as she reached the split-rail fence that separated the two properties and let herself out through the gate. Usually she didn't bother, but he supposed she was acting with modesty now for the sake of his mother, who would not think very highly of a young woman hoisting herself up over a fence and down the other side.

"Don't forget, Clayton," *Mamm* said, interrupting his thoughts, "Maisie and Joan and their families will be joining us tonight."

He felt a surge of anger well up within his chest. "*Ya*, at *Daed*'s request," he snapped. "I haven't forgotten."

His mother sighed, as if she already knew the evening was going to play out badly. "Your father wants to have a few things in place for you when—" She stopped for a moment, her voice breaking as she added softly, "When the time comes."

He glanced her way, feeling guilty for having taken his frustration out on her. Clearing his throat, he pushed back the anger and spoke in a far gentler tone.

"Everything is already in place," he said softly. "*Daed* doesn't need to worry about any of it. I'll be fine. You and I will be fine."

She looked up at him, her eyes swimming with tears. "You will hear him out, though, won't you? This is important to him."

"*Ya*. I will listen to what he has to say."

His mother nodded, turning away to dab at her tears with the hem of her apron. As she did, Clayton's gaze returned to the retreating form of Miriam Beiler, who was now almost to her own house. When she turned the final corner at the back and disappeared from view, he realized that his mother had been watching as well.

"I understand a suitor is coming to supper at the Beilers' tonight," she said, her voice heavy with implication.

Clayton didn't reply. Instead, he turned and began limping toward the clock shop. He knew what *Mamm* was really trying to tell him.

He just didn't want to hear it.

TWELVE

Supper was a much noisier and more chaotic affair than usual, and Clayton was relieved when it ended and most of the children were sent outside to play in the last of the day's sun. Only the two youngest remained. All of the leftovers had been put away, a fresh pot of coffee had been made, and now Clayton, his parents, his sisters, and their husbands were all seated in the big front room. The two toddlers were on the rug nearby, quietly entertaining themselves with a basket of toys *Mamm* kept handy for when little ones came to visit.

"I'll get right to it," *Daed* began. "I want to make sure Clayton and *Mamm* will be able to keep the business going and tend to all the day-to-day details of the house and the land once I'm gone." He reached for his wife's hand as he said this and gave it a squeeze. Her eyes immediately glistened. "I want to know I have everything in order before another day goes by, and that's why I asked you all over tonight." He looked at his daughters and their husbands with purpose and conviction.

Clayton had just opened his mouth to speak, ready to assure his father that there was no need to worry, when Maisie beat him to it.

"Roger and I have been talking about this," she said, turning toward her husband.

He gave her a nod and then looked to *Daed* as he took it from there.

"With Reuben coming on fifteen and Fern nearly thirteen, they are good, responsible workers. Maisie and I have decided we can spare them a couple afternoons a week so they can help out in the barn and in the clock shop. On Tuesdays I can come along too." He looked toward Joan and her husband, adding, "Solomon, you said Thursdays were good for you folks, *ya*? And some of your boys can help with morning chores on Mondays and Fridays?"

"*Ya*," Solomon and Joan replied in unison.

As Roger continued, clarifying with Solomon the details about who would handle which chores when, Clayton looked over to his father, who was listening intently, seeming pleased and surprised that his children had already talked all of this over and come up with some solutions. Clayton's eyes went to Maisie and then Joan, both of whom were just sitting there, beaming proudly, as their husbands controlled the discussion. When they were finally done, Joan added that although she was planning to be here on Thursdays, there were a few coming up that might be problematic.

"*Ya*," Solomon said, looking at *Daed*. "But not to worry. I'll be filling in for her here on those days."

Again Clayton opened his mouth to interject, but his father filled the gap. "Well, it's a great relief that you four have already thought things out so thoroughly—"

But before he finished his sentence, Maisie cut in again. "We've talked to the others too," she said, referring to her other sisters and their families.

Roger nodded. "Katrina and Pauline promised to come when they can, but they couldn't commit to specific days or times. And Dorothy and Libby both said either they or one of their older children could get here once a week or so to lend a hand—at least until the tobacco starts coming in and everyone's needed at home."

"Best of all," Maisie added, "everybody is willing to start right away, even next week if you'd like." With a smile, she sat back and crossed her arms over her chest, as if there was nothing further to talk about.

"Oh, my," *Mamm* said, as the tears that had formed earlier finally slipped down her cheeks.

"I don't know what to say," *Daed* murmured gratefully, tearing up a little himself.

"You don't have to say anything," Roger replied. "Don't give it another thought. We'll see to it that Clayton and *Mamm* are in good hands. I promise."

Maisie, Joan, and Solomon nodded in agreement with him.

Clayton hadn't felt this invisible in a long time. No one had even looked his way or so much as intimated he might have something to say about their grandiose plan to swoop in and take over his life. Hot anger rose up inside him, and he knew he had to tamp it down before letting loose his own opinion. As he silently counted seconds to gain control, the others rose from the sofa to embrace *Daed* and *Mamm* and assure them all would be well, no matter what happened.

"Wouldn't anyone like to hear what I have planned?" Clayton said finally, but no one seemed to notice. "I'm speaking here," he said, louder this time, bridled anger making it sound as if he were pushing his voice past sand.

"What was that, son?" *Mamm* asked, her grateful tears shining on her face.

When he replied, it was in a shout. "I'm trying to tell you people about *my* plans!"

Every head in the room now turned toward him. His sisters unwrapped their arms from around their parents and stared at him, wide-eyed.

Daed seemed to be the first to realize what was going on. "Of course, son. Of course we want to hear your ideas."

He sounded sincere, but Clayton couldn't keep the anger from his voice as he spat, "I don't have 'ideas,' *Daed*. I have a plan. And because the clock shop is going to be *my* business and *Mamm*'s care *my* responsibility, I would appreciate being heard."

Roger and Maisie and Joan and Solomon all retook their seats. Clayton's outburst nearly echoed from the walls as an awkward silence filled the room.

"We didn't mean to sound as though you wouldn't have a say in any of this, Clayton," Roger offered a moment later, his voice calm but assertive.

"Didn't you? Because it sure seemed like it to me."

"Clayton, your sisters and their families have gone to some trouble to come up with a way to help you and *Mamm*," his father said gently. "It sounds like a good plan to me."

"But I don't need their help. I didn't ask for it and I don't want it."

"Why don't you tell us what your thinking is, then," Roger said, leaning forward, elbows on knees, acting as if his mind wasn't already made up.

Clayton cleared his throat, reminding himself to choose his words carefully. "I would be happy to have your boys come by a couple times a week to help with afternoon chores if they wish, and my nieces are welcome to pitch in as well. But I don't need anyone to do morning chores before the shop opens. I can handle all of that myself. And as to—"

"But there's a lot to be done in the mornings, Clayton," Roger said, his voice even and low. "You needn't wear yourself out before your day at the shop even begins."

"*Ya*—" Solomon started to chime in, but Clayton interrupted him.

"I get up at five every day. The shop doesn't open until nine. We have two horses, two pigs, one cow, and a dozen chickens. Do you really think it takes me four hours to do the morning chores?"

"Clayton," *Daed* said his son's name with a measure of caution in his voice.

Clayton turned to his father. "*Daed*, you and I together did the chores in an hour. Recently, I've been doing them alone in well under two."

"*Ya*, but—"

"But what? I could open the shop at ten o'clock instead of nine and we'd lose no business. That would leave me with *five* hours every morning to take care of this homestead and *Mamm*. That's more than enough time, even for a helpless cripple like me."

"Clayton!" his mother exclaimed.

Her scolding tone was so clear that the two children playing on the floor looked up, as if to make sure it wasn't them who had done something wrong.

Maisie leaned over the coffee table and gave her brother's good knee a gentle pat. "Clayton, we're not saying you're not capable of doing it all, we're just saying you shouldn't have to."

"Why shouldn't I have to? You all take care of your homes and businesses on your own. I'm not married and I don't have children. This home and this shop and *Mamm* are my only responsibilities."

Maisie narrowed her eyes. "*Daed* and *Mamm* are our parents too. And you're our brother. Just because we have our own families to care about doesn't mean we've stopped caring about this one."

"But you're inventing a need where one doesn't exist," he shot back. "I haven't asked anyone for help."

"Remember, though," *Mamm* said to him, her voice wavering. "We're not just talking about now. We're talking about…down the road. In the future."

Clayton took a deep breath and let it out slowly, reminding himself that this wasn't easy for any of them.

"Look," he said, more softly now, "I would appreciate help with the vegetable garden this summer, and actually it would be great if someone else could do the chores here on Saturdays because that's my busiest day in the shop. But beyond that, there's nothing else I need. If you people insist on helping, then fine, come help *Mamm* clean the house or cook or can. But I have everything else under control. I really do."

Tension hovered in the room, silent now except for the two toddlers giggling together as they played on the floor.

"What about the shop itself?" Roger asked finally.

"What about it?"

"You're saying you don't want help in there either? At all?"

"I already have help," Clayton said, looking to his mother.

She nodded. "That's true. I'm always here to pitch in on Saturdays and whenever things get busy."

Clayton met Roger's eyes with his own. "What I'm saying is that I'll be the one managing the business, not you and not Solomon. And not any of my sisters." He looked to *Daed*. "You are leaving the management of the clock shop solely to me, are you not?" he asked. "That's what you've always told me."

Daed nodded silently, a mix of emotions on his face.

"And after working with me for all these years, do you honestly think I can't handle it on my own?"

The look on his father's face was a mix of confidence and doubt, hope and dread, as though he wanted to fully believe Clayton could handle everything that would come his way, but he couldn't quite get there.

Saddened, Clayton turned back to the others. "As the future sole proprietor of the shop, I'm saying that if additional staff is needed, I'll take care of it. I'll hire who *I* want to hire."

Clayton could see a shimmer of hurt in both of his sisters' faces.

"We're not trying to run your life, Clayton," Maisie said. "We're—"

"Then don't."

The conversation came to an end. After a long silence, someone said something about needing to get home and the others piped up in agreement, each of them acting as if there had been no conflict at all between them. As Clayton remained in his chair, the others rose and gathered their things. They left the room in clusters until all that remained were Joan and Maisie and their two children, who were still picking up the toys from the floor.

"You know what I think?" Maisie said suddenly, her cheeks flushed and her tone soft but defiant. "I think you already have someone in mind to hire for the store."

Clayton blinked, feeling as if she had read his mind.

"If he does, Maisie, that's between him and *Daed*," Joan said, looking embarrassed.

"I don't know," she replied, her eyes narrowing. "I feel like there's something Clayton isn't saying here." Turning back toward him, she added, "So who is it, *bruder*? Who are you planning to hire once *Daed* can no longer help?"

Clayton stared at his oldest sister and considered telling her there was no plan, or it wasn't any of her business. But she was a shrewd and insistent woman, so finally he forced himself to answer her question in the most neutral, matter-of-fact tone he could muster.

"Miriam Beiler," he said with a shrug. "She needs a job, and she's right next door, which would make it convenient for both sides."

As soon as the words were out there, Joan and Maisie both froze.

"And I've been thinking maybe Titus or Obed might like to apprentice with me," he continued, pretending he hadn't noticed, "which would help with this too, because as long as someone else is around, there wouldn't be anything inappropriate about Miriam working with me when *Mamm* isn't in the shop."

Still Clayton's sisters did not reply, so finally he looked from one to the other, and he was startled at the intensity of emotion showing on their faces.

"That *really* isn't a good idea," Maisie said softly, shaking her head from side to side. "Titus already works with his father, Clayton. And Obed would never want—"

"It's not our business, Maisie," Joan whispered, a small wooden horse clutched tightly in her hands. Then she returned her attention to the children, kneeling down and tossing the horse into the basket of toys.

"Think about it, Clayton," Maisie said, still standing there looking at him. "What good would come of Miriam working for you? You'll only end up getting hurt."

He was trying to come up with a reply when Joan spoke. "I think Maisie's right, Clayton. It wouldn't be fair to you."

"Fair?" he exclaimed. "What exactly are you implying?"

Joan exhaled slowly, sad-eyed as she met his gaze.

"You've been sweet on Miriam ever since the Beilers moved in next door," she said softly. "Offering her a job now would only set you up for heartbreak."

He wanted to respond. He wanted to refute his sisters' assertions with enough authority that they would realize they were being ridiculous, that he'd never thought of Miriam as anything other than a friend. But the words wouldn't come. Instead, he felt the anger inside him slowly shifting into something else, something more like a terrible ache.

When he said nothing in response, Joan returned the toy basket to the closet, and then they both told Clayton they would see him later as they herded the children out the door.

He stayed where he was, listening to the laughter and chatter wafting in from outside as kids were rounded up and horses were strapped in and everyone prepared to go home. He was still sitting there ten minutes later when his mother came back into the room. From the look on her face, she knew exactly what had transpired between him and his sisters. No doubt, Maisie had shared every word.

Embarrassed, he rose, turning his attention toward the window just as the last of the buggies pulled away.

"The Beilers would never agree to Miriam working at the shop," *Mamm* said, wringing her hands in front of her.

"Miriam is a grown woman."

"Even so, they don't want her spending so much time here…with you. Her mother told me that today, Clayton. They want her to settle down and get married, maybe even to the man who's having supper at their house tonight."

Clayton did not look at his mother, but he could tell she was crying as she said words that she surely knew were stinging him to the core. He swallowed the knot that swelled behind his Adam's apple.

"Miriam won't marry somebody just because her parents want her to," he barked.

"And she won't marry you, son."

Tears sprang to Clayton's eyes, but he turned away before his mother could see.

"I know she won't," he managed to mutter. Then, without another word, he limped to the stairs, gripped the railing, and began to move slowly upward, step by leaden step.

Thirteen

Over the next few days, Clayton found himself wishing he could relive the evening his sisters and their families had come to supper. Though he and *Daed* still quietly worked side by side in the shop, the silence between them seemed forced now instead of natural. Clayton had apologized the morning after for losing his temper, and *Daed* had forgiven him, but it was clear his father didn't know which plan—the family's or Clayton's—was the one to go with. This weighed on him.

And it seemed to weigh on *Mamm* too. She insisted on helping Clayton maneuver the wheelchair from the house to the shop, even though he tried to convince her she didn't need to. It was almost as if she wanted Clayton to know she wouldn't be forgotten or pushed to the side as everyone tried to come up with the best course of action for when *Daed* left this earth at last.

The worst part of the fallout from that evening was finding out that it was no secret among his parents and sisters that Clayton had feelings for Miriam Beiler. He had never so much as hinted to anyone how he felt about his next-door neighbor, and yet apparently they all knew. Even Miriam's parents had suspicions, or why else would they tell his mother they didn't want their daughter spending so much time with Clayton? It was as though they were saying they didn't want a possible suitor seeing Miriam hanging out at the Rabers' so much and getting the wrong idea.

As if anyone would. Miriam was only a friend. She had never given Clayton any indication she was attracted to him. And why should she? He wasn't near good enough for someone like her. At least *she* hadn't picked up on his feelings for her. Surely if she had, she would have long since said something. Miriam was the most transparent person he knew. If she realized how his heart raced whenever she was near, she would have brought it up. Wouldn't she?

All of these troubling thoughts stayed on Clayton's mind—the tension between him and his parents, the way he had left things with his sisters, and the fact that his private thoughts were no longer private. Four days after the disastrous conversation, he was gathering eggs in the violet predawn when *Mamm* was suddenly in the coop with him, taking the basket from his arm.

"I can do this," he said quickly. "You don't want the wood shavings in here to set off your asthma." Her sensitivities were always worse in the spring and summer.

"I won't stay but a few minutes. You gather. I'll hold the basket."

Clayton reached his hand into a nesting box and pulled out three eggs the color of coffee and cream.

They worked in silence for a few seconds and then his mother spoke. "This situation with you, *Daed,* and your sisters can't stretch out indefinitely. We need to come to some sort of agreement. Your father doesn't want to rush you, but he doesn't like having unfinished business lying about right now. I'm sure you can understand that."

Clayton inhaled heavily. He did understand, but he didn't know how to fix what was amiss.

"They just can't have that much involvement with the way I do things here," he said in as gentle a tone as he could produce. He placed two more eggs in the basket. "I know I'm slower at the chores than anyone else is, but I do get them done. And as far as help with the shop, why can't it just be you and maybe Miriam for a few hours a week? She's right next door."

His mother pursed her lips together. "Miriam may not always be next door."

"I know that. But she is right now. And there wouldn't be anything inappropriate about that if I also took on an apprentice."

"An apprentice?" *Mamm's* eyebrows raised, and Clayton realized she hadn't been in the room when he'd posed the idea to his sisters. At the time, Maisie had made it sound like neither boy would be available or interested, but he had a feeling she was just using that as a reason to keep him and Miriam apart.

"*Ya*. I was thinking maybe Titus or Obed."

Mamm looked away for a moment, toward the coop's open door and the glowing dawn sky. "Even if something like that could be worked out, I'm afraid for you, for what might happen if Miriam were around more often than she already is. It would be more difficult than you think. Do you really want to spend your days listening to her go on and on about her latest suitor? Do you really believe…"

Her voice drifted off. Clayton looked down at the dozen or so eggs in the basket. Some were speckled, some weren't, but they were all smooth and warm to the touch. Speckled or not, they would all look the same on the inside. And they would all break the same.

"I know you don't want to talk about this," she continued, "but I can't stand by and say nothing. I truly don't want to see you get hurt, son. There's already been too much of that in your life."

They were quiet for a moment. Outside a rooster crowed, slicing the morning air with his age-old salute to daybreak.

"She's just a friend, *Mamm*. She's not in love with me. She's never been in love with me." He thrust his hand under the last roosting hen, and the bird cackled at his intrusion. He pulled out an egg and placed it in the basket.

"There's a young woman up near Ephrata who lost her husband last fall to a terrible fever. She has three young boys to raise, sons who are already a help around the home and farm. They say she's a very nice person."

Clayton couldn't believe his ears. Was his mother actually being as intrusive as Miriam's parents had been lately with her?

"What are you getting at, *Mamm*?"

"I hear she's a nice person," she said again, as though Clayton had asked her to repeat what she said, not explain it.

"*Mamm*—"

"Her name is Lillian, and she's just a year or two older than you are. Twenty-nine, I think."

Clayton turned to look at his mother directly in the eye. "Are you suggesting I court this widow? Is that what you're saying?"

"She's too young to be alone. And her boys need a father."

"I don't know her. And she doesn't know me."

"But you could maybe find out more about her, Clayton. You could try."

"Are you forgetting something?" He nodded to his misshapen leg. "Do you really think whoever this Lillian is that she'd want to marry someone like me?"

"Why do you always do this? It's not as if you're a helpless cripple. You have a good job at the clock shop. And you are a kind and decent man. Her sons could be a big help to you. The oldest is already nine. Once he's a bit older, he could become the apprentice you were talking about."

Clayton's eyes narrowed as he stared at his mother. "So that's what this is about," he hissed. Then he turned and lumbered out of the henhouse, his mother following close behind.

"Clayton, wait. What do you mean?"

"You want me to court this woman—this complete stranger—because marrying her would give me instant sons to do all the things you and everyone else think I'm not capable of doing!"

"That's not what I'm saying—"

"It's *exactly* what you're saying!"

"You've never even *tried* to court anyone. I know you've always thought no one would want you, but I don't think that's true. And I am ashamed at myself for not telling you this sooner. The right person for you is out there, Clayton. I'm sure of it. But you don't even try—"

"Because I'm not good enough!" he yelled, kicking his bad leg at a pile of sawdust near his feet.

"Because you're in love with someone you can't have!"

Tiny bits of pine shavings settled on their shoulders as Clayton and his mother stood and glared at each other.

"Is this what you came out here to say?" he asked in a low voice, his jaw tight. "That I need to convince this widow to marry me because no one else will? That's why you're out here?"

Clayton's nostrils were flaring and the veins in his neck pulsed with anger. He knew it was a transgression to speak to his mother this way, but he was so furious he couldn't help it.

Mamm's eyes were glistening, and he considered apologizing as she looked at him. But then she spoke.

"I came out here to tell you that you and your father and your sisters need to come to an agreement. It's not fair to your father to ask him to wait to decide these things."

Mamm was letting the matter of Miriam slip back to the private place within his heart where it had been for the last five years, the place where it belonged. But her voice was no longer angry. It was sad. Clayton pretended not to notice.

"Titus or Obed can help with afternoon chores on Fridays and Saturdays," he answered, his temper finally under control again. "The older nieces can be on hand to pitch in with the vegetable gardens, but only when we need it and ask for it. I don't want Maisie and Joan helping in the shop or in the barn. And if we need a worker in the shop, I want to pick that person myself."

"Maisie and Joan just want—"

"Maisie and Joan treat me like a child." As soon as he said it, Clayton wondered if she was thinking they treated him like a child because when he lost his temper he acted like one. "Look, *Mamm*. I'm not against getting help, I'm really not. I'm just against getting help when it isn't needed. And I'm especially against getting help from people who tend to take over and boss me around and act like they know better than I do how business should be handled. I'm fine alone. We're fine, you and me."

His mother hesitated and then tried a new approach. "Regardless, Miriam won't be able to come work for you anyway. She got a new job cleaning and cooking for a man and his wife in Lancaster."

Since the evening of the disastrous supper, Miriam had not been by the shop or barn. Clayton thought it was because her parents had told her to stop hanging out over here, but he had secretly been hoping that either she would not be offered the job or that her parents would insist she not take it.

"How do you know that?"

"Abigail told me. Miriam started two days ago."

Clayton turned back to the roosting racks and stared at the empty spaces where the hens had slept the previous night. "Well, then. I won't ask her. That should make everyone happy," he said gruffly.

"None of this makes anyone happy," his mother murmured, her voice thick in her throat. "And it still means you don't have any help lined up for the shop."

Clayton absently rubbed his stubble-covered chin. The tiny fissure that had opened in his heart at hearing Miriam had gotten the new job was already closing. She wouldn't have wanted to work with him anyway. It surely would have seemed too slow and uninteresting. She had said to him once that the constant ticking of the clocks was like being inside someone's sleepy dream. He was a fool to even have entertained such a thought and twice the fool for stating it out loud to first his sisters and now his mother.

"We'll just take it one day at a time," he finally said. "You can still help me in the shop on Saturdays, can't you? And busy summer afternoons? And if it gets to be too much for just the two of us, I promise I will hire someone. If one of the nieces or nephews wants the job, I've no problem with that. But it won't be charity. It will be a job, and I will expect that person to treat it as such—and to treat me as their boss. But I don't want it to be Maisie or Joan. It wouldn't be a job to them. It would be coming to my rescue. And I just can't have it that way."

Mamm nodded resolutely. "And you will tell your father this is what you have decided?"

"I will."

She hung back a moment as if there was more she wanted to say, but then she hiked the egg basket higher on her arm and walked up to the house.

Clayton finished the rest of the chores—mucking out the horses' stalls, feeding and watering, and checking on Rosie, and then he went back inside to clean up, shave, and have breakfast with his parents.

Daed said little as Clayton explained he'd finalized his plans for managing the home and business. When he was finished, his father wiped his mouth with his napkin and set his fork down.

"All right, son. If you think this is the best route to go, I'll stand with you."

"It is the best route."

"Then the rest we will leave to God."

After breakfast, Clayton went out to the barn for one final check on the animals before starting the workday. He was surprised to see Miriam standing at Rosie's railing. She was wearing a blue dress the shade of a robin's egg. Her *kapp* was pinned carefully in place and her shoes were polished.

"*Gud...gud mariye,*" Clayton sputtered.

"Hi, Clayton. I had a few minutes before the bus comes, so I stopped by to check on Rosie. Guess she hasn't had her calf yet. I thought maybe you'd forgotten about me wanting to know. "

How could I forget anything you say? "Nope. She hasn't had it yet."

Miriam wheeled away from the railing. "I got the job in Lancaster," she said, her expression humble but her tone almost proud.

"I heard. *Mamm* told me."

"You wouldn't believe how beautiful their house is, Clayton. I've never seen so many pretty things. Look." Miriam reached into her bag and pulled out a decorated hair comb. It sparkled in the morning sun that angled across the barn from the loft window.

"It's called cloisonné. Brenda gave it to me. She got tired of it."

Clayton could only stare dumbly at the glittering hair decoration in Miriam's hand. He'd seen clocks set in cloisonné before, but he'd never come across a hair ornament constructed of it. It was the fanciest and most worldly thing he'd ever laid eyes on. Surely her parents didn't know she had it. "What are you doing with that?" he asked, instantly worried for her.

"Don't go crazy on me, Clayton. Not you. I'm just enjoying it for the moment. Look how it shines in the sun."

But he could only look at her, at how beautiful she was as she stared at the trinket in her hand.

"Brenda has a bunch of stuff she wants to give away," Miriam continued, her gaze still on the hair comb. "I was helping her go through things yesterday afternoon. Clothes, shoes, scarves, jewelry, hair stuff, earrings. She has so much stuff that she actually gets tired of it. Can you imagine?"

"No. I can't."

"She said she would give it all to me if I was allowed to have it, which she knows I'm not. So she said I could take the comb because it was little and I could stash it away somewhere. Here. Touch it."

Clayton reached out a tentative hand and ran a finger along the tiny mosaic pattern. The metal teeth of the comb were cold. "What are you going to do with it?"

"I'm not going to wear it if that's what you mean, silly." She laughed. "I'll hide it away somewhere and take it out when I want to look at it."

Clayton was about to ask why when Miriam seemed to think of something else and touched his arm. "Oh, my! I almost forgot to tell you! Brenda has a beautiful clock she got for a wedding gift when she was married. I think it's the prettiest clock I've ever seen, all carved with roses and such. You would love it. I wish I could show it to you."

Despite his other concerns, it warmed Clayton to his core to think Miriam had seen something in the *Englisch* woman's house and thought of him. For a moment he could not speak. "*Ya?*" he finally said, instantly wishing he'd thought of a more intelligent response.

"And guess what else? She has tickets to the theater in Lancaster tomorrow afternoon. It's a matinee. Douglas—that's her husband—he doesn't care for that kind of thing, so Brenda asked if I wanted to go with her. I could hardly speak I was so excited! She thought I was offended that she'd asked and started to apologize. I had to stop her and tell her I would most definitely like to go with her. She thought that was so funny. Then she told me it was a musical, and that she thought I would like it because she's heard me singing when she and Douglas get home from work."

Clayton listened with growing concern. Miriam sounded very happy with her new job, which was so different from her last one at the furniture store. But surrounded by such fancy goods and wealth? Bringing home outlandish trinkets? Going to the theater with her *Englisch* employer? How could anything good come from any of it?

"What?" she said, a hint of frustration in her voice when she noticed the expression on his face.

"Nothing," he replied quickly. "I just…I want you to be safe, Miriam. I want you to be happy, yes. But I want you to be safe too."

She laughed. "Safe? What a funny thing to say. It's just a play. And it's just a hair comb. And it's just a job. It's not as if I am in the play or wearing the comb or becoming *Englisch*."

"*Ya*, but—"

"It's nice for right now, you know? It's not always going to be this way. Especially if my parents have anything to do with it. That man they want me to court? He asked to take me on a buggy ride after work tonight. And my mother said I would without even asking me. See what I mean? If I don't have something fun and exciting to look forward to during the day, I'll explode." She glanced out toward the brightening sky. "I have to go now or I'll miss my bus." She swung away from him, dropping the hair comb back into her bag.

"Bye, Clayton," she called over her shoulder.

She was gone from view before he found his voice. He didn't think she heard him tell her to have a good day.

FOURTEEN

As April drew to a close, it became clear to Clayton and his family that *Daed* would likely not survive to the end of the summer. The change was gradual at first. Throughout the month of May, he began to rise later in the morning and would often fall asleep after supper in his favorite chair while reading his Bible. His skin grew paler and his appetite waned. By the beginning of June he didn't have the energy to go to the shop anymore. And while *Mamm* had been telling him all along he didn't need to be there every day— or at all, for that matter—the first morning he chose to stay at the house with her, she broke down in tears and excused herself to the canning room to count jars.

Clayton's six sisters and their families still came over for dinner every Sunday, but the conversation around the tables no longer centered on the weather or the price of feed or the goings-on in the county, but rather on the many good times they had all shared. After the meal, *Daed* would sit in his armchair enjoying his grandchildren, hugging them, telling stories to the littler ones, and giving words of advice to the older ones. Clayton found it hard to be in the room when he was doing this. It was obvious *Daed* was passing on what he could to the next generation and that he believed he would soon be gone from them.

On one of those Sunday afternoons, Clayton and his father explained together to Maisie and Joan and their husbands how the caring for the home and the shop would be handled once the inevitable happened, a conversation for which Clayton was immensely grateful. Maisie was not in favor of their "let's wait and see" approach, but Roger finally deferred on her behalf, saying they would do as asked. Joan didn't agree with the plan either, and she made Clayton promise that the minute he or *Mamm* changed their minds, all they had to do was send word and she and her oldest children would be there to lend a hand. Clayton's other sisters and their husbands also assured him that he and *Mamm* weren't to hesitate a moment to ask for assistance with anything. In turn, he assured them that he had no problem asking for help when it was needed. He just didn't think it would be.

"Won't you be lonely in the clock shop all by yourself?" Joan asked in a final appeal.

"With all those clocks to keep me company? Not a chance," he'd replied with a smile, ending the conversation on a positive note.

Their weekend family get-togethers, bursting with noise and activity, were in stark contrast to Monday mornings when Clayton would walk down to the shop alone. He would pretty much remain that way throughout the day except for the occasional customer. His mother didn't feel right leaving *Daed* by himself in the house, even for a few minutes. Sometimes Maisie or one of his other sisters would stop by to give their mother a rest and to bring over a casserole or a crock of stew, but *Mamm* never strayed far from the house. She came down to the shop only on the rare occasion to ask Clayton a question or bring him a snack. Over time, he found himself pushing his end-of-the-day chores to five o'clock after he closed up. This meant his normal workday was now well over twelve hours. He didn't mind, and again he declined to accept assistance from his sisters' children, though both Maisie and Joan offered. Between handling all the clock repairs on his own, working on new time pieces, and waiting on customers, the workday flew by.

As it turned out, though Clayton greatly missed his father's presence in the store, he realized that working by himself wasn't all that different. The two men had always been so absorbed in their own tasks that they had barely interacted for much of the day anyway. Now that Clayton was manning the place alone, he came to appreciate the solitude.

He had taken down the curtain that hid the back room, and after a while he found that he no longer wanted or needed to shy away from tourists who simply had to know why he limped so badly or what had happened to his face. The more he answered their nosy questions, in fact, the less angry he would be that they asked. Likewise, the less angry he got, the less he would lose his temper and say something impolite. He found out rather early the first week he was alone in the shop that the majority of the curious didn't ask about his scarred brow or oddly bent leg at all. They just looked at him with questions in their eyes, and he pretended not to notice.

He also found a rhythm with the chores, one that surprised him. His days were not at all unpleasant, and the time it took him to tend to the animals, both in the mornings and the afternoons, started growing a little shorter as he fell into a routine.

Still, on most evenings, by the time he finished with the chores it was already well past supper. *Mamm* would keep a plate warm for him, and he would usually eat it in the living room with his father, telling him about his day—who had come into the shop, what new repairs he was working on, and what new projects he had started.

Though *Daed* continued to grow weaker, he seemed to thrive on these conversations, and it was obvious to Clayton that the man's confidence in him was growing. Clayton was so glad, because he really didn't want his father to spend his last days worrying about what might happen once he was gone. Instead, *Daed* needed to see that all would be well, that life would go on, that Clayton was capable of providing for *Mamm* and handling whatever might come their way in the future.

He was to learn that that goal had been achieved on a Sunday afternoon in mid-May. About an hour before dark, just after his sisters and their families had gone home from an afternoon visit, he walked back into the house to find his father sitting in the entryway, waiting for him.

"Clayton, I need to talk to you about something. Would you roll me down to the shop?"

Intrigued by *Daed*'s intensity, he readily agreed and retrieved the wheelchair. As he helped the man settle into it, he noticed a piece of paper rolled up in his father's hands. He decided not to ask about it. If his father wanted him to know what it was, he would show him.

As they headed down the driveway together, *Daed* cleared his throat and began speaking. "I need to apologize to you, son, for having doubted your ability to handle the store, the chores, and everything that goes along with running this homestead. I've seen how well you're doing with all of it, which is why I've decided to…" he paused and then smiled. "Well, you'll see."

They reached the bottom of the hill, and *Daed* asked Clayton to roll him behind the shop and around to the far side of the building. Situated between the clock shop and the Beilers' driveway, the grassy lot held a single shade tree at its center with an old picnic table underneath. Clayton and his father used to share lunch there on warm spring days when the sun was shining and the shop wasn't busy. As Clayton rolled his father toward there now, he realized they would never share another one of those lunches again.

Clayton's heart ached at the thought and at how he'd taken for granted such wonderful moments in the past. His sadness only increased when he realized he would never share times like that with a son of his own either. He would never have a son at all.

Forcing such thoughts from his mind, he parked the chair under the tree and then sat on the bench as directed, resting his elbows on the rough wood of the table. Once he was settled, his father began to speak.

"As you know, my parents didn't leave this homestead to me in their will. Instead, they signed the deed for it over to me while they were still alive, to avoid inheritance tax issues. And though technically it all became mine the day we signed on the dotted line, that deed protected them as well by establishing their right to live here until their deaths, even though they no longer owned the place."

Clayton nodded, familiar with what his father was saying. Deeding land rather than willing it wasn't an uncommon practice in the Amish community. The only part people found odd was the bit about reserving the right to live there till death—as if there were any question. But *Englisch* lawyers always insisted on that clause, and so the Amish usually went along with it.

"Anyway," *Daed* continued, "as you also know, the homestead becomes your mother's once I'm gone, but eventually she'll be doing the same thing for you and your sisters that my parents did for me. She'll pass along the homestead to you to possess and occupy during your lifetime. You understand what I'm saying? This place will be yours to use for the rest of your life, but once your mother signs it over to all of you, even though your right to live and work here for the rest of your life will be legally protected in the deed, this homestead will not belong to you alone. Your sisters will own it jointly with you."

"I understand, *Daed*."

"I know you do, and as long as things go on as usual, it doesn't really matter anyway."

"So why are you telling me all of this?"

Daed looked at him, his expression unreadable. "I'm telling you this in case things *don't* go on as usual." He coughed, the rattling sound like sandpaper on a clock's casing. Then cleared his throat and kept going. "In the future, if you ever wanted to make changes to the place, your co-owners would have the right to step in and have a say on how things are handled. Do you understand what I'm getting at?"

Clayton shook his head. Everything his father had been saying made sense, but he just didn't see why it mattered.

"Because you will share ownership with your sisters," *Daed* explained, exhaling slowly, "I worry about them meddling once your mother and I are gone. Specifically, I'm concerned about the shop. Say it does well and eventually you want to expand. With your sisters as co-owners, they would have to give their permission for you to do any new construction to the property. And knowing how protective they are—and how much they tend to underestimate your abilities, not to mention your determination—chances are they would be very conservative in allowing that."

Clayton nodded again, still trying to figure out what his father was getting at.

"The thing is, I don't want you to *ever* have to go through another conversation with them like the one we had back in March." *Daed* looked down at the ground, his features filled with guilt and regret. "We were all wrong and you were right. I should never have involved your sisters and their husbands that way. And I certainly shouldn't have allowed their opinions to overshadow yours."

"*Daed*..." Clayton began, but he couldn't finish.

"I believe in you, Clayton. Since that day you've proven yourself fully capable of everything you said. That's why I've decided to do something else before I pass on. Something legal and binding."

Daed's face suddenly took on a smile. Eyes twinkling, he held out his hand and added, "Got a dollar?"

Clayton hesitated, frowning, but he could see that his father was serious, so he dug into his pocket, produced a single bill, and handed it over. In return, *Daed* gave him the rolled up paper he'd been holding in his other hand.

His brow furrowed, Clayton unrolled the paper. It was some sort of document, a legal agreement between *Simon Raber* and *Clayton Raber,* a transfer of land from one to the other for the price of *$1.* The land was listed as *Lot 23, Ridge Road, Ridgeview, Pennsylvania.*

"This still needs to be notarized, so I've arranged for a notary to come by tomorrow afternoon, when your mother will be over at Joan's. After that, you'll have to file it with the county. But then it'll be official."

Stunned, Clayton finally found his voice. "What's 'lot twenty-three'?"

His father waved a hand, encompassing the area around them. "That's this part here, from this side of the parking lot to just short of the barn, and from this side of the store to the Beilers' pasture. Right around an acre total, which isn't much. But by deeding it over to you now, I'm ensuring that however this little rectangle of land gets used in the future will be *your* prerogative—and yours alone. It's my way of saying I believe in you, son. It's my way of saying I'm sorry I doubted you before."

Clayton looked down at his father's gnarled hands, at the deed, at the tract of land that was to become his, and he was unable to come up with words. He was dumbfounded.

Without question, he knew this wasn't necessary. It was going to be all he could do to keep the store running and the chores done, much less grow and expand the business. But this gesture, and the way his father was looking at him now, meant more to him than almost anything anyone had ever done for him.

"And *Mamm*? She's in agreement?"

Daed shrugged. "I'm sure she would be if she knew about it, but I haven't told her because I don't want your sisters to know. Why create division in the family now when temperatures are already running a little hot?"

Clayton understood and agreed.

"This can be between just you and me," *Daed* continued. "It'll probably come out eventually, but for now I just want you to hang on to the deed yourself for when—or if—the day ever comes that you need it. Does that make sense?"

Clayton nodded, tears suddenly filling his eyes. Then he leaned over and wrapped his father into a fierce hug, something he hadn't done since he was a boy.

"Thank you," Clayton said, barely above a whisper. He held their embrace for a long moment before letting go and rising from their treasured lunch spot.

They were quiet as they went back up to the house, both lost in thought. Clayton hadn't realized how much he'd needed his father to have confidence in his abilities—not just so the man could have peace in his final days, but to be able to go on after death parted them. As they headed back up the hill, Clayton felt a new sense of purpose and a deep satisfaction in knowing that *Daed* had come to believe in him at last.

Fifteen

During the final weeks of his father's life, Clayton had hoped that being busy from sunup to sundown would give him little time to think about Miriam. Apart from a wave now and then across the little pasture, he had barely spoken to her in two months. They'd had just three actual conversations, in fact, all of them brief and none of them satisfying. Each time, Miriam had gone on and on about what was apparently her latest obsession, the theater. Once her boss had taken her to her first matinee, Miriam said, she had loved it so much that she'd actually gone back a few more times by herself. The whole situation made Clayton very uncomfortable—her enthusiasm for the stories and the actors and the costumes and the music and the fancy sets—not to mention it wasn't exactly a topic he knew or cared anything about. During their first conversation on it, he'd just stood there, trying to cautiously listen but mostly thinking about how pretty her lips were when she spoke and how brightly her eyes sparkled when she was animated.

The last time they had talked, she launched into the same topic, and he considered interrupting her to point out the issues inherent in her obsession and indeed with the *Englisch* world overall. But he held his tongue, fearing he might start to sound like a rooster, crowing the same song day after day. In the end, the only chiding he did was about the way she spoke of her boss,

Brenda Peterson, as if the woman were a best friend rather than an employer. In response, Miriam had simply laughed.

"A person can be both, you know," she'd quipped, but a momentary flash of irritation in her eyes told him the subject wasn't up for discussion.

Sadly, nothing seemed to make any difference in the way Clayton felt about Miriam, not his heavy grief over his father, her silly enthusiasms, or the lack of time they had spent together lately. He still found his thoughts frequently wandering in her direction, especially when he would see her taking in laundry or coming home from a buggy ride with her suitor, whom Clayton had learned was named Vernon Esh.

Clayton thought of Miriam when he saw a kerosene lamp glowing in her bedroom window across the small field that separated them. Or when he lay in bed at night unable to sleep. He had begun to pray every day that God would make the feelings he had for her go away. He *implored* God to take them away, but nothing seemed to change inside of him. If anything, his feelings for her had intensified, and this made no sense to him whatsoever.

When Rosie started to calve at a few minutes after sunset on a warm summer's eve, Clayton had hesitated a moment before going over to the Beilers' house—only to be told that Miriam was working late in Lancaster that night. Hours later, around midnight, he heard a car door slam outside, which likely meant Miriam's boss had finally brought her home. But by then Rosie was already nursing her newborn and Clayton was in bed and nearly asleep.

He had hoped to catch her before she went to work the next morning to tell her about the new calf, but he never saw her. Perhaps that was God answering his prayer to be delivered of his attraction, he thought. Perhaps it was to happen slowly, like this. It was almost like an escapement in a clock, he decided, where each swing of the pendulum would cause the gear train to advance in a small, fixed amount. Over time, those incremental advances added up, just as perhaps over time, these missed moments with Miriam would add up, ultimately lessening his feelings for her.

To Clayton, it seemed that he was facing two difficult goodbyes at the same time. One was the imminent passing of his beloved father. The second was the much-needed demise of his affection and fascination for Miriam. He truly wanted no part of either farewell, but he had no choice. *Daed*'s days were numbered, and Clayton was just as sure that he should not continue to feel this way about Miriam, especially now that she was being courted by another man.

And she was definitely being courted. He knew that because he'd seen the fellow's buggy show up at her house almost every Friday and Saturday evening for weeks. Clayton didn't know where they went on their dates, but more than once he'd watched from his bedroom window as Miriam came out of the house and headed off with Vernon into the night. Sometimes they would stay out till ten or eleven, and sometimes he'd have her home by nine.

The first time Clayton had seen them was on a warm Friday night, not long after supper, when he was alone in the kitchen just finishing up the dishes. His mother was in the next room tending to his father, and Clayton was standing at the sink, absently drying a glass, when he noticed a beam of light angling across the dark yard outside, an indication of a vehicle of some kind pulling in at the Beilers' place.

Curious, he put the glass on the shelf, closed the cabinet, and walked to a different window to get a better look. Trees partially blocked the view, but from where he stood he could see the front corner of what seemed to be a courting buggy sitting in the driveway, the horse still hitched up but the headlights now off. The driver was striding toward the side door of the Beilers' house, but before the man got there, the door swung open and a woman emerged. Even in the dark, Clayton could tell by her faint silhouette against the white clapboard that it was Miriam. Squinting, he watched as she approached the driver, and then the two of them walked together back toward the buggy. They became obscured by foliage as they went, but Clayton knew that the man was likely helping Miriam up into her seat before going around to the other side and climbing in next to her.

They were too far off for Clayton to hear any conversation between them, but through the open window he could make out the faint crunch of tires on gravel as the horse began to move again. The buggy's lights popped back on, and the beam swept in a wide arc across the grass as they made a U-turn in her driveway. Even after the buggy was down the hill and out of sight, Clayton stayed there at the window for a long time, listening until the distant *clip-clop* of hooves on blacktop faded away, leaving behind only silence and darkness.

An hour later, he was up in his room for the night, dressed for bed but perched on the window seat with a book in hand, telling himself he was there to read, that it was purely coincidental that this particular window offered a clear line of sight to the Beilers' house and driveway and yard. A light outside caught his eye.

Clayton quickly extinguished the small kerosene lantern that hung from the wall next to him. Then he returned his attention to the world beyond the window, to the sight of the same buggy he'd seen earlier, finally returning Miriam to her house.

In the past hour the moon had emerged bright above the horizon. From his unobstructed, second-story viewpoint, he saw the horse come to a stop. The lights flicked off. The man and the woman climbed down from the buggy and walked to the door.

As the guy leaned in to kiss Miriam on the cheek, Clayton knew he should look away, that he should close the shades on his pain and frustration and just forget all of this. But he couldn't tear himself from the open window and the scene unfolding before him.

Even after the buggy drove off, he remained where he was, stiff and tired but unable to move. He stayed there at the glass, staring into the dark, trying to pray but mostly just thinking. About Miriam. About the hollowness in his stomach. About the literal ache of loss. He spotted a flickering glow behind the shade of the second window from the left, top floor. Her bedroom. Five minutes later, the light went out.

Wearily, Clayton rose from his perch and made his way across the room to his own bed. It was still quite warm, and as he folded the bedspread down and slid onto the mattress under a single sheet, he chastised himself for having spied on his lovely neighbor. What right did he have to watch her comings and goings? None at all, and that was that.

Yet the very next night, he found himself back at the window again, waiting and watching until she came home. By the end of the following weekend, which once again included outings with her Amish suitor two nights in a row, Clayton recognized a sad sort of rhythm. The beam of headlights catching his attention. The buggy turning in and pulling to a stop. The man and woman walking to the door. The woman going inside. The woman's bedroom light coming on. The woman's bedroom light turning off. The lonely man limping over to his own bed.

Clayton tried to stop watching for her. He really did. He tried to tell himself it was a waste of time to long for a woman who would never be his, but he just couldn't help it. He was *drawn* to her, like a magnet, unable to leave his place at the window, unable to find sleep until he knew she was there across the narrow field, second room from the left on the top floor, also asleep.

By the time the following weekend rolled around, Clayton didn't even bother with the self-recriminations anymore—or with the pretense of reading. He simply got ready for bed, twisted off the light, and resumed his post at the open window, waiting and watching for Miriam to come home. It was a chilly night, but he didn't even gather a blanket around himself for warmth. He just sat there and waited.

Eventually the buggy appeared, as usual, and Clayton slid into the rhythm of it all yet again as he watched the walk to the door, the closing of the door, the buggy driving away, the light coming on upstairs. As the light turned off again, he let out a deep sigh and tried to find the energy to go to bed himself.

But he wasn't tired. He was restless. He knew if he were to crawl into bed, sleep would not come to him. He padded across the darkened bedroom, opened his door, and within a few minutes was at the mudroom door, opening it to the starry night. He stepped outside in his bare feet and for a few minutes just stared at the expanse of the vast heavens above him. The sky at night looked calm and serene. He wanted to drink in that peaceful strength. He wandered over to a pear tree and leaned against its trunk, the branches a leafy bower above him. A few minutes passed, and he was just about to go back inside when he detected movement at the Beilers' house to his right.

Someone was at the side door and then running down the driveway in the darkness. It wasn't until the person was almost to the road that Clayton spotted a car pulling up to the curb with its lights off and its engine idling.

He stepped out from the branches. Miriam? Was it Miriam running toward the car? The running person swung open the car door to get inside, and the light that came on confirmed Clayton's fear. It was her.

Worse, she was dressed in *Englisch* clothing.

Flummoxed, he watched as the car began to creep forward. Not until it was well down the street did its lights come on. Whoever it was hadn't wanted to be observed—at least not by the people inside Miriam's house.

But who did she know that owned a car? Was it her boss, Brenda Peterson, the woman who seemed to be her friend? It had to be. What other *Englischers* did she know? Clayton spent the next hour hovering by the pear tree, waiting for Miriam to return, but she never came. Finally, furiously, he limped back to his house and his bedroom.

Why had he insisted on watching her? What did it matter to him what she did or who she was with? It was none of his business. He was just the next-door neighbor, the guy with the hideous face and the crooked leg who pined over the beauty with the auburn hair and the lilting voice.

Once in bed, he lay awake for a long while, trying to convince himself that this was it. He was done with her. But it was no use. Every sound of the night outside his half-open window snapped him to attention, and when he finally heard soft footsteps running across gravel, he leapt from the bed, hobbled to the window as fast as he could, and confirmed that Miriam was finally home.

The car that brought her drove off quietly into the night, but no flicker of light ever came on in the second-floor bedroom. Clayton could picture her at that very moment, sneaking around her room in the dark, getting ready for bed as quietly as she could, hiding away her *Englisch* clothes. No doubt, she had a place where she stashed them, some secret place where no one else would ever think to look.

With a heavy heart, he told himself he needed such a place as well, a secret place where no one would ever look, a place he could hide his pain.

<hr>

When the next Friday night rolled around and after his parents were asleep, Clayton was again at the pear tree when Miriam turned out the light in her bedroom. Sure enough, less than an hour after making his way in the dark to the tree, a car without its lights on pulled to a stop at the curb down at the main road. From where he stood, Clayton could almost make out the driver. He was about to take a step from the shadow of the branches when he heard the side door at the Beilers' house open.

Miriam was dressed in *Englisch* clothes again, and Clayton watched as she sprinted in the dark toward the car. Clayton squinted, trying to see the person at the wheel. The light inside came on, and he could make out the square shoulders and short, dark hair of a man.

A man.

So it wasn't Brenda, Miriam's boss. And he knew it wasn't Brenda's husband, because he'd seen that guy bring Miriam home from work before, and he drove a bigger, much fancier car.

This was someone else, someone Miriam knew that he didn't. If only he weren't disabled, Clayton thought, then he could dash down there in the darkness and see for himself, up close. The car pulled back onto the road, only then turning on its lights. What was going on?

Was Miriam safe?

Clayton returned to the house but was too worried about her to sleep. He propped himself up with pillows on the window seat, watching for her return. For hours he stared off into the night, waiting for her to come home. He must have fallen asleep at some point, because he awoke with a start just before dawn, his neck sore and his bad leg throbbing. Certain he had slept right through Miriam's return, he stood and stretched for a moment before heading to his bed. But as he leaned down and began to gather up the pillows, something outside—some movement—caught his attention. With a start, he shifted back down onto the wide wooden sill and peered out into the night. The car was back—only this time it had actually pulled up the drive and was sitting not too far from the Beilers' house.

It remained there in the driveway, rumbling faintly, headlights off, for several minutes. The dark night was shifting into gray and the outside world slowly began to take shape. Clayton wondered what she was doing in there, though he felt sure he knew. Then, finally, its passenger door swung open and Miriam stepped out. After shutting the door quietly, she dashed toward her house, smoothing down her loose, messy hair as she ran.

Miriam's hair.

Clayton had never seen it unbraided before. As livid as he was at this man who didn't even have respect enough to walk her to the door, he couldn't help but be captivated by her hair. So beautiful. So alluring. So utterly indecent being worn down like that. Miriam well knew it should be braided and tucked away under her *kapp*, not loose and free, on display for all to see—for anyone to see other than her husband in the privacy of their home.

Clayton didn't know what to do with all he'd witnessed. It seemed to him Miriam was mixed up in something that could hurt her. He wanted to protect her, but he didn't know how. She wasn't yet a church member, so he was not obligated to speak to the bishop about it. Maybe he should say something to her himself, one Christian to another as the Bible directed. Then again, what would she think of him if he did? He'd be the creepy neighbor who spent his lonely nights spying on her every move.

Clayton remained a while longer, watching his breath fog the glass. Why did he care so much? What Miriam did on her *rumspringa* was none of his business. Perhaps God had allowed him to see what he had seen to help him get over her. *I just need to let it go.* He rubbed the fog from the window with his sleeve and stood to stretch his leg. *I need to focus on life ahead of me without my father, not on Miriam or my feelings for her.* He decided to dedicate his thoughts to prayer and fasting for his father's declining health. He would continue to ask God to take his feelings for Miriam away, once and for all.

And he would never, ever watch for her at the window again.

Sixteen

In the days that followed, the long stretches of solitude at the shop in between customers presented Clayton with the best opportunities to lay his heart open before the Lord. He often whispered his prayers aloud as he worked, though that wasn't his usual way.

"Please have mercy on my father, O God," he would pray. "If it be Your will, spare his life. Restore his health." Despite himself, he couldn't help but add, "And please, please, take from me these feelings I have for Miriam. Please take them. I do not wish to dishonor You or her. Please take them."

Even so, day after day *Daed* grew weaker while Clayton's affection for Miriam grew stronger.

Then, on the sixth of July after a supper of ham loaf, succotash, and chunky applesauce, *Daed* settled into his armchair while Clayton helped clear the table and *Mamm* prepared a dessert tray to be served in the living area. She had made a chocolate cake—*Daed*'s favorite—and had just cut a slice when she called over to ask him if he wanted a little vanilla ice cream to go with it. When there was no answer, she asked Clayton to see if he had fallen asleep.

Clayton found his father looking as if he had indeed only nodded off, serene and peaceful, his hand on an open Bible in his lap. But there was no question.

This time he would not be waking up.

The next few days were a blur as the Amish community sprang into action, doing the many things they always did when one of their members passed away. Neither Clayton nor *Mamm* had any chores to handle. There was no work to get done, no meals to prepare or clocks to fix, or anything else that would pull them away from time spent with their loved ones, time spent comforting, mourning, and fellowshipping together. Any task that could be handled by someone outside the family was simply taken care of. A sign went in the shop window, saying it would be closed for a week. The cow was milked, the lawn was trimmed, the eggs were gathered, meals were served, and so much more, the logistics and efficiency of these quiet workers functioning in the background, unseen, like a sophisticated gear train in the finest Hentschel clock.

When *Daed*'s embalmed body was returned home by the mortician, Clayton and his brother-in-law Solomon were the ones to dress him in burial clothes. Clayton had thought that would be the hardest part, but in a way it wasn't difficult at all. If anything, it helped remind him that *Daed* was long gone, that this was only an earthly vessel that had held his soul for a time.

It was on the second day after *Daed*'s death that Clayton realized he hadn't seen Miriam yet at all. Her mother and other relatives had been in and out quite often, helping out in numerous ways, but Miriam herself had stayed away, and Clayton wasn't sure if it was because she was busy with work or because she held their friendship in such little regard that she didn't even consider pitching in with the others worth doing. Perhaps that was another click in his escapement, another advance in the gear train of his diminishing feelings for her.

But then came the funeral itself, when he spotted her sitting across the room, among the other women. He saw her again at the graveside, and that time her cheeks were a vivid red, her eyes wet and swollen. Something beyond the death of a neighbor was bothering her, that much was obvious. In that moment, as heartbroken as Clayton was for his own loss, all he really wanted to do was go to her and ask if she was all right.

They didn't have a chance to speak until later, back at the house, when friends and family were milling around, talking and crying and laughing and eating and sharing memories of Simon Raber. Clayton had just helped hitch up the wagon for a departing cousin when Miriam approached him to offer her condolences. As she did, he realized it was the first time in many weeks that he had been within inches of her. And even though his heart was still full of grief at the passing of his father, he sensed a happy trembling inside as she took his hand in hers and spoke words of comfort.

"I'm so sorry, Clayton," she said, her voice soft and melodic. "Your father was such a good man. I know you will miss him terribly."

Clayton could sense that she was sincere, but there was a strangeness about her voice, further convincing him that something else was troubling her, something that had nothing to do with the current situation at all.

"*Danke*, Miriam." Had she quit another job? Had Vernon proposed? If so, were her parents now pressuring her to accept?

She looked up at him with a wordless gaze that answered none of his questions.

"Would you like to see Rosie's calf?" he asked, regretting his question the second he blurted it out. Offering to show his neighbor a new calf on the day of his father's funeral seemed in poor taste, but he wanted to talk to Miriam away from the others, and it seemed a perfect excuse.

"Oh!" she replied, and Clayton could tell she had completely forgotten about having wanted to be there for the birth. "It's happened already?"

"Yes," he said, equally startled. Had she not seen the calf out in the field with its mother? "I came over to your house the evening she started calving like you asked, but you were working late that night. I'm sorry you missed it."

"Oh," she said again. She looked away, as though mentally sifting through the succession of days since she and Clayton had last talked about Rosie and calling to mind the evening she had worked late and the calf was born. "Yes, I would. I would like to see it."

"Okay."

Clayton looked for his mother. He spotted her through the kitchen window, inside, surrounded by a group of other women her age. "Come on, then," he said, limping toward the barn. Miriam followed.

They walked slowly, and not only because of Clayton's complicated gait. Miriam appeared to be in no hurry, even though she had been anxious to see the calf moments earlier.

"Job okay?" Clayton asked, not looking at her.

"What?"

"I, uh, just asked if the job was going okay."

"It's fine."

A few more seconds of silence hovered about them as they continued across the yard.

"The little calf is doing well," Clayton said. "Though he's never more than inches from his mother's side."

He wished he could just say what he wanted to with Miriam. He could be blunt with everyone else, but not with her. And Miriam was never quiet around him. She was either talking or singing, though she was doing neither at the moment, and Clayton could not bring himself to ask what was bothering her.

They reached the barn and stopped at the open doors, peering inside the cavernous structure. Rosie and her calf, easily visible from the doorway, were lounging in their stall as the afternoon sun angled down and bathed the animals in filtered light. The cow and her youngster, a pale orange-brown bullock *Mamm* had named Butternut, regarded them with languid stares. Rosie flicked her tail, and the bullock nestled closer to his mother.

"What's its name?" Miriam said, smiling now for the first time since she had arrived at the house.

"My *mamm* calls him Butternut."

Miriam chuckled. "For the squash?"

Clayton nodded, returning her smile. "His color does sort of remind you of it."

Miriam folded her arms across the front of her dress. "I'm so glad you haven't separated him from his mother yet. I hate that part. I know it has to happen, but it's still hard to watch—or listen to. Can you imagine what it must be like to have your child taken from you?"

"Uh, no. But—"

"I heard it one time, at my uncle's dairy farm, when some calves were taken from their mothers. It was the saddest sound in the world."

"I suppose."

She inhaled deeply, seeming to draw strength from the tableau of mother and offspring before her.

"Anyway, I'm glad you didn't do it right away, like some."

"Well, at the moment there's plenty of milk for us and Butternut. But there will come a day when he will have to be weaned."

"*Ya*, but not yet."

"No. Not yet."

They stood there for a few more minutes, Miriam lost in thoughts Clayton could not read.

The words he wanted to say rolled around in his mind like a windmill in a storm. *Who were you running off with late at night? Where were you going and what do you do there? Why are you so quiet now?*

He knew he couldn't ask these things. It seemed so pathetic, him watching her from the window night after night. If he voiced his concerns, Miriam would have a few choice questions for him in return, ones he wasn't ready to answer.

He glanced over at her. Without warning, an image came to him, the same image he had been trying to erase from his mind for weeks.

Miriam in the early dawn light. Her hair down and flowing behind her as she ran.

It had looked so inviting, so fascinating, and yet it was a violation of the Amish way. He was not meant to observe her loose, flowing hair like that. But he had. And he hadn't been able to forget about it since.

"Will you and your mother be okay?" she asked, interrupting his thoughts. "You're not going to sell the shop or the house?"

For a second he couldn't answer. Her concern for him and his mother rendered him momentarily speechless. Then he managed, "We…we'll be fine. We have a lot of family we can call on. And we're not selling anything."

"Good. I'm glad. I can't imagine your not living here or working down at the shop."

"I can't either." *It's all I have.*

She turned her head to look at him. "You know, I always thought someday that I would buy one of your clocks."

I would give every clock I have to you.

She took a step away from the open barn doors. "But I'd want a pretty *Englisch* one and you probably wouldn't sell me one of those." She flashed him a half smile.

Words of response hung in his throat, unuttered.

She patted his arm and laughed as she swiveled away from the building, but the sound was without mirth. "I'm only kidding, Clayton." She started to walk past him, her unspoken burden clearly back on her shoulders.

He turned awkwardly and took a lumbering step to follow her, his balance precarious for a second. Miriam saw and reached back to steady him. Normally he hated to have someone help him regain his footing when he started to falter, but her hands on his arms felt like heaven, and he wished she would never let go.

They stayed that way for several seconds, her arm looped easily around his. Then she released him, and the moment was over. They began walking back toward the house together. Ahead of them, another buggy was arriving, and several others were leaving.

"I wish I were like you," Miriam said dreamily.

Clayton cocked his head to look at her. He couldn't have heard her right.

"No, I mean it. You don't try to change what you can't change. You just accept it. You live with it."

He laughed uneasily. "I wouldn't say that, exactly. I'm known for my temper."

She waved the air with her hand as if to sweep away that last comment. "No, I know that. I've seen you angry. It's just that…even when you don't like something, even when you're angry about it, in the end you just let it come because you know you can't stop it."

Clayton felt his face grow warm. Her compliment was not only too good, it wasn't true. It couldn't be true. Miriam shouldn't be like him. There was no merit in allowing something unwanted to come just because that was easier than trying to stop it.

He very much wanted to stop Miriam from doing…whatever it was she was doing.

He wanted to take her in his arms and tell her not to marry Vernon Esh.

He wanted to look her in the eye and beg her to never see the man in the car—whoever he was—again.

Clayton was about to say she was wrong about him, but he'd waited too long to respond.

"Do you remember last year when I came down to the clock shop one day to tell you I had gotten the job at the furniture store?"

He nodded wordlessly.

"You were working on a grandfather clock that seemed as big as a house. Your father said something about time that day, that we can use it or misuse it or waste it, but we can't stop it. The sun will come up and the sun will go down on every good day and every bad one. That's how you are, Clayton. You're steady. Constant. As constant and enduring as the rising and setting of the sun."

He tried to speak, to say that's not who he was, but her words had stolen away every thought in his head.

She took his silence as agreement and gave him a final nod. Her parents and brothers and their families were coming out of the house now. The

Beilers, a dozen of them, approached to offer words of comfort. When they had said their final goodbye, they started for Norman and Abigail's next door. Abigail put her arm around her daughter's waist as they walked away. Miriam looked back once as they neared the path between the properties. She smiled and mouthed the word "goodbye," as though she were leaving him forever.

Seventeen

The first full week after his father's passing was like a strange dream, Clayton thought, the kind where a person's surroundings were both familiar and unfamiliar at the same time. The house was unchanged, yet without *Daed* there it felt completely different somehow. The shop, as well, seemed both unchanged yet inextricably altered, starting with the Raber and Son Clockmakers sign above the door, which was all wrong now. Clayton would not contemplate changing it, but he found himself staring at it often, wishing the sign's words were still true.

Each day, while he worked at the shop, all sorts of food made its way into the kitchen of the house—casseroles and loaves of bread and trays of sweets and more, all lovingly prepared and delivered by members of the community. And though Clayton appreciated how such efforts were temporarily lessening his mother's load, he had to admit that most of it tasted a little off somehow—not bad but different from what he was used to.

Chores were the same way. Though the complete takeover of those first three days had come to an end, somehow things kept getting done here and there. Friends and neighbors were obviously still popping by to handle various tasks. And even though Clayton knew this, each time he walked up from the shop at the end of the day to find the horses returned from the pasture, or Rosie milked, or the chickens gathered into their coop, he was startled. It always took a moment to remember that folks were just trying to be nice and lessen his load during this difficult time.

Until it struck him one day that it wasn't "folks" who were still doing all of this. It wasn't the community or friends or neighbors. It was family. His family. His sisters, finally getting their way by slipping in while he was at work under the guise of community concern and doing the chores they had said all along he wasn't capable of handling.

The evening he figured it out, he had come into the barn straight from a full day in the shop, smelling of varnish and sawdust and linseed oil. But with nothing that needed doing there, he remained untouched by the additional odor of animals and hay and earth.

His steps heavy, Clayton said only four words to his mother when he went into the house. "Who did the chores?"

She looked up from where she stood at the sink, her expression distant and vague as she named two of his sisters.

The very thought made Clayton furious, and he demanded to know why she had let them do that.

Mamm, who still seemed in a state of quiet bewilderment at *Daed*'s passing, simply answered that Clayton's sisters were dealing with the loss too, and allowing them and their children to help was one way they were able to cope.

"It doesn't hurt you to let them help," she added as she reached into the cabinet and pulled out two plates.

Clayton didn't know how to tell her that somehow it *did* hurt. Coming into the house well before dark and with no outside chores to do meant a very long, quiet evening with just his grieving mother for company.

"They won't be coming into the shop, if that's what's bothering you," she added when he gave her no reply. "They know how you feel about that." Then she looked up at him. "Unless you have changed your mind."

"I haven't."

"But you'll let me come help you?" Her voice sounded tired, as though she wanted to do so but hadn't the energy just yet.

"When you feel up to it. There's no rush."

"But Saturday will be busy."

He nodded.

She sighed gently as she served up a plate for Clayton and then one for herself. "I will come down to help you on Saturday."

Anger at his own selfishness roiled up within him. It was because of him that *Mamm* felt forced to work in the shop so soon after losing *Daed*. "I can ask Joanie. Or one of the nieces. It's just one day a week. I'll take care of it."

His mother stroked the back of *Daed*'s chair. It was pushed fully under the table, without a place setting in front of it. "How I wish you would, Clayton. I know I shouldn't be sad, but I just miss him. I miss him."

Clayton limped to his mother's side as quickly as he could and put an arm around her as silent sobs shook her body.

"I thought I had prepared myself for this," she murmured as she struggled for control. "I thought I had given this whole matter over to God. I thought I was ready to walk this road."

"I'll ask Joanie. I promise," Clayton whispered, unable to think of anything else to say to comfort his mother. He didn't think there were other words that could. Sorrow wasn't a time for words.

She shook her head, swallowed heavily, and sniffed. "No. No, I will help you. I want to do this for you, Clayton."

"But—"

She patted his chest lightly, just over his heart. "I understand how you feel. I didn't until I began living in this house without your father, but now I know how hard it must be for you to be working in the shop without him and how awkward and strange it would be to have new people in there right now. I will come, Clayton."

"All right," he said softly.

The days slipped by, and before Clayton knew it another week had passed. Now that the chores were no longer being done for him, he was able to keep busy until sunset, and his work went by more quickly. But sometimes it felt is if time were creeping by. Each day meant another one without *Daed*.

Another one without Miriam.

Clayton was thinking of her late one Sunday afternoon, almost two weeks after the funeral, when he went to the kitchen sink for a glass of water and saw Norman and Abigail Beiler walking across the yard toward the house. They carried nothing in their hands, and Miriam was not with them.

"Looks like Norman and Abigail are coming by," he said to *Mamm*.

"Goodness. I don't think we have room in this kitchen for any more food."

"They're not bringing food."

Mamm slid a plate into the sink of sudsy water. "Well, then. If you'll get one of the cakes we've been given, I'll start a pot of coffee."

He was at the pantry still deciding between a strawberry angel food cake and an applesauce spice cake when the knock came at the door. He reached for the angel food and set it on the counter next to the coffeepot. "I'll let them in," he said.

He crossed the kitchen and headed for the open main room and the front door, greeting Miriam's parents and inviting them inside. Immediately, Clayton could see that they both wore worried looks on their faces. Distraught looks. Were they angry with him? He couldn't imagine why. He hadn't seen Miriam since the funeral, so they couldn't possibly think he was messing up their plans with Vernon. Except for the day of the funeral, she hadn't come over even once, not for weeks.

"Won't you sit down?" Clayton said, as polite as he could as he motioned to the sofa. *Mamm* appeared then and welcomed them as well, saying she had a pot of coffee going and they were just in time for dessert.

"That's very kind, but no, thank you, Lucy," Norman said, as he and Abigail seated themselves onto the couch. Clayton noticed that Abigail had a crumpled handkerchief in her hand and her eyes were slightly puffy.

"Is everything all right, Norman?" *Mamm*'s brows had furrowed with instant concern. She could see as easily as Clayton had that the Beilers were upset about something.

"No," Norman answered sadly, and Abigail squeezed her eyes shut.

Clayton's heart skipped a beat. "Is Miriam okay? She's not hurt, is she?"

Neither of the Beilers looked his way as they shook their heads.

Mamm came to Abigail's side, taking *Daed*'s armchair next to her. "Then what is it? What has happened?"

Abigail blotted her nose with the handkerchief. She opened her mouth and closed it again, unable to say anything. Or unable to find the right words. She lifted her head to look at Clayton, who was still standing in the middle of the room. He couldn't read the look on her face, but it occurred to him that perhaps the Beilers needed to speak to his mother alone.

"I have some work to do outside. I'll just be going if you'll excuse me." He turned on his good heel and had taken only two halting steps when Norman spoke.

"Please stay, Clayton."

Norman's voice was hopeful but adamant.

Clayton turned back around to face his neighbors.

"Please?" Norman said, less forceful this time.

Clayton hobbled fully into the room and lowered himself into the chair *Mamm* usually sat in after supper.

After a few seconds of silence, Norman cleared his throat. "We have a problem. And we don't know if you will help us, but we know we have to ask. As hard as it is *to* ask, we know we must."

"Norman, Clayton and I are happy to help you in any way we can," his mother said, her own woes pushed aside for the moment. "You know that."

He shook his head. "Wait until you've heard me out, Lucy. We've come to ask no small thing."

Beside him, Abigail sighed and looked up at her husband. Her eyes were shimmering with ready tears.

"What is it that we can do for you?" Surprise made *Mamm*'s words sound airy and unsure.

"It's not what you can do, Lucy. It's what Clayton can do."

Norman turned his head to face Clayton. So did *Mamm*. Abigail glanced at him and then quickly looked down at the handkerchief in her hand.

"Me?" Clayton exclaimed, his mind instantly awhirl. What could a disabled man like him do for the Beilers?

Norman rubbed his beard with one hand, lost in thought. "The thing is, Clayton, we've…Abigail and I have known for some time that you are fond of Miriam."

Heat rushed to Clayton's face in an instant. He said nothing.

"And she's always been fond of you."

"As…as…a friend," Clayton stammered. "We're just friends. I've barely talked to her in weeks. I hardly ever see her anymore. She…she hasn't been around like she used to be. You have my word!"

"She hasn't," *Mamm* replied in her son's defense, her voice as earnest as Clayton's had been.

"No, I know that," Norman said, shaking his head as if Clayton had completely misunderstood him. "Her attentions have been, uh, elsewhere. We just…she…" He expelled the air from his lungs, apparently unable to say the words to finish his sentence. The pained look on his face made it appear as though he had already said them, and they had been appalling to utter.

"She what?" Fear that something dreadful had happened to the only woman he had ever loved made Clayton's voice quaver.

"She…" Norman began again but then stopped.

"What?" Clayton heard the desperation in his voice but didn't care. Something was terribly wrong. "She *what*?"

Abigail lifted her gaze to him, the shimmering tears slipping down her cheeks unchecked. "She's with child."

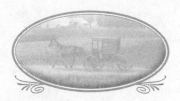

Eighteen

The silence in the living room was broken only by the gurgling of the percolator in the kitchen as it produced coffee that none of them would be drinking. For several seconds no one said anything. Norman stared at a speck on the rug. Abigail's eyes were closed in obvious distress. *Mamm* was stone still. As the impact of Abigail's announcement slammed into Clayton, a thousand warring thoughts somersaulted in his head—and only one image, that of his beloved Miriam in the arms of another man. Heat rose again to his cheeks, blistering hot this time with equal parts anger and shame. He did not want to picture her kissing another man, lying with another man, and he did not want to imagine who that man was. But he couldn't help it.

"Vernon Esh?" his mother said in a hushed voice, assuming the one who had done this was Miriam's Amish suitor.

But Clayton knew it was not Vernon. It was the man in the car, the one who took her away late at night after her dates with Vernon were done. It was the man who waited for her in secret, who disappeared with her for hours, who dumped her back out on the driveway before dawn.

Clayton felt the fingers of his right hand curl into a fist, as though that man was in the room and Clayton was preparing to slug the living daylights out of him. He covered the fist with his left hand to hide it and quell his rising rage. It was not the Amish way to respond with violence to any kind of provocation, not even to condemn a man's immoral dealings with a young, unmarried woman.

But how dare that man touch Miriam? How dare he take what did not belong to him? How *dare* he?

"It wasn't Vernon, Lucy," Norman was saying to *Mamm*, though Clayton could barely hear him over the roaring in his ears.

"It wasn't?"

"It wasn't Vernon," Norman said again, softer this time, as Abigail swallowed back a sob.

Clayton's voice stilled in his throat, waiting for a name. But no one said it aloud, and he realized he was relieved. He didn't want to hear it. Better this person remain always in his mind as just a shadowy figure inside a car.

"The father of the child is *Englisch*," Norman continued. "He was a performer Miriam met in Lancaster, at the Fulton. An actor. He was in town for the run of a play. They became friends, so she says."

"Friends?" *Mamm* whispered, and again Abigail choked back another sob.

"So she says." Norman repeated, with a slow shake of his head. "The man and the play are gone now, on to another city. He knows what his actions have resulted in, but he wants nothing to do with Miriam or the child."

"Oh dear Lord!" *Mamm* murmured, and then she bowed her head in silent lament.

Both of Clayton's hands were balled into fists now, and his chest heaved with outrage and anguish.

His sweet Miriam...

"How could a man do such a thing to a young girl and then just leave her?" Abigail murmured, her voice breaking on the last three words.

"Because he's *Englisch*!" Norman exclaimed, his voice now breaking too.

Because he's an animal! Clayton thought. *Miriam, Miriam...*

"And now Vernon wants nothing to do with Miriam either," Norman went on, wiping his glistening cheeks with his weathered hand.

"Oh, Norman! Abigail!" *Mamm*'s mother-heart was breaking for her neighbors and their only daughter.

Clayton had never felt such a blinding ache before, not even when *Daed* died. His father's passing had been expected, though not welcomed. This was not like that at all. Clayton had always known Miriam would someday bear another man's child, but he had never considered it would happen like this.

He was still trying to wrap his head around this knowledge when he realized Norman had said his name.

"*Ya?*" Clayton looked up at Miriam's father.

"We've come to ask if you would be willing to help us. Help Miriam. We wouldn't be asking if the situation weren't so dire. We don't know what else to do."

"Oh!" *Mamm* said, as she realized ahead of Clayton what Norman was about to say.

As she turned to her son with dread and wonder etched in her face, it also became clear to him why the Beilers had come over.

"We know you're fond of our Miriam," Norman said, repeating his words from minutes earlier, but this time with a heaviness in his tone that made them seem forged of iron. "We know you're a man of character, and that you would treat her with kindness and respect. The babe she is carrying needs a father and a name. Miriam needs a name. We are humbly asking if you might give her yours, Clayton. Please. Would you consider marrying her?"

For Clayton, time seemed to stand still in the room. It was as if an invisible curtain had been drawn across the moment and the earth was no longer spinning on its slow journey around the sun. For a clockmaker, it was a sensation he was wholly unfamiliar with. Clayton was aware that the Beilers were looking at him—Norman, earnestly, and Abigail, over the tips of her fingers as she dabbed at the tears in her eyes. His mother was looking at him too. Her eyes were wide as she sat forward in *Daed*'s chair.

Daed.

Oh, how Clayton wished his father were in the room hearing this conversation. He would be in this frozen, timeless moment with him. *Daed* would know what he should do.

Clayton could barely make sense of the request that had been placed before him. He had only ever wanted one woman. He had long since divested himself of any notion that she would ever be his. Ever. It was not to be.

And yet now Miriam was in trouble, and here was her father begging Clayton to take her, remove her disgrace, and give her unborn child his name. Marry her.

"I know it's a lot to consider, son," Norman continued when Clayton said nothing. "Believe me, we don't take lightly what we're asking. But you...you've always cared for her. If you still do, perhaps you could find it possible to look past this terrible mistake she has made. If anyone could, it would be you."

Clayton looked over at *Mamm*. Her face was awash in questions but she said nothing. It was not her decision to make.

"Does Miriam know you are over here asking me this?" Clayton said as he turned to face the Beilers again.

"Yes," Norman answered.

"And how does she feel about it?"

Norman exhaled as if releasing a breath he'd been holding for weeks. "She knows you can help her, Clayton. She knows Vernon won't. And she knows this *Englisch* man who took from her what she had no right to offer him won't, nor do we want him to. I wish to never see that man. Ever."

"Are you saying Miriam will marry me if I ask her?" Clayton replied, barely able to say the words.

Norman nodded. "She will."

For several long moments, Clayton just sat in his mother's chair letting that notion swirl about in his head. *Miriam will marry me. Miriam will marry me.*

He did not think about the fact that she was pregnant, unwed, and desperate, only that it was possible he could marry the woman he loved. That he still loved.

Despite what she had done, and with whom she had done it, he still loved her. She carried an unborn child who needed a father and a name. Perhaps there would be more children down the road, Lord willing.

A wife he loved and children of his own! These were but daydreams he'd seldom allowed himself to dwell on. And now both seemed inconceivably within his grasp.

But would Miriam really have him? He would not be part of some scheme to see her married. If she was not truly willing, or if she loved this *Englischer* the way he loved her, he would not be party to it.

Norman started to rise. "I know you and your mother probably want some time alone to—"

But Clayton cut in before Norman could finish his sentence. "I'd like to talk to Miriam, please."

Norman nodded once, relief evident on his face, and retook his seat. "She was hoping you would. She's waiting for you in your barn. She said you and she have had lots of conversations there while you and your father did chores. I told her the two of you could have the house to discuss this in private, but that's where she said she wants to talk to you if you're willing."

Clayton rose from his chair. He headed slowly for the mudroom and his straw hat hanging on the hook by the door. As he slipped it on his head, he glanced into the living room. Three sets of eyes were watching him. *Mamm* tipped her chin to him, a silent gesture that communicated she would stand behind whatever decision he made, but he could see that her eyes, even from across the room, were filled with concern.

He opened the mudroom door and stepped gingerly into the gathering dusk. Inside his being he felt both numb and invigorated, as though his mind and heart were dueling for supremacy. His brain was saying "go slow, go slow," but his heart was shouting "all you ever wanted, all you ever wanted!"

As he limped across the yard, he prayed the third verse of Psalm 43 silently, over and over, as he was unable to find his own words for pleas for divine guidance.

O send out thy light and thy truth: let them lead me…O send out thy light and thy truth: let them lead me…O send out thy light and thy truth: let them lead me.

He expected to find Miriam at Rosie and Butternut's stall, but there was no sign of her anywhere in the barn. She wasn't with the horses, either, nor was she near the hogs. Had she changed her mind about him and gone back home? Had he both gained and lost her in mere minutes?

"Miriam?" he said gently, hoping against hope he was not too late and somehow she could hear him.

"Up here, Clayton."

Startled, he looked above him. She was peering down at him from the hayloft.

"What are you doing up there?" he asked in astonishment.

"I like it here. It's quiet. It's above everything."

Her voice sounded sad and resolute at the same time.

"Do you…I…I came here to talk to you."

She closed her eyes for a second. When she opened them, they were shimmering in the elongated rays of twilight. "Do you hate me now?"

Clayton found he could not speak. He shook his head.

She nodded as if he had actually said much instead of nothing at all. "Will you come up here? I know you can climb this ladder. I've seen you do it."

"If that's what you want."

Miriam answered by moving from the ladder, clearing the way for him. He *could* climb the ladder. It just took him twice as long as a normal person.

In the summer, the loft was empty for the most part except as a place for storing odds and ends that didn't need to be kept inside the house or weren't used very often. In the winter months it housed hay and straw for the animals. Clayton or his father only needed to toss down bales once a week or so.

He grabbed the rungs, taking his time to steady his disfigured leg before taking the next step. He was glad she wasn't hovering at the top when he reached it. She was sitting back a ways on an old trunk filled with horse blankets.

Clayton eased himself over the top of the ladder and stood. Several mismatched kitchen chairs were hanging on hooks on the rafter above him. He pulled down one and set it near her. Then he settled himself on it, grateful for the few seconds of silence to collect his thoughts. When he was seated, he looked up at her. She was staring at the only window in the loft— a pane of glass on the west side that was covered with dust, grime, and old webs. Nothing could be seen on the other side except diffused light.

"So you know?" she said, not looking at him.

"*Ya.*"

"And you know what my parents want you to do?"

"I do."

She sighed gently and turned her head to look down at her empty hands in her lap. "Is that why you're here?"

"I'm here because I want to know what *you* want."

She laughed lightly, mirthlessly. "I don't think this is about what I want anymore."

"It is where I'm concerned."

She said nothing, unwilling, it seemed, to consider that she still had a choice in the matter.

"Do you love this man, Miriam?"

She hesitated a moment before answering. "I thought I did. I mean, I thought he loved me. I was wrong."

He closed his eyes against the sting of her candor. "Do you love him?" he said again.

"I won't lie to you, Clayton. I've never lied to you. I did love him. But I am trying hard to love him a little less every day." She reached a hand up to her right eye and flicked away a tear.

Clayton let those words settle over him. They still hurt, though not as much. But he was not finished. "Do you want to be with him?"

At this she raised her head and looked into his eyes. He forced himself not to look away from their penetrating beauty.

"No," she whispered.

There was such pain and longing in that one, barely audible word. He could feel it even from several feet away. "Are you saying that just because your parents are insisting you marry me?" He could feel emotion thick now in his throat, and tears were springing to his eyes, just like the ones shining in hers.

Miriam shook her head slowly, never taking her eyes off him. "I don't want to be with him," she said softly.

"Why not?"

She shrugged and fingered away another tear. "Because he doesn't want to be with me."

Several moments of silence hovered between them. Outside, dusk was giving way to night. The light in the barn was growing dim.

"So you don't hate me?" she asked for the second time, her head turned toward the diminishing light outside the window.

"I could never hate you, Miriam."

She sighed again. "Because you're Amish."

"Because…because I love you," Clayton said, as a strange burst of courage coursed through him. "I've always loved you. And not just as a friend. I am in love with you."

She slowly swung her head around to face him again. In her eyes Clayton could see that his confession hadn't completely surprised her. "Maybe you were before, but I don't see how you could be now. You deserve someone better."

"As do you. I'm a wrecked man with a bad temper."

She shook her head. "You're not wrecked."

Again there was silence.

"I know you don't care for me the way I care for you," he said a moment later. "But I promise I will do my best every day to give you a good home and many reasons for affection to grow. I hope it will. I promise I will be a loving father to this child and to love you as Christ loves His church. I promise not to bring up to you or to others the reason we married ever again. I promise to be to you all that a good husband should be, and I will give you all the time you need to think of me as your husband."

Again she turned her head and her gaze sought the opaque world outside the dirty pane of glass. A look of profound loss covered her face. Clayton was sure she was going to tell him she appreciated very much his offer to cover her shame and provide for her and her unborn child, but she could not accept.

Then she turned her head to face him again.

"You really do want to marry me?" she said, her tone hopeful for the first time since he'd climbed up the ladder.

"With all my heart."

NINETEEN

The next afternoon, Clayton closed the shop an hour early and took Miriam to the home of Uriah Weaver, their bishop, who was waiting for them along with two of the church's ministers. As they all sat in a circle of chairs in the Uriah's living room, Miriam made a full confession and repented of her sin. Clayton knew how difficult the encounter was for her, and he was deeply grateful for the men's kind demeanor throughout. Both Clayton and Miriam breathed a sigh of relief when Uriah told them he'd decided that she would not be required to confess to the entire church—nor would any disciplinary measures be taken—because her sin had been committed prior to membership.

Of course, everyone in the church would know the reason for the marriage anyway, simply because the ceremony was going to fall outside the time frame of the Lancaster County wedding season. Amish couples were wed only in the fall, usually in October or November, and weddings that took place in any other month were generally considered to be "fast-tracked" because of a child on the way.

Clayton didn't care about the knowing stares and whispers they were going to face. This situation had happened in their community before, with others, and it would happen again. What mattered was that Miriam had confessed and repented, so now the issue was to be forgiven and forgotten. All he cared about was that people not be hurtful to her, for he knew she didn't need others rubbing salt in her wound.

Because of the time frame, Uriah offered to accelerate Miriam's membership classes as well, condensing down the sessions so that she could be baptized into the church in just three weeks. The subsequent days flew by in a flurry of activity, Clayton juggling his duties at the shop and his usual chores while making time whenever he could to be the one to drive her over to Uriah's for her nightly membership instruction.

Miriam had given up her job, of course, but between her pursuit of church membership and her preparations for the wedding and their new life together afterward, she stayed quite busy as well. Before they knew it, the three weeks had passed, after which she was indeed baptized.

Two days after that, on a beautiful, sunny Tuesday morning in August, Miriam Beiler and Clayton Raber were married by the minister inside the Beilers' home in front of a small gathering of family and friends.

As Miriam stood next to Clayton, she seemed so petite and fragile to him and yet so beautiful. She spoke in a soft voice that was sapped of its usual vitality, yet she looked into his eyes without hesitation as she promised to support her husband, have love and compassion for him, and not part from him until death.

After that, as Clayton listened to the minister read the marriage prayer from the *Christenpflicht*, he wished for the hundredth time that *Daed* had been there to go to for counsel as he'd made this decision. From the moment Clayton told his mother he had agreed to marry Miriam, *Mamm* had been supportive but apprehensive, as if she, too, wished Simon were there to consult.

"You know you don't have to do this," she had said when Clayton returned to the house after speaking with Miriam in the barn. "Just because she's in trouble doesn't mean you have to be the one to get her out of it. She made the decision herself to do what she did."

They had been sitting at the table sipping the coffee she had made when she thought the Beilers were coming over for a social call. The cake still sat untouched.

"I know I don't, but how can I not? You know how I feel about her."

"And how does she feel about you?" *Mamm* had asked gently. "Did you ask her that?"

Clayton had only hesitated a moment before answering. "I know she doesn't love me like I love her, but I also know love can grow. And I will give her the time she needs for that to happen. It might. And even if it doesn't, it will be enough for me just to have her in my life and not married to some-one else."

Mamm had cupped her hands around her mug, drawing its warmth into her palms. "But will it be enough for *her*?" she murmured.

Clayton couldn't answer that.

He turned now to his bride as the minister concluded the wedding por-tion of the service with the exhortation to "go forth in the name of the Lord. You are now man and wife."

After that they returned to their seats on opposite sides of the room for the rest of the service, which would take another few hours and would be simi-lar to regular church on Sundays except for the smaller number of people in attendance. The entire time, throughout every sermon and song and prayer, three words kept reverberating in Clayton's head, over and over: *Man and wife, man and wife, man and wife.*

Afterward, there were subdued yet sincere words of congratulations from the Beiler brothers and their wives, and slightly more robust congratula-tions from Clayton's six sisters and their husbands and older children. Maisie looked on him with far too much concern, and Joan as well, for that mat-ter. He could see in their eyes that they thought he was making a mistake. Katrina, the one sibling who foisted on him the least amount of unwanted pity for his condition, seemed genuinely happy for him. His three other sis-ters wore expressions too difficult to read. All of them knew Miriam was car-rying a baby that wasn't his. And all of them knew Norman and Abigail Beiler had asked Clayton if he would marry their daughter and that he had agreed.

The wedding meal was by design smaller and less elaborate than those held after fall weddings, but Clayton found himself enjoying it more this way. After a while, even Miriam seemed to relax and act like herself, though he noticed she barely touched her roasted chicken and didn't even sample the sweets and cake and other desserts that came later. He told himself that her appetite had waned because of the baby or maybe just the excitement of the day. What he wouldn't allow himself to think, no matter how many times his mind tried to go there, was that she wasn't eating because the very thought of being Mrs. Clayton Raber was making her physically ill.

Eventually, he excused himself and slipped away, needing to get some air and a little peace and quiet to process his thoughts. The meal was being served out on the lawn, so he went around to the front door of the Beilers' home and managed to slip in without being seen by anyone in the kitchen. Stepping into a small side room, he lowered himself onto a nearby chair, leaned his head back against its padded upholstery, and closed his eyes.

Thankfully, the room was silent and still, and for a long moment he just allowed himself to grasp the fact that he was married—*married*—and not only that, but to the woman of his dreams.

Lord, is this why You didn't answer my prayer to take away my feelings for Miriam? Because You knew that eventually I would find myself in this position? After a long moment, a wide grin spread across Clayton's face as he added, *Thank You, God, for always knowing and doing what is best. Amen.*

He opened his eyes but remained where he was, listening to the sounds of distant laughter and chatter and clinking of silverware and dishes coming through the open windows from outside. Several rooms away, he could also hear a few women in the kitchen, clanking and banging and chatting, but even their noises were distant and muffled. It wasn't until he was about to get back up and rejoin the crowd that he realized someone was coming his way, two voices engaged in conversation, the sound growing louder the closer they came. With his bad leg, he couldn't exactly slip out gracefully, sight unseen, and his mind raced as he tried to think of how he could explain his presence in here when everyone else—including his beautiful new bride—was out there.

Fortunately, just as the two interlopers reached the room where he was sitting, they stopped short, slid open a closet just inside the doorway, and began pulling out boxes and checking their contents. It was two teenage boys, and from the sound of things, Clayton decided they had been sent here on a hunt for more drinking glasses, though so far all they were coming up with were extra tablecloths and silverware.

The boys were perhaps ten feet away from where Clayton sat, but they were so absorbed in their task—and their conversation—that they didn't even notice him. He decided to remain still until they were gone, hoping they would never even realize he was there.

Clayton couldn't remember the boys' names, but they were Miriam's nephews and cousins to each other. Maybe fourteen or fifteen, they were both on that narrow precipice between child and adult, where they could be admiring a girl one minute and catching crawdads the next.

At first, Clayton didn't pay much attention to their conversation itself. He was more focused on the cracking of their adolescent voices as they talked. But then he heard one of them—the gangly one, all joints and long limbs—say something that made him start: the words "pity marriage." *Pity marriage?* Had the kid really said that?

He must have, because the other boy immediately shot out a forceful "*Shhh!*"

"Well, that's what they're calling it," the first one objected, his voice defensive but not quite as loud. "Everyone knows it's true."

Clayton sat there, completely still, expecting the blood to begin boiling in his veins. But instead he found an odd calmness falling over him, as if he'd finally discovered the cure for his own insecurities. Yes, he may be a monster and a freak to the rest of the world—a man to be married only out of pity, never love—but at least Miriam Beiler had thought enough of him to unite her life with his. Necessary or not, that still said something, that perhaps he wasn't completely worthless after all. If these families gathered here today considered it a pity marriage, then that was their problem. One of the things he'd always loved most about Miriam was that she'd never ever once pitied him. And hers was the only opinion that mattered now.

Clayton was pondering these things when he noticed that the room had grown silent, and when he looked over at the boys, he realized they had spotted him. They were both frozen in their tracks, eyes wide, boxes in their arms and fear on their faces.

"Hey, Clayton. Been there long?" one of them squeaked.

He hesitated, wondering if he should let them off the hook or not. Perhaps not, he decided, given their ages. Perhaps it was time they learned to act a little more like men.

"Why do you ask?" he replied, sitting up in his chair and fixing his gaze on them.

The boys shared a glance but didn't reply.

"Are you afraid I might have overheard what you said? Because I did. And you should not have said it."

The primary offender swallowed hard. "I didn't mean it."

Clayton took in a breath and let it out slowly. "Didn't mean *what*? That your aunt married me out of pity?" he growled.

The second boy shook his head and blurted out, "We weren't talking about *you*."

Clayton's eyes narrowed. "What do you mean?"

That kid glanced at the other and then back at Clayton. "We were talking about her. Miriam. *You* married *her* out of pity. Because of…Well, you know. Somebody had to do it."

And there it was, the familiar anger that began coursing through Clayton's veins. How dare these children speak of Miriam that way? How dare they speak of her at all? His head filling with a roaring sound, Clayton rose from the chair and took a wobbly step toward the boys, fists clenched at his sides. He knew full well how menacing his features could seem, especially when he was angry, and he used that to his advantage, leaning in close and speaking in a tightly controlled whisper through teeth clenched with rage.

"Don't you *ever* talk about my wife like that again. Do you understand me?"

"Yes, sir—"

"Is something wrong here?"

The words came from someone else, and Clayton looked up to see the gangly one's father hovering in the doorway.

"Yes, there's something wrong here," Clayton snarled. "Your son is repeating things he shouldn't say, things he probably overheard from someone else."

The man's face hardened, but before responding, he patted the boys on the shoulders and told them to take out the glasses and that he would handle things here.

They didn't have to be told twice. Once they were gone, the man—his name was Perry, Clayton remembered, and he was Miriam's oldest brother—crossed his arms over his chest and suggested that Clayton calm down. But he said it in such a composed, condescending tone that it only made Clayton more furious.

"Calm down? Miriam is my wife. You and the rest of this family will speak of her with respect!"

Perry exhaled slowly, as if he found Clayton's anger tedious or boring. "What did my son say that has you so upset?"

At least Clayton had the presence of mind to lower his voice before giving his reply. "He called this a 'pity marriage,' implying I married Miriam out of pity because of her…condition."

From the guilt that flashed briefly across the man's features, Clayton knew exactly where the term had originated.

"Well, it's not being completely disrespectful if the kid's just stating the facts."

Behind Perry, several faces appeared, nosy women from the kitchen who had come to see what was going on.

"Take it back!" Clayton growled. Party noises outside the window became quiet as those nearby strained to listen.

"Oh, come on," Perry growled back. "I'm just telling you like it is. There is nothing to be celebrated about *this* wedding. Nothing. It's a joke."

"Perry, I will not tolerate you speaking to Clayton that way." Abigail pushed her way into the room past a trio of women. "If you only knew what this young man has done for your sister—"

"Abigail," Clayton faced his new mother-in-law, his gut clenched with apprehension, "you don't need—"

"Let me get this straight," Perry interrupted him. "The way you see it, *Mamm*, Clayton Raber is the *hero* in all this?"

"He…yes. Yes, he is," Abigail stammered. "You *know* the child's not his, Perry," she whispered through clenched teeth.

The man turned to Clayton, shaking his head. "Well, you sure got the better end of that deal, didn't you? It's a perfect arrangement! She's desperate for a husband, you're desperate for a wife, so why not throw it all together and slap marriage vows on it?"

Clayton's anger slowly drained from his body, and in its place shame flooded inside, more for Miriam's sake than for himself.

The thing was, as cutting and inappropriate as his new brother-in-law's words were, they held a few kernels of truth. Miriam had been in need of a name. Clayton had been in want of a wife. But the part Perry left out, the part he didn't know, was the only part that mattered. Clayton *loved* Miriam. And someday, God willing, she would come to love him in return.

TWENTY

I should have warned you about my brother," Miriam said later as she and Clayton stood in the driveway and waved to their last departing guest. "I sometimes forget he was already grown and gone when my parents and I moved here, so you never got to know him. He's always been like that."

As the last buggy went down the hill and out of sight, Miriam's hand dropped to her side, and for a moment Clayton considered taking it in his. But he refrained, not just because public displays of affection—even for a brand-new husband and wife—weren't common among the Amish, but also because he couldn't be certain Miriam would find such an action comforting.

At least the scene with Perry had ended about as well as could be expected. Among those who had heard the argument via the open windows had been the minister who had conducted the ceremony. As soon as things began heating up, he had gone out and retrieved Uriah from the tables in the yard and filled him in, and the bishop had immediately taken the situation into hand.

Uriah had told everyone to calm down and then he addressed them all as a group. His voice even and calm, he said that whatever may or may not have taken place prior to this marriage had been confessed and repented in private with church leaders, and that was sufficient given the *Ordnung* and its rules regarding nonmembers.

"Because there has been repentance, there must now be forgiveness—as complete as the forgiveness the Lord gives to us every time we ask for it."

After that, the crowd had returned to what they had been doing before things started falling apart, pretending as if nothing unusual had even happened. Perry disappeared soon after, gathering up his family and saying they needed to get on the road. Once they were gone, tensions lessened considerably.

As for Clayton, he had done the only thing he could think of. He sought out Miriam, whom he looked for everywhere and finally found up in her bedroom. She was moving slowly and calmly as she placed her belongings into cardboard boxes.

"*Wie bischt du?*" Clayton said softly, hovering in the doorway. Glancing over at the window, he realized that although he had imagined this room a thousand times, this was the first time he'd ever seen it from the inside.

"I'm fine," she'd replied, not even glancing his way as she folded a nightgown and tucked it into an open box. "I just thought I'd finish getting ready to go. We can bring these things over to your house as soon as the reception is over and everyone leaves. Should I bring my hurricane lamp?"

Clayton hadn't been sure how to respond. Should he bring up the incident or just follow her lead and pretend it hadn't happened? Before he had to decide, however, she paused and spoke.

"I'm okay, Clayton. Really. It's going to happen. I figure even if word gets out all over Lancaster County, it'll be the latest gossip only until some other big scandal comes along."

He nodded, wondering if that was just bravado speaking or if she really meant it. Hoping it was the latter, he stepped farther into the room and surveyed the open boxes on the bed. Among her personal belongings—shoes, clothes, papers, and books—she'd also packed a number of items he and *Mamm* already had at their place, such as board games, flashlights, candles, linens, coat hangers, and so on. He started to tell her as much but then stopped himself. If it made her feel better sleeping on sheets from her own house or cooking with pots she'd been using her whole life, then so be it. In a way, he felt guilty for ripping her from her home, as if maybe he should have offered his name and nothing more, not even a life shared under the same roof. Perhaps that would have been her preference.

"How about you?" Miriam had asked, interrupting his thoughts. "How are you doing?"

Feeling his face flush with heat, he looked down at the ground. "I'm angry at myself. At my temper. I don't know why I still let it get the best of me." Meeting her gaze, he added, "I am working on it, though. I am. I promise."

Miriam gave him a sweet half smile. "You didn't say anything down there you should regret, not from what I heard. It's going to happen. And I hate to see you worrying so much about what other people think."

"I don't care about what people think."

A tiny grin lifted the corners of her mouth. "Of course you care about what people think, Clayton. Why else would you lose your temper the way you do? Everybody cares about what people think."

He'd swallowed hard and then finally gave her a nod and a smile in return. "Okay. Well, right now, what people are probably thinking is, 'Where are the bride and groom?' I suppose we'd better get back down there."

Miriam sighed, her petite shoulders sinking under the weight of that thought. "Suppose we'd better," she had echoed, and then together they returned to the party and spent the next hour acting as if no one had said anything that day they were going to regret.

Now, with their last guest gone, Clayton knew he needed to apologize to Miriam's parents for his outburst earlier.

As they stepped back inside, Clayton spotted Norman at the kitchen table, both hands cupped around a mug of coffee as he stared off into space. The house was otherwise quiet, the only sound the ticking of a clock on the wall.

Miriam gave Clayton a knowing look and then headed up the stairs to her room. He approached his new father-in-law.

"Everyone gone?" Norman asked, snapping out of his daze.

"*Ya.*"

Norman took a sip of his coffee, grimaced, and put the cup back down. "It's cold."

Clayton hesitated, wondering if he should sit or offer to make the man a new pot or just say what he needed to say and then leave Norman to his thoughts.

"Guess it's time to move over Miriam's things," Norman said, and Clayton could tell he was trying to sound matter-of-fact. "Need any help with that?"

"No, we'll be fine. But thanks anyway."

Norman rose from the table and headed to the sink with his cold cup of coffee.

"I'm sorry I got into that argument with Perry today," Clayton blurted out. "Really sorry."

Norman didn't turn around as he poured the contents of his cup down the drain.

"From what I hear, it wasn't your fault. Perry was in a snit. I've never known anyone to have wider mood swings than he does, from up to down and back again. It's not the first time he's spouted off over something that on a different day wouldn't bother him at all. He's the one who should be apologizing, son. But not to me."

"We both said things we shouldn't have."

Norman put his hands on the counter, bracing himself as he looked out the kitchen window toward the wide sky that lay beyond. No weight had been lifted from his shoulders that day. "Perhaps it would be best if we forget the words spoken between you two. Go help your wife, Clayton. We just need to move on. All of us."

The late afternoon air was alive with the sounds of crickets, grasshoppers, and birdsong when Clayton and Miriam started out with the first load a few minutes later. They each carried a box—Clayton's heavy with books and papers and Miriam's lighter with quilt padding and sewing materials and such—as they made their way across the wide expanse of grass to Clayton's home.

They were silent as they went, but he felt that was more from exhaustion than awkwardness. They were too tired to talk. When they reached the house, they set their boxes down on the porch and immediately headed back for the next load. As Clayton hobbled along the best he could, he realized Miriam was having to adjust her pace to match his own slow gait.

The move ended up taking them three trips total, the last one being the easiest as there were no more books or cast iron pots or anything else heavy to lug. In fact, Clayton was able to hoist the final three boxes together. Miriam had just a few last items of clothing draped over her arm and carried in her free hand a covered wicker basket.

As they were leaving the bedroom, she said to go ahead and that she would catch up. She wanted to tell her mother they were leaving. Clayton did as she asked, and when he reached the bottom of the stairs, Norman was there to greet him.

"Looks like this is it," Clayton said, again hoisting the boxes to rebalance the load.

"Let me get the door for you," Norman replied as he stepped ahead of Clayton.

"*Danke.*"

As Norman held the door open and Clayton limped down the step onto the porch, the top box shifted in his arms, and a few of its contents threatened to spill out. Norman thrust out his free hand to steady it.

"I got it," Clayton said when his footing was secure again.

"*Ya*," Norman replied, nodding once and slowly lowering his hand.

The two men stood for a moment on the threshold between inside and outside.

"If there's ever anything I can do…" Norman began, but then his voice fell away.

"We'll be fine," Clayton said quickly, filling the weighty void.

"*Ya*, but I mean down the road. If there's anything you need, or Miriam needs, I want you to know we're right here. We still love our daughter. And we will be good grandparents to the child."

"Of course," Clayton said slowly, unsure what the man was wanting from him. Forgiveness? Reassurance? Some sort of promise or guarantee? He was about to offer all three when Miriam emerged at the bottom of the stairs, her mother right behind her.

The four of them shared a quick, awkward, and final goodbye, and then Miriam hiked up the load of clothing higher on her arm, and she and Clayton set off for the last trek across the yard. When they reached the fence, she opened the gate and they both stepped through. As she closed the latch behind them, he glanced back toward her house and saw that Abigail and Norman were still there, standing on the porch side by side, watching them go. Even from a distance, Clayton could read their expressions, which were similar to those he'd seen displayed by Maisie and Joan and others that day. Even by *Mamm*. Worry that a mistake had been made seemed stretched across their faces like a veil.

When they got to the house for the last time, Clayton's mother emerged from the mudroom to hold open the door as they came inside.

"When you're done bringing up all these boxes and settling in," *Mamm* said, gesturing toward the stack they had left on the porch, "I've some sliced ham, pickles, and poppy seed loaf. Just let me know when you're ready."

"*Danke*, Lucy," Miriam softly replied.

"*Danke, Mamm,*" Clayton added, taking in his mother's expression in a single glance. Concern and apprehension were written all over her face.

Part of that, he knew, was her consternation about what might happen next. Neither she nor he had been certain of Miriam's intentions regarding sleeping arrangements, and so she had prepared the guest room "just in case." Clayton hadn't been comfortable asking Miriam ahead of time if she would share his room with him right away. He was not going to insist that she did.

Mamm stayed in the kitchen as the two of them climbed the stairs, Miriam first and Clayton limping behind her, taking his time on each step so that he didn't lose control of the boxes. Miriam reached the landing and waited for him. There were several bedrooms down a short hallway, and a bathroom.

"Which one?" Miriam said, without emotion and without looking at him.

Clayton felt a warm current of blood rush to his face even before he answered her. "Where do *you* want to sleep, Miriam?"

She turned her head to stare at him, a strange mix of surprise, appreciation, and sadness on her face. "Where do *I* want to sleep?"

He looked at the boxes in his arms. "I won't make you…I mean, you don't have to be…with me just yet. If you don't want to."

He could feel her eyes on him.

"Is that what you want, Clayton? Do you want me to sleep in another room?" she asked softly.

Clayton lifted his head to meet her gaze. "No."

After a few seconds, Miriam looked off toward the hallway and the doors. "Which one is yours?"

"The one at the end."

Miriam started for it and Clayton followed. She stepped inside, and he realized this was the first time she'd seen his room as well.

The day before, he had installed a new row of clothing pegs and made space in the wardrobe, all in hopeful and yet fearful anticipation that this would be her choice. Last night he and Roger had brought in a bureau that Maisie was donating to the cause, and they placed it against the far wall next to the pegs. Otherwise, Clayton had left the cleaning and final decorating to his mother. Now as he came into the room and stood behind Miriam, he was pleased to see that the space was immaculate, the wood furniture gleaming, the quilt on the bed crisp and colorful.

On the bedside table sat a new kerosene lamp with a shiny chimney, and next to that was a little vase of teacup roses. A larger vase of the same roses sat across the room atop the bureau intended for Miriam. Beside the bureau, Clayton was surprised to see one final addition he hadn't expected, a wood-and-fabric screen, its three zigzagged panels offering a small bit of privacy for dressing and undressing. Like the roses, Clayton thought it was a wonderful touch.

Miriam's eyes went to the clothing pegs nearby, which held Clayton's straw work hat and all of his pants and shirts, and then to his bureau, the top of which sported a small round container holding a man's hairbrush and a pack of Wrigley's spearmint gum, already opened. Sweeping her gaze around the room, she spotted the second bureau and the screen and the empty pegs and headed there. She placed the basket on the floor behind the screen before taking a moment to hang her clothes along the pegs. Then she turned her attention to the bed, hands on hips, as she asked Clayton which side was his.

"Excuse me?" he asked, startled. With a flush of heat, he realized he was still just standing there in the doorway, frozen, the three boxes in his arms.

"Which side do you want?" she repeated, gazing down at the mattress.

Clayton found that he could barely speak. "I don't care, Miriam."

She nodded and then gestured toward her corner of the room.

"Anywhere over there is fine," she said, and then she turned slowly to the foot of the bed and sat down on it. Exhaling heavily, she surveyed the room.

Their room.

Clayton set the boxes down against the wall as she had asked and then crossed to the bed as well, wishing for all the world that he could do so without limping and drawing such attention to getting there. He sat beside her, wanting to say just one more thing, needing to say one more thing before their life as husband and wife truly began.

"I will share my bed with you, Miriam. But I won't...I don't think we should...I could never force myself on you. I want our bed to be..." But he could not finish. He could not find the words to tell her he did not want to give his body over to her or to take hers as his own if she still loved another man.

Miriam reached up with a hand and wiped away a tear that had started to slip down her cheek. I would sleep in the other room..."

"That's not what I want from you."

"Then what?"

She let the hand at her cheek fall to her lap, and Clayton reached over to cover it. *I want you to want to be with me*, he wished he could say.

"I just want you to be happy," he said instead.

They sat that way for several long moments. Miriam sniffed back her tears and then took in a deep, cleansing breath.

"Would you mind giving me a few minutes alone to put my things away? We can bring up the rest of the boxes later."

Clayton didn't know if this was a good sign or a bad one. "Of course," he replied, after a second's hesitation.

He released her hand and stood awkwardly to his feet. At the door, Miriam said his name. He turned to her, and she remained seated on the bed with her hands in her lap.

"*Danke*," she said, and her eyes still shimmered with tears.

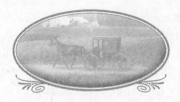

Twenty-One

The next morning—the first full day of his wedded life—Clayton stood in front of the mirror and enjoyed the unique and thrilling experiencing of shaving only his upper lip. Today his beard would begin to grow, never to be trimmed or shaved again now that he was married. Something about the simple act of running the razor over just the mustache area and then putting it away, all done, filled his heart with joy. As a symbol of marriage and commitment, a beard was something Clayton had never, ever expected to have in his lifetime.

His happiness quickly dissolved, however, as he emerged from the bathroom and Miriam rushed in to take his place, one hand covering her mouth as she barely managed to close the door behind her. He spent the next half hour hovering there in the hallway, listening to the horrible sounds from inside and asking her over and over if she was all right. The youngest of his siblings, Clayton had never lived with a woman who was in the family way, and no one ever talked about the specific biology of it. He'd heard vaguely of "morning sickness," but this horrible retching had to be something far more serious. It was nearly more than he could bear.

Finally, his mother convinced him to come downstairs and let Miriam be. Once he was in the kitchen, she thrust a cup of coffee in his hands and told him the barn chores would take his mind off what was happening in the bathroom.

"By the time you come back in, Miriam will probably be done," she added. "Done? Done with what?"

"Done getting sick for the day," she answered forthrightly. "It's normal, Clayton. Don't fuss about it. It's normal."

He had stomped outside with his coffee, mumbling there was nothing at all normal about what was happening upstairs.

When he came in nearly an hour later, Miriam was sitting in the living room with a cup of tea, watching the sun rise, and his mother was preparing a chicken for roasting so the oven could be turned off before the worst heat of the day arrived.

"Sorry about all that." Miriam took a sip of her tea, regarding him over the rim of the cup, and then she returned her attention to the pearly-rose hues of first light outside the big front room window.

"Are you all right now?" Clayton asked, noting how pale she seemed.

Miriam shrugged. "For a lot of women, this would have ended by now. But my mother had the morning sickness long into her time, so I suppose it may be that way for me too. I should have warned you. It only started about a month ago."

Clayton wanted to go to her and lay his hand on her shoulder and tell her he was sorry she had been so sick, but he didn't know if he should. Everything about Miriam was suddenly very new and strange to him. When he had awakened in the darkness that morning and felt the warmth of her back against him, he could only lie there in astonishment at the raw and shattering reinvention of her presence in his life. He had known and loved her for five years, but being married to her was like meeting her for the first time every few minutes.

"You can come down to the shop with me today if you want," he said when his voice returned to him. "If you're feeling better, that is."

She seemed to think on it a moment before turning her head from the window to face him. "I don't know the first thing about clocks except that they all do the same thing, the same way, and they always have. I doubt I'd be much help to you."

She started to turn back to the window and her cup, but then she bolted from the chair and took to the stairs, sloshing tea onto the braided rug at her feet. A moment later, the sound of her retching wafted down to him.

Within a few days, Clayton had resigned himself to rising many minutes before Miriam stirred so that he could be outside already when she awoke and the horrible morning ritual began. He also took his time so that if there was a round two, he'd miss that as well.

When he awoke on Saturday, darkness still covered the county. The only clue that dawn was not far off was the strident crowing of the rooster outside. Miriam did not move as Clayton rose from their bed, but for her sake he still took his shirt and pants to the bathroom to change in there, as he had since the day they were married.

At the top of the stairs, he spotted a light burning in the kitchen. *Mamm* was already up. The aroma of fresh coffee met him on the first step and grew in intensity as he descended. When he rounded the corner into the kitchen, he saw that his mother was at the table with a mug in her hands and her head bowed as if in prayer. The windows were open, and the only cool breeze likely to be felt that day was ruffling the curtains. He was about to make his way outside through the front room door when she spoke.

"You can come in, Clayton."

He stepped into the kitchen. "I thought you might be praying."

"Just thinking."

He said nothing as he poured himself a cup of coffee.

"Is…are things right between you and Miriam?"

Clayton sipped the coffee despite its heat to quell his embarrassment. "As right as they can be, I guess. It's early yet. Not even a week since the wedding." What did she expect him to say? Was she asking him about their private life behind his bedroom door? Did she know he and Miriam had not been intimate and she was concerned about it? Surely she was not asking him about that. Impossible.

When he said nothing else, she exhaled heavily. "I think you should invite her down to the shop, Clayton, like you said you wanted to do back when…back when *Daed* was still with us. She needs something to do. It's hard for me—and for her, I think—when it's just the two of us here all day. Except for the morning sickness and various chores around the house, she spends a lot of time out in the barn, mostly up in the hayloft. It's not wise for her to be climbing up and down that rickety ladder to get there. Now that she's your wife, she should be the one coming down to help you at the shop anyway, not me."

"*Ya,* but I'm trying not to rush her, especially with her being so sick. I don't think she's quite ready to come to the shop with me yet."

"The sickness is done by midmorning and then she's fine the rest of the day." *Mamm* sipped from her cup and then set it gently back down on the table. "She'll come if you tell her to."

"It's not like I haven't mentioned it—"

"*Ya*, I heard how you mentioned it the other morning. You said she could join you if she wanted to. That's not the same as telling her to come because you need her there."

Clayton could certainly use some assistance. The last few days had been busy with the summer season in full swing, busy enough that he had sensed his slowness on his feet was a detriment. He couldn't transition fast enough from work area to the retail side to the back room. He had kept customers waiting several times, something *Daed* said was never a good practice.

"All right. I'll ask her."

"You mean you'll tell her."

Clayton swallowed another sip of coffee and then set the half-empty cup in the sink. He left without responding. He didn't need his mother instructing him on how to manage his wife.

He returned to the house an hour and a half later with a container of milk fresh from Rosie's ample supply and a full basket of eggs. Miriam, pale and haggard looking, was sitting at the table with just a glass of water in front of her. *Mamm* wasn't in the room.

"Can I get you anything?" he said as he set the eggs and milk down.

Miriam shook her head and then changed her mind. "Wait. Do you have saltines? Sometimes crackers help."

Clayton opened the door of the pantry and withdrew a Nabisco tin of Premium Saltines and set it down next to her. "Do *we* have saltines," he corrected, lifting the corner of his mouth in a gentle smile. "This is your home now too, Miriam. Anything in this house is yours. Open any drawer or cupboard or closet you wish to find what you need."

She smiled weakly in return and reached for the tin. "If only it were that easy."

"It is that easy."

She said nothing as she popped open the lid and extracted a waxed paper sleeve, unwound the twisted top, and pulled out four crackers.

Clayton cleared his throat. "I was thinking it would be good if you could come to the shop with me today. Summer is a busy time down there, and I, uh, could use the help."

Miriam swallowed a bite, coughing a little at the cracker's dryness. "You want *me* to help you? Wouldn't you rather have someone who knows what they're doing? Like your mother or one of your sisters?"

"I'd rather have you. I can teach you what you need to know to serve the customers. I think you'll like it, actually, and I don't doubt you'll be good at it. We've a lot of *Englischers* who come in, and you've been in their homes. You know what they like."

"I've only been in a couple. Four at the most."

"That's four more than I've been in."

Miriam licked salt off her lips and nodded slowly. "All right, Clayton. If you really want me to."

He felt a tremendous sense of relief. This would satisfy *Mamm* and would bring Miriam into the part of his life where he spent the most hours of his waking day. "I really do."

"Okay, then. I'll start today?"

He smiled. "*Ya*. Why don't you come down around noon, as long as you're feeling well by then."

"All right."

"*Gut*. Maybe you could bring our lunches with you, and we can eat there together."

She took another bite of cracker and washed it down with a sip of water. "Okay," she rasped, and the very thought thrilled Clayton's heart. Just two months ago, he had rolled his father out to the old picnic area and thought sadly that he would never share it with anyone again. Now look how God had blessed him! He had a wife he loved and a child on the way that was to be raised as his. He couldn't imagine anything that could make his life more complete.

He was about to leave when she spoke again.

"Listen, as long as we're talking about what I can do around here, I have to tell you that it hasn't been easy finding my place."

His heart sinking, Clayton lowered himself to the chair next to Miriam's.

"What do you mean?" he asked, his gaze fixed on hers, terrified of whatever she might say next.

She glanced around and then lowered her voice. "It's your mother," she whispered.

Clayton exhaled, his heart filled with relief. As long as Miriam's problem wasn't with him, they could find a way to work it out.

"She's not exactly thrilled to have me around," Miriam added.

"Don't be silly. She's fine with having you here."

Miriam gave him a stern glance. "You're not around all day, Clayton, so you don't know what it's like. She doesn't want me doing any of the cooking, and she hovers around like a persistent bee whenever I try to do any cleaning. I finally decided to try pitching in outside, out of the way. Then yesterday she told me she didn't want me doing any barn chores either. Other than working in the garden, that doesn't leave much."

He was sorry to hear this, but he wasn't exactly surprised. Despite having raised six daughters, *Mamm* had always been very protective of her position as matriarch of the house.

"Like yesterday afternoon," Miriam continued. "Your nephew Titus came by with his little sister to deliver some supplies for the animals. I was helping them put stuff away when we realized the storage area was kind of a mess, so the three of us set about cleaning and organizing the tack. Then all of a sudden your mother showed up and told me I shouldn't be out there at all."

"Uh…well, in your condition maybe…"

Miriam cut in, relieving Clayton of having to find the right words to complete his sentence.

"I'm just having a baby, Clayton. Women have been doing this since the dawn of creation. I am not going to faint dead away from washing and organizing a few halters and lead ropes."

"*Ya*, but…" Clayton let his words fade. He had no idea what a woman should or shouldn't do when she was with child.

"I'm perfectly capable of doing my fair share of the chores around here."

"Well, maybe what she was talking about was just climbing up the ladder to the hayloft," he ventured, feeling as if he were being stretched between two forces larger than himself.

"She told you about *that*?" Miriam's eyes widened in anger.

Clayton sensed his own temper flaring. "Told me about what?"

"That she doesn't want me on the ladder to the hayloft."

"Miriam, I don't see why—"

"I like the hayloft. I told you that already. I like it up there."

"Yes, but the ladder is—"

"The ladder is just a ladder! Did you not just tell me this home was now my home too?"

Clayton let out a long breath. "I did."

"And did you mean it?"

"Of course I meant it."

"Then if I want to clean *our* tack supplies, I should be able to. And if I want to climb up and sit in *our* hayloft, I think I should be able to do that too. Believe me, the time will come when I won't be able to do either. I'm smart enough to know when that time gets here."

She was right. He could see that now. "I'll talk to my mother. But do be careful on the ladder. And don't overdo it. Will you promise me that?"

She nodded as she crunched on another cracker, which she swallowed hastily. "I don't think Lucy likes me very much. She wishes you had never said yes to my parents."

For a second Clayton could only sit there and stare. Then he glanced behind him to make sure his mother wasn't coming down the stairs. He lowered his voice. "That's not true. She likes you very much. She always has."

"You mean she used to like me. Until I ruined your life. And hers, apparently."

Instinctively, Clayton reached for Miriam's shoulders to force her to look at him. "You did *not* ruin my life. You didn't ruin hers. She doesn't wish I had never said yes to your parents. She's just adjusting to having a new person around. Give her time."

Miriam shook her head. "She doesn't like me, Clayton. I can see it in her eyes."

"What you see in her eyes is grief over losing my father. That's all. Okay? The rest will work itself out in time. And if it doesn't, well…"

"Well what?" she asked, sounding hopeless.

He met her eyes and gave a slight grin. "Well, there's room out back for a little *daadi haus*. If I have to, I'll build one for her and move her out there myself."

Miriam giggled, and the sparkle that flashed in her eyes for the briefest of moments made Clayton's heart sing.

"And even if she did feel that way, I don't," he continued, growing more serious again. "I don't, Miriam. You married me, not her. And I have no regrets. I never will."

Tentatively, he reached and drew his wife close. It felt awkward at first, but then she relaxed and rested her head on his chest.

"Sometimes I think I am dreaming," she whispered.

"Me too," he said, speaking the words into her hair.

Twenty-Two

Miriam had visited Clayton in the clock shop a number of times over the years, more so when she was younger and didn't have an outside job. As a teenager, sometimes she would bring down a plate of cookies or a basket of muffins and then just linger in the showroom for a while, listening to the gentle ticking that filled the air or running her fingers along the beautiful edges and lines of the *Englisch* clocks that surrounded her. As she grew older, she had come less and less until she hardly ever showed up any more. Clayton couldn't remember the last time she'd been there.

Now, as he heard the back door swing open just before noon, he found himself almost feeling nervous. Would she still love it here? Would she enjoy working alongside him? Would she, too, find the days flying by with all that was to be done?

Fortunately, she'd come during a lull in customers. Clayton was at the worktable, putting the finishing touches on some complicated mechanics, so he set down his tools, stood, and was about to head into the back room to greet her when she appeared in the doorway, an oversized lunch pail in her hands.

"No more curtain," she commented, looking up over her head to where it used to hang.

"I took it down once *Daed*...once I started handling the store all on my own." *Once I could no longer run and hide from the curious stares of my customers.*

Miriam looked around, taking everything in. "The place seems smaller without your father in it," she said, her eyes landing on the far side of the worktable. "I suppose that doesn't make sense. It should seem bigger with one less person here."

"I know what you mean, though," he replied, realizing in that moment he hadn't moved his father's chair. It still sat there at the far end of the table, as if *Daed* might return any second, take a seat, and get back to work. "I feel that way too every time I come in."

Clayton reached out a hand and took the pail from Miriam, noting the familiar anticipation in her eyes as she gazed toward the showroom area ahead. Though it wasn't a huge space, they had managed to get the most out of it. Mounted practically floor to ceiling were all of the wall clocks, interspersed here and there with the grandfather clocks. At the center were glass-fronted cases that held the mantel clocks, carriage clocks, Chaucer clocks, table clocks, chronometers, and other small, non-mounting timekeeping devices.

To Clayton's delight, Miriam moved there now and began doing what she'd always done when she came to the store: stroll along the displays, walking slowly and admiring each clock individually. Both Plain and fancy clocks were available, but Miriam lingered only over the fancy ones, pausing at the prettiest and most ornate and studying them with awe.

All around, gentle sounds of ticking and clicking filled the air like a symphony, though Clayton rarely ever noticed or heard it anymore. He knew some people didn't like the sound, that they considered it more a distracting, untimed cacophony. But he could never understand that. He loved the way his shop sounded. He also loved the way it looked, the dozens of swinging pendulums like tiny little hands waving hello each time he glanced their direction. He even loved how the room smelled—fresh cut wood, varnish, linseed oil, all of it. The whole shop entranced him. From what he could tell of Miriam's smile, she seemed to feel the same way.

Thank goodness.

There were still no customers by the time she'd made the rounds of the room, so Clayton suggested they lock up for half an hour and eat outside at the picnic table. As they headed off together, he explained to her how the schedule usually worked, saying he and *Daed* used to eat lunch at home every day but that for the past year or so there seemed to be a lot more tourists coming to Lancaster County, especially in the summer and fall, and because many of them seemed to be interested in Amish-made clocks, traffic at the store had been steadily increasing. *Mamm* would send something down with them in the mornings, and they would close for a quick half hour at midday, eating out here under the trees or in the shop, depending on the weather.

They sat across from each other now, and Clayton watched as Miriam unloaded the food she'd brought, a delicious spread of red beet eggs, *boova shenkel* perogies still hot from the stove, sliced apples, and crackle top cookies. Thinking of their conversation earlier, he didn't ask if she'd made any of it herself, but he had a feeling at least the cookies were hers.

"This is great," he said before biting into the fried potato-and-meat pie.

"It really is," she replied, and when he looked up at her, he realized she wasn't talking about the food. She was gazing at their surroundings—the beautiful old oak tree, the grassy slope of the lawn, the cloudless blue sky. "I never noticed you sitting out here before—and I grew up right next door."

Clayton swallowed. "That's why I like it. It's kind of hidden, even though it's in the middle of everything."

It pleased him deeply that she liked this little part of the homestead as much as he did. As she picked at the food in front of her, taking tiny bites here and there, he considered telling her about the last time he'd come here with his father, when the man had deeded him this rectangle of land as a vote of confidence. *Daed* had said it was "just between the two of us," but Miriam was his wife now. Had *Daed* suspected that Clayton would ever end up married, he probably would have added, "and your future spouse too, of course."

But before he could begin his tale, Miriam began to speak, and the conversation headed in another direction.

"Brenda had the most beautiful backyard. Did I ever tell you that?" she said, her eyes taking on a dreamy, faraway look. "She had this one thing…She called it a pavilion but it was really just a screened-in gazebo. I used to love to go out there and sit in it whenever I had a break. It was so lovely, looking out over the pretty flowers and trees and even a little man-made pond. Can you imagine that, Clayton? Having a pond dug in your own backyard just because it's pretty?"

He wasn't sure how to respond, so he just gave her a nod and took a big bite of perogie. Truth was, he couldn't imagine a more *Englisch* thing to do. What was so wrong with taking a walk to see a God-made pond?

Miriam gave a heavy sigh and the wistful look on her face faded away. Both made Clayton uncomfortable, so before he lost her again, he launched in about work and she seemed happy for the distraction.

As they finished their meal, he filled her in on the basics of manning the front counter—how to handle the customers, how to fill out the paperwork, what to do with the money, and so on. She seemed to take it all in stride, and from the questions she asked, he realized that her past work experiences were going to be helpful to her here—not just her year at the furniture store, but even the short-lived job with Brenda Peterson. More than most Amish women, Miriam had spent time with finer things. As he'd already told her, she knew what *Englischers* wanted.

Once they finished up and went inside, Clayton used the last few minutes to show her around the back room. He started with the will-call area, made up of shelves where the repaired clocks waited until they were picked up by their owners. Next to that were the various supply bins and supplementary tools. On the other side of the room was the small desk where he handled all the paperwork and the odds and ends of running a shop.

Looking at it now through her eyes, he realized he'd let the room get rather messy in the past few months. The showroom was always immaculate so the pieces would look their best, and the worktable area stayed clean and organized or he'd never get anything done. But back here had been primarily his father's domain, and since the man's passing Clayton had been so busy he'd let a lot of it slide.

The messiest part was the desk area, where piles of papers had accumulated so much that they had begun spreading to other surfaces as well. There were papers filling the chair, covering the filing cabinet—even stacked on top of the kerosene heater. He pointed that out to Miriam, saying they would have to be sure to remove that particular pile once things turned colder lest they switch on the heater one day and end up burning the place down.

"Kerosene?" she asked, leaning forward to look. "Why not coal?"

Clayton said they used to use coal but that the dust created too many problems with the clocks. If the building had a basement where the coal dust could be contained, the furnace could have gone down there, and then it probably wouldn't have been a problem. But because the back room was their only option for where to put it, they'd finally had to take it out altogether and replace it with a kerosene heater instead.

"The old coal bin's still here, but we don't use it anymore." He gestured toward a long metal handle attached to a knee-high, pull-down door imbedded in the far wall. "Kerosene's not as efficient, but with this unit back here and a second one in front, we manage to get by."

He went on to point out the stack of supply catalogs and the bins of spare parts, concluding his tour with the last shelving unit, a tall one near the door that held all of the clocks awaiting repair.

"This room's kind of...interesting," Miriam said when he was finished, taking in the equipment, clock parts, and shelves with their bulging contents.

"Interesting?"

She ran her finger across the top of the desk, outlining its edge. "Do you sit here much?"

He shrugged. "Well, sometimes I make lists of things we need from the catalogs. And I write up the invoices to be mailed when repairs are finished. Otherwise, not really."

Miriam moved the stack of papers from the desk chair and sat down. "I could do those things for you."

Clayton hesitated only a moment. Her interest surprised him. "Okay."

She touched the surface of the desk, flitting through the papers, random tools, and odds and ends. Her fingertips came away gray.

"Sorry. It's gotten a little dusty in here—even without the coal."

"I can take care of that."

He sensed a subtle longing in her voice and in her countenance. He wasn't sure what to make of it.

"Would you mind if we thought of this as my desk?" Miriam asked tentatively. "I'd like to have a little place to come to that's just mine." She looked up quickly. "I mean, I know you need this desk for the shop, but I could do the things at it that you do. I could take care of the mail and correspondence, and the ordering and the invoices." She turned her head toward the shelves. "I could tidy up and keep everything dusted." Then she swung her head around to face him again. "If you're worried about me going up into the hayloft, then...I still need a little place to be me."

"Of course you can think of this desk as yours," Clayton said as elation filled him. It was too good to be true. Miriam wanted to be here in the shop with him. Sitting at his desk. Straightening his supply shelves. Sending out the bills and notices. Sharing in his day-to-day world.

Anything I have is yours.

"*Danke.*" She sighed audibly, thankful, it seemed, that she didn't have to explain what she meant by "needing a place to be me." He wasn't entirely sure he knew, but he didn't care. If Miriam wanted be at the shop, that was enough for him.

"Consider this whole room yours if you want," he said. "You can spend as much time back here as you want."

"I won't leave you out there alone when customers come in. I promise."

"I'd appreciate that," he replied, glad he had taken down the quilt that had served as a curtain at the doorway. The thought of seeing Miriam every time he walked past the opening was exhilarating.

He felt his face flush with color at the thought, so he covered it by moving to the repair shelf and reaching for the next broken clock to be worked on. It was *Englisch*, painted a shiny white enamel and festooned with rosebuds and etched with gold filigree. He took it into his hands and turned awkwardly with it. Miriam stood from her chair and steadied his arm as he regained his footing.

"*Danke.*"

"That clock is so pretty."

Clayton looked down at the appliance in his hands. The profusion of flowers and glistening gold accents were a bit much for him, but he nodded and replied that yes, it was a very pretty clock.

Miriam reached out to touch its smooth surface as if to memorize its loveliness. Then she let her hand fall away. "When will the first of the afternoon customers start coming?"

His eyes widened. "Um, probably as soon as we remember to unlock the door and let them in," he said with a sheepish smile.

Sure enough, when the two of them reentered the front room, they could see a car already waiting in the parking lot outside.

"I'll get it," Miriam told him, straightening her shoulders and putting on her best greet-the-customers smile. "You can get back to your work."

As Clayton hobbled over to the table and set the clock down, Miriam headed for the door, humming a song as she went.

She ended up handling the customer just fine. She had to look up a clock's invoice, collect the balance on the repair, and then retrieve the correct item from the will-call area. Miriam managed to do all three with charm and poise, and as Clayton pretended to work nearby, it was all he could do not to grin. Some days he just couldn't believe how blessed he was to have her as his wife.

Once they were alone again, she turned her attention to cleaning up and organizing the back. As she worked, Clayton heard her begin to sing softly. It was a tune he did not recognize, an *Englisch* song about someone named Mr. Sandman making dreams come true. She sounded happy, and tears stung his eyes as he realized it was the first time he had heard her sing since her life changed forever.

It was the most beautiful sound he'd ever heard.

TWENTY-THREE

Despite some days of relentless rain and strong winds that caused trouble all over Lancaster County, Clayton and Miriam settled into the second week of married life. At times she seemed content, almost like the old Miriam who used to sit in the barn and happily chat with him and *Daed* as they did their chores.

At other times, it seemed she felt as though she were serving a life sentence without parole. An expression would come over her face, a mix of sadness and longing so severe that it left no doubt to Clayton what was on her mind: the betrayal of her former lover, the actor, the father of the child growing inside her. Clayton would spot her in the clock shop or in the kitchen, a customer receipt or a pie recipe sitting forgotten beside her, her hand on her stomach and her eyes far off and unfocused. At those times, such a vivid glimpse into her unhappiness would pierce his heart like a sword.

Part of the problem was that even as she yearned for all she could no longer have, he had finally gotten everything he'd ever wanted. Now that she was his wife, Clayton was *allowed* to love her, a freedom of the heart that had opened some tiny bud within his chest and burst it forth into full bloom. No longer the pathetic, lonely neighbor pining for a woman he could never have, he was now that woman's husband. She still wasn't yet his lover, but he knew that surely that would change in time. For now, it was enough that she was his life mate, his true love, and his best friend.

Sometimes, Clayton had to admit, there were glimmers of hope, brief hints that Miriam was slowly falling for him in return. He would see it in the sparkle of her eyes when he made her laugh or in the admiration in her gaze when she watched him work. He would hear it their whispered conversations some nights as they lay side by side under the covers, chatting softly before drifting off to sleep. He would feel it in the warmth of her body on those mornings he awoke to find her cuddled against him, her soft, even breaths fluttering like butterfly wings against his shoulder.

In those moments, it took all the strength he had not to wake her and request she be his wife in every sense of the word. But each time he resisted, knowing she must be the one to come to him if that level of physical intimacy was to mean anything to her at all. He prayed often for patience and self-discipline.

And then he prayed some more.

Throughout the month of August, as Miriam seemed to vacillate between closeness and distance, love and indifference, somehow Clayton learned to take it all in stride. The way he thought of it, getting her to love him was like getting the teeth on a gearwheel sawed. It was a difficult and intricate process. If the sawing were rushed, the small blade could snap or a tooth could break loose from the wood. But when the clockmaker went slowly and steadily, giving the blade enough time to stabilize and adjust first before proceeding, the resulting gearwheel would come out strong, sturdy, and beautiful. Miriam just needed time to do that—to stabilize and adjust. Then their life together would become as strong, sturdy, and beautiful as a well-made gearwheel for the finest clock.

The first of September—exactly three weeks after their wedding—was one of the good days. Clayton had just gotten back from morning chores and was getting cleaned up before heading down to the shop. Miriam was awake but not yet out of the bed when he came into their room after his shower, and he chatted easily with her as he stood at the mirror and combed through his wet, unruly hair.

He was just dropping the comb back into its holder when he heard her gasp behind him. Turning around, Clayton saw that she was sitting on the edge of the bed, her hand on her stomach and her mouth open in shock.

"What is it? What's wrong?" he demanded, wobbling over as fast as his bad leg would carry him and dropping awkwardly to his knees on the floor in front of her. Was she in pain? Was something the matter with the baby? What did she need him to do?

She looked up, and as their eyes met her face broke into a radiant smile. Without a word, she reached out and took his hand and placed it over the solid bulge of her belly. He let her hold it there, but he wasn't quite sure what she was doing.

"Do you feel that?" she whispered, her voice full of awe.

"Feel what?"

"The baby. It's moving."

Clayton's heart leapt to his throat. Miriam was fine. Her baby was fine. The baby was moving.

"I don't know," he whispered in return. "What is it supposed to feel like?"

She placed both hands over his, slid it over just slightly, and then continued to hold it there. "It started last week, really, but I wasn't sure that's what it was. It just felt like a little flutter at first. But this…this was an actual kick."

As she said the word "kick," Clayton thought he could feel the slightest something shift under his hand, like detecting the gentlest poke of an elbow through a thick pile of quilts.

"There! Feel it?" she said, and because there was so much eagerness in her voice, he nodded and said yes, he absolutely did feel it.

In that moment, as he knelt before her, Clayton could easily forget all of the obstacles between them. He could forget that her affections were divided, that her life with him was not the life she'd wanted, that the child she carried inside her had not been conceived with him.

Instead, as she slowly lowered her forehead and rested it against his, all he could remember was that this woman was his wife and this child was to be his child, and there was not one single other thing in the entire world he wanted or needed beyond that.

A few nights later, as they were getting ready for bed, Miriam called to him from across the room, asking for his help with something. He glanced over to see her standing in front of the bureau, fooling with her hair, her *kapp* hanging from the hook nearby.

"One of the pins is stuck in my braid and I can't get it out. I just need you to pull the comb through the tangle until the pin comes lose."

He finished putting away his suspenders, slid the drawer shut, and then limped over to her. Taking the comb from her hand and moving into position behind her, he stood there for a moment, unsure of how to help or where to begin.

She smiled in the mirror. "Is everything all right back there?"

"You may be surprised by this, Miriam, but I don't often style my hair." His eyes narrowed as he examined the tangle. "The only combing I've ever done is to a horse's mane, and they don't generally wear braids or pins—or *kapps*, for that matter."

Miriam's eyes crinkled with her laugh. "It's not so different from that. Just pull the comb through until the hair falls free."

"All right. I'll try." His brows knitted in concentration, he stuck the comb in the tangle and began to tug.

"Ow! Gently, Clayton!" she said with a laugh. "Let me show you. You have to come at it from the side."

She placed her hand over his and started the comb at the top of her head. Then she led it down the back of her hair, along the side of the tangle, to the very ends that hung well past her shoulders. She showed him once more, moving closer to the tangle this time and catching just the edge of it as she went, and then she released his hand.

"Now you try."

He did as he was shown, trailing the comb through her long auburn hair from the top of her scalp to past the middle of her back, until the motion felt natural. When he looked in the mirror to ask if he was doing it right, he saw that her eyes were closed, her lips parted. He continued to comb, long after the tangle had loosened and the pin had dropped to the floor. She didn't ask him to stop.

He remembered the night he had seen her run from the car, her loose hair trailing behind her, seductive and forbidden. He'd had no choice but to watch her from a distance and imagine what it was like. What did it smell like? What did it feel like?

Since the wedding, he'd seen it down and loose plenty of times in the privacy of their bedroom, but for the most part he'd tried not to look, knowing to do so might tempt him beyond all reason. But now not only was he looking at her hair, he was touching it, touching *her*. And here she was, in the flesh, standing before him and seeming to enjoy his touch. It was like a dream.

It was more than he could bear.

Silently, he set the comb on the bureau and then returned his hands to her head and inserted his fingers among the strands of her hair. Holding his breath, he slowly ran them downward through her thick mane, scalp to tips. Inhaling deeply, he pulled the bottom of her hair toward him and pressed it to his face and breathed her in, breathed in cinnamon and wildflowers and hot sun. Easing her hair to one side, he exposed the back of her neck, soft and white and curved like porcelain. He gripped her shoulders, wanting to lean in and kiss her right there at the nape, to press his lips against her skin and feel the heat of her at his mouth.

For a brief moment, he closed his eyes, and when he opened them again he realized Miriam was watching him in the mirror. Her cheeks were flushed, her expression unreadable.

"Clayton," she whispered, and then her eyes darted away. "I…can't."

Releasing her shoulders, he took a step back and rubbed his neck, trying to catch his breath. "Then when?"

The question came out with more force than he'd intended. He took a deep breath and blew it out slowly. "I'm sorry. I want you to feel comfortable. And ready. You know that."

She hesitated for a long moment and then moved to the foot of the bed, sat, and patted the covers next to her. He joined her there, knowing she had something to say, fearing that by pressuring her he'd only succeeded in pushing her further away.

He was about to apologize again when Miriam said something he hadn't expected to hear.

"It's not that I don't want to. Sometimes I do, you know. Sometimes I desire you…quite strongly." She snuck a glance at him before looking back at her lap, her cheeks flushing a vivid pink. "I don't know, Clayton, maybe it's just…I don't want you seeing me like this. Not the first time."

He didn't understand. "Like what?"

"You know…" She slid her hands to her ever-growing stomach and rested them there. "Like this."

Understanding slowly dawned on him. She was embarrassed about her body, about how the tiny life form inside was slowly changing it into something she no longer recognized. If only this encounter had happened sooner! In the past week or two, her middle had seemed to cross some sort of line, going from just the slightest bump to a perceptible bulge. Though she'd never been more beautiful to him, he could understand why she might feel insecure about it.

But she had no reason to. His mind spinning now, he tried to think of a way to make her understand that she couldn't be more wrong, that he loved every inch of her body, big or small, and wanted only to show her exactly how much.

"Miriam," he began. "You're beautiful this way. And every way."

She didn't respond, but she didn't pull back either.

"If you had any idea…" he said, and his voice trailed off into a guttural sort of chuckle mixed with a deep moan. How could he put into words the ache that he lived with from morning to night, the ever-constant desire to take her as his wife and possess her completely?

He was about to try again, to pull aside her hair and this time just follow his instincts and start kissing her there. But as he was about to do so, she rubbed the sleeve of her nightgown across her eyes and he realized she was crying.

"Oh, Miriam," he said, freezing in midstride. After a long hesitation, he exhaled slowly, his desire ebbing only slightly. What was he supposed to do now?

He produced a handkerchief from his pocket and put it into her hands. She pressed the cloth to her face, the whimper that accompanied that movement nearly breaking his heart in two. Bad timing or not, when she hurt, he hurt. It was that simple. Without a word, he wrapped an arm around her shoulders and pulled her close.

Miriam went willingly, her silent tears turning to audible sobs as she buried her face in his chest. He didn't know what this was about or how he could help, so he simply held her as she continued to cry.

A while later, when her trembling shoulders finally stilled, he pulled her in even closer for a hug and gently kissed the top of her head.

"When you're ready, my love, and not before," he promised in a whisper, and then he let her go.

She was so spent that he practically had to put her bed as he would a child. He helped her stand, and then he pulled back the covers and held them as she slipped between the sheets. After tucking the quilt in around her, he leaned forward and gave her one final kiss on the forehead.

"I don't deserve you, Clayton," she whispered.

But before he could think of a reply, she was asleep.

Clayton tossed and turned for much of the night, his emotions sliding back and forth between desire and joy and fear and dread like the steel sphere in a Congreve clock. When a woman said she didn't deserve you, what was she really saying? That she didn't want you? Or that she did but just needed more time?

Long after midnight, he was still awake, trying not to listen to Miriam's breathing or the steady beat of his own heart, when he finally decided to get out of the bed entirely and go for a walk. It wasn't something he made a habit of, but the moon was out, the room was stuffy and hot, and if he didn't take some kind of action soon he feared he might go crazy.

As he pulled back the covers to leave, his hand accidentally bumped into Miriam's, startling her partially awake. She stirred, mumbling something he couldn't understand.

"Sorry," he whispered. "Go back to sleep."

"Okay," she sighed, her voice thick with slumber as she turned his way and nestled against him.

Clayton stayed where he was, waiting for her to drift back into a deeper sleep before continuing to extricate himself.

But then he felt her shift again, this time sliding her warm hand into his and slowly intertwining their fingers together. She sighed, though whether from sleepiness or contentment, Clayton wasn't sure. It didn't matter.

Abandoning his plan, he relaxed against her as well and stayed right where he was, finally able to call it a night. As he drifted off to a much-needed rest, one thought filled his mind. *Perhaps there is hope after all.*

The next day, about an hour after lunch, a woman came into the clock shop for the third time in four days and announced she'd finally made a decision. A wealthy tourist from Florida, she and her husband were staying at a nearby inn, visiting the region together in the morning and then splitting up each afternoon so that he could golf and she could go shopping. The first time she'd come into the store, on Monday, she had introduced herself as Florence Upton and explained she was looking to buy a clock for her husband for their upcoming anniversary. She wasn't sure what kind he would like, so Miriam had spent nearly an hour with her, discussing the various features and designs and mechanisms of the many clocks in the showroom. When Mrs. Upton finally left without purchasing a thing, both Miriam and Clayton figured that was the end of it.

The next day, however, she returned, having discreetly picked her husband's brain the night before and narrowed down the choices from all that she'd seen. The problem was that she liked the design of one but the utility of another and the sound of yet another. That was when Clayton had stepped in to help, suggesting that they combine elements of all three and custom build exactly what she wanted. Mrs. Upton had been delighted, and the two of them set about doing just that. As they talked and Clayton sketched, he knew the end result wasn't going to be cheap, but judging by the quality of the jewelry she wore, he figured cost probably wasn't an issue.

Decisiveness was an issue, however, and when all was said and done, there were still several elements she simply couldn't make up her mind on. In the end, she told Clayton she wanted to sleep on it but that she'd get back to him with her final decisions tomorrow.

She never showed up, however, and Clayton assumed that meant their exchange had been a complete waste of time. But now, Thursday, she was back and ready to take the plunge at last.

"With all the rain yesterday, Homer never went golfing, so I couldn't slip away," she explained as she came toward the counter. "So sorry about that." She set her purse on the wide wooden surface and rested a hand on top of it. The cluster of diamonds on her ring finger caught the sun's rays and scattered them in prismatic pinpoints across the room.

"After much consideration, I really do know what I want. For the case, the Windsor cherry with inlays and not the tiger maple. For the drawer, the recessed latch and not the keyed lock. For the chimes, Westminster and not Whittington."

"Wow, you sound a lot more certain today than you were when you left here on Tuesday," Miriam told her with a smile.

Mrs. Upton nodded, replying that a good night's sleep—or two—always made everything clearer.

Because it was a custom clock, Clayton wrote up the order himself, double-checking each element yet again and then totaling the price. He announced the final figure, a hefty amount that would have given many of his customers pause, adding that he would need half up front as a deposit and the other half once the clock was done.

"Or if you pay in full now," Miriam chirped from beside him, "we'll ship it at no extra cost."

"Then you have a deal," the woman replied, digging her wallet from her purse and writing out a check for the entire amount without batting an eye.

Before she left, she made a point of thanking them both for their patience. "Whenever I have decisions to make, I drive poor Homer crazy with all my dithering. I know I'm not easy to work with."

"I think it just shows how much you care, Mrs. Upton," Miriam replied. "You want to get things right."

She nodded emphatically. "Especially on this clock. It's for our fortieth anniversary. I really wanted to do something special for him."

Her eyes sparkled as she spoke, and Clayton recognized what he was seeing. It was the same sparkle his mother had always had for his father, the sparkle he dreamed of someday seeing in his own wife's eyes for him.

"You'll know exactly what I mean when the two of you eventually get there," she added with a wink to Miriam. "Forty years of marriage, and my heart still flutters when he comes into the room. I'd say that makes me one very lucky woman."

Clayton was so touched by her words that he had to look away. Would Miriam ever grow to love him like that? In forty years, would she still be pining after the man who had stolen her innocence and then disappeared on her? Or by then would she finally have come to understand that God's plan for her life was the perfect plan and His will for her mate had been the perfect choice for her?

Such questions filled Clayton's mind until Mrs. Upton drove off and Miriam's cool exterior gave way to complete exuberance.

"This is amazing, Clayton!" she cried, waving the check in the air and doing a little dance. "I can't believe a person would pay this much for a single clock!"

His questions faded away and he couldn't help but grin, enjoying her display of enthusiasm.

"And it's going to be so beautiful too! I cannot *wait* to see it once you've finished. This is just so amazing!"

Despite her excitement, she managed to finish out the transaction by putting the paperwork and the check in their proper places. After that, he returned to his table and she went back to her dusting. As she made her way around the room polishing each clock and dusting the shelves, she hummed and sang and occasionally took a few dance steps, her mood the lightest it had been in quite a while.

And though part of Clayton loved seeing her this way, another part was bothered by it. He wasn't sure whether she was thrilled with the infusion of cash or thoughts of the clock that cash was paying for. Either way, this was the side of her that had always concerned him, and he wasn't sure how to take it now.

Fortunately, he didn't have much time to ruminate. The rest of day ended up being quite busy, thanks to a busload of tourists who descended upon Ridgeview's tiny downtown, scattering customers from the clock shop on this end to the cabinet store on the other and everywhere in between. Together, Clayton and Miriam managed to sell eight clocks, including one of Miriam's favorites, a tiny, jewel-encrusted Sheffield with a matching leather case.

By the time they locked the door behind the final customer, Clayton was exhausted but Miriam was still flying high. As he cleaned and oiled and put away his various tools and she straightened up the counter area and totaled out the cash drawer, she once again returned to her singing, belting out the Mr. Sandman song as she worked. And though she had a beautiful singing voice, something about it just didn't sound quite right.

TWENTY-FOUR

Clayton's concerns stayed with him throughout the next day. For some reason, he found himself watching Miriam as she worked and seeing things more clearly than he had before. The devotion with which she polished the clocks was something closer to worship. The flash of disappointment after selling off a favorite piece was bordering on covetousness. And the gaze she gave Clayton when she stopped to watch him work was something less like wifely contentment and more like hunger. She loved the clocks and the clock shop, yes, but it wasn't because she enjoyed dealing with the public or working alongside her husband or selling heirloom-quality pieces that folks would love and enjoy for generations.

It was because by being in here, she was surrounded by beautiful things, by fancy things. By *Englisch* things she wanted for herself.

These thoughts were still running through his mind as they headed to the shop on Saturday morning. *Mamm* came along with them as well. Things had been so busy in the shop that Clayton had had a feeling the three of them would be needed. Saturdays were usually busy, but if another tour bus showed up on top of the regular customer traffic, then they would definitely want the extra help.

His plan worked in theory. But what he hadn't counted on was that his mother would be as possessive and bossy with Miriam in the store as she was in the house. More than once he heard her snip or scoff at Miriam and then show her the "right" way to do something. After several contentious hours, he knew he had two choices. He needed to either lay down the law with his mother and tell her to back off or not invite her to work with them again.

He posed that thought to Miriam as the two of them slipped outside for a quick lunch during the noon lull. *Mamm* had eagerly offered to man the store while they did, which made Clayton more than a little suspicious. He had a feeling that even as they ate their corned beef sandwiches out here, his mother was hard at work reorganizing as much as she could in there.

"So which is your preference?" he asked, taking a bite of his sandwich. "Should I lay down the law with her now? Or just never invite her to work with us again?"

Miriam smiled and said it didn't matter to her. She was just glad he had noticed.

"I couldn't have missed it, and I'm really sorry about all of it."

At the bottom of their lunch pail sat two beautiful, ripe oranges, and Miriam set about peeling them and dividing out the slices. "To tell you the truth, Clayton, for today I'd just as soon take off myself and leave her with you in the shop."

His eyebrows rose. "Are you feeling okay? Do you need to go home and lie down?"

She sucked on the tip of an orange slice and then pulled it, like a lollipop, from her mouth. "I'm fine. I'm not really tired. Just tired of her. Tired of the noise and confusion. Taking the afternoon—especially if she's not up at the house—would be lovely."

Clayton's heart warmed at the thought of what Miriam described. Yes, he could see how nice that would be, the chance to putter around, maybe clean a little, maybe cook their supper, all without comment or criticism.

"Of course," he said, and the relief on her face made him feel guilty that he hadn't been the one to think of it.

At the end of the day a neighbor stopped by the store in the hopes that Lucy would be there, and the two women were busy chatting when Clayton was ready to close up. Gently ushering them outside, he locked the door behind them and then went about cleaning and closing out after a long but profitable day.

His mother and her friend were still visiting when he was ready to head up to the house, so he just locked the back door of the shop and then came around the side of the building to give *Mamm* a wave. She waved back, barely breaking stride in the conversation, so he continued on up the hill by himself.

It had been a beautiful summer day, the sky a rich blue dotted with perfect white fluffy clouds. He had chores to do and animals to tend, but it struck him that maybe he would take his wife for a buggy ride while it was still light out. There were some hiking trails nearby, including one that ran along a beautiful bubbling creek, and after six days in a row of being cooped up in the shop, the thought of strolling along that creek under those trees with Miriam at his side was too appealing to resist. Fortunately, she was a spontaneous person and probably wouldn't hesitate to jump on it once he shared his idea.

To his surprise, when he arrived at the house she wasn't inside anywhere. There were no smells or sights of some bubbling stew or baking bread or any other kind of kitchen work. He decided that maybe she was out in the barn, so he went there, expecting to find her talking to Rosie or brushing the horses or yet again organizing the tack closet.

Instead, she was nowhere to be found there either—or so he thought. He was just about to turn and leave when he heard the soft strains of her humming, coming from above.

She was in the loft. Again.

What was it about the place that held such fascination for her? He didn't want to be like his mother and condemn her being up there outright, but he did have his concerns. The bigger Miriam grew, the more her center of gravity was shifting. One of these days, if she wasn't careful, she was going to fall off that ladder just like *Mamm* had said.

Clayton took a deep breath and blew it out, reminding himself what she'd told him about the loft and what it meant to her. As her husband, he should want that for her if it made her happy. As her husband, he should try to understand what it was really about.

With a smile, he quietly crossed to the ladder and then began climbing, softly and slowly, hoping to surprise her at the top. He knew if he called up to her that she would come down to him, but it was time for him to do this, to join her there, to see what a place of one's own actually involved.

It was slow going, but finally he reached the top of the ladder. As he paused to catch his breath, he saw Miriam with her back to him, kneeling in front of the old trunk where they had kept the spare horse blankets, only now the blankets were stacked in a neat pile next to it.

Miriam, still humming away, was seemingly lost in her own world. On her hands she wore a pair of white gloves with sparkly, diamond-like button closures at the wrists, and her humming turned to singing as she pulled them off, finger by finger, and then daintily laid them across her knees.

She then turned her attention to the trunk and thrust her hands inside.

Shocked by the sight of those gloves, Clayton shifted his weight, causing a floorboard to creak. She snapped her head around as she yanked her hands from the trunk.

Her eyes were wide with surprise and fear at being discovered, but when she saw that it was her husband rather than her mother-in-law, she seemed to relax somewhat, her expression slowly changing over to something more like sadness and loss.

"What are you doing?" Clayton asked.

"Nothing. Can you please just let me be for a minute?"

"Why?" He took a step toward her. Miriam shrank back a bit before turning toward the open lid on the trunk and slamming it shut. Then she stared up at him, almost defiantly, determination creeping into her expression. It was obvious to him something was in there she didn't want him to see.

Anger, swift and unsettling, swept over him in a rush. Things had been going so well. He thought they had been making progress. He thought they had been moving toward the kind of love and affection a husband and wife should share. Now he realized it had all been a lie, that having a place of one's own merely meant having a place to keep secrets.

"What are you doing?" This time curiosity didn't lace his tone. He heard the anger in his voice and so did she. Miriam leaned back against the trunk as he strode awkwardly toward her.

"Nothing," she said, but her voice, her manner, and her posture told him she was lying to him.

He tipped his head toward the gloves in her lap. "Where did you get those?"

Miriam glanced down and startled—she had forgotten she'd laid them across her bent knees. When she looked up again, dread and longing were both etched across her face. "They're nothing, Clayton! Brenda gave them to me. She didn't want them anymore. They're just a pair of gloves."

"They are fancy."

Her eyes pleaded with him. "Please, Clayton. Don't make more of this than need be. I am not wearing them. I just like looking at them."

She was definitely lying now—she'd had them on when he first came up here! He took another step toward her. "What else is in the trunk?"

Miriam sat up straight on her knees and put a protective arm across the top of the closed lid. "Nothing important!"

She looked so childlike and afraid that it was almost more than he could bear. Despite her protestations and her lies, she seemed so vulnerable and desperate in that moment that Clayton felt his anger ebb somewhat. He lowered himself awkwardly to the floor beside his wife.

"We cannot have secrets from each other, Miriam."

She opened her mouth as if to protest but then closed it again. She turned to face the trunk. The look in her gaze told Clayton that whatever was inside, it was precious to her.

"Show me what you have in the trunk."

For a long moment she did nothing. Then she looked down at the gloves and fingered a shimmering button.

"Everything that makes me happy is always taken from me," she finally whispered, but not to him.

Clayton reached out and covered the hand that Miriam held over the gloves. He could feel the silky satin just under his fingertips.

"Miriam," he said softly.

She exhaled deeply and her shoulders slumped as she lifted the lid with her other hand.

Clayton leaned over and peered inside. Down in the bottom sat an array of fancy items. A sky blue hat with a netted brim and silk forget-me-nots woven into its band. A nearly empty perfume bottle with a sparkling pink sprayer. A rhinestone bracelet in need of polish. A butterfly-shaped brooch of gleaming green and blue. A beaded evening bag with a missing clasp. And more.

He had never seen such extravagant items. As a member of the Amish church, Miriam had no business having them. She had taken vows. She had pledged to live a life apart from the world, vows of separateness and simplicity.

"Where did you get these?" Anger was seeping back into his tone. And fear for her.

Miriam didn't look at him. "I told you! Brenda didn't want them anymore. She was going to donate them to a thrift shop. I said I knew somebody who would enjoy having them, so she let me take them."

"Somebody who would enjoy having them?" he echoed. Clayton wanted to believe that that *somebody* was someone other than Miriam, even though deep down he already knew she had meant herself.

She sighed heavily, angrily. "Yes, *I* wanted them. *I* wanted to have them.

Not to wear or use or show anyone. I just wanted to be able to look at something beautiful from time to time. Is it really so terrible that I wanted to have a tiny little part of the world out there in here?"

Clayton was quiet for a long moment as he considered her words and genuinely tried to process her question. Was it so terrible that she'd lied to her husband? Yes. Was it so terrible that after all that had happened to her out in the world, her heart hungered for it still? Yes. Was it so terrible that she'd hung on to fancy things despite having taken vows to the contrary?

Yes.

"Miriam, you took a vow before God and the church," he finally said, as gently as he could manage. "You know what the Bible says about storing up treasures here on earth. Our treasures are to be stored in heaven."

The defiance in her countenance seemed to melt somewhat. "I know."

"Then you know that you cannot hold on to these things. You *must* know I cannot let you keep them."

Miriam looked up at him, perhaps sensing for the first time that Clayton had a role of authority over her she had not considered until now. It seemed she had suddenly realized he was more than just her rescuer from a scandalous situation, more than just someone who would be the father to her child from another man.

He was the one she had married. She had vowed to love and support her husband, just as every Amish wife had done in all the decades there had been Amish wives.

Clayton saw the depth of this realization as she stared at him.

"Can't I keep them for just a little while longer?" The distress in her voice at the imminent loss of that which she found dear made part of him want to take her into his arms and another part of him want to shove that trunk over the edge of the loft and let it crash to the concrete floor below, destroying everything inside it. Her attitude toward these *Englisch* trinkets put her on precarious ground.

"What would be the good in that?" he asked, his tone a mix of gentle counsel and solemn authority.

Miriam hesitated only a moment. "It would give me time to get used to the idea of not having them."

"*Not having them* would get you used to the idea of not having them, Miriam. You must know I am right about this."

For several long moments she just sat there with the gloves on her lap.

Then she picked them up by the wrists and dropped them onto the hay-strewn floor.

Before he could reach for her, she rose to her feet and headed for the ladder.

"Miriam," Clayton called after her.

She turned to face him, and it seemed the light had gone out in her eyes. "Do what you think you must, Clayton."

"Miriam!" He exclaimed angrily as he struggled to his feet.

But by the time he got to the ladder, she was stepping off the last rung and running out of the barn.

Twenty-Five

For the next several days Miriam barely said a word to Clayton, not even to ask what he had done with her treasures. He'd wanted to burn them that very night with the week's rubbish, but he hadn't been able to figure out how to carry out that plan without his mother noticing. Miriam still slept next to him in their bed, but she made sure their bodies no longer touched. And when she came down to the shop in the morning, she arrived after he did and stayed in the back room until customers came, at which time she would emerge and plaster a semi-cordial smile on her face while she waited on them.

If that wasn't distressing enough, it seemed other people noticed the animosity between them. Thanks to Uriah's speech at the wedding about forgiving and forgetting, their closest friends and family members no longer seemed to be whispering about them behind their backs. But for the members of the church who hadn't been there that day, Clayton and Miriam Raber remained the big topic of conversation—and now that it appeared their marriage was in trouble, there were even more sideways glances and whispered comments.

Clayton didn't know what to do about it, nor did he know how to get rid of those *Englisch* trinkets in the hayloft. He wished they would just disappear on their own, along with Miriam's displeasure.

Mamm witnessed firsthand the tension between the two of them, but she made no mention of it until Wednesday morning, when she appeared in the mudroom at daybreak as Clayton was sitting on the bench, pulling on his work boots.

"I don't mean to pry, son," she said softly. "Your marriage is your business. But seeing as I let you agree to this marriage without doing much to talk you out of it, I'm going to speak my mind. I don't know what's come between you and Miriam, but if she's been unfaithful to you in her heart, I think you should go to the bishop. If she still loves this other man, Uriah needs to step in and handle it from here, maybe even require another, more public confession and repentance from her."

Clayton nearly dropped the boot he held in his hand. Hot anger pulsed inside him in an instant. "Unfaithful to me?" he exclaimed. "What would make you say that? How can you even *think* that of her?"

Her tone turned defensive. "She hasn't been a proper wife to you, Clayton. I *know* she hasn't. And she's barely spoken to you for days. She barely speaks to anyone. She walks around with her hand on her belly, stroking that child and looking off into the distance like she's waiting for that *Englisch* man to come rescue her!"

Clayton rose to his feet as swiftly as his disfigured leg allowed. He was only a few inches taller than his mother, but she shrank back from him as in his anger he seemed to now tower over her. "You *will not* speak of Miriam that way." He could scarcely get the words past his lips.

She was instantly flustered. "I only meant—"

But Clayton cut her off, raw emotion now lacing his words. "You *cannot* speak of Miriam that way. She is my wife. She is your daughter-in-law. And that baby will be your grandchild."

Mamm's eyes turned glassy with tears. "I just…I just don't want you to get hurt, Clayton. I'm afraid she is going to hurt you!"

"She is not the one hurting me right now."

The two of them were quiet for a moment. When she spoke, a tear ran unchecked down her cheek. "I just can't help feeling that we all made a terrible mistake. That we stepped outside of God's will and took things into our own hands—and far too quickly."

For half a second Clayton wished he could turn to *Daed* and ask him if that's what had happened. *Had* they all made a terrible mistake? Had they acted in contradiction to what God desired for their lives? Clayton couldn't imagine it to be so. In fact, he realized now, he had known exactly what God would have him do the moment Miriam's parents stated their request on that life-changing day. He didn't need his father to affirm what he had decided, what he had pledged. What God had *led* him to do.

"It was no mistake, *Mamm*, I can promise you that. But even if it were, Miriam and I are married now. I took my vows. What's done is done."

His mother seemed to grapple for a response, finally having to go with a repeat of her earlier words. "She's not been a proper wife. She doesn't deserve you."

"Deserve me? *Deserve* me? Is that how Christ loved us? Did He wait until we were perfect before He died on the cross for us? Do we *deserve* His grace?"

Mamm wiped her cheek as she shook her head. "No, son. We don't," she whispered. "But that doesn't mean Miriam can continue to treat you this way. She took vows too. To support you. To love you."

"And I will give her as many reasons as I can to want to make good on those vows."

Mamm had nothing at the ready to say in reply. Clayton sat back down on the bench, slipped on the other boot and tied it tight. Then he stood, grabbed his hat off its peg, and opened the mudroom door.

His mother reached out her hand and laid it across his forearm just as he stepped onto the threshold. She opened her mouth to say something else, but then closed it. He hesitated only a moment before walking out into the half-light of dawn.

Clayton went down to the shop early that morning, alone, not bothering to get cleaned up after doing his chores and not waiting for Miriam to go with him. Apparently, she hadn't appreciated that, because she never showed up at all. Opening time came and went and Clayton remained alone.

As far as the store went, he didn't care. Things were always their slowest midweek, and he passed the first few hours of the workday with just two customers and no sales.

He was glad. Alone at the table, he poured all of his anger and frustration and confusion about his wife into his work, finishing up several quick repairs so that he could start on the order for the Uptons. Theirs was to be a real showpiece, a highly polished and buffed wood mantel clock with brass bushings, beveled glass panels, and satin black Arabic numerals on a silver chapter ring. Its base would be larger than the norm, large enough in fact to sport a single hidden drawer in the front panel, one that could be opened using a recessed latch in the back. Mrs. Upton wanted the drawer for her husband's smoking supplies, and she especially liked the fact that the compartment and the latch were both virtually unnoticeable, as that would keep the grandchildren out of the tobacco.

The case was to be constructed primarily of Windsor cherry and would have inlays made from ten different species of hardwood and veneers, including Padauk, Sycamore, Kingwood, Avodire, Silver Gum, and more. He started there, with the wood, going into the back room and looking through his supply of small beech planks. He chose the most flawless one he could find and pulled it from the pile. It wasn't until he turned to go that it struck him how nice everything looked in here. He hadn't bothered to look before, but he saw now that Miriam had really tidied up the place. There was no dust, the stacks of papers were gone, and the wood shavings had been swept from the floor. He hadn't even noticed.

A short while later, he was sitting at the machinery area behind the table, carefully sliding the band saw through the perfect, unmarred piece of beech when he realized he wasn't alone.

Miriam had arrived and was now standing beside him.

Turning off the saw, he paused to look up at her questioningly. In response, she actually met his eyes for the first time in days and managed to give him a small if somewhat melancholy smile.

Something had changed. For the better. There was an apology in that smile, and he wondered what had caused her sudden change of heart. Was she finally starting to understand that he was right in insisting she give up those fancy *Englisch* things? Perhaps the Lord had managed to convict her where Clayton had not.

Whatever it was, her wordless apology extended to a covered plate he now saw she was holding in her hands. She hadn't spent the morning away from the shop in order to avoid him, he realized. She'd spent it in the kitchen, baking up something that smelled like heaven. Peeling back the tinfoil, Miriam revealed a batch of blueberry muffins drizzled with lemon icing—his favorite, as she well knew—and then she spoke.

"I guess you could call this an edible apology," she told him, as if any explanation had been needed.

He took the plate from her with both hands and closed his eyes for just a moment, the kindness of her gesture healing some broken chink deep inside him. When he opened his eyes again, he was about to tell her that he was sorry too, that he loved her and only wanted what was best for her, when he realized she was on the verge of tears.

"What?" he asked, setting the plate aside before rising to stand in front of her. "What's wrong?" Looking at her now, he realized there was something she needed to tell him.

Blinking away the wetness at her eyes, she shook her head and finally let it out. "I…they're gone. The things in the trunk. I took care of them. I just wanted you to know that."

Clayton was stunned. The chore he had been both wanting and dreading to do was done. He was so relieved—and yet he also knew that *he* should have been the one to complete that task. Suddenly, he felt as though he'd failed her.

"On Sunday afternoon," she continued, oblivious to his guilt, "when I was coming back from visiting with my parents, I slipped into the barn and went up to the hayloft to see if they were gone yet. I thought you would have removed them already, I really did. I didn't expect to see them there still."

"You shouldn't have had to be the one to take care of that. It should have been me. You shouldn't have had to climb that ladder again, Miriam. I'm sorry."

She laughed lightly and wiped another tear away. "You're too good to be true, Clayton. You really are."

Again, words failed him.

"Look. I am the one who brought them here. I'm the one who had to get rid of them, not you."

"Where…how did you…" Clayton didn't know how to finish his question without making it sound as if he didn't trust her that the deed was truly done.

"Remember the covered basket I carried the day I moved in here, the day we were married?"

He nodded. She'd brought it on their final trip over, and it had still been in her arms when he showed her the bedroom they would share.

"I'd been hiding the trinkets in there—at least until I found a better place up in the hayloft."

Her eyes welled with fresh tears, but she brushed them away in frustration. "So yesterday, when I knew I'd be going to Bird-in-Hand with my mother, I went up to the hayloft with the basket and loaded them all back into it. My mother didn't think twice when I told her I needed to stop by the thrift store on our way into town to drop off some donations."

"So now they are gone," Clayton said.

"So now they are gone," Miriam replied.

The two of them were quiet for a few moments, each lost in their own thoughts.

"You did the right thing," he said, hoping she felt the same way and that the awful tension between them would now be history.

Miriam didn't say anything to that, and suddenly Clayton was assailed with new doubts. If she didn't think so, then had they really made any progress here at all?

"Are you still angry with me?" Clayton asked, his tone just a little too gruff.

A fresh set of tears glimmered at the corners of her eyes, breaking his heart anew. He never, ever wanted to make her cry.

"I'm sorry, Miriam, I—"

She held up a hand to stop him.

"I was never really angry at *you*, Clayton. I was just…angry."

He thought about that and finally gave her a nod. He understood. He forgave her.

"There's something else I want to tell you," she added. "I…" She paused, needing a moment or two to search for the right words to complete her sentence. But then she just shook her head as though they had been impossible to find.

"What? What do you want to tell me?" Clayton leaned forward, desperate to know that it wasn't that her heart still beat for someone else.

"Miriam?"

When she looked up, he found he could not read what her eyes were communicating. She gestured toward the plate of blueberry muffins. Then she placed a hand on Clayton's chest, raised up on tiptoe, and gently kissed him on the cheek. A tiny peck. The slightest brush of her lips against his skin.

For several minutes after she turned from him to walk back to the other room, Clayton could only stare at the blueberry muffins, the table, the beech wood, and his empty hands as he replayed that kiss over and over in his mind.

The rest of the day, the two of them were quiet with each other but no longer contentious, as if they just needed to think and heal a little longer before they could get back to who they had been before.

Late that afternoon, about an hour prior to closing, Clayton went into the back room of the shop to find Miriam with her head bent over the desk, writing on lavender-colored stationery. He cleared his throat to let her know he was there, and she startled, quickly placing both hands over the page.

"Yes?" she said, obviously trying not to look as flustered as she felt.

In an instant his stomach lurched. Were there to be more secrets between them already?

"What's that you're working on?" he asked in a voice filled not with rancor but disappointment. He might as well learn the truth now and get it over with.

She looked down at her hands and the words they covered. "Just some paperwork."

He exhaled slowly. "If it's just paperwork, then why are you hiding it?"

Miriam hesitated for a long moment, and then her shoulders seemed to droop in surrender. "It's only a letter, Clayton."

A letter? His pulse surged. To whom? Someone on the outside?

Miriam looked up at Clayton, and she must have seen his thoughts reflected in his features. "It's not what you think. I'm writing it…to you."

"Me?" he replied, at a complete loss as to why she would do that. Unless she was considering leaving him.

"Why are you looking at me like that?"

His next words were slow in coming and stitched together with fear. "What must you put in a letter that you cannot tell me straight out?"

For a second or two she just stared at him. Then understanding filled her eyes. "Do you really not trust me at all anymore?"

"What does the letter say?" he challenged, barely able to squeeze the words from his throat.

"Look. It's just…Sometimes when I want to tell somebody something complicated, it's easier to write it down before I utter the words aloud. So I decided to put it on paper first. I'm not even sure if I'm going to give it to you or not. I just need to spell things out this way, for my own sake. Haven't you ever done that?"

Clayton peered deeply into his wife's eyes and prayed she was telling him the truth. She seemed completely sincere, though after having learned she was capable of keeping secrets—or at least one very big secret—from him, he was having trouble believing her now. He considered insisting that she let him read the letter for himself just so he could know for sure. But after all that had passed between them in recent days, he feared doing so would endanger the new peace they had managed to find.

"No, actually, I haven't," he replied softly.

She folded the sheets of stationery in half and rose slowly from the desk, slipping the letter into her bag. She took a step toward him and looked him fully in the face, holding his gaze tight on hers before she spoke.

"Don't give up on me now, Clayton. Not now. Please? I need you to trust me."

I am trying to trust you. He was afraid to say the words out loud.

"Please?" she said, her eyes pleading. "Please, Clayton?"

When he still said nothing, she reached toward him and placed a hand on his cheek, her fingers just inches from the old wound on his brow. Then, before he had moment to prepare himself for it, Miriam rose up on tiptoe, leaned forward, and pressed her lips to his in an exquisite kiss that was as soft and gentle as it was demanding.

Time seemed to withdraw to some faraway place as he kissed her in return, and in that frozen moment Clayton was aware only of the warmth of her mouth, the tenderness of her touch, and the beating of his own heart.

"Don't give up on me," she whispered as she broke away from him. Then she turned and walked from the room, leaving him stunned and speechless and still.

That evening after supper Miriam seemed pensive. The kiss between them continued to linger on Clayton's lips, as it surely must have on hers. She was kind and attentive to him, but she would not make eye contact. He sensed her growing apprehension and found that it was fueling his own unease. They were like two strangers meeting for the first time, polite but cautious toward each other. His mother was quick to pick up on the tension. Throughout the evening, as the three of them went about their normal routine of relaxation and reading and devotions and prayer, *Mamm* kept looking from him to Miriam and back again, an expression of concerned curiosity on her face.

As he brushed his teeth before retiring to the bedroom, Clayton realized he already knew what was weighing on Miriam. After the intensely physical moment they had shared that afternoon, she no doubt feared he had expectations for that night.

But he didn't. He knew she wasn't ready to give herself completely to him yet. Their kiss had been wonderful—and it had awakened every nerve ending in his body—but it was a far step from there to the shared intimacy he wanted for the two of them. There was also the matter of the encounter they'd had just last week, when Miriam confided that she was embarrassed for him to see her in her current condition. He'd been thinking a great deal about that conversation, because he was certain that no matter how many times he might try to convince her otherwise, she was never going to believe him when he said she was beautiful.

He knew all too well how debilitating it could be to feel unattractive.

He also knew there was something he could do, a step he could take that might help her in this regard. And though he'd rather do anything than what he was about to do, he knew that it had to happen eventually anyway. He placed his toothbrush in its holder and opened the bathroom door.

When he walked into their room, Miriam was sitting on the edge of the bed, her hands folded in her lap. She looked up at him as he stepped inside, and he could see the mix of sadness and resignation in her eyes. She was not happy about the way she felt, he could see that. But she couldn't pretend she was ready to be his wife in every sense of the word when she wasn't. When he moved toward her, she dropped her gaze back to her hands.

"Miriam, please don't worry," he said, coming to her side and sitting down next to her. "I'm not…I don't expect anything to happen tonight just because you kissed me today. I told you from the beginning I would wait until you are ready."

It seemed she had not heard him. He was on the verge of repeating what he'd said when she whispered two words.

"Thank you."

For a few moments they just sat there, side by side, in silence.

"I don't feel pretty," she continued, her gaze still on her lap and the bulging evidence that she was with child. "I don't feel like a new bride. I feel…ruined. I love this child, but I look down at where my waist used to be and all I see is the evidence of what I did. I can't…I'm not…"

"Shhh," he whispered, putting an arm around her. "It's okay. I understand. More than you might think."

"Really?" She looked up at him.

He nodded. "Really."

Clayton took her hand in his as he sent a quick prayer heavenward, asking the Lord to help Miriam see God's love for her through what he was about to do.

"Do you remember that time, years ago, when you came out to chat with me at the chicken coop and I told you all about my accident?"

She was quiet for a moment, thinking. "*Ya*, I do. It was right after we moved here. Your scar made you seem so mysterious and intriguing. I wanted to know where it came from."

"Do you remember how difficult it was for me to share it with you?"

"*Ya*. I had to keep pressing you. But you got it out eventually."

He could hear the smile in her voice, but he couldn't look at her. Not yet. "It was hard for me because I hadn't told that story to very many people—not in that much detail. Sharing it with you should have been unpleasant or embarrassing, like it was with everyone else. But instead it was just…natural. I felt I could tell you anything."

"You *can* tell me anything," Miriam replied, and Clayton felt her eyes on him.

He swallowed hard.

"Can I *show* you anything?" he asked, his voice just above a whisper.

"Of course." Her tone was tentative but trusting.

With his heart pounding so hard in his chest he felt sure she could hear it, Clayton leaned down and began to roll up the pajama pant on his deformed leg. Even though they had been married for nearly a month, he'd managed to keep his bad leg out of view. Each night before bed, he'd changed his clothes in the bathroom, and despite the heat he'd worn his longest pajamas. Once in the bedroom, he would wait for Miriam to get settled and then he'd twist off the bedside lamp before removing his socks and quickly thrusting his feet under the quilts.

No one had seen his leg in years, not even his parents, as he always kept it covered, kept it hidden, kept it to himself. But now he was exposing the disfigurement to his wife.

He didn't look at her as he waited for her to respond. She was silent as her eyes took in the crooked bones, the folds of scar tissue, the mangled mess that was his left leg.

"Clayton," she finally whispered, but he could tell from her tone that she wasn't really speaking to him. She was speaking to Clayton the little boy, five years old, atop his pretend water tank horse. She whispered his name again and then he felt the warmth of her fingertips at his knees. He turned his head to look at her, and she was gazing at the deformed limb as if it were the most ordinary thing she'd ever seen.

Again, she touched a scar, one lower down this time, then again, gently, the same way she'd touched the scar at his brow so many years ago. She hadn't been there at the wreck or by his side in the hospital or on the playground at school where the other kids ran and jumped and played and he could only watch from the sidelines. Yet with each scar she touched now the memories, the pain, the losses of the years since ticked away. It was if the clock of his life was being rewound. Her touch was healing his very soul.

Clayton knew she needed the same kind of healing touch on her own life—and that it was not a thing to be rushed.

He lay awake for more than an hour after they finally turned out the light, savoring the remnants of Miriam's gentle hand on his body, unexpectedly the most intimate and loving encounter he'd ever known.

Twenty-Six

The first day of October began cool and crisp, but thanks to September's lingering temperatures, by noon the clock shop was growing stuffy and Miriam was making her way to the side windows to open them.

On the worktable in front of Clayton was his favorite project of late, the nearly finished cherry mantel clock for the Uptons. But he looked up from the clock now and watched his wife slide open the window closest to him. A brisk breeze ruffled her dress and brought with it the scent of fresh-cut hay. Clayton was mesmerized by the sight of her pausing there at the window, one hand on her rounded middle. She was nearly six months into her pregnancy—there was no mistaking it now that she was with child. Miriam stood at the window with her eyes closed as she breathed in the sweet autumn day.

That was when the idea came to him. Ever since their big argument in the hayloft, he had been wondering how to provide her with a place of her own, something more personal than the back room of the clock shop. He hadn't understood what she'd meant the first time she'd said it, but over the past month he'd come to realize that what she really needed was a private place to go off to be by herself once in a while, away from the demands of daily life. He'd put an end to her visits to the hayloft, and though she still considered the desk area in the back room of the shop to be "hers," that bit of space was hardly adequate for a personal retreat.

As she relished the gentle breeze wafting in from outside, it had come to him in a flash. A gazebo. He would build her a gazebo.

A place of her own.

It wouldn't be fancy like the one Brenda Peterson had. There would be no embellishments or curlicues or any other kinds of *Englisch*-type of adornments. But a small, simple structure with a wood frame and screened walls would allow her to enjoy the outdoors for all but the coldest of months while protected from rain and insects—not to mention people who might otherwise intrude. Best of all, he already owned the piece of land where it would go. Out under the shade tree where the picnic table sat now was the perfect spot to put it.

When his father died, his sisters' husbands had promised they would be there for Clayton whenever he needed them. While he hadn't availed himself of that offer to any great degree, this was one time he was going to take them up on it. With six able-bodied men, plus their teenage sons, he knew the project would come together quickly. One afternoon to pour concrete, and one day to build the structure.

He sketched out the plans that night by moonlight as Miriam slept.

Clayton and two of his brothers-in-law broke ground on the project a week later, on an unseasonably warm autumn afternoon when Miriam was off shopping in town. Working together, the men managed to dig the holes and pour the concrete in under two hours. By the time she returned, Clayton was back inside the shop, working away on the Uptons' clock and acting as if he'd been there the whole time.

Over the next few days he finished that clock, and it turned out beautifully. As was his custom, the final step was to carve his initials and the citation for his favorite Bible verse into the bottom, which he did now. After prepping the surface, he took out his favorite chisel and carefully etched into the wood his mark:

CR
Ecc 3:1

Pulling back to give it a look, he realized he was no longer alone. Miriam was standing nearby, watching him as he carved, mesmerized.

"You finished it," she said, stepping forward to get a better look.

"*Ya.*" He traded the chisel for a jar of liquid and a fine-tipped brush, and then he carefully painted over the letters and numbers until they were covered fully in the sealant. "All done."

"It's perfect. Shall I pack it up and ship it in the morning?"

"*Ya.* If you can get it over to the post office first thing, it should arrive well in time for the Uptons' anniversary."

For a split-second, an odd expression crossed Miriam's face, one Clayton could not read. But before he could ask if something was wrong, the store's front door swung open, the bells chiming, and a small group of customers came inside.

Later that afternoon, Miriam slipped into a quiet mood that Clayton chalked up to exhaustion due to her condition. She looked pale and listless to him, and he realized she hadn't eaten much the last few days. He wondered if that was normal for a woman in her sixth month of pregnancy.

At closing time he grabbed her by the hand and told her he wanted to show her something. He hadn't been planning to reveal the gazebo to her until it was finished, but he needed something now, something big enough to snap her out of this somber, distracted mood. She came willingly but without much interest—until they rounded the corner and she saw the odd cement squares protruding from the ground.

"What's going on here?" she asked, sounding perturbed that someone had messed up her favorite little picnic spot.

Clayton couldn't suppress his grin. "It's a surprise, something I decided to build for you—with a little help from the guys. We got this done the other day while you were off with your *mamm*. Now all we have to do is wait a few weeks for the concrete to cure, and then we can start framing it out."

"Framing what out?" she asked, shaking her head. "What is it?"

"It's a gazebo. I mean, it *will* be a gazebo when we're done with it. And it's yours, Miriam. It will be your special place. All yours." He watched her face with equal parts anticipation and apprehension as she absorbed his announcement.

Miriam blinked. "A gazebo?" Her tone was impossible to gauge. Clayton had thoroughly surprised her, but he couldn't tell if it was a good surprise.

"I know how much you liked the one at Brenda's house. This one will be sort of like it. Not as fancy, of course, but sturdy and screened in, and perfect for sitting in and just being by yourself when you need to be."

"By myself," she said, not so much a question as an echo.

"*Ya*. Your special place won't just be an old desk in the back room or up in a dusty old hayloft. It will be here. And it will be yours."

She at last turned from the footings sticking out of the ground to look at him.

"You're making this for me?"

"I am."

A slight smile lifted the corners of her mouth. "You don't have to go to all this trouble, Clayton. I know how much this spot means to you."

He put both arms on her slim shoulders. "I *want* to do this for you, Miriam. I realize it doesn't look like much now, and the concrete's still wet, but when it's built, it will—"

She silenced him with a gentle kiss to the cheek. "It's the nicest thing. Really. Thank you, Clayton. I'm overwhelmed." She looked down at the nearest footing. "It's still wet, you say?"

He nodded, trying to ascertain if she was truly happy or not.

"Then you should put your mark in it, the same way you sign your clocks."

Clayton stared down at the gray, malleable foundation. "But it's not my gazebo. Why don't you sign it instead?"

She turned to look at him again. "Can't we share it? It should be *our* gazebo."

Though she still hadn't rewarded him with the exuberance he had hoped for, the fact that she wanted to share the gazebo with him lightened his heart.

"Then I suppose we'll need a new mark. One that stands for the both of us."

Miriam grabbed a nearby stick and knelt at one of the footings as together they decided what their mark might be. Once they had chosen, she wrote in the cement the letters *MMCR* for "Mr. and Mrs. Clayton Raber" and the citation for Mark 1:35, a Bible verse perfectly appropriate for a place of one's own:

> *In the morning, rising up a great while before day, he went out,*
> *and departed into a solitary place, and there prayed.*

The next morning, when Clayton came in from doing the chores, he learned from his mother that Miriam had gone on to work extra early. At first, he wondered if she was down at the gazebo site, already eager to spend time in that "solitary place," just like the Bible verse said. But then he remembered a brief exchange between the two of them before falling asleep last night, something about her going in first thing to get the Uptons' clock ready for shipping and him bringing the buggy down when he came later so she could head right on out to the post office as soon as he got there.

Sure enough, when he reached the shop at his usual time and stepped inside the back door, he spotted the box on the desk, wrapped and addressed and ready to go.

"I thought I heard you coming down the hill," Miriam said as she came through the showroom doorway and retrieved her purse from the shelf. "Carry it for me?" she asked, gesturing toward the package.

"Sure." Clayton set down his things, scooped up the box, and then carefully carted it out to the buggy, setting it on the floor inside.

Miriam seemed preoccupied as she walked around and climbed in from the other side, so he didn't try to make conversation. Instead, he just unhitched the horse from the post, handed her the reins, and watched as she drove the buggy away.

Her odd mood seemed to linger even after she was back, and she was silent and distracted for much of the day. Clayton spent the afternoon on a complex clock repair, though as he worked his mind kept going back to a niggling, disturbing thought, one that had to do with that day last month when he'd come upon his wife in the back room writing a letter. She had said she was just working out her thoughts on the page, and yet, Clayton realized now, she had not shared those thoughts with him at any point since, nor had she given him the letter. Their kiss that day had been pure heaven, but looking back at it now, he had to wonder if his tentative trust had been misplaced.

As he finished his repair now, fixing the erratic rack and snail movement of a porcelain Waterbury clock, he decided he had waited long enough. He would ask her again about that letter, soon.

He waited until they were in bed that night, the lights extinguished and the two of them lying side by side. The covers were off and the windows were open to let in what small breeze might come to cool off the room. It took him a full ten minutes to summon the words.

"Miriam, remember last month when we were at work and I came into the back room and you were writing me a letter?" he whispered into the dark.

But she made no response.

He turned his head toward hers and could just make out the confines of her profile. Her eyes were closed, the rising and falling of her chest slow and even.

"Miriam?"

No response. She was asleep.

Turning on his side, he prayed that God would show him how to let her know she could tell him anything—and that he would be able to hear whatever it was she found so hard to say.

Clayton wasn't aware he drifted off, only that the next thing he knew, Miriam was calling for him in a dream. They were in the pasture between their houses, and she was screaming his name, over and over, but he couldn't get to her. He looked down at his legs and saw that both were now disfigured lumps of scar tissue and mangled bone. He could not run to her. He couldn't move—

"Clayton!"

He awoke to the sound of Miriam's screams from down the hall.

He heaved himself out of bed, knocking over his bedside lamp as he struggled to find his footing. The glass chimney shattered, and broken bits skittered across the hardwood floor. He smelled spilled kerosene as he grabbed his flashlight from the dresser and stumbled toward the bedroom door.

Throwing it open and moving into the hall, he realized he was hearing his mother's voice now as well, low and soothing as she tried to calm the still-screaming Miriam. Flipping on the flashlight, he hobbled forward through the shadowy hallway until he reached the open door of the bathroom. He came to a stop and directed the beam inside.

In the jerky half-light he saw Miriam doubled over on the bathroom floor, groaning in pain. His mother was kneeling beside her, and all around their folded knees was a growing puddle of blood.

~~✺~~

Clayton had only been in an *Englisch* hospital one other time in his life, after the buggy accident, when a doctor with a hawk-like nose and a bushy moustache told his parents that he'd been able to save the leg, but it would never function normally again.

Now, as Clayton sat next to Miriam's bed, holding her hand as she stared out the window at the soft light of dawn, the fear he had felt in this place as a child came flooding back to him.

The hospital was where you found out everything was different, but you didn't know what that difference really meant, or how it would change your life. You didn't know how it would change you, only that it would.

"What was it?" Miriam whispered now, her tone void of expression.

"Miriam," Clayton whispered back, afraid to answer her.

"I want to know what it was."

Clayton swallowed back the growing ache in his throat. "A girl."

"Did you see her?"

Clayton had not asked to see the tiny stillborn child Miriam had been carrying. It had not occurred to him to ask. "No."

"Where is she? What have they done with her?"

Clayton didn't know. Was he supposed to know? "I'm not sure."

Miriam's eyes closed as tears pooled and then slid down her cheeks. A nurse came into the room to do a quick exam and told Clayton he could wait out in the hall.

He hesitated. The nurse's timing couldn't have been worse. "I don't think I should leave her. Can't it wait just a few minutes?"

The nurse opened her mouth to reply, but Miriam filled the space with an answer of her own.

"It's okay, Clayton. I'd like some time to myself, anyway."

He was startled. Alone? Now?

"Really," she pressed. "You can go. And you don't need to rush back."

The request fell off her lips softly, but it felt like a load of bricks hurled at his heart. "Miriam?" he asked, certain she couldn't possibly mean what she had said. She hadn't even looked at him.

She just turned her head more fully toward the window.

The nurse smiled compassionately at him and nodded for him to leave.

"Aw, don't take it out on him, honey," he heard the woman say to Miriam as she pulled a curtain around the bed. "It's not his fault. There's nothing he could have done to save the child."

Clayton hesitated, listening, but Miriam did not respond.

"Sometimes it just happens. I've been in this job a long while and I can tell you that you didn't do anything wrong either. Trust me. You and your husband will be able to have many other children."

Still Miriam said nothing in response. Clayton continued on into the hall, lost in thought. He knew what had happened was God's will, but knowing it and believing it on the inside were two different things.

He hovered just outside the doorway for a while, wondering what he should do once the nurse was finished. More than anything, he wanted to go back into the room to be with his wife, but he also wanted to respect her wish to be alone. He was still waiting, still debating with himself, when Miriam's mother came rushing down the hallway, her *kapp* strings flying behind her.

"Where's my daughter?" Abigail demanded when she reached Clayton.

He nodded to Miriam's room. "She's in there, but the nurse is with her right now."

She pushed past Clayton and went inside.

At least that answered his question. Miriam had wanted him to stay away so she could be alone, but as long as her mother was here, she wasn't alone anyway. Once the nurse was done, he was definitely going back in.

From where he stood in the hall, Clayton could hear the murmur of the nurse talking to Abigail. He wanted to get the facts as well, so he moved closer and listened as she said that Miriam's vital signs were good despite the loss of blood and that she was a very lucky young woman. The room fell quiet after that, and Clayton imagined the look Abigail was giving to Miriam, knowing luck had nothing at all to do with this.

He heard the nurse speak again, breaking the silence as she tried to reassure Abigail with the same words she had used for Miriam. "Your daughter and her husband will have plenty more children, Mrs. Beiler. You don't need to worry about that."

Then, with a *swoosh* of metal rungs along the steel rod, the nurse pushed away the curtain and exited the room, moving past Clayton in the hallway with an efficient nod, her attention already shifted to her next patient.

He stepped back into the room, but the sight of his wife and mother-in-law was blocked by the curtain, which the nurse hadn't managed to slide fully out of the way. Not realizing he was there, Abigail spoke to her daughter.

"I'm glad you didn't tell her the child wasn't his. It's none of her business."

He froze.

"Why would I?" Miriam responded listlessly.

"Oh, Miriam," Abigail said, and from the scrape of the chair, Clayton knew she was taking a seat next to the bed. "This is so awful. Here you went and married Clayton to save yourself from disgrace, and now that the child is gone, the entire marriage was for nothing."

Abigail's words stung, but the silence that followed—Miriam's silence—cut him to the quick.

She didn't defend their marriage. She didn't say what a good husband he was or how well they were getting along or that affection for him was growing. She didn't say a word.

Clayton turned and went back into the hall, nauseated. He slumped against the wall and sank to the floor.

The look he had seen in her eyes, the touches on his arm, the late nights talking, her body against his. He was certain she had begun to fall in love with him.

Had he been wrong all along?

Clayton became aware that *Mamm* was there in the hallway. Having returned from the cafeteria, she was now seated on a bench with her forehead resting on an upturned hand. A handkerchief was pressed into her palm, and her eyes were puffy and red.

"Oh, how I wish we could turn back the clock," she said softly, more to herself than to him.

"You know that's impossible," he replied, and then he stood, intent on finding a quiet place to pour out his heart to God and remind Him that he did not want to turn back the clock. Not for a second did he want to turn it back, not if it meant Miriam would no longer be his.

Twenty-Seven

Miriam was released from the hospital a few days later, in time for the funeral on Monday afternoon. As with their wedding, the event was not done in the usual Amish way. Neither family had any desire to spread the word about the loss of the child, so there was no visitation period, no endless comings and goings of friends and neighbors taking over the chores, no gathering of Amish men to dig the grave. Instead, Miriam's father had dug it himself alone in the Amish cemetery, not far from the still-bare mound where Clayton's own father had been laid to rest just months before.

At the family's request, the funeral was a private affair, attended by only seven people: Uriah Weaver and his wife, Norman and Abigail Beiler, *Mamm*, Miriam, and Clayton. Uriah handled the ceremonial portion of things, addressing the family for a while at the house and then saying the usual brief words graveside. As Clayton listened and attempted to comfort his grieving wife, all he could think about was how tiny the grave was, how very much it reminded him of the holes he had dug for the gazebo. As there would be no post-funeral meal, Uriah and Norman stayed behind at the cemetery to finish up there while Clayton took his wife and mother back home. Once at the house, *Mamm* went to the kitchen to start on supper, but Miriam headed straight to bed. Clayton spent the remainder of the afternoon at the closed shop, alternately praying and pouring his grief into the making of a new clock.

In the coming days, though Miriam rose and dressed each morning, she seemed overly tired. Clayton urged her to take it easy, reminding her that the doctor had told them both she had lost a tremendous amount of blood. She was also still mourning the death of her child, and likely would be for quite some time to come.

Eventually, she seemed to rally, at least somewhat. Two weeks after losing the baby, she began coming down to the clock shop again—not to work, but just to go through the mail and sit at her desk and stare off into space. She usually came near the end of the day so that she and Clayton could walk back up to the house together. As they did, sometimes she would reach out and take his hand, as if she could draw strength into her body from his. Occasionally, he still felt her crying at night, her silent sobs shaking the bed, but it was happening less and less.

Clayton grieved the loss as well, though he tried not to burden Miriam with his darker moments. Instead, he took those to God, who blessed him in return with much peace amid the pain. By the end of October, the autumn leaves were at their peak, a sight Clayton had always loved. Each time he noticed them now, he reminded himself of the constancy of the seasons, of how fall gave way to winter and then back around to spring.

Once or twice as he hobbled down the hill toward the shop, bundled in his dark coat against the rain, he thought about his unfinished gazebo on the far side of the building, about the concrete that had cured more than enough now to be built upon. A part of him wanted to keep going with the structure and get it finished, but a bigger part felt oddly reluctant. In the end, he decided he would wait and get back to it once Miriam was well again. The days were colder and shorter now anyway. It was a project best revisited in the spring.

Even *Mamm* seemed subdued and saddened these days, though Clayton suspected there was more than a little guilt wrapped up in her grief. She really had behaved poorly to Miriam before, but at least she seemed to be making up for it now.

Once word got around about what had happened, as they all knew it inevitably would, community members responded by reaching out to them as well. At first Miriam welcomed those who stopped by with food, accepted invitations to the occasional outing, and even returned to worship services. Clayton was relieved, glad to see that love and grace and fellowship were helping both of them get through the hard days.

Or so he thought.

About a month later, there was a change in Miriam. Suddenly, rather than finding comfort in her community, she began to withdraw from it instead. She canceled plans, refused to make new ones, and once even closed the door in a startled visitor's face. Out of the blue, she wanted nothing to do with anyone anymore, not even her own parents. Not even him.

Though physically she seemed recovered, Clayton knew something was definitely wrong. Her emotions vacillated from snappy and churlish one minute to detached and carefree the next. Yet even her calm times were odd. A strange look would come into her eyes, and she was easily agitated and overwhelmed.

As Clayton's concern for her grew, he knew he needed to do something, but he had no idea what. When he awoke on an unseasonably warm Tuesday in November, he made the impulsive decision to close the shop for the afternoon and take Miriam out for a buggy ride. Maybe it was the shorter days that were getting to her and all she needed was a little fresh air and sunshine.

Not surprisingly, she resisted his idea at first. No, she didn't need to get out. No, she didn't want to see any of their friends. No, she didn't want to go shopping or hiking or on a picnic. She just wanted to be left alone.

Clayton finally managed to talk her into a brief ride for an ice-cream cone, but only if they went all the way down in Strasburg, she said, where they were less likely to run into anyone they knew. As he helped her on with her sweater, he glanced over at *Mamm*, who was at the stove stirring a big pot and had heard their exchange. He expected her to give him her familiar look, the one that said Miriam wasn't being a proper wife. Instead, all he saw on his mother's features was concern. She was as worried about Miriam as he was.

A few days later, Miriam chose not to get out of bed—and ended up staying there for more than a week.

"A woman needs time to recover from her child's death," *Mamm* told Clayton when they talked about it, a response he found condescending.

Of course he knew that, and he was prepared to give Miriam as much time as she needed. He just wanted to make sure she was okay.

As the days continued to grow progressively shorter, not only did Miriam sleep far too much, she nearly stopped eating and drinking. Fearing there was something more serious going on than just grief, Clayton finally insisted on contacting the doctor. The man made a house call that very night, but after a thorough examination, he announced that Miriam's body was perfectly healthy.

Outside, at the car, he was more forthcoming with Clayton, explaining that this was not a physical issue, but that sometimes grief affected people in odd ways and she just needed a little more time.

Clayton thanked him for his help, and over the coming days he tried to keep the man's words in mind. But it was hard to do so when his wife stopped eating almost entirely. When she refused to dress or bathe. When her face grew devoid of almost all expression and she would just stare blankly for hours.

One night she surprised him by having a full piece of toast and almost an entire bowl of chicken-and-rice soup. As he carried the empty dishes back down to the kitchen from the bedroom, he allowed himself to feel a small spark of hope. Perhaps she was finally getting better.

Mamm noticed the change in appetite as well, so each day following she tried to make the evening meals progressively heartier. On the night supper consisted of baked ham, pole beans, and corn bread, Clayton went upstairs to speak to Miriam, hoping to convince her to come down and eat with them at the table instead of in bed alone.

He stepped into the room, expecting her to be sitting up in bed as she had been for the past few nights. But his heart sank when he spotted Miriam, lying down with her head fully covered by the blankets. As he knelt next to her and pulled the covers aside, she turned toward his movement. Her eyes were open, but it was as if they weren't really seeing.

Clayton was devastated.

"Miriam?" He placed a hand on her arm and gave it a gentle shake. "Please, Miriam. You were doing so well."

When she didn't respond, he simply laid his head on the pillow beside hers, tears welling in his eyes. "Please come back to me," he whispered.

After a long moment, she finally responded, her voice soft but hoarse. "Clayton."

His head jerked up. "*Ya*? Are you okay? What is it?"

She stared at him, and he could almost see her eyes slowly bringing him into focus. "I'm sorry."

He frowned. "Sorry? For what? Don't be sorry."

She drew a breath and let it out slowly. "I am, though. I'm so very sorry you married me," she said dully.

Miriam's words hit him in the chest like a hammer. Clayton struggled to stand, and she was saying something else as he hobbled from the room, but he couldn't hear a sound beyond a roaring in his ears. He stumbled down the stairs and out the front door, the cold November wind blasting his face.

All this time he had been hoping that she was slowly learning to love him, and it turned out that Miriam was sorry they'd ever gotten married at all.

He lumbered across the yard away from the house without a coat, ignoring his mother's calls from the doorway. When he reached the barn, he went inside, retrieved the horse, and hitched him to the buggy.

By the time Clayton got to Uriah's house, his lips were blue and his body was trembling violently. Uriah took one look at him and pulled him inside, wrapping him with blankets and seating him next to the fire as he instructed his wife to heat up soup and coffee.

When she brought both, Clayton couldn't taste a thing but he ate and drank as instructed, like an obedient child. At some point, the mug and the bowl were taken away. The children were ushered from the room. The bishop's wife disappeared and the two men remained alone.

Uriah turned his kind eyes upon Clayton. "What troubles you, brother?"

Clayton wasn't sure how to say what he'd come to ask. Finally, he summoned his nerve and blurted it out.

"I want to know where the church stands on annulment."

Once the words were spoken, Clayton looked away, not wanting to see the shock in Uriah's face.

The man didn't respond at first. Instead, he stood to get more wood, set it on the fire, and poked it until the flames crackled with intensity. He sat again. When Clayton gained the nerve to look up, he saw that his bishop was neither angry nor horrified.

He was sad.

"Why would you want your marriage annulled?" Uriah's tone wasn't accusing. It was empathetic.

Clayton ran his hand through his hair, fumbling for the words. "It's not for me. It's for Miriam. She…she's sorry she married me. Sorry any of it ever happened."

Uriah nodded but did not reply, so Clayton continued.

"I don't know how to explain this, but it's like she's dying of grief. She hasn't been the same since she lost the baby. Maybe if she can be freed from our commitment, she can finally begin to recover again. To find a new life. To be happy." Tears burned Clayton's eyes as he admitted the full extent of his shame. "The marriage has yet to be consummated, if that makes a difference."

Uriah turned again toward the fire, and Clayton prepared himself for whatever answer might come.

Finally, Uriah spoke. "You're familiar with the story of our Lord's birth."

Clayton nodded, though it had been a statement, not a question.

"Then you'll remember this part," the man continued. "Joseph was already betrothed to Mary when he learned that she was with child. He sought to divorce her, as was his right by Jewish law. He planned to do so in the way that was best for her, privately, so she would not be stoned. He thought it was the right thing to do. But then the Holy Spirit visited him in a dream and told him he was to do no such thing. He took Mary as his wife, and Jesus was born."

Uriah grabbed the poker and stabbed at the fire from where he sat.

"Their betrothal was not consummated either," he continued. "But God still saw it as a union, one pleasing to Him, one He commanded them to keep."

Clayton leaned back in his chair, his heart doing an odd leap. "You're saying that annulment is against the *Ordnung* no matter the reason?"

"I'm saying that sometimes God calls us to stand firm in situations we don't fully comprehend."

Clayton stared blankly ahead. His heart began to race. He hadn't wanted to come here, hadn't wanted to ask for a way out. He'd done it for Miriam's sake because he knew it was her desire.

But if annulment was as forbidden by the church as divorce, then maybe the two of them still had a chance. He didn't want her to feel trapped, but if she knew he had at least tried to release her from this marriage—from this *mistake*, as she saw it—then maybe she would begin to understand how very much he loved her and wanted her to be happy. He loved her enough to let her go.

Clayton said none of this to the man across from him. He simply dropped the blankets from around his shoulders and stood. Uriah looked up at him, seeming perplexed by the obvious relief on Clayton's face, but he rose without comment.

"You've helped me more than you can know," Clayton said, shaking Uriah's hand.

"Well, I don't know how much help I'd be if I sent you home without a coat," Uriah replied with a smile. Then he pulled one from the peg by the door and held it out to Clayton. "You can give it back to me at church on Sunday."

Back at home, Clayton was relieved to see that his mother had gone on to bed. The house was dark, and he was quiet as he made his way up the stairs. In the bedroom, Miriam's sleeping form was snug under the covers in the dark, but he sat on the edge of the bed, placed a hand on her slender arm and gave it a gentle shake.

She opened her eyes, and when she realized Clayton was there beside her, she sat up.

"Where did you go?" she said, her voice accusatory and relieved at the same time.

He just looked at her for a long moment, the only sounds the wind rattling at the windows and a clock ticking steadily from the hall.

"I went to see Uriah. To ask him about an annulment."

"You did *what*? Why?"

"For you, Miriam. You were sorry you married me, so I thought maybe if the *Ordnung* permitted the dissolution of our marriage, then I could give you that. You could be free. You could be happy again."

Her expression went from shock to hurt. "Who said I was sorry I married you?" she demanded.

He gaped at her, blinking. "You did. Right here. Just a few hours ago. You said, 'I'm sorry that you married me.'"

Now it was her turn to gape. "That's not what I meant, Clayton. I'm not sorry I married you. I'm sorry you married me. I'm sorry for your sake, not mine."

"What?"

"I was apologizing to you for all I've put you through."

Clayton couldn't believe what he was hearing. He pulled his wife into his arms and held her tight. And though she didn't exactly reciprocate, neither did she push him away.

Finally, he let her go, telling her they could talk more in the morning.

But sleep did not come easily for either of them. Lying in the dark, Clayton waited for her steady, even breathing to begin beside him, but it did not. Instead, after a while, she spoke.

"Your mother told me something tonight I never realized. She said you were the one who arranged for the baby's burial. Is that true?"

"*Ya*," Clayton replied, though he didn't understand the question. Burials for stillborn children weren't common in their district, but they were allowed.

"Why did you do that?"

"You asked me where they took her. When you were still in the hospital. So I found out for you and then made all the arrangements from there. Was I wrong?"

Miriam's eyes filled with tears. He was about to apologize, but then she turned his way and curled herself against him.

"You weren't wrong," she whispered.

And then she drifted off and slept in his arms for the first time since coming home from the hospital.

TWENTY-EIGHT

Hours after Clayton returned from Uriah's house and he and Miriam had at last fallen asleep, he was suddenly jarred awake. She was no longer in his arms but was instead thrashing about in the bed next to him.

"Miriam? What is it?" He blinked, unable to see her in the darkness.

She whimpered in reply.

He sat up and lit the small lantern on the bedside table before turning to see his wife sitting up in the bed, eyes wide with terror, hands frantically swatting at the coverlet.

"Miriam," he said, louder now. "What's wrong?"

"Look! Don't you see them?"

Clayton held the lantern closer, but all he could see was her slapping at the rumpled bed linens. "See what?"

"The bugs! Hundreds of bugs!"

"Bugs?" Clayton saw nothing, but he set the lamp back on the table and got to his feet, ready to protect his wife from whatever creatures had invaded their bedroom. He grabbed the coverlet and tore it from the bed. He was about to carry it downstairs when she cried out.

"Now they're on me!"

He threw the coverlet down and lit the lantern on Miriam's side of the bed. But even with both lights shining, he still couldn't see any bugs.

"Where?" he said, watching as she frantically ran her hands down her arms. "I see nothing."

"They're everywhere!" Wriggling free from the sheets, she jumped to the ground and began swatting at her torso, her legs. Except that there was nothing there.

"What kinds of bugs?" Clayton asked. Maybe the insects were too small to see without brighter lighting—like chiggers or bedbugs.

"Giant ants!" she cried. "Beetles. Locusts. Look!"

She thrust out both arms, as if the proof was crawling all over them.

He saw nothing but the sleeves of her nightgown.

"Miriam," he said in the calmest, most even tone he could muster, "there aren't any bugs."

She was about to argue the point, but then she hesitated, looked down, and slowly crossed her arms over her chest. Her expression hardened.

"There were bugs. They may be gone now, but they were here."

"I think maybe you were having a nightmare."

She shook her head, her lips a thin, tight line. "It wasn't a nightmare. I was—I still am—wide awake."

Clayton wasn't sure what to do or think. What had just happened? He offered to change the bedding and put the offending linens outside, where any bugs would die overnight in the cold. Her nightgown too. When she didn't respond, he walked over to her bureau, opened a drawer, and pulled out a clean nightgown.

She took it from him without a word and walked behind the screen to change. As Clayton stripped the bed and replaced it with clean sheets and blankets, he felt as if he were moving in a fog. He kept his eyes open for bugs, but somehow he knew he wasn't going to find any.

"Done," he said, smoothing the sheet at the corner. "Whatever was there before isn't here now."

She came from around the screen in her fresh gown, handing him the one she'd just taken off. He grabbed the other linens as well, and lugged the whole pile down the stairs and outside, just in case. He half expected *Mamm*'s head to be peering over the banister as he came back inside, but fortunately all the activity had not awakened her.

When he returned to their bedroom, Miriam was still standing where he'd left her, but now her stubborn expression was gone. In its place was a look of fear and sadness. Her eyes brimmed with tears. She moved toward him, and then her body slumped, as if she could barely hold up her own weight.

Stepping forward, Clayton pulled her close and held her as she began to sob. She buried her face against his chest, her fragile shoulders shaking with each ragged breath. For a long while they stayed like that, clutched together in the semidarkness, she continuing to cry, and he comforting her even as his mind raced to make sense of what had just happened.

"It was a nightmare," he told her—and himself—again, stroking her silken hair. "Just a bad dream."

For the next few days life hinted at a return to normal. Shaken by the incident with the bugs, Miriam finally stopped taking to her bed during the days. She managed to get cleaned and dressed each morning, and she started eating at the table again with Clayton and his mother. Weak from inactivity and the weight she had lost, she didn't come back to work yet at the clock shop, but Clayton convinced her to walk with him each day after lunch, just for the fresh air and the sunshine.

As heartened as he was by these simple changes, he was still worried, especially as Thanksgiving neared. Miriam's moods were still so unpredictable, and the family was to gather at Joan and Solomon's home for the big meal. He didn't want his wife making a scene and embarrassing them both or saying something she would regret and berate herself for later.

On the morning the holiday arrived, Clayton could see that Miriam was having one of her strange days when she was angry one moment and teary the next. He silently prayed all the way to Joan and Solomon's that God would intervene and settle his wife's anxious heart. To his relief, she didn't scream that there were bugs crawling all over Joan's kitchen while all the women were getting the food ready, but she seemed on the verge of bursting into a rage the entire day. Everyone else seemed to notice it too, though courtesy kept anyone from asking outright if one of them had done something to offend her.

While they were slicing pimpkin pies and dabbing on whipped cream, Miriam, in front of nearly everyone, told Maisie that Clayton's mother had the day before locked her out of the house in the cold without any shoes—on purpose—which Clayton's mother then vehemently denied. Not five minutes later, Miriam announced she had a stomachache and she wanted to go back home. That very moment. The rest of the family said their goodbyes with pasted-on smiles and concerned gazes as Clayton helped Miriam into their buggy.

As they clopped along, he asked her why she said what she did about *Mamm*, and she seemed to have no idea what he was talking about. When they got home, she went up to the bedroom, closed the door, and didn't emerge for several hours. But when she did, she was smiling and pleasant, curious to know if it was too late to go back to Joan and Solomon's for some pie.

~⦵~

The following morning, after Clayton had done the morning chores, cleaned himself up, and eaten breakfast, he found that Miriam was still asleep. Before leaving for the shop, he asked his mother to keep an eye on her despite what Miriam had said about her at Joan and Solomon's.

"She's still not her old self," he said, defending her strange behavior.

"You're telling me," *Mamm* said sarcastically.

"Please, *Mamm*?"

His mother sighed. "You know I will, Clayton. She's my daughter-in-law. I have to leave for my quilting group at eleven, but I'll make sure she eats something before I go."

It wasn't Miriam's breakfast that concerned him, it was her soundness. Clayton didn't say that aloud. He just placed his hat on his head and added, "Come and get me if she seems any worse, okay?"

His mother patted his arm and assured him that of course she would let him know if anything required his attention.

Clayton passed a quiet morning at the shop, glad for the escape and sad for being glad about it. At least he could pray as he worked. He remained in prayer for most of the morning, in fact, and by lunchtime he was feeling a bit better. Whatever was wrong with Miriam, God was in charge. God would provide. God would see them through this, no matter the outcome.

At noon, he locked up the shop and headed home under a white and oddly heavy sky. The paper had said there was a fifty percent chance of snow today, but looking up now, he changed that percentage to one hundred percent. No doubt they were in for their first snowfall of the season. Judging by the portent in the air, the flakes would begin falling soon, within a few hours at the most.

When he arrived at the house, he found it empty. After a quick search of the rooms, he remembered that *Mamm* had her quilting group today. Miriam must have gone with her, a development he found encouraging. If she was willing to get out and interact with others, she must be at last on the road to recovery.

He was a little surprised that neither woman had thought to leave a lunch for him, but after rooting around in the icebox, he managed to pull something together. He was on his way back to the shop when he spotted the buggy coming up the drive. He gave a smile and a wave, and though his mother did the same in return as she pulled past, he realized with a start that Miriam wasn't with her.

Unease gripping his stomach, Clayton reversed course, following on foot the path of the buggy all the way to the barn. By the time he got there, *Mamm* had already managed to unhitch the horse, one of several skills *Daed* had insisted on teaching her not long before he died, saying that if he couldn't be around anymore to do these things for her, she'd better learn to do them for herself.

"Clayton," she said, surprised but pleased when she saw him come in the barn door.

"Where's Miriam?" he demanded, his voice harsher than he'd intended.

"I don't know. When I left, she was in the kitchen and about to make your lunch. I know what you said earlier, but she seemed fine to me. More than fine. Her hair was neat, her dress ironed, her mood greatly improved. Almost like the Miriam we used to know."

Clayton hesitated, unsure what to think—or do, for that matter. On the one hand, she'd been acting so erratic these days that there was no telling what she might have gotten into now. On the other hand, she was a grown woman, one who had freely come and gone as desired from the day she moved into their house.

He cast a glance up at the loft. He could see one corner of the old trunk, which was there as always, but otherwise the space seemed empty.

"Miriam!" he called out, just in case, but there was no sound, no movement in response.

"What's wrong?" *Mamm* asked, her brow furrowed.

"She's not in the house, and she left no lunch waiting. I don't know where she is."

Again, his eyes went to the loft. Just to be sure, he crossed to the ladder and began climbing, ignoring his mother's protestations.

"Clayton! Slow down! You'll fall!"

He made it three quarters of the way up without incident, high enough to see fully into the loft.

It was empty save for numerous bales of hay and the old trunk.

"Maybe she went over to her parents' house," his mother offered as he climbed slowly back down.

"Would you go and see?" he asked, his heart leaden with worry. "I'm going to check the shop. Maybe she slipped into the back office and I didn't notice."

"If she's not at the Beilers', I'll come down and find you," *Mamm* said as they parted ways outside the barn. "If she is there, I'll send her down instead."

Clayton took off, moving as fast as he could along the sloping drive. As he went, the first flakes of snow began to fall.

He reached the shop and unlocked and flung open the back door, but Miriam wasn't there. He moved into the front room and peered out each window in succession, not even sure what he was looking for. She wasn't out at the picnic table—not that she would be at this time of year. She wasn't out on the street. She wasn't in the parking lot.

He wanted to hurry over to the Beilers' himself and not wait for his mother or Miriam to come to him, but he knew that would be a mistake. If it was *Mamm* who came, she would return via the pasture and past the barn down their own driveway, and if it was Miriam, she would take the shortcut down the Beilers' driveway. Either way, he would run the chance of missing them. Better he wait down here, so he closed up the shop and simply stood out back, where he could look in both directions.

After several agonizing minutes, he saw his mother carefully making her way down the incline to the shop. He hobbled toward her.

"Norman and Abigail haven't seen her for days," she said when they were within a few yards of each other. "But they understand our concern. They're going to check around to see if she's at a friend's or…or the cemetery."

Even as she spoke, Clayton's attention was drawn to his left, and he saw the Beilers' buggy heading down their driveway toward the road, Miriam's father at the reins. After a moment's pause, Clayton continued hobbling toward the barn as his mother tagged along behind, insisting that Miriam probably just went off shopping or out for a stroll or something and that she would be back soon.

"It's thirty degrees out here with a big snow on the way, *Mamm*. Who goes for a stroll in weather like that?"

He knew he was being harsh, not to mention disrespectful, but he couldn't help himself. After weeks of keeping his temper in check, it sprang full force from his chest. He was angry.

Angry at his mother, for leaving his wife home alone despite his concerns.

Angry at his body, that he couldn't run and find her.

Angry at God, for allowing his beloved wife to turn into a madwoman.

Angry at himself, for no longer believing that all would be well in the end.

He opened his mouth to apologize for his tone, but as he looked back down the hill, he saw that a car was turning into the clock shop's parking lot, a vehicle he recognized. The car of Miriam's former employer. At the wheel was an attractive, elegantly dressed woman he assumed was Brenda Peterson.

Next to Brenda, with no *kapp* and her hair hanging loose around her shoulders, was Miriam.

TWENTY-NINE

Relief flooded Clayton at the sight of his wife, safe and sound in the front seat of the *Englischer*'s car. But that momentary jolt of joy didn't last long as his eyes focused on Miriam's haggard appearance. Had she walked all the way to Brenda's without a coat? Had someone come for her? Who? His heart was pounding with equal parts anger and worry as he started back down the hill.

"Stay here," Clayton said curtly to his mother. As he went, he saw Brenda emerge from the vehicle. He quickened his awkward pace as she seemed to spot him and began walking his way. The two of them met in the middle, *Mamm* behind them and Miriam in front of them, neither one close enough to hear what they might say.

"Mr. Raber," the woman said, extending a gloved hand. Clayton caught a whiff of expensive perfume and saw that her lips were painted a deep red.

"It's Clayton." He briefly shook her hand, looking past her to see Miriam still sitting in the passenger side of the car thirty yards away.

"I'm Brenda Peterson. Your wife worked for me this past spring."

"*Ya*. I know who you are. Thank you so much for bringing her home." He started to step around her, but she reached out a hand to stop him.

"Don't you want to know how I've come to have Miriam in my car?"

"I will ask her myself, *danke*," Clayton replied as politely as he could. He had no desire to discuss his and Miriam's troubles with an *Englisch* woman he didn't even know.

"She hitched a ride, Mr. Raber. From a total stranger. I don't have to tell you how dangerous that can be."

Clayton swung back around to look at her as embarrassment, fear, and indignation swarmed inside him.

The woman's countenance softened. "Look. I know what happened with the baby and all. I know it's been hard. But Miriam is wondering if she can stay with me for a little while."

"Stay with you?"

"Actually, it was my idea. Maybe for a month or so. Maybe longer. I suggested it to her and she agreed."

A thousand angry responses swirled in Clayton's head. When he couldn't decide on one, Brenda went on.

"She's so unhappy right now, and I know you did a great thing by offering to marry her when she…well, you know. But with the loss of the child, I think it's just been a bit too much."

How dare you come here and say such a thing to me? Clayton wanted to demand of her. But his mounting anger had rendered him speechless. He was aware that his mother was now standing a few inches behind him.

Brenda continued. "I think she's just a bit mixed up, is all. She's certain Russell is in town again—"

"Russell?"

"The actor, the one she…saw for a time last spring." At least the woman had the decency to blush. "Miriam thinks he's come back into town to appear in the Christmas show. Today she was found banging on the stage door at the Fulton, demanding she be let in so that she could see him."

At these words a searing pain in his gut nearly sent Clayton to his knees. "Do not speak that man's name," he managed to utter through his clenched teeth.

"I can understand how you feel about him, but that's not the point."

"The *point*?" Clayton echoed, incredulous. Hurting. Livid.

"Yes. The stage manager recognized Miriam as being my former housekeeper, and he called me rather than the police, which he could have, you know. She wouldn't stop banging on the door. Whether Russell is actually in town or not, I doubt he would have wanted to see her."

Do NOT say his name! Clayton screamed inwardly.

"Here's what I think, Mr. Raber. I think she just needs a quiet place away from everything to come to terms with all that's happened to her. She's sad and lonely."

"She's my wife!" Clayton roared, finally finding his voice.

"Well, yes, you married her, but that doesn't mean she's not sad and lonely. She can't help it if she still loves that other man. It doesn't matter how much you don't like hearing it. You can't help who you love, Mr. Raber. That's how love is."

Clayton took a step toward the woman, surprising himself with how strong he felt on his two legs, the normal one and the imperfect one. She cowered in front of him. "That is *not* how love is. Love doesn't chase after a monster like that actor who treated Miriam as if she is worthless."

Brenda's eyes widened, and she took a step back, fearful. "Look, all I'm saying is that girl in my car is hurting. You can't fix that kind of pain with a marriage of convenience. You can't make her love you. Not like this. Give her some time, and maybe—"

Clayton would hear no more. "You and I are done here." He moved past the *Englisch* woman but had taken only one step toward the vehicle ahead of him when he saw that the passenger side of Brenda's car was empty, the door ajar.

"Miriam!" Clayton yelled as he looked from side to side. Where could she have gone in so short a time without him noticing?

He stumbled toward the car and then to the parking lot of the shop and the main road. Brenda caught up with him in no time.

A tour bus was parked at the curb on the other side of the clock shop parking lot and a little crowd was gathered at its open doors. The snow began to fall more heavily now, as if sprinkling the people in ticker tape. Clayton looked for his wife among them and didn't see her.

"Miriam!' he called out again.

A friend Clayton recognized, the *Englischer* who owned the insurance company across the street, was in the throng of people, and he turned now to Clayton.

"Clayton! I was just about to come looking for you. It's your wife. She's sitting inside that bus and won't get off. The tour company wants to get going."

"She's *what*?" Clayton said, though he'd heard every word perfectly. He just couldn't believe it.

"She's on the bus," the man said, pointing to the coach.

"Oh, my!" Clayton heard Brenda exclaim from behind him.

He turned to her. "I meant what I said. You and I are done. I'll take care of this."

Brenda's eyes flashed with anger. "You mean like you have been taking care of it already? This is what you call taking care of something?"

Clayton ignored her taunting questions and pushed through the crowd. The driver was standing on the first step, clearly at a loss as to how to get the unticketed passenger off his bus. He stepped aside so Clayton could move past him and up the rest of the stairs. Miriam was sitting in the front row just behind the driver's seat. Her hair was tumbled about her shoulders in tangles and there was no sign of her *kapp*. She held a fistful of dollars in her hands and was clutching them and staring straight ahead. Her eyes were vacant and wild.

"Miriam," he said when he was fully inside. "Time to go home."

She would not look at him.

He took another step forward and put his hand gently on her wrist. "Let's go home."

Her skin felt clammy beneath his touch. She looked down at his hand and then again at the empty driver's seat in front of her.

"I have no home."

The air stilled in his lungs. *God, help me.* "Yes, you do," he insisted, calmly but firmly. "Your home is with me."

"I *have* no home," she said again, her tone defiant.

He reached out again, more firmly this time. "Miriam, please."

Miriam shrank in her seat. "Get away from me!"

Helpless, Clayton looked back toward the open bus door. *Mamm* was there now, but Brenda was nowhere to be seen. Clayton figured she had finally realized that his and Miriam's personal lives were none of her business—either that, or she'd finally gotten a glimpse of Miriam's deranged mental state and realized this was all much more than she was willing to handle.

In addition to the passengers milling around the bus, curious bystanders had begun to accumulate and were now standing around watching. It wasn't often you saw an Amish woman with her hair askew, arguing with her husband inside an *Englisch* touring coach.

"There's Norman," *Mamm* cried, glancing out toward the road. She whirled away, waving frantically at the buggy that was about to pass by.

Clayton returned his attention to Miriam. Instead of reaching toward her, he offered his hand as if to ask for a dance. "Here, Miriam. I'll take you home. Everything will be all right."

She turned her head toward his outstretched hand and then gazed up at him, her eyes shiny with anger. "Everything will *not* be all right," she hissed.

And then she fixed her gaze upon him and said words that left him dumbfounded.

"You *wanted* my baby to die!"

For a few moments he could only stare at this stranger who was Miriam, the woman he loved. His wife.

When he found his voice, he sensed the same rage inside him that was building in her. Rage at the world, at the fragility of the human body, at God that He had taken not only the child from Miriam but also her ability to be reasoned with.

"Come," he said curtly, leaning toward her. "We're going home."

"Get away from me!"

"Everything okay?"

Clayton turned to see a familiar face, a manager of one of the stores along the strip, peering up at him. All Clayton wanted was get Miriam home and away from these people. They didn't know her. They didn't love her. "We'll be fine, thanks," he struggled to say. "My wife is…she's not been well."

The man looked uncertain, as if trying to assess the situation, but then *Mamm* returned with Norman in tow, so he stepped aside. Miriam's *daed* was about to come up and join them when the bus driver decided to take matters into his own hands.

"Excuse me, sir!" he barked, and when Norman turned, the man pushed past him and climbed on to the bus.

A heavyset fellow with a starched blue uniform and bright red cheeks, the driver looked from Clayton to Miriam and then leaned forward to speak directly to her.

"Ma'am, this has gone on long enough. You don't have a ticket to ride this coach."

Miriam startled a bit and then looked down at the money in her hands. "I can buy a ticket."

"This is a private tour. I'm afraid you'll need to get off. Now."

When she made no move at all, Clayton again tried to grasp her hand. "Let's go, Miriam."

Her chest began to heave with anger, frustration, and unshed tears that now rimmed her eyes.

The next instant she bolted from the seat and shoved her way past Clayton and the driver.

"Leave me alone!" she yelled, nearly knocking over her own father in her haste as she pushed through the doorway and seemed to move in the general direction of home.

Clayton struggled to get off the bus as quickly as he could. By the time he reached the pavement and broke free from the throng, he saw that his wife was just about to round the corner ahead of him.

"Miriam!"

She stopped, whirled around, and stared at Clayton for a long, tense moment. The snow that had been falling in a gentle flurry was starting to intensify, as though it wished to cover the ugly confrontation with grace and beauty. Miriam seemed to notice for the first time that the crowd included people she knew and who knew her. Her eyes went to Clayton's mother and then to her own father, both of whom had moved forward and were now flanking Clayton on each side. Her eyes returned to her husband.

"I know what you're thinking, Clayton!" she yelled. "You wish you had never married me! You hated my baby! You wanted her to die!"

There was a collective gasp, the loudest of all from Clayton himself.

As Miriam spun around and kept going, he needed to call after her, but the words seem to stick in his throat. The astonished people, with snow dotting their shoulders and heads, murmured to one another, and someone asked if perhaps the police should be summoned. Norman charged after his daughter, and by the time Clayton caught up with them, they were at the base of the driveway. Clayton cupped Miriam's elbow with his hand and gave it a tug. "Let's go home. Now."

Miriam cried out as if he'd struck her. Jerking away, she moved backward, flailing her arms at her sides, as if to demand some room.

Torn between fury and heartbreak, Clayton watched as myriad emotions passed across her face. Then, finally, her shoulders slumped and she sank to her knees in the quickly accumulating snow. A cry of anguish erupted from her throat.

"What is it, Miriam?" His mother pushed past Clayton and Norman and knelt down. She spoke in a clipped tone, one that told Clayton she also, was struggling between anger and sorrow.

"What's wrong, Miriam?" she repeated. "Why are you acting this way? How could you say such things to Clayton?"

But Miriam only rocked back and forth, clutching her empty abdomen as sobs racked her body.

"Let me take you home, daughter," Norman offered, and Miriam only cried harder.

"Her home is with me," Clayton growled.

"Clayton," his mother said in warning. But he would hear none of it.

"She's my wife! I am her husband. Her home is with *me*!"

Clayton knelt by Miriam and put his arm around her shoulders. To his surprise, she allowed him to pull her to her feet.

"I don't want it to be like this," she whispered.

"Like what?" Norman asked, leaning in, with a suspicious eye toward Clayton.

"I don't know…" her voice trailed away.

"Come, Miriam," Clayton said, attempting to take a step forward with her, but she didn't budge.

"Stop it, Clayton. Just stop it!" She shook his arm off her shoulder. "Leave me be. All of you!"

Then she turned from the three of them and hurried up the drive, slipping twice in the gathering snow. When she reached the dividing point where one direction led toward the Beiler house and the other to the Rabers', she hesitated.

A few seconds later she turned and went into the barn.

Clayton started to follow, but *Mamm* reached out and stopped him. He swung around angrily.

"*What?*" he roared.

For a moment the woman looked terrified, as though she thought he might strike her in his rage.

"What, *Mamm*?" he said again, not quite as loudly this time.

"Do what she asked. Just let her be for a bit," his mother said, her eyes bright with alarm. He realized she was actually afraid of him, of what he might do. Of how angry he was in that moment.

Maybe because he'd never *been* as angry as he was in that moment.

He tried to calm himself, but it was impossible, especially when he looked at his father-in-law. The grief etched on Norman's face made it obvious he wished he'd never asked Clayton to marry his daughter.

Clayton had never felt so alone in his life. A cry of utter frustration was boiling up inside him, and if he didn't let it out, he would explode. Leaving the two of them there, he took off as fast as his deformed leg allowed and headed for the house. Because of the snow, he slipped and fell several times on the way but finally managed to make it. Once inside, he continued up the stairs to the bedroom, slammed the door shut, and lowered himself to his knees on the floor by the bed. Reaching for a pillow, he pressed it to his face to absorb the roar of his anguish.

Thirty

When Clayton's outburst was finally over, he stayed where he was, on the floor, for a long time. He was spent. Exhausted. Beyond himself.

But he was also in pain, he finally realized, not just in his bad leg but his good one too. He looked down and saw that he had scraped his knees on the gravel on the way up the hill. His pants were torn on both sides, and the skin he glimpsed underneath was bloody and raw.

He didn't care. He hobbled over to the window seat, collapsed onto the bench, and leaned his head against the glass. What was he going to do?

Across the field, now nearly covered in a blanket of white, sat the Beilers' house, and as he looked over at it, he saw that several buggies were in the driveway. Great. Gawkers and busybodies who had heard what happened and come to get the scoop from the in-laws, no doubt.

He shifted and closed his eyes against the image of supposedly well-meaning friends and neighbors gobbling up the details of this terrible day.

Clayton knew he needed to check on Miriam. He knew he shouldn't leave her out there in the cold barn for too long. He knew she could very well run off again the longer he waited.

But for some reason he simply couldn't move. If God was testing him, or teaching him, he didn't get it. He had failed. The moment those horrible words had spewed from Miriam's mouth, he knew he'd failed.

You wish you had never married me. You hated my baby. You wanted her to die.

He thought of that night not so long ago when he'd misunderstood an apology, taking it for regret and going off half-cocked to Uriah's house, only to learn later what Miriam had really been trying to say. He had made a mistake that time, but there was no mistaking this. She couldn't have been clearer.

You wish you had never married me.

You hated my baby.

You wanted her to die.

If Miriam honestly thought those things, then not only had he failed as a husband but as a future father. A fellow human being. A Christian. He had tried so hard for so long, but now he knew the truth. In all ways he had failed utterly as a man. For the first time since his father's death, Clayton almost felt glad that he was gone so that he hadn't had to witness the shameful scene.

He opened his eyes and shifted again, the cold from outside beginning to permeate through the window to his bones.

Clayton needed to understand. Yes, Miriam was grieving. Yes, her behavior had been alarming lately in numerous ways, but the things she'd said to him out there today went beyond any of that. They had come from her core, from her very soul. She lost a child, and now not only did she blame him for the loss, she had even managed to convince herself that it was what he'd wanted all along.

And now he needed to go to her and somehow get her to come back inside the house with him.

He could hear voices, and he wished he could climb out the window rather than walk down the stairs and run into whoever had come calling. But that wasn't an option, so he slowly eased himself off the wooden seat and headed for the door.

Mamm was just reaching the top of the stairs as he swung it open, and her eyes widened at the sight of him.

"Are you okay, Clayton? What happened to your pants? Is that blood?"

He had forgotten about the state of his clothes, but what did that really matter now? He motioned for her to come in the room, and then he closed the door behind her so they could speak privately.

"It's nothing," he said dismissing her concern. "I need to check on Miriam. She's probably still in the barn."

"I think that's a good idea. I imagine she's had time to cool off by now." After a beat she added, "Have you?"

Clayton took in a breath and looked away for a moment. *Mamm* really had no idea what he and Miriam were going through. No idea at all. "Who's down there?" he asked, ignoring her question and gesturing in the general direction of the living room.

"Roger and Maisie. And a few friends."

He raised an eyebrow.

"They're here to help, Clayton. They care about us, about you."

"That may be true for Maisie and Roger, but don't kid yourself about the others."

"Clayton!"

"I have to check on my wife," he said gruffly. Then he moved around his mother, opened the bedroom door, and headed down the stairs. He crossed the main room, past the Amish gauntlet, ignoring all of the people gathered there. He yanked open the mudroom door. He shrugged on his coat and grabbed Miriam's coat too.

He was surprised to see how much snow had already accumulated when he stepped outside. Taking a deep breath, he set off for the barn, careful this time to move more slowly and not lose his balance on the slippery ground.

As soon as he walked through the wide barn doors, he could hear Miriam's voice. The room was dark and cavernous, so despite the cold outside, he propped one of the two doors partially open for the light, and then he stepped further in and came to a stop, listening. Just as he'd expected, she was up in the hayloft, at the moment singing softly to herself a tune so happy that it couldn't have been less fitting for this day.

His heart heavier than it had ever been in his life, Clayton crossed over to the ladder and began to climb. Though he didn't even bother trying to be quiet, she didn't seem to notice his approaching presence. But then the singing came to a stop, and a voice floated down to him.

"Please go away."

Miriam sounded less angry than before, though just as adamant.

He ignored her request and kept climbing.

"Go away, Clayton!"

He continued. Just as he topped the ladder he heard a solid *thunk*. Miriam was at the trunk, wrapped in one of the horse blankets. He realized the sound had been the closing of the lid.

"Go away, Clayton!"

Ignoring her words, he heaved himself onto the loft floor and rose slowly to a standing position.

"I said no! Go away!"

Still ignoring her, he tossed Miriam's coat to the side and walked across the hay-strewn floor in her direction.

"Don't come any closer!" Her shouts reverberated against the slanted wooden walls.

"Miriam," he said in as calm a voice as he could muster. "I just want to help you."

"No, you don't!" she yelled, angrily. "You're trying to trick me. You want to take away all my treasures and bury them with my baby!"

He stopped in his tracks, wincing at the mention of the baby in that way, but he could not ignore her comment about her treasures.

Her treasures.

The trunk.

Clayton hadn't ever come up to the loft to check that those *Englisch* trinkets were really gone. He'd taken Miriam at her word that she'd gotten rid of them.

How foolish he had been.

He began hobbling forward again, his eyes on the trunk.

"Open it!" he said through clenched teeth.

She looked up at him. "No. Stay where you are!"

"Open it, Miriam!" he commanded, his voice booming in the cavernous room.

"No!"

"*Miriam!*" he bellowed, undone at the wound she was inflicting. The act of hiding some worthless baubles could not begin to compare with the accusations she'd made against him today. Yet somehow those baubles shone in his mind more brightly than anything else that had happened. They represented all that was wrong—all that had ever been wrong—between them.

After one final step, he lunged at the trunk and threw the lid open himself, his vision so clouded with rage that it took a moment for him to see what was inside.

Nothing.

He sank to his knees, stunned. There was nothing inside. The trunk was empty.

Clayton looked again at Miriam, and only then did it register that she was clutching something and had been since the moment he got there. With a quick glance at the trunk, he knew what it must be. She may have gotten rid of all the other things, but she had kept back one single, undiscarded treasure, something she had been unwilling to part with.

He thrust out his arm, palm upward. "Give it to me, Miriam."

"No!" She clutched both hands to her chest.

He saw the crazed look in her eyes and in a flash realized he might be wrong. Perhaps she only *thought* she was holding something. Like the bugs, was this too just a figment of her imagination?

Clayton's mind raced, uncertainty clouding his thoughts. He had to take a minute, had to consider his next move. What was he going to do? How were they ever going to survive this? How could they possibly move on from this day?

Lord, show me!

And then in an instant, clarity fell across him. Miriam was in desperate need of help. She was sick. Something was wrong, something inside her brain. He didn't know what it was, but there had to be a doctor out there somewhere who could treat her, maybe someone from the new Mennonite mental hospital over in Mount Gretna. Whatever it took, he would get her the help she needed.

He had to. She was his wife. He would care for her, no matter what came their way, until the day she died, just as he had promised he would. And he would do so with all the love and tenderness and strength the Lord would provide.

That's how they would move on from this day.

Clayton saw Miriam with fresh eyes as he took in her desperate state, and he knew he would never leave her side, not physically and not emotionally, no matter how dark the situation looked. And she needed to understand that.

"Miriam," he began, trying to make his voice as calm and gentle and non-threatening as possible.

She shifted, the horse blanket falling from her shoulders, but she wouldn't meet his gaze.

"Here's what we're going to do," he continued in the same even tone. "I know what our doctor said about your condition, but I think he was wrong. I think we need to find you a new doctor, someone who can—"

Suddenly, she sprang to her feet, startling him as she made a mad dash toward the ladder.

Time suddenly stretched to an elongated pace. Clayton saw the next few seconds play out with such blinding accuracy, it was almost as if he was seeing them before they actually happened.

The wildness of her movements. The unknowing miscalculation of her steps. The mere inches of hayloft floor that separated her from the open air and the barn floor below.

She was running too close to the edge.

"Miriam!" he screamed, reaching forward to pull her to safety. But in her terror, she saw him grabbing for her and in response, she jerked away.

Her scream as she fell was one of complete surprise.

His scream as he watched her fall was one of utter horror.

Clayton yelled her name as he hobbled forward and looked over the edge.

His wife lay on the concrete floor below, her neck at an odd angle, her eyes open and unblinking.

"Miriam!" Clayton screamed again.

He continued to scream as he fumbled to descend the ladder, falling when he was nearly down and landing on his shoulder with a crash against the unforgiving ground. From outside the barn door he heard the sound of running feet and yelling. Harsh light fell over him as both doors were flung open wide. People in silhouette were coming inside. Stunned, he crawled to Miriam's still form, screaming her name, and cutting his palms on the shards of a tiny, broken, porcelain bird that lay in pieces by her open hand.

Thirty-One

Clayton would never be able to recall how he managed to make it through the horrible first days after Miriam's death. That time would always be a numb blur of formless minutes and hours. He knew he would always remember being forcibly pulled away from her body when others came running and saw her there. He would remember the sound of an approaching siren. He would remember a policeman asking him what had happened prior to Miriam's fall, if it was true that he and his wife had been fighting. But when a sheet was pulled over her lifeless form and it finally became clear to him that she was gone, Clayton felt as though he had fallen into a dark, cold cave where time did not exist.

He would remember Miriam's stricken parents, three days later, sobbing aloud at the funeral.

He would remember seeing his wife's casket in the living room, the same place where his father's casket had sat just last summer, the same place the baby's casket sat in the fall.

He would remember Maisie looking at him strangely all that day.

He would remember a lot of people not looking at him at all.

But he would never remember sleeping alone in his bed the night Miriam died or how the shards of the broken bird ended up in the drawer of his bedside table or why he even went up to the hayloft thinking he could talk some sense into her the day she fell.

What he would remember from that time, what would haunt him for years upon years, was the moment two uniformed Lancaster police officers came to the house two days after the funeral, slipped handcuffs on his wrists, and arrested him for the murder of his wife.

Clayton lost count of how many times he had to go through the same set of facts. He sat in a hard chair in a small, stuffy room for hours, recounting for the detectives exactly what happened the day Miriam died—over and over and over again. Each time, when he got to the part where she fell, one of them would nod, jot a note or two, and then say, "Okay, let's run through this again."

Clayton just didn't understand. Did they really think the story was going to change on the third go-around? Or the fourth, or the fifth? For hours, they alternated between being kind and helpful—"You look thirsty, would you like some water?"—and being angry and cruel—"Do you honestly expect us to believe that you harbored no resentment whatsoever over the fact that your wife was pregnant with another man's child?" Through it all, the best he could do was to try to remain calm, no easy feat, and tell the truth as best he could remember it.

It didn't help that Clayton wasn't even sure if he should be speaking to these men at all. What did the *Ordnung* say about how to behave when falsely accused of a crime? He had no earthly idea. Amish fathers were often arrested in Lancaster County for refusing to send their children to public high schools, and everyone knew how they were supposed to behave. They were told to emulate the martyrs of the church, conducting themselves with dignity and nonviolence while refusing to acquiesce to government regulations that violated their beliefs.

But those men weren't being charged with murder.

Clayton tried to think of Bible verses that might guide him, but the only one that kept coming to mind was from Isaiah, about not defending himself at all: *He was oppressed, and he was afflicted, yet he opened not his mouth: he is brought as a lamb to the slaughter, and as a sheep before her shearers is dumb, so he openeth not his mouth.*

Clayton definitely felt like a lamb to the slaughter, but was that what he was supposed to do, not open his mouth in his own defense? Or did the verse apply only to the coming Messiah, to His interrogation by Pontius Pilate? He just didn't know.

In the end, he decided his only option was to tell the truth, and so that was what he did. And did again and again and again until even the words "And then she fell," no longer wrenched his heart to utter.

"Okay, Mr. Raber," Detective De Lucca said once the other man had left and the two of them were alone. "Let's run through this again."

And so they did.

"You and your wife had an argument on the street a few hours before she died. A dozen people heard her say that you wished you had never married her, that you hated the baby she lost as a stillbirth, and that you wanted that baby to die. Is that correct?"

"It is correct that that's what she said. But none of it was true."

"Uh-huh." The man stared at him, as if that might somehow change his answer. "She was trying to leave you that day, wasn't she, Mr. Raber? Isn't why she was on that bus?"

"She wasn't feeling well. She was…different after she lost the baby."

The detective looked down at his notes, flipped back a page.

"At the request of Miriam's parents, you agreed to marry their daughter because she was with child and in need of a husband to hide her shame?"

Clayton exhaled slowly. "I married her because I loved her."

"And she loved you? Is that what you're saying?"

Why did the man keep asking him this, over and over? Clayton's jaw clenched as he responded, "That is not what I am saying."

"She was, in fact, in love with someone else, was she not? The real father of her baby?"

"No."

"No?" De Lucca jerked back, as if physically struck. "Your own mother says differently, Mr. Raber. So does your wife's former employer. In fact—" The detective looked down, flipped a few pages, and looked up again "—this employer, Brenda Peterson. She was very adamant that Miriam was ready to do almost anything to get away from you to be with this other man."

Clayton pinched the bridge of his nose. "My wife was ill, Detective."

"Your wife was in love with another man."

What else could he say? "I don't know about that."

De Lucca's eyes narrowed. "You don't know if she was in love with another man but these other women do?"

Clayton sighed. "Miriam never said she was in love with him. She told me she thought she had been, but he didn't love her in return. And that every day she loved him less."

De Lucca nodded and seemed to back off for a long moment. Then he spoke. "Yet you never consummated your marriage."

Anger surged in Clayton's chest. How could that be any of the state's business? Who had told the detective this? His mother? Abigail? Brenda Peterson? "What kind of man would I be to force myself on a woman whose heart was divided?"

"Her heart was divided. Is that how you put it?" De Lucca didn't even wait for an answer as he scribbled something on the page. "So you do admit she loved this other man."

Clayton shook his head, but before he could speak the detective continued, coming at him with a new fact he hadn't thrown out there until now.

"You tried to get the marriage annulled when she lost the baby, isn't that right?"

Clayton's jaw dropped open. How did the man know *that*? Had Miriam told *Mamm* and *Mamm* told the detective? Had Uriah somehow volunteered that information to him directly?

Clayton swallowed hard and gave an honest answer in return. "I asked the bishop about it, yes."

"You asked about getting an annulment from the woman you say you *loved*?"

Clayton feared he might cry, but to his relief the tears didn't come. "It was just a misunderstanding. I thought it was what she wanted."

"Because she loved another man."

"No!" Clayton pounded his fist against his knee. "No, no, no. She was learning to love *me*. She just needed more time."

De Lucca sat back and eyed Clayton, silent as the echoes of his outburst ebbed away. Clayton knew he shouldn't have lost his temper, but considering what this man had been putting him through, he could have done much worse. He pressed his lips together, waiting for the next question. After a beat, the detective came at him from a different angle.

"You and your wife were fighting on the day she died. First in town and then in the hayloft. Correct?"

"She was upset. She was ill. I was trying to help her."

"By yelling at her?"

"I didn't yell."

"Your nephew heard you, Mr. Raber. As did your sister and brother-in-law, your mother, and six of your fellow church members." De Lucca flipped back a number of pages and then read aloud what those people claimed to have heard them say. "'Go away. Stop it. Don't come any closer.' Those were some of the things she yelled at you. They said it sounded like you were insisting she show you something or give you something."

"I already told you. We had a history there. Earlier in our marriage, she had been hanging on to things she shouldn't."

"Like her love for another man?"

"Detective—"

"You've always had quite the temper, isn't that true, Mr. Raber?" the man said, startling him with the sudden shift. "Do you know that's what people say about you?"

Clayton put his hands in his lap. "I didn't kill my wife. It was an accident. She was running too close to the edge and she fell."

"It's a nice story," De Lucca said, closing the notebook, clicking his pen, and sliding it into his chest pocket. "But that's all it is, a story. The truth is that you were angry with your wife because she was in love with someone else. You didn't want anyone else to have her. It's the oldest crime of passion there is."

"I loved my wife."

"I'm sure you did, Mr. Raber. That's why you killed her. Because she didn't love you in return."

Clayton had seen photographs of the Lancaster County Prison in the newspaper many times, but nothing could have prepared him for the sight of the incongruous and absurd structure in person. Looming up from the earth like a giant medieval castle, the building was at least two hundred feet long and made of heavy sandstone blocks, with turrets and towers and other castle-like embellishments. Clayton almost expected to see a dungeon inside, but once he passed through the heavy iron doors, shuffling painfully in his ankle shackles, the interior looked normal, like any other jail might.

Processing took forever, but eventually the shackles were removed and he was handed a stack of folded linens—one bottom sheet, one top sheet, one pillow case, and one rough navy blue blanket—and escorted to a cell by a uniformed guard. The man didn't say a word, though he grunted impatiently at the hindered speed of Clayton's gait as he hobbled along behind him. Clayton had expected to hear the jeers and catcalls of other prisoners, but this particular hallway was quiet and empty, and he wondered if he was being segregated because he was Amish—or because he was a suspected murderer.

When they reached his cell, the guard swung open the door and waited for Clayton to step inside. Then he pulled the door shut again and locked it with a key, the click of the bolt as it slid into place cutting him off like a cleaver from any hope of freedom.

Without even so much as a nod, the man turned and walked away, his heels clicking against the hard floor as he walked, much faster now than before. Clayton wondered if the man had ever dealt with an Amish prisoner before. Then again, whether he had or not, probably the only Amish men who had ever been prisoners in here had been arrested for the sake of their faith in matters of civil disobedience. Clayton had been charged with something else entirely.

Dazed, he limped to the cot in the far corner and lowered himself onto the bare mattress. The springs creaked beneath his weight as he sat and looked around at the damp stone walls, the dingy tile floor. The toilet in the corner.

His home seemed so surreal now. He should be in the clock shop at the worktable at this very moment, polishing the wood of some finished clock, listening to Miriam hum in the back room.

Miriam.

Pain struck him anew, like a shattering kick in his ribs. Clutching the stack of linens to his chest, he rocked back and forth, just trying to breathe. He could still see her lying there, unmoving, her beautiful hair fanned out around her. The image was so vivid, he felt as though he could reach out and touch her even now. But he couldn't. She was gone. And he was trapped, locked in a cell, accused of her murder.

He wished with all his heart he had fallen instead.

Clayton crumpled to the cold tiles, and to his knees in supplication. *Lord, why have You allowed this? Why am I here?*

He knelt there for a long while, pleading with God to answer him. His knees grew numb, but still he knelt, his bad leg eventually throbbing with pain. He pulled himself up from the floor to lay on the cot, his mind sinking deeper and deeper into hopelessness.

A few hours passed and Clayton, tired of feeling, closed his eyes. Just before his body surrendered to sleep and his mind became still, a thought popped into his head, a Bible verse he had memorized as a child.

Remember the word that I said unto you, the servant is not greater than his lord. If they have persecuted me, they will also persecute you.

Clayton eyes snapped open.

If Jesus Himself had been accused of crimes He hadn't committed—was even crucified for them—then who was Clayton to believe he was above wrongful imprisonment? Perhaps the Lord wasn't punishing him but instead was inviting him into a more intimate understanding of His sufferings, an intimacy that could only be cultivated through the refining fires of persecution.

Clayton was comforted by this thought, but still his heart ached. His mind was still burdened by doubts and fears. But stronger than these was a feeling of peace, that regardless of the result of the trial to come, the only opinion that mattered was God's, and God knew the truth.

God knew he was innocent.

Three days later, Clayton was resting on his cot after yet another meal of beans and canned fruit and congealed soup when he heard a clatter in the hall. He limped to the cell door and pressed his face against the bars, trying to see what was causing the commotion.

It was the same guard he usually saw, but this time he was bringing in another prisoner. And though the guard, true to form, said not a word, the man he escorted was about as noisy as a person could be. He was complaining and stumbling, and as they drew closer, Clayton recognized the soured smell of alcohol.

The guard locked the man in the cell directly across from Clayton, and he found himself feeling oddly pleased. As much as he didn't relish witnessing the raucous behavior of a drunken man, he'd been so isolated that even this was better than nothing.

The man tossed his linens toward the cot and then stood where he had been left, rocking back and forth and singing to himself. Then he looked over, noticed Clayton, and grew silent.

He stared for a long moment, his body swaying back and forth. "You're him, ain't you?"

Clayton blinked. "Excuse me?"

The man barked out a laugh, as if he couldn't believe his luck. "You're *him*. The one all over the news. I don't believe it." Another laugh, this time with a slap to the knee. "They done stuck me in here with a murderer. Not just any murderer—a famous murderer. A famous *Amish* murderer." Shaking his head, he moved to the cot and half sat, half collapsed onto it. "Don't that just beat all."

Lying back against the mattress, the man covered his eyes with one arm and almost immediately let out a loud snore. He was asleep.

An hour later, when he finally stirred, Clayton spoke. He had been waiting.

"What are they saying about me?" he asked, not truly sure that he wanted to know. If even his mother was against him, telling the detective all sorts of personal things about him and Miriam, then he could only imagine what "facts" were being spread all over town by everyone else.

The guy ran a hand down his face, sat up, and spat toward the corner.

"What do you mean?" he grunted, only slightly less inebriated than before.

"You said I was famous. How? What are they saying, exactly?"

He laughed. "What do you think? A picture of them taking you away been on the front page of every paper in town, 'Amish Clockmaker Kills Wife in Jealous Rage.'"

Clayton swallowed hard as the man continued, rattling off a series of mistakes and misconceptions and outright lies. "Somebody said she never even slept with you, not once, 'cause she was in love with another man. She was carrying his child. Is that true?"

Clayton did not reply.

The drunk burped and wiped some spittle from his chin with his sleeve. "I said, is that true? You never been with your own *wife?* Is something wrong with you, boy?"

Clayton pursed his lips, closed his eyes, prayed for deliverance from this torment.

To his great relief, he heard what sounded like another snore, and when he looked over at the man again, he realized he'd collapsed back against the cot and was once again out.

Weariness settled onto Clayton's shoulders like an iron yoke. He lay back on his cot as well and stared up at the ceiling.

Heavenly Father, whatever happens I accept the plans You have for me. The servant is not greater than his lord.

〜〰

On the fifth day of his incarceration, Clayton heard the main doors down the corridor open and close. He assumed another prisoner was being ushered in, but then the guard was standing in front of his cell and unlocking the door.

"Let's go. You're being released," the guard said, as casually as if he'd announced the lunchroom would be serving French fries today.

Clayton stared at him.

"Come on, Raber. Get up. I have other inmates to manage."

His mind numb, Clayton slid his feet into his shoes, stood, and followed the guard down the hall, hobbling as fast as his legs would carry him. As if in a dream, he was processed out of the prison, far more quickly than he'd been processed in. He was given back his clothes and possessions. He signed some paperwork and then changed in the dress out room.

"What has happened?" he kept asking. But the only answer he got was that he was being released. No one seemed to know or care why.

Before he knew it, Clayton was standing outside the jailhouse in his black felt hat and dark coat, blinking in the sun, trying to understand what had just happened. He turned to speak to the guard who had let him out, but he was already gone. Stunned, he looked around for someone else to ask when he spotted a familiar face leaning against the sandstone wall nearby as if he'd been waiting for him.

It was the lawyer, the fellow who had been assigned by the court to defend Clayton. They had met only once, here at the jail the day after his interrogation, and their entire conversation had consisted of Clayton recounting all he'd shared with Detective De Lucca and this man shaking his head as if to say, *You told him that?*

Now he had a broad smile on his face and a cigarette in his hand. He offered the cigarette to Clayton, who declined.

"Congratulations, Mr. Raber," the lawyer said, putting the cigarette between his own lips instead. He flicked open a lighter, cupped his hand around his mouth, and lit up.

"Please tell me what's going on," Clayton said, for some reason sounding angry even though he wasn't.

The lawyer blew out smoke in a long, satisfied stream. "Charges were dropped. Officially speaking, the prosecutor decided there was insufficient evidence to go to trial."

Clayton blinked. Insufficient evidence? So why had they arrested him in the first place? "I don't understand."

Another drag, another exhale. A long, heavy pause, and then what almost felt like a secret shared in a low voice. "A credible witness came forward who said they saw the whole thing."

A witness? But he and Miriam had been alone. Who could possibly have seen them?

"Who?"

"Don't know. The person asked to remain anonymous. But the police must have believed whoever it was, because after taking a statement they decided to drop charges and close the case. You're a free man."

He took Clayton's elbow as if to usher him forward away from the jail doors, but Clayton would not budge.

"What witness? Who?" he insisted. Theoretically, someone could have observed their encounter from down below in the barn. The hayloft was open, after all, and they were for the most part standing close enough to the edge to have been seen.

But no one had been down there. No one else was in the barn with them.

"Does it matter?" the lawyer asked, seeming vaguely irritated. "The point is you've been released."

"Why remain anonymous, though? If someone saw what happened, why wouldn't they speak freely?"

The man sighed, impatient with Clayton's persistence. "I don't know, Mr. Raber. But if I were you, I'd just count my blessings and never look back."

Clayton spent the first few days of his return home in solitude, praying and mourning. Though he had expected to be welcomed back into the bosom of his family and community, he quickly realized that matters were unfolding in the opposite direction. Apparently, not only did the newspapers and *Englischers* who read them believe he'd been guilty and had simply gotten away with it, but everyone in his community—and his family—did too.

Even his mother seemed to have her doubts. She moved over to Maisie's the same day he came home, claiming his sister needed some extra help around the house. But Clayton knew the truth. She thought he was guilty, that he was a killer. And now a part of her was actually afraid of him.

Oddly, the only ones who seemed willing to believe him and move on were the very people who should have harbored the most anger toward him: Miriam's parents. Though he could tell it was hard for them to be with him— to even look at him—at least their words were kind and they made an effort to see that he was fed. In the absence of his mother, Norman brought over a dinner plate each afternoon and left it in the kitchen for when Clayton came home from the shop.

At first, he assumed that the community and his family members needed time. Miriam's death had been a shock, and maybe their consternation was more about that than about some perceived guilt of Clayton's. He hoped things would get better. But even being at worship service was strange, different. Almost as if he were officially shunned, the people wouldn't quite look at him, barely spoke to him. Whispered about him constantly. Even Uriah, his wise bishop, treasured friend, and trusted confidant, now regarded Clayton with a mix of skepticism and mistrust.

Except that he wasn't shunned. He wasn't dealt with by the church in any way at first, almost as if they were still trying to make up their minds about Clayton Raber and the truth of what happened that day.

He'd never felt so alienated and alone.

At least he had his clocks, he thought. But then it seemed the town, too, had made up its mind, and without the support of local customers, his business began to decline. Still, he tried to hang on, telling himself God knew the truth and that was what mattered. Clayton hoped that in His sovereignty He would reveal that truth to others in time.

But the longer that seemed to take, the more Clayton withdrew. Unable to bear how he was treated at church, he stopped going altogether. Stopped trying to contact family members. Finally even stopped opening the store on any sort of regular schedule. Not that it mattered. Business had dwindled to a trickle.

He knew what folks were saying about him. Some believed he'd purposely pushed Miriam off the loft, hoping the fall would kill her. Some believed he pushed her in anger, not realizing the fall would take her life. But whether they thought it was an accident or intentional, they all believed he'd pushed her. They all blamed him for what happened.

Oh, Miriam. If only I had fallen instead of you.

One day he was visited by Uriah and three of the ministers, who had come to inform him that his prolonged lack of attendance at church had become unacceptable. They were putting him on probation, and if he didn't come to the next Sunday meeting, he might be excommunicated.

He knew that was just an excuse. What they really wanted was for him either to go away entirely or to confess and repent for having killed his wife. The fact that the police and the court system had declared him innocent made no difference to them. After all, some of them had been there. They had heard it for themselves. They had witnessed Clayton's temper and seen Miriam's anguish and known their marriage was headed for disaster from the very start.

It was obvious to him they believed he was guilty. Clayton tried to defend himself, tried to share the same sorts of facts he'd shared with Detective De Lucca, but nothing he said made any difference, not even the news that there had been a witness who had seen the whole thing and sworn to his innocence.

"The police know I didn't do it. They dropped all charges."

"We are to be a peculiar people," Uriah said, shaking his head slowly. "What the state concludes and what we know to be true are separate matters."

Clayton's eyes filled with tears, but he was not ashamed.

"How could you think I killed her?" he asked, looking from one man to the other. "I loved her. I wanted to help her. She was sick."

No one would look at him, so he spoke to Uriah directly.

"I told you how irrational Miriam had been acting. You saw how much her suffering pained me, how much I loved her."

The man sighed, and in that sigh Clayton knew that all Uriah chose to remember was the night Clayton had come and asked him for an annulment once the baby died.

"I think we sometimes do strange things for the people we love, things that seem best at the time," Uriah said, tears in his own eyes as he finally met Clayton's gaze.

Clayton felt his hands ball into fists. "I can't confess to something I didn't do, Bishop."

No one spoke a word in reply.

The men left Clayton's home in sorrow, the matter unresolved. Clayton did not go to church that Sunday, and three days later he was informed of his excommunication.

After that, he devoted the lonely hours to making clocks, the one thing he still had left, but even this began to seem meaningless. Each morning, he found himself more and more reluctant to enter the shop. Christmas came and went without much fanfare, and then he stopped going to the shop altogether.

He couldn't spend his days working on gears, wheels, and pendulums that reminded him every second that he would spend the rest of his hours alone, without his family, without his community. Without Miriam. No one was coming into the shop anymore anyway, except those who wanted their repaired clocks returned to them as well as those who wanted their not-yet-repaired clocks returned. The only tourists who stopped by were those curious to get a glimpse of the Amish man who had murdered his wife and gotten away with it.

With sinking clarity, Clayton realized there was nothing left for him in Ridgeview, nor in Lancaster County. The one person he wanted to share his life with was gone, and everyone else had turned their backs on him for good.

Clayton knew he had to leave. He would tell *Mamm* to sell the shop if she wanted, sell the land, the house, the property—he didn't care. Sell it all. She'd be set for the rest of her life, money-wise. She could stay with Maisie if she wanted, maybe use some of the funds to help Roger put in a little *daadi haus* over there. Either way, she wouldn't have to live alone at the homestead among its miserable memories once he was gone.

Yes, she would be sad for a while at the loss of the home she had shared with *Daed*, and she might even be sad that Clayton was gone, but in the end she would be cared for and spared of any visual reminders of what had happened here. She could go on with her life, investing it in the lives of her daughters and their families. She wouldn't need Clayton's company anymore. And her asthma would be monitored by Maisie's watchful eye. In time, she would be happy again.

As for Clayton, he would set out for somewhere else and make for himself as quiet and simple a life as he could.

It wouldn't be an Amish life. It couldn't be an Amish life, but it would be a Plain life, one as pleasing to God as he could make it out among the *Englisch*.

It would be the solitary life he was already living here, but without the constant looks of mistrust from strangers, the ongoing rejection by his church and loved ones, and most of all the reminders of Miriam and of his loss. He was done.

Done with anger.

Done with love.

But he would get by. A quiet life of solitude, somewhere far from here, would require neither.

PART THREE
Matthew

Thirty-Two

The once-beautiful clock bearing Clayton Raber's initials was the first thing I saw when I awoke the morning after Amanda and I discovered it in the back room of the tack shop.

At first my wife hadn't been overly thrilled to have the dusty clock in the cottage, much less in our bedroom, but I really wanted to have it near me before I turned it over to Clayton's family members. To make her feel better, I'd checked it for spiders and bugs and had found neither.

I was eager to get to the Helmuths'. I wanted to see Joan Raber Glick—the only living sibling of Clayton Raber—face-to-face to see if she could help me figure out where her brother was living now. *If* he was living now. Regardless of what she'd told the Starbrite hotel people, I had to believe she had some idea of where he might have gone when he left Lancaster County so many years ago. Now that I had this old clock we'd found hidden in the wall of the back room, I hoped I finally had a chance of convincing Becky Helmuth to let me in to speak with her mother.

Fortunately, Noah agreed to work both my shift and his at the shop so I could slip away first thing, even though it was Saturday, our busiest day of the week. At Amanda's insistence, I wasn't even going to swing by the store first lest I get caught up in things there. I was just going to take the clock and go.

When I came in from morning chores, hungry for breakfast, I was astounded at what awaited me on the dining table. Next to a steaming plate of eggs and corned beef hash sat the most beautiful, shiny, elegant, gleaming clock I had ever seen.

"Is that the same clock we found last night?" I asked, stepping toward it and carefully lifting it in my hands to get a better look. The piece was magnificent, a work of art in wood.

"I think it's made of cherry," she said, "but other kinds of wood are in there too, all inlaid together. That's what makes the design."

I ran a finger over the front panel of the clock at its base. She was right. Now that the dust and cobwebs were gone, what had looked last night like some painted-on decoration was actually not painted at all. The various colors in the design came from the different kinds of woods that had been used to make it.

"Does it still work?" I asked, realizing that if it did, it might possibly be worth a lot of money.

"Well, I don't know, Mr. Zook," Amanda replied with a wink. "What time is it?"

I looked at the beveled glass on the front of the clock and then over at our modest little kitchen wall clock and realized that the two timepieces matched perfectly. All I could do after I had gently set the clock back down was sweep my wife into a big hug and thank her for making the most of my chances today at the Helmuths'.

An hour later I pulled into their driveway with the clock nestled on the seat beside me, wrapped up in a clean swath of fabric. I left it bundled as I gently lifted it out and carried it up to the front door. I knocked more loudly than usual, hoping that maybe Joan would answer. But she didn't. Becky came to the door, and when she saw me, she had the same stern look on her face as she had the last time I saw her.

"Wait! Please. Before you close the door on me, let me show you something." I held up the bundle so she could see it and then peeled back just a corner of the fabric to reveal a bit of the gleaming reddish brown wood underneath.

"It's a clock, Becky, a beautiful old clock with the initials *CR* on the bottom. My wife and I found it last night. It was hidden in the back room of the tack store in an old coal bin I don't think anybody has seen the inside of in decades."

She seemed surprised and somewhat interested—until I added, "I was hoping I could show it to Joan."

Becky's eyebrows lifted, as if she were appalled I would stoop so low as to use an old family heirloom as barter to gain a visit with her mother. But before she could refuse and once again send me away, I pulled off more of the fabric and then raised the clock so she could see the bottom.

"Look, there it is," I said, pointing to the initials. "'*CR. E-c-c 3:1.*' I know this is Clayton's signature because I've seen it plenty of times before. He made this clock and then for some reason hid it in the old coal bin in the back of his clock shop."

For the first time since I'd met her, Becky seemed somewhat less than sure about what she should do. Tentatively, she held out one finger and touched the letters that had been carved into the wood, as if she were reaching back through time to touch the hand of her long-lost uncle.

"Clayton made this clock," I repeated, keeping my tone even and gentle. "I know your mother would want to see it."

Before she could reply, another face—an even older, female face—appeared behind her. Thin and frail, the woman leaned on a cane, and her *kapp* seemed too big for her withered head.

Surely this was the woman I'd been so desperate to see. This was Joan Raber Glick.

"What's this about Clayton? Who has heard from Clayton?" the woman said, her voice quavering.

Becky sighed under her breath. "No one has, *Mamm*."

"What did that man say about a clock? Has he a clock of Clayton's? I want to see it."

"*Mamm,*" Becky began, but the old woman interrupted her.

"You there!" she said to me, as she opened the screen door with a shaking hand. "What did you say about a clock?"

I looked at Becky, who gave a resigned sigh. "Bring it on in then. She won't rest until she sees what you've brought. She's already heard too much."

Trying not to grin, I came directly into a large sitting room. Becky helped her mother into an armchair and directed me to sit on the couch.

"*Danke.*"

Becky sat beside me but closer to her mother. "Sarah, maybe you could bring us some lemonade?" she said to her granddaughter, who had just come into the room. The young woman nodded and headed off for the kitchen.

"What did you say your name was?" Joan asked, looking at me with a furrowed brow.

"Matthew Zook. I'm from Ridgeview."

"Zook, from Ridgeview," she echoed, and her eyebrows furrowed even more.

"Yes, ma'am."

"Zook. From Ridgeview." She turned to her daughter. "A Zook bought the Ridgeview homestead from my *mamm* when Clayton left."

"*Ya*," I said. "That was my grandfather. Isaac Zook."

She turned back to me. "I grew up in that house!"

"So did I," I said with a polite smile.

"Been a while since I've been by there. A long while."

Becky pointed to the clock, clearly wanting to get on with the business of why I had come. "Tell her what it is that you have there."

Turning to Joan, I unwrapped the clock and held it so she could see it. Then I repeated what I'd already told Becky, that I was sure it was one of Clayton's clocks. "It has his initials engraved on the bottom. It was hidden in an old coal hamper in the back room of what used to be his clock shop, a room we've always used for an office. We're doing some remodeling, and last night my wife discovered this inside the bin."

Joan asked to hold the clock. I rose from my chair and took it to her. She ran her hand along the glossy wood before trying to turn it around to see the bottom. I helped her maneuver it. She traced an arthritic finger over the *C* and *R*. While she was admiring the clock, our lemonade arrived. Sarah placed the three glasses on the coffee table in front of us and then quietly slipped from the room.

"Clayton's clocks were so well made," Joan murmured. "Much finer than *Daed*'s, though I never said so to his face. Or to Clayton's." She struggled to turn the clock back over, and again I assisted her. "*Daed* was a tradesman, but Clayton was an *artist*."

I nodded in agreement. Certainly, this was the most beautiful clock I had ever seen.

The three of us sat in silence, Joan admiring the clock, seemingly lost in a thousand private thoughts, while Becky watched her mother's face. I waited patiently, praying I would know the right moment to ask my next question, one that might reveal to me the answers I needed in order to find Clayton.

Finally, when Joan's watery eyes met mine, I launched in, giving her a simplified version of the property issue I was facing now and my need to find her younger brother in order to straighten it out. The whole time I spoke, she just stared at me blankly, and I wasn't quite sure if she followed what I was saying or not.

"Bottom line, Mrs. Glick," I said, trying to simplify even further, "I very much need to find Clayton or my entire livelihood will be in jeopardy. Is there any way you can tell me how or where I might locate him?"

The question hung in the air for a moment, and then she shook her head. "Clayton didn't own that land," she said. "Before he died, *Daed* signed the deed over to all the children, not just my brother."

I glanced at Becky, who merely shrugged in return. Again trying to keep things simple, I added a few more details, explaining about the specific part of the homestead in question and even mentioning the quitclaim deed. When I was finished, Joan didn't reply. Almost as if she were disappearing inside herself, she simply looked off in the distance, her wrinkled lips pursed in thought.

This wasn't getting me anywhere.

Glancing around the room, I knew it was time for Plan B. Even if Joan was too old to understand what I was saying, at least I could question Becky now in Joan's presence. My hope was that if she knew her mother was right there listening, she might be a little more forthcoming.

"Becky, I'll ask you again. Do you know where I can find Clayton Raber?"

"Like I said the other day," she replied, reaching for her lemonade, "no one around here has seen the man in sixty years."

I nodded, letting that sit there for a moment.

"So when you say no one has seen him, does that mean you don't know where he is? That you haven't heard from him in all this time?" I leaned forward in my seat. "Or are you just speaking literally, that you haven't *seen* him?" My implication was clear. Was she hiding behind a turn of phrase?

As I waited for her reply, Joan closed her eyes, the clock still in her hands, and her feeble shoulders began to shake. "It was all the fault of that girl he married," the old woman said, her voice breaking. "She was nothing but trouble, that Miriam. When God took that child from her, she went plumb crazy, she did. She deserved what happened to her. If it weren't for her..."

"Crazy?" I said. "She went plumb crazy?"

"*Mamm*," Becky interrupted, patting her mother's arm, "you don't have to tell him anything."

But Joan went on as if her daughter weren't even there.

"Clayton had a temper, and we all knew he was upset because Miriam didn't love him. She loved that *Englischer*," Joan said, spitting out the last word as if it were dirt in her mouth. "They fought the day she died because she made a terrible scene in front of a crowd and he had to practically drag her back home after she threatened to run away. It was like she'd gone crazy—and it just kept getting worse and worse. Oh, if only he'd never married her!"

The woman began to sob.

"Now you've done it," Becky said angrily as she jumped from her seat. "You've made *Mamm* cry with all your questions." She rushed to the woman's side and patted her arm, but tears continued to stream down Joan's aged cheeks. Becky remained beside her, speaking in a soothing tone. Then she remembered me, and with a fierce gaze she asked me to leave. I stood slowly, looking toward Joan. Somehow I just knew that words had gone unsaid here, words Joan almost seemed to want to say now, but for some unknown reason couldn't bring herself to do so.

There was something she wasn't telling me.

"It's time for you to go," Becky insisted.

Reluctantly, I offered a quick apology for having upset things, and then I headed for the door.

I was on the last step of the porch when I heard someone run up behind me. It was Sarah, and she held the clock in her arms.

"My grandmother told me to give this back to you," she relayed, though she seemed confused by the request. "She told me to tell you we want nothing to do with the clock or Clayton Raber."

Sarah transferred the clock into my arms as if it were a sickly baby, and then she went back up the porch steps and disappeared into the house.

THIRTY-THREE

The next morning was a church Sunday, and though my heart was heavy from all that had come the day before, I tried to put aside the failure and disappointment, seeking comfort instead in the sermons, the prayers, the songs, and the fellowship with other believers.

Once the service was over, I was feeling much better. After rearranging the benches, we all shared in the usual light communal meal and were discussing the shop's expansion delay when the talk turned to Clayton Raber, startling me out of my short-lived sense of peace.

"Does it bother you to go in the barn, knowing a woman died in there—and so violently, no less?" one of the women asked.

"Different barn," I muttered, not bothering to explain that my grandfather had taken down the one big barn decades ago, building in its place the two barns that were there now—a medium-sized one for the feed store and a smaller one for our horses.

"Still, what's it like working and living in the same place *he* worked and lived?" another person asked, saying "he" with force, almost as if it were a bad word.

I looked to Amanda on my right and then Noah on my left, hoping one of them would respond more graciously in the moment than I might.

"Makes no difference to me," Noah answered confidently.

Nodding in agreement, I slathered a cracker with homemade peanut butter and shoved it in my mouth. I didn't want to talk about this.

I didn't want to get into any of it, not even to mention the beautiful clock we'd found, which was now sitting on our bedroom dresser until we figured out what to do with it. Mostly, I just listened as the older folks in the group tossed around the facts of the story—or at least as they had always believed them. About the only good to come out of the conversation was when someone mentioned Clayton's motive. Though I'd been familiar with the tale since I was a child, I'd never been told the supposed reason for the alleged murder. According to the folks here, Clayton had loved Miriam but she'd been in love with someone else, so that's why he'd killed her.

As the five of us rode home together in the buggy afterward, I asked my parents for clarification on this new bit of information. Though it was a delicate subject, I managed to garner from them several shocking new facts, including that Miriam was in the family way when she and Clayton married, and that although the child wasn't his, he married her anyway to save her from shame and give her baby a name. Sadly, they said, she did not carry the child to term and it was eventually stillborn.

Just the thought of that created a knot in my stomach, one that stayed with me the rest of the day.

The next morning was Amanda's seven-month checkup with the midwife. As I drove her to the birthing center, I kept my focus away from the tragic details of Clayton's life and directed it to Amanda and our own baby instead. Steering the buggy away from Old Philadelphia Pike and its busy lanes of traffic, we took the back roads to get there and made good time. Amanda was her usual talkative self on the way, but for some reason she, too, managed to avoid the one topic we'd been consumed by lately: Clayton Raber. It seemed as if we discussed almost everything else but that.

We reached the birthing center ten minutes early, which gave me ten minutes to try to talk her out of her plan. Though I had agreed to be present during the birth of our child, Amanda wanted me to come into her appointments with her from here on out, an idea I did not relish. I really didn't need to be that directly involved with what was basically a matter between her and the midwife, but she insisted, as she had for the past few weeks, saying that all modern Amish husbands were taking a bigger part in the birthing process than ever before.

"Yeah, it's the 'process' part of that equation I'd rather avoid," I said, and she slugged me on the arm.

"Tough luck, buddy," she said as she began to climb from the buggy with some help from me. "If I have to deliver this child, the *least* you can do is be there with me."

As much as I'd rather stick with the old-fashioned approach to the matter, thank you very much, I knew that when Amanda Shetler Zook set her mind to something, there was no stopping her. I finally agreed, though once we were both inside, all signed in and sitting in the waiting room, I began to doubt that decision.

I looked at the other women—no men, only women—all at various stages of pregnancy, at the flowered paper on the walls, and at the posters of mothers playing with their babies, and I suddenly felt very out of place. Fortunately, it wasn't long before the nurse called us back.

As I tried to stay out of the way, the nurse checked Amanda's vital signs and then helped her onto the examining table—which really looked more like a big fancy chair to me—and directed me toward a stool in the corner. I sat as instructed, wondering how long this was going to take. Somehow, the other visits had been a lot easier when all I'd had to do was drop my wife at the door and then kill a little time at the diner across the street with a cup of coffee and some pie.

The midwife entered, and she and Amanda chatted as easily as if they'd known each other for years. My wife seemed knowledgeable about everything, though many of the words and phrases they used sounded like a foreign language to me. The midwife had an odd little device attached to her belt, and after they talked for a while, she helped Amanda lay back even farther on the table chair and arrange her clothing so that her bare stomach was exposed.

I was mortified—this was way too intimate for me—but both women seemed perfectly comfortable with whatever was happening, so I forced myself to hover in the background and not do or say anything stupid.

The midwife pulled a part of the device loose, though it stayed connected with a cord. Then she pressed it against Amanda's stomach and moved it here and there as both women grew silent.

I felt as though we were supposed to be waiting for something, and I was feeling so antsy I was just about to ask what that was when I heard the strangest sound come from the base of the device, almost like a heartbeat after running, pulsing in a rapid but steady beat.

"What is that?" I whispered, thinking surely it couldn't be what I thought it was.

Both women smiled my way and I knew. And though I'd never heard anything like it before, it almost sounded familiar to me, as if I already knew and loved what I was hearing.

"That's your baby's heartbeat, Mr. Zook," the midwife said, smiling at me.

My baby's heartbeat. It was such a beautiful sound—and one that brought me tremendous relief. In a way, I realized, I'd been holding my breath since yesterday afternoon when I learned Miriam Raber's baby had died during the pregnancy. I didn't know what caused such a tragedy to happen, but at least now I knew that my own child was alive and well, its heart pumping to beat the band.

The rest of the visit wasn't so bad after that, and it was deeply reassuring to hear the midwife say that both mother and child seemed perfectly healthy, with everything progressing as expected. When we returned to the waiting room, I noticed two other fathers there now, one of them Amish, which also made me feel better.

I paid at the window while Amanda studied a wall of brochures—information, no doubt, about pregnancy and childbirth and nursing. As we headed out, I saw that she was carrying one of the brochures in her hand but didn't think much of it. It wasn't until we were in the buggy that I noticed her animated expression.

Something was up.

"What is it? Why are you smiling? What are you not telling me?"

Amanda's expression grew intense. "I think I know why Miriam Raber was acting so weird right before she died."

A part of me didn't want to hear it, didn't want to think about babies and death and tragedies that ripped families apart. But Amanda insisted I take a look, so before we pulled out of our parking spot, I took the brochure from her hand.

It was a glossy, tri-fold piece of literature with a bright purple title on the front that said *Warning Signs of Postpartum Depression & Psychosis.*

"What is that?" I asked, staring at the words that sounded scary even without being totally sure of what they meant.

"It's an illness a woman can get after she's had a baby, Matthew. Or if she's pregnant and loses the baby. It's a mental illness, which tells me it probably wasn't always diagnosed properly in years past. They didn't know as much then as they do now."

"Okay," I said, waiting for her to explain.

"The important part is right here," she said, flipping open the page and pointing to a list of symptoms. "Look at this. It says that postpartum psychosis can make a woman feel like she's going insane."

I scanned the page, my eyes absorbing the words as quickly as they could. According to the text, postpartum depression could begin soon after giving birth and might include symptoms such as feelings of sadness and inadequacy, a sudden withdrawal from family and friends, frequent crying, or even thoughts of suicide. I flipped to the next page and read it out loud.

"'Postpartum psychosis is a rarer and more extreme version of postpartum depression.'" I looked up at Amanda, who prompted me to go on. "'It can include symptoms of delusions, hallucinations, thoughts of harming the baby or yourself, and severe depressive symptoms.'"

It was all making sense. This explained what Joan had been talking about when she described Miriam's strange behavior after the baby died. No wonder Clayton had tried to tell his family that Miriam was sick. They all believed she was simply pining away after the *Englischer* she was still in love with. But it wasn't that at all. She really was sick.

I'd stake my store on it. Miriam Raber had postpartum psychosis.

"Amanda, this is it," I said, my eyes still fixed on the brochure.

"I know! It says if a woman has postpartum psychosis, she needs to be hospitalized. It won't go away on its own. It only gets worse."

I looked up at my brilliant wife. "Miriam probably had this and no one knew it. Joan said she just kept getting worse and worse."

Amanda nodded, pleased to have solved a riddle that had lasted for sixty years. And we were both relieved to know what really happened to Miriam back then. It had a name. Though rare, it was a true medical condition.

"*Danke*," I said, reaching for her hand and giving it a squeeze. She smiled in return.

We decided to go straight to the Helmuths' with the brochure. I felt hope growing in my chest, hope that maybe this information would soften Becky's heart enough for her to let me back inside to see Joan for one more try. I figured it wouldn't hurt either to have my sweet, charming, delicate pregnant wife in tow, just as a reminder that our livelihood depended on finding Clayton Raber.

When we got there, Becky was outside in her squash garden with a rake in her hands. She looked up as I drove in, set her rake down, and came toward us. I helped Amanda out of the buggy.

"What now?" Becky asked, frustration on her face and in her voice.

"We stopped by because I have something new to tell you," I said.

"I'm sure it's nothing I want to hear," she replied, her words biting.

Ignoring her words, I motioned to Amanda, who quickly produced the brochure. "We think we've figured out why Miriam Raber started acting so odd after she lost the baby. We think maybe she had this illness."

I added, "Amanda saw this today at the birthing center in Gordonville, and we decided to bring it right over."

Becky stared down at the brochure's glossy front as if it were poisonous to the touch. She looked up at me with the same venom in her eyes. "How many times do I have to say this to you? *Stay away from here*. You're upsetting my mother, me—the whole family!"

"I just thought you would want to know," I said. "Please take it. Joan would want to know what it says."

Becky turned around as if she were going to stomp off without it. Then she faced Amanda and, in one swift motion, ripped the brochure from her hand. She scooped up her rake and propped it against the house as she entered through the door, which she slammed soundly behind her.

After the shock of our encounter wore off, Amanda let out a whistle. "You weren't kidding, Matthew. These people are difficult."

She looked over at me, cautiously, perhaps expecting me to be upset or angry, but I returned her gaze with a smile.

"It may look hopeless now," I said as I helped her back into the buggy. "But I think once she reads the pamphlet for herself—if she does—she'll be grateful for the information. This might even change her whole attitude."

"I sure hope so."

After we returned home, Amanda lay down for a nap, and I made my way to the store to relieve Noah for a break. I stayed busy while he was gone, but once he returned I went into the back room and checked the pile of the day's mail stacked on my desk, hoping there might be a response to my information request for the police file on the death of Miriam Raber, the one I'd submitted online on Friday. It was supposed to take five days, the website had said, but I was feeling optimistic.

It wasn't there.

I sat at my desk and studied the pile of papers before me. I wished I could talk to someone who was involved back then, a detective, police officer—anybody. They probably wouldn't remember where Clayton had gone when he left Lancaster, but at least they could confirm whether he would have been required to give them his new address, and if that address would have gone into the police record. Otherwise, there was no reason to wait for the stupid information request anyway.

So much for doing things the Amish way. As it turned out, face-to-face conversations with real people were no better than the fancy *Englisch* computer-related searches and tracking technology. Apparently, no one was going to find Clayton no matter what method they used. I sighed heavily. The Amish network had let me down.

I returned to the front of the store, my mind still going over other avenues to try, other possibilities. I wondered if the old newspaper reports would have had the name of the detective or detectives involved with the case. Though it would take a lot of time and trouble, I could try going to the Lancaster library to find that information—but then a thought struck me.

Didn't cops have a sort of network, kind of like the Amish did? I'd read about it before, a "brotherhood of the badge" or something. The officer at the police department hadn't been all that helpful, but maybe I could ask the one policeman I actually knew personally, one who helped us out in the past.

The officer's name was Nick Iverson, and he'd been the one to respond last fall when we had a theft at the store. It was our own fault, really. *Daed* had forgotten to put away an outdoor display of Amish-made birdhouses one night, and they ended up disappearing by morning. I was really frustrated—and maybe I shouldn't even have involved the police—but it was just one more loss to our diminishing finances, a good several thousand dollars of inventory down the hole. At least the church allowed such an action on my part, and Nick ended up being sympathetic and respectful. He even helped track down the stolen items, acting on a hunch. It turned out, thanks to a big local football rivalry, that the items had been taken by some spirited teens who had been planning to put them in the individual lockers of the opposing team members. Apparently, the thieves' mascot was a blue jay, and the birdhouses were to serve as an intimidation technique, a sort of symbolic calling card.

Remembering all of that now, I called the station and asked for Nick by name. The woman on the other end told me where I could find him, saying he was working an event at a local firehouse. I thanked her for the information and hung up, deciding to go over there and speak to him right away.

Fortunately, the young police officer remembered me and didn't seem bothered by my tracking him down to ask for some help. The event turned out to be some sort of fund-raiser, and as soon as there was a break in traffic, he was able to take a few moments to speak with me.

Once I had his attention, I explained the situation with the expansion, the property dispute, and my resulting need to find the man who had lived in my house before his mother sold it to our family.

"I'm not sure how I can help you, Matthew. The police don't keep tabs on people."

"This one, they may have." I proceeded to give Nick the basic story about Clayton Raber. "What I'm wondering is if the police report would have included Clayton's forwarding address. Would he have been required to give it in case they needed to reach him in the future?"

Nick thought for a moment, obviously intrigued by my dilemma. "It depends on how 'closed' the case actually was. You'd have to get a look at the report yourself."

"I filed a request for it, but they said it can take up to five days. I was hoping to talk to the detectives sooner than that."

Nick let out a short laugh. "Forget five days. Yeah, you'll hear back in five days, but all that letter will say is that the records are old and it will take thirty days to process your request instead. You said fifty-five, right? I highly doubt anything that ancient has been computerized."

I rubbed the back of my neck and sighed. "Thirty days? I can't wait that long, Nick. Is there any way you could find out for me who handled the case back then? If the person's still alive, maybe they would remember something about where Clayton might have gone."

He studied me for a moment, concern in his eyes. "I know you need to find this guy for the sake of your business, but the fifties were a long time ago. Whoever investigated the case is probably long gone by now. Dead, I mean," he clarified.

"Maybe so, maybe not. What I've been told is that Clayton Raber is more than likely still alive. We just don't know where."

Nick was quiet for a moment, and then he nodded. "I can talk to some of the older guys on the force. One of them might know. How can I reach you if I find out something?"

I gave him the phone number to the tack shop but told him to feel free to stop by the store or the house if that were easier—or faster.

"Okay, I'll try to get back to you soon as I can, one way or the other."

With that, we shook hands again and parted ways. I should feel hopeful, I told myself as I unhitched the horse, but I knew he was right. The fifties were a long time ago. Chances were, everyone connected with the case back then was long gone by now.

THIRTY-FOUR

All Tuesday morning I worked in the store, making certain to always be within earshot of the phone if it rang. I hated waiting around for a call when I could be out searching for more clues about finding Clayton, but Nick Iverson was the best lead I had right now, and he'd said he would get in touch with me as soon as he could.

Amid all of the waiting, a part of me also kept hoping Becky might call. Surely she'd read the brochure by now. Would the new information it provided be enough to get her to open up to me? After watching her walk away from us yesterday, I didn't want to go back over there today. But maybe—just maybe—she would come to me this time.

A man could hope, anyway.

I found some busywork to occupy my scattered mind, but after rearranging the shelves and sweeping up some dust that had gathered on the floor, there was nothing left but more waiting. I stood at the window in the back room and looked out across the yard, at the resort next door that was growing bigger and louder by the day. I watched a workman in an orange vest hammer a stake into the ground. With each pound, I felt the knot in my stomach growing larger. I inhaled deeply and breathed out again, trying to remind myself that God was in charge. I simply needed to trust in Him.

In Thee I put my trust, I prayed, but the words felt rote. Empty. Hollow.

I tried again, saying it aloud this time, though keeping my voice low enough that no one else would hear.

"In Thee I put my trust," I whispered, trying to mean it.

But I felt as though I were talking to the air. Was I really trusting God in this matter at all?

I shifted uncomfortably. In the beginning, I'd put the entire expansion into His hands again and again. But somewhere along the way—as soon as the first big problem cropped up, really—a part of me had ceased to do so. Instead of surrendering my burdens to Him, I'd been gathering them up and clutching tightly onto them.

Trust. I needed to trust and let it go. I knew this in my head. My heart, however, was suddenly filled with terrible questions.

What if He has something else in mind?

What if He doesn't come through for us on this?

What if He can't always be trusted?

Shaking such faithlessness from my mind, I reached up and slammed the shutters on the window, blocking out the view of next door. These were thoughts better explored later when I was alone and could think more clearly.

"Mail's here." I turned to see Noah coming into the room with a small stack of letters and flyers and catalogs in his hands.

He was heading toward the desk with them, but I intercepted him and took the pile from him with a quick thanks. After he was gone, I began flipping through it. Halfway down, I spotted what I'd been waiting for: an envelope, addressed to me, from the clerk of court.

I tore it open and read the letter eagerly, only to find that Nick had been right. According to this, my request for the case file of Miriam Raber was going to be delayed "up to thirty days." The records were so old they weren't in the system and would need to be retrieved from a remote facility. I shoved the letter in my pocket, my heart heavier than ever as I went back out to the front of the store and told the others I was going to lunch.

I'd just reached the house when a police car pulled up behind me, Nick at the wheel. He parked and climbed from the car, and I greeted him with renewed hope and then invited him for lunch, gesturing toward the house.

"Thanks, but no. I only have a minute. I found the names of the detectives who were on the Raber case. One of them passed away twenty years ago, but the other is still alive. He's in a nursing home in Ephrata. His name is Ralph De Lucca, and he was the lead detective."

My heart soared as he handed me a yellow Post-it Note with a name, address, and phone number written on it. I was still staring at it when Amanda emerged from the house.

"Judging by the smile on my husband's face, I'd say you just made his day," she said, coming to join us.

Nick smiled and tipped his hat. "Ma'am. How are you?"

"Just fine. Good to see you again, Officer." Turning to me, she added, "Well? Was he able to come up with a name?"

I said yes, indeed, and flashed the paper toward her so she could see.

Amanda thanked Nick as well and also invited him to stay for lunch. "I have a nice pot of potato soup on the stove and a blueberry-peach pie baked just this morning."

Nick put a hand to his stomach and gave a groan. "Aw, man, I'm sure it would be wonderful. But I need to get going."

Amanda nodded. "I had a feeling you might say that. So here." With a smile, she raised her hands and I realized she was holding about half of the pie, wrapped up in foil. "For you and your wife," she added, giving the package to Nick.

He took it gladly and thanked her, inhaling the scent of cinnamon and pastry, saying he remembered her delicious pie from last fall. Amanda smiled and waved away the compliment, replying it was nothing and that we appreciated his help.

"Yeah, thanks again," I said, pumping Nick's arm in an enthusiastic handshake. "I was just about out of options."

"Glad to do it, Matthew. I don't know if it'll pan out, but it's worth a shot, I guess. We cops can be pretty tight lipped while we're on the force, but ask any retiree who's been out of it for a while about an old case, and he'll likely talk your ears off."

That very afternoon, the car I'd hired to take me to Ephrata was dropping me off at the front door of the nursing home where Ralph De Lucca, the detective who had been in charge of investigating Miriam Raber's death, now lived. He and I had spoken briefly on the phone earlier, and though he sounded elderly, he also seemed quite lucid. He'd invited me on over, adding, "It's not like I'm going anywhere."

The large brick building looked nice enough, with purple and white flowers bordering the path that led to the front doors. I entered the lobby and told the woman at the front desk I was here to see a Mr. De Lucca. She smiled and gestured toward the waiting area by the front window.

"I believe he's been watching for you," she said.

I looked over to see a man sitting in a wheelchair right at the glass, peering intently toward the parking lot, eyes studying each person who came and went.

"Mr. De Lucca?" I said, stepping toward him.

He turned, his face wrinkled into a scowl but his eyes bright. "Yes?" he said, looking vaguely peeved at having been interrupted.

"I'm Matthew Zook. We spoke on the phone?"

I held out a hand to give his a shake and watched several emotions wash over his features in succession: surprise, that the guy he'd spoken to earlier turned out to be Amish; concentration, as he tried to match that information with the fact that I was here to discuss an old case; and recognition, as he most likely made that match and decided which case I had come here to discuss. Being a homicide detective, Clayton Raber was likely the only suspected murderer Mr. De Lucca had ever investigated who also happened to be Amish.

He suggested we chat in the day room, so I rolled him down the hall and soon we were in a bright, sunny area with numerous small groupings of chairs, most of them empty.

"Everybody's at bingo right now," he explained, waving toward a seat near the window. "We shouldn't be interrupted in here for a while."

I rolled him into place and then had a seat, meeting his rheumy blue eyes with my own.

"Like I said on the phone," I began, "I'm here to ask you about a case you handled back in 1955. A man named—"

"Clayton Raber. I figured as much as soon as I saw you."

I nodded, relieved that he was apparently as sharp as I hoped he would be.

"Do you remember the case?" I asked. And though I was prepared to explain the reason why I needed to know, he jumped right in and started talking. As Nick had predicted, it sounded as if this guy could go on for days.

Before he went very far into the tale, however, I managed to stop him, saying that my main concern was tracking down Clayton Raber now. "I need to find him, and I'm hoping maybe you've kept tabs on him over the years or at the very least got a forwarding address from him back when he first left the area."

"Nope and nope," he said, dashing my hopes in three little words.

He didn't seem to notice how crestfallen I was because he just kept going, telling me all about the incident from his point of view, how the original responders hadn't realized it might be a crime scene and had ignored procedure, allowing any possible evidence to be trampled away in the immediate aftermath. By the time he was assigned to the case, though, enough suspicious statements had been made by others that De Lucca went into it certain the man was guilty.

"But I was wrong," he added with a shake of his head. "That poor man was innocent."

I was surprised at the conviction with which he said those words. "How can you be so sure?"

"There was a witness."

My eyes narrowed. "A witness?"

"Yep. And the man's story completely corroborated with what Clayton told me, that Miriam had been acting crazy, that she really did accidentally fall, and that Clayton tried to save her from falling. He didn't push her off."

"I don't understand," I said, still surprised by this news. "Who was the witness? How come you believed him but nobody else seemed to?"

"Because said witness asked to remain anonymous."

I sat back in my chair. "Anonymous? I don't understand."

The detective surprised me by rolling his eyes. "This guy was in the barn when it happened, but no one knew it, and as soon as she hit the ground, he took off running. He didn't say anything to anybody for days, not until he read in the papers that we'd arrested the woman's husband for murder."

"At least he came forward then, right?"

Again, the old man rolled his eyes. "Yeah, with a high-priced lawyer in tow. Said he wanted to make a statement but would do so only if we would keep his name out of the papers."

How odd. "Why? What did it matter?"

De Lucca shook his head. "The guy was a stage actor and thought he was the next big thing. He didn't want any sort of scandal attached to his name. Apparently, Miriam had shown up at the theater earlier that day and made a big scene demanding to see him. He'd managed to get her removed from the premises, but then later he'd gone out to the Rabers' house to tell her to leave him alone. Said he was going to tell her husband too, and demand that he control his wife."

"Why was she trying to see him?" I asked, thoroughly confused.

"Did I leave out that part? Sorry. He was her ex-lover, the one who had gotten her pregnant before she married Clayton. Guess she was hoping the actor might give her an encore." He snickered at his own joke.

I closed my eyes for a moment, absorbing that thought, knowing the poor woman had not been in her right mind by that point. There was no telling what sort of delusion had taken her to the theater that day or what would have happened had she lived. What a tragedy all the way around.

"So this actor gets to the clock shop but it's closed. Then he walks up the hill toward the house. He hears a bunch of yelling and recognizes Miriam's voice. Follows the sounds to the barn. He's down below, trying to see who's up in the loft and what's going on when he realizes it's Miriam and her husband having an argument. He's down there watching and listening, waiting for the right moment to interrupt and have his say, when the whole thing goes down. She fell, and he took off like a rabbit, terrified of what it might look like if his presence there made the papers. What a schmoe. He really thought he was the next William Holden or something. But you tell me, ever heard of 'Russell LaRousseau'? Please. Maybe a scandal would have done his career some good."

Clayton. Innocent. I felt another smile stretch across my face as I helped the last customer of the day load sacks of feed into his truck. The late afternoon sun was in my eyes as he pulled out and a buggy turned into the driveway and took his place. I couldn't see who was at the reins until it was practically in front of me. Lifting my hand to shield my gaze from the glare, I was about to say we were closed when I realized it was Becky Helmuth.

Trying to contain my excitement, I secured her horse and then positioned myself to help her down from the buggy. Instead, she shook her head, saying this would only take a moment.

I was so happy to see her, I was about to burst with my news, to tell her everything that I'd learned from the detective. But she seemed to have something important on her mind as well, so I let her talk first.

"I was on my way home from town, and I just wanted to stop by to say thank you for the brochure you brought us yesterday." She hesitated and then met my eyes. "It answered a lot of questions for us. And it gave my mother much peace."

I was moved by the emotion in her voice. "I'm glad to hear that."

"You were right. The brochure described exactly what happened with Miriam. *Mamm* says it was terrible. She was obviously deranged, but it wasn't like she was running a fever or anything. Now that we know what was probably wrong with her, it explains so much." She lifted her hand to her face and wiped at her eyes. "My mother said Miriam's brother Perry had strange, unpredictable moods. He could be extremely happy one week and horribly depressed the next, likely what we'd call bipolar these days. The brochure said a family history of that sort of thing is usually present for women who have postpartum psychosis. That has to be what was up with Miriam. The family just didn't know it."

"Your mother was able to handle this news?" I asked, stepping closer to the buggy. I prayed she had.

"*Mamm* feels both better and worse now. Better that she understands what was happening with her sister-in-law back then. Worse that it just makes it that much sadder. We can't go back in time and change anything."

She sighed heavily.

"Anyway, that's why I came by, to thank you for the postpartum psychosis information." She took the reins in her hands, and then she paused and looked at me again. "But I also needed to ask you something. No offense, Matthew, but please stop coming over. You have to quit upsetting my mother. We can't help you find her brother. I hope you'll respect that."

"I do respect your wishes," I began cautiously, "but before you set that in stone, there's something I need to tell you too. I have huge news. Really significant information I wanted to share with your mother. I think everything will change once the two of you hear this."

Becky continued to watch me, the reins tightening in her hands. I removed my hat from my head and held it in my hands.

"Clayton *is* innocent."

She looked as if she were about to protest, to tell me once and for all to stay away from her family, to stop mocking their tragedy with my haphazard guesses, but I pushed forward before she could cut me off.

"I tracked down the detective today who was in charge of Clayton's case. That man is still alive. Do you know why they dropped the charges against your uncle?"

"Insufficient evidence."

"No. They dropped the charges because there was a *witness*. A man came forward who saw the whole thing as it happened."

Becky's eyes narrowed skeptically, but she didn't interrupt so I kept going.

"The thing is, the witness was willing to talk to the police, but otherwise he insisted on remaining anonymous. That's why nobody else knows it, but it's true. The guy saw everything. Clayton did not push Miriam. She fell." I locked eyes with Becky. "Clayton is innocent."

She didn't speak for a long moment. She just stared straight ahead, stunned, the reins she had been holding laying limp in her lap. "The family always hoped that it was so, but no one could say absolutely for sure whether he'd done it or not. When he left town, everybody figured that confirmed his guilt, at least for those in the community."

"The community excommunicated the guy. No wonder he left town."

She considered this for a moment. "My family has never stopped praying for him, though. Praying for repentance and reconciliation. Now you tell me there is proof that he was innocent after all." She paused to soak in that thought. "My *onkel* really was innocent? Then you're right. My mother definitely needs to know."

After a pause, she turned to me again, a flash of something like guilt in her eyes.

"Matthew, there's something I have to show you. It's at the house. Maybe you should come over."

I swallowed hard. "I'll leave as soon as I lock up here."

"Can you give us an hour? I need to break this news to my mother." Her voice grew faint, almost weary. "I just don't know how she's going to take it. She'll be thrilled, of course, but also…"

She didn't have to finish that thought. I understood. But a part of me feared that if Joan reacted poorly to the news about Clayton, then Becky might change her mind and once again send me away empty handed. I couldn't risk that this time, not if there was something she needed to show me, something that would help me find Clayton at last.

"What is it you want me to see? I just want to know before I come."

She hesitated, that flash of guilt returning now in full. "My mother actually *has* heard from Clayton over the years. Just a few times, mind you, and not in a long while. But now and then he would send her a letter. She saved them all."

"The envelopes too?"

She smiled slightly. *"Ya.* The envelopes too. "

"And they have a return address on them?" I asked, hope surging in my chest.

"Sort of. There's a post office box, not a street address. A town up in the Poconos."

"That's better than nothing," I said, thankful for any bit of information at all. Even just knowing the town made me that much closer to finding him.

Becky turned from me, her eyes searching the distance. "I'm sorry I didn't tell you sooner. I just…I didn't…"

"It's all right. I understand."

She looked at me again. "You can read those letters when you come. They might help you narrow things down better."

"That would be an honor. I'll be over in an hour."

She gave a somber nod in reply, and then she was gone.

Thirty-Five

Becky was bringing in clothes off the line as I once again drove my buggy into her farmyard. Chickens scattered at my approach, and a pair of golden-haired little girls walking a baby goat on a lead rope laughed as the goat tried to chase them. Probably two more of Joan's great-grandchildren. As I tied up my horse to the hitching rail, Becky walked toward me.

"*Mamm's* out on the back porch," she said, as she brushed a few wisps away from her brow. "Come on. I'll take you."

I followed her around the side of the house to the ample porch that looked out over the Helmuth acreage and hundreds of grazing and bleating goats. Joan sat dozing in a rocker with a lap blanket over her knees. An embroidery hoop with a half-finished project rested on the table beside her, along with a small stack of yellowed envelopes poking out from underneath.

Becky laid a hand on her mother's shoulder. "Matthew Zook is here, *Mamm.*"

The older woman lifted her head and slowly opened her eyes.

"What?"

"Matthew Zook. He's here."

Joan looked over at me in obvious consternation. Whoever I was, I had disturbed her nap. But then she seemed to remember who I was and why I had been invited out.

"You've come about Clayton," she said, still frowning at me, but with less you've-interrupted-my-nap rancor.

"*Ya.*"

"He's come about the letters, *Mamm*. Remember? We have those old letters of Clayton's?"

Joan turned to face her daughter, looking as cross at her own flesh and blood as she had at me. "Letters?"

Becky pointed to the little pile of envelopes on the table beside her mother. "Those letters. Remember?"

The old woman swiveled her head to look. "Oh. Those." Her features softened as she stared at the envelopes.

"Matthew's the one who told me that *Onkel* Clayton was innocent. He said the police detective told him there was a witness who saw the whole thing. And that it was definitely an accident."

Joan closed her eyes, and I could see she was overwhelmed with emotion, a mix of sadness and guilt and regret. Then she opened her eyes and tipped her head back to study my face. "I know you now. You live in my old house."

I nodded. "I do. I grew up there."

"And you know where Clayton is?" Her tone was so hopeful.

"I don't yet. But I'm trying to find him."

"That's why he needs to read the letters, *Mamm*," Becky said.

Joan turned her head toward the table again and reached out a bony, shaking hand that was mottled with age spots. She wrapped her fingers around the envelopes and lifted them. Then she swung her arm around. "Sit right here, young man. By me."

Becky nodded to a wooden ladder-back chair that was just a few feet away. I pulled it close to the old woman and sat. Becky leaned comfortably against the porch post and folded her arms across her chest.

Joan thrust the five envelopes toward me. The return address was for a post office box in Mountain Gap, Pennsylvania. I had no idea where that was, but I was sure I could find out.

"Read them in order," Joan instructed. "And speak up. I don't hear so well anymore."

"I read them to you yesterday, *Mamm*," Becky interjected.

"Well, I don't remember yesterday."

I hadn't expected that I would read them aloud, but it didn't seem to matter one way or the other. "I don't mind," I said.

The letters were postmarked March 1956, April 1956, August 1960, January 1973, and November 2001. I sorted them in order and then set down all but the oldest one. I opened its flap and gently removed the yellowed, fragile paper inside it. I began to read.

March 21, 1956

Dear Joanie,

I hope it is okay that I write. I thought someone should know where I ended up and that I am fine. Saw in the Budget that the home place was sold to a family that will do something good with it. The Zooks sound like nice people. There hasn't been a local tack and feed shop in a while, and I'm glad they are opening one. Hope you and the others are well.

As for me, I am in a town up in the Poconos, not far from Palmerton, where I have been taken in by a pastor and his family. (You will be happy to know that.) The church is called Mountain Gap Fellowship. As it is a Plain church, we've much in common faith-wise. They aren't Amish, of course, but I suppose I am not Amish anymore either, though I still feel like it most of the time. Pastor Gunderson, his family, and his church have been very kind to me. They know what the newspapers have said about me, but they believe me. I don't write that to make you feel bad. I just want you to know I am welcome here. He is a very good man. He reminds me of Daed.

I've said this a hundred times, I know, but

Miriam's falling was an accident, Joanie. I didn't push her. I saw that she was too close to the edge and reached out to catch her but I couldn't. I did not push her.

I know this has been hard for Mamm. It's been hard for all of you.

I hope you will not think me forsaken by God. He has been watching over me.

Give Mamm my love.
Clayton

April 30, 1956

Dear Joanie,

I got your letter and I understand. Whatever Maisie thinks is best for Mamm. The last thing I want to do is make this harder for her.

People in the church are bringing me their broken clocks to fix. And Pastor Gunderson wants me to make him a clock for his study. He helps me get the right tools at auctions and such. It feels good to work again. I just wanted you to know that. Maybe you could tell Mamm for me, if you think it would be all right. If not, then don't.

I still think I did what was best, even though it means I'm away from you all. If I was wrong for leaving, I pray God will overlook my ignorance. In my heart I wanted to do right by the family.

Your brother,
Clayton

P.S. If you ever want to write me now and again, you can. Unless you tell me to, I won't make trouble for you by writing you back. I don't want to cause problems with the bishop or the church (or Maisie).

August 12, 1960

Dear Joanie,

God bless you for writing me to tell me of Mamm's death.

I am sorry it has taken me two months to thank you for letting me know. It's been hard. I hope and pray she did not suffer and that she was able to fully forgive me for all my wrongs.

We can be done now, you and I, if it will be easier for you to let me go.

You have been a true sister, Joanie.

Clayton

January 14, 1973

Dear Joanie,

I saw in the Budget about Maisie's passing. Very sad news, but especially for you as the two of you were always very close. Hope you are doing well otherwise.

I'm still here in Mountain Gap and things are fine, though there have been some changes since I last wrote. I work for a local merchant, doing small mechanical repairs. We don't get in many clocks, so I've had to expand into watches and music boxes and portable kitchen appliances and such. I'll always love clockmaking—and I still do it on the side—but doing it full time made me miss Daed so much, and Miriam too, that it's actually easier this way.

Money-wise, I'm getting by, not that I need much anyway. I still live Plain for the most part. God provided a home for me through a fellow church member, where I do have electricity. But I've found most other Englisch things unnecessary. Telephones, cars, new clothes, and the like.

My church community here is still very supportive. I've learned over the years that if you lose a family, somehow God finds a way to make you a new one if you let Him.

I miss home. And you. These days my biggest heartache is to know that when I, too, pass on, I won't be buried with family, at Miriam's side, but off in another part of the state, in a cemetery that is not Amish.

Otherwise, I am happy enough. Hope you are too.

No need to write back.

Clayton

August 14, 2001

Dear Joanie,

It's been a few years since I last wrote. I was thinking of you this week and wanted to say Happy 80th Birthday. I wonder if your family will be throwing you a party. Hope you are well.

Saw in the Budget a few years ago about Solomon's passing. I'm so sorry. I know he was a good husband to you.

As always, no need to write back. Just wanted to send birthday wishes your way.

Your brother,
Clayton

When I finished reading the last letter, a heavy silence fell across the three of us. Joan was looking out onto the horizon, and Becky was staring at the ancient papers in my hands. When I placed the fifth letter back in its envelope, Joan filled the wordless void with a heavy sigh. Unsure of what to do with Clayton's letters, I was grateful when Becky leaned forward and held out her hand for them. She set them back on the table as Joan watched.

"I only wrote twice, after his first letter," Joan said, not looking at either one of us. "Other than that, our communications over the years were strictly one-way." She had a distant look in her eyes. "I should have written to him. I thought about sending Clayton a note for his eightieth birthday, as he had done for mine, but with the church and everything, well, contact had to be limited, you know."

I wanted to say the right words, to comfort her in her grief. But a tightness took hold of my chest. Despite the excommunication, the man was never shunned. Joan would likely have been allowed to write to her brother, especially if it were used as an opportunity to try to bring him back into the fold. Her words now were just an excuse, one she told herself to make her feel better about not writing. The truth was, she hadn't kept in touch all those years because she thought he had killed his wife and gotten away with it.

I felt a surge of anger toward her, but as I watched her now, tears streaming from her eyes, shoulders stooped and hands gnarled and dotted with age, that anger began to melt away. This woman had been trapped for years by grief and prejudice, torn between condemning and believing her baby brother. It wasn't right, what she had done. But if God could forgive her, I must do the same.

Still, I couldn't help but think about all the wasted years, Clayton's unanswered letters that could have been face-to-face encounters, and the family and the community that hadn't believed him.

If only the clockmaker could turn back the clock.

Becky patted her *mamm* on the shoulder for comfort and then looked to me. "So, Matthew, what happens now? If you find him, I mean."

The question wasn't hard for me to answer. "I'm going to give him his clock, explain about the property issue, and ask him if he would be willing to sign the quitclaim deed. If necessary, I'll pay him for the land. Of course, I'll tell him the whole truth, about how the resort people are also looking for him and that they could offer him much more money than I can. But I'm hoping he'll sign with me. It's what his mother intended, you know?"

"When you see him, will you tell him I love him?" Joan asked in the most lucid tone I had yet to hear from her.

"Yes, ma'am. I'd be happy to."

"And ask him if—" She paused, her eyes filling with fresh tears. "If he might find some way…to forgive me." Her voice broke and she again turned away, her shoulders shaking with sobs.

Leaning toward her, one hand on her bony arm, I assured her I would tell him that as well when I saw him. She gave no reply, and I knew there wasn't much else I could do for her. I looked to Becky, and her eyes met mine. It was time for me to go.

With a final pat to the sniffling Joan, I rose from my chair and followed her daughter down the back porch steps to the path that would lead me to the buggy.

We walked in silence a few paces.

"You thought Clayton was innocent all along, didn't you?" she asked once we'd rounded the corner, her voice sounding sad and lost.

"I guess I did. Though I can't say why. Just a feeling."

"A feeling," she echoed.

"Maybe it's because I was on the outside looking in that I saw it the way I did," I offered. "He's not my blood relative, but he was once a member of this community that I love. He grew up in the bedroom that eventually became mine. He used to make clocks in the shop where I now run my business. I feel a strange affinity for him. I always have."

Becky shot me a glance as we walked. "This has become more to you than just a property dispute." It was a statement, not a question.

After a beat I nodded, trying to think of how to reply. "Especially now that the truth has been confirmed, I feel that it's up to me to right this wrong. He really was innocent. People need to know that. And he needs to know that people know that."

We were now at my buggy.

"You're a good man, Matthew Zook," Becky said as I climbed inside it. "Do what you can. And go with God's blessings."

Thirty-Six

Back at home, I pulled out a map of Pennsylvania and found the town of Mountain Gap. It was in the Poconos, as Clayton had said in his letter, but just barely. It was located at the very beginning of the mountain range, past Blue Mountain and right off of the Northeast Extension. I calculated the mileage and decided it was nearly eighty miles away. Not a cheap trip, by any means, at least not via hired car, especially if I ended up having to stay somewhere up there overnight, all the while racking up costs in food, gasoline, and a hotel. But no train went up that way, and the bus route was so roundabout it turned a two-hour drive into a fifteen-hour journey. I just couldn't imagine that. Staring at the map, I wondered if I could afford to go there.

Then again, I told myself how could I afford *not* to go there? Each day the expansion wasn't finished and open to customers was a day we lost money. If I took this trip and found Clayton, then that might just be the end of the matter, in which case the cost would be worth it. Surrendering to the wiser option, I called the company I used most often to hire a car and driver.

The next morning, as I headed northeastward toward my destination, I began to think about Clayton and how he had ended up where he did. Had he stepped off a bus in Mountain Gap by some random choice, or was that just where his travel money ran out? Had he been to other towns along the way where he had stayed briefly and then moved on after someone recognized him? Was this the place he started his new life because he had truly run out of options? Or was this the place where people finally stopped whispering, "Isn't that the Amish man who pushed his wife off a barn loft to her death and got away with it?"

We hit the Northeast Extension at Allentown, and about twenty minutes later entered a tunnel that looked as if it went straight through a mountain. When we came out the other side, I couldn't help but gasp.

"Beautiful, isn't it?" the driver asked. "I love this view, the way it just pops out at you like that."

I agreed, my eyes following the lush and green landscape as it slipped past the window. It *was* beautiful, but it was so much more. Peering around me, I began to understand why Clayton may have settled here. Because of that tunnel, it felt like a completely different world on this side, as if nothing back there could touch you once you came through. In the space of that single transition, the terrain changed from rolling green hills to downright mountainous, with craggy rocks on all sides, meandering creeks far below the road, and tiny towns nestled among the foothills. After all he'd been through, Clayton would have felt safe here, I thought, like he'd left the old behind and could start anew.

We took the first exit and wound our way around to the town of Mountain Gap. I had asked the driver to take me to the church Clayton mentioned in his letter to Joan, which was the only address I had to go on thus far. The 1940s-era tawny brick church and white steeple sat on a large lot with an expansive lawn, trimmed trees, and a sign out front with letters that could be moved around to say what you wanted. Today's message was: *His mercies are new every morning*.

Only two cars were in the parking lot, but at least someone was there. One of the cars was an older model Buick, well cared for but dated. I'd seen plenty of these drive through Ridgeview, and the passengers were nearly always gray haired. That was a good sign, as I needed to be able to talk to someone older who may have an idea of whom I was trying to find.

The driver dropped me off at the church's office entrance, handing me a slip of paper with his cell phone number on it before I got out and telling me to give him a call when I was ready to be picked up. I'd had to hire the man for the whole day, so while I was inside trying to track down Clayton Raber, this guy would be seeing the sights or eating or otherwise killing time while he waited to hear from me.

Amanda had packed up the clock carefully and put it in a canvas bag, so I lifted that from beside me now, climbed from the car, and headed inside. I opened the door, and a pleasant-looking woman seated behind a desk smiled up at me. The nameplate in front of her told me her name was Denise. She looked to be about thirty or so. Perhaps not the gray-haired owner of the Buick I was hoping for.

"Good afternoon," she said cheerfully but with obvious curiosity as she took in my Amish garb. "Can I help you?

I smiled back at her. "I sure hope so. I'm trying to locate a man who may or may not be a member here now but definitely was at one time. I'm hoping he's on the church roster, and if not that someone in your congregation remembers him and will perhaps know where he might be living now, if he is indeed still alive."

"Oh, well, it's possible," she answered brightly. "How long ago was it? We have some older members who have lived here all their lives."

"This would have been sixty years ago."

"Wow! Sixty years!" she said, but then she seemed to have thought of something. Her smile grew bigger. "Wait a minute. Would this person happened to have been raised Amish, like you?"

"*Ya.*"

"Would it be Clay Raber you are looking for?"

My heart just about slammed into my stomach. "*Ya!* Do you know where he is?"

"Sure do. He lives about five miles outside of town. He comes to church here every Sunday. My in-laws bring him. And my next-door neighbor mows his lawn."

I was stunned nearly beyond words. I'd hoped so desperately that Clayton might still be in the same place he ended up all those years ago, but just in case he'd moved since that last letter, I'd steeled myself for bad news.

Now I'd been given the very best news of all.

"He's still here," I said with a huge grin.

Denise laughed, obviously happy to have so easily made my day. "Oh, yes. Clay has been here for ages. He's one of our oldest members, bless his heart. And one of the dearest. Are you family?"

"Well, not exactly. I live in the house he grew up in. I have a property matter I need his help on." Glancing at the bag, I added, "And I have something that belongs to him."

She tipped her head in wonderment. "He's never had anyone Amish ask about him that I can recall. I'm a little surprised you're here."

I wasn't sure what she meant. "Surprised?"

"Well, we all know he was raised Amish, and he still lives Plain, but he's never made it seem as though, you know…" Her voice trailed off without finishing her thought.

"Does he have family here? Did he ever remarry?" I asked, still trying to wrap my head around the notion that Clayton was living just five miles from where I stood.

"I don't believe so. I've only been here for the last fifteen years, but—" A figure appeared in the doorway to the rest of the offices. A woman with silvery-gray hair stood there, her gaze on me. Denise went on. "Oh, Bonnie can tell you. She's known Clay nearly her whole life, haven't you?"

The woman named Bonnie was still staring at me, and I could see that a dozen thoughts were running through her head.

"You know Clay Raber?" she asked.

"I live in his old house. I have something that belongs to him. And I need to talk with him about an important property matter."

She regarded me for another moment, as though she were sizing me up. It was easy to see she was being protective of Clayton, and it took me a second to realize that must mean she cared about him and didn't want to see him get hurt. Bonnie looked old enough to know what had sent Clayton away from his home and family six decades ago.

"Perhaps you would like to come on back to the library with me so we can chat," she said.

"Sure." I nodded to Denise, whom Bonnie clearly wanted to exclude from this particular conversation. "Thanks for your help."

She smiled but said nothing.

Bonnie led me down a short, carpeted hallway past a set of restrooms and a door labeled "Sanctuary," finally coming to a stop at the last door on the right, marked "Library." She stepped inside and motioned to a reading table with four wooden chairs pushed neatly around it.

We sat, and I placed the bag on the floor next to me. When I was settled, she extended her hand.

"I'm Bonnie Dryer, by the way." Her tone was cordial, but there was only a faint smile on her lips.

I shook her hand. "Matthew Zook."

"And you're from Ridgeview?"

"*Ya.*"

She paused a moment. "No one from Lancaster County has ever come to see Clay before," she said, inviting me to explain myself.

"No one knew where he was," I replied, as politely as I could. "He's been gone a long time. And it appears he and his sisters did not keep in touch."

"How did you find him here, then?"

"His one surviving sister received a few letters from him over the years. One of them mentioned this church. That's pretty much all I had to go on. That and a Mountain Gap P.O. box number."

"I see. And you've come to talk to him about a property matter?"

"That's right," I said, and for about the tenth time in less than a week, I laid out the whole issue—only this time I threw in every detail I could think of, feeling that the better she understood the problem, the more likely she was to help me with the solution.

I even pulled out copies of the conflicting survey maps and the as-yet-to-be-completed quitclaim deed. Once I'd gone through everything, I left my visual aids out on the table and waited for her to respond.

"Sounds like you've had quite the search trying to hunt him down," she said, studying the maps.

"My business depends on it, ma'am."

She handed back the map and leaned forward in her seat, her posture telling me she'd made a decision.

"I know why Clay left Lancaster County. I know what happened to his wife. She died in a tragic accident that was not his fault, but everyone back home thought it was. I don't want that past coming back to haunt him now."

I saw the protectiveness in her eyes, and it touched me. Indeed, when Clayton Raber lost one family, God had managed to give him another.

Taking a deep breath, I told Bonnie the rest of the story, the part about growing up in Clayton's room and feeling such a strange kinship and believing he was innocent even before my talk with Detective De Lucca confirmed it. Apparently I managed to convince her that I meant her dear friend no harm, because once I was finished, she rewarded me with a genuine smile.

"How did he end up here, if I may ask?" I said. "I mean, it's a beautiful area, but why this? Why here? Or maybe you were too young to remember back then."

"Oh, I remember. I was fifteen when Clay first showed up."

There was such a dreamy tone to her voice that I waited, hoping she might go on. A moment later she did.

"I'm the one who found him on the church's doorstep in the rain one early Monday morning. My father was the pastor here, and he and my mother and little brother and I lived in the parsonage that used to be next door. I had gotten up to let the dog out, and I saw a man huddled under the eaves of the church trying to stay out of the rain. Millie saw him too and started barking at him. Clay had been asleep, and he startled awake when he heard her. He saw me and Millie and told me I didn't need to worry, that he'd be on his way. But I could see that he had been there all night in the rain. And I could tell he was an Amish man. When I saw him start to limp away, I assumed he'd been hurt. I knew my papa wouldn't have wanted me to turn my back on someone who needed help when it was in my power to give it. That's not how I was raised.

"I asked him if he needed a doctor and he just shook his head. Well, I thought, maybe he didn't need a doctor but he sure needed to get in out of the rain. So I asked him if he needed a warm place to dry off, and he just kept trying to hobble away, saying he'd be on his way. Millie was barking the whole time, and I didn't realize that my papa had stepped out onto the porch and had seen what I had seen.

"'Come now, friend,' Papa said. 'Wherever you're headed will be nicer to get to once you've dried off and had some breakfast.'

"Well, Clay stopped and turned toward us. I don't know if it was the way my papa said 'friend' or the thought of breakfast that made him stop, but stop he did. And I saw the longing in his eyes even from fifty feet away. Then Papa asked him where he was headed. Clay took his time answering. 'Nowhere,' he finally said. And Papa said something like, 'Well, nowhere's a place that can always wait.' And so he came inside."

Bonnie paused a moment, breathed in deeply, and I could see that she remembered the day Clayton arrived as if it were yesterday.

"Papa gave Clay dry clothes to change into as everything he had on and in his duffel bag was wet. Mama laid out all of his clothes on the drying rack in the kitchen. He didn't say much as he ate, and the more Papa asked him questions, the faster Clay chewed so he could be finished, get his own clothes back on, and leave. At some point Papa realized who Clay was. I saw a look pass over my papa's face, and I knew he had suddenly figured something out. It had been in all the daily newspapers, the story of the Amish wife who had died under suspicious conditions and that there was insufficient evidence to charge her husband in her death. Clay saw that look pass across Papa's face too. He stood up and started to thank my mama for the fine breakfast and could he please have his own clothes back so he could be on his way and trouble them no longer.

"Now, my papa always had a way of seeing into peoples' hearts. Some said he had the gift of discernment. I don't know if he did, but I do know he was the smartest man I ever knew. And the kindest. He told Clay to please sit back down. His clothes weren't dry, his food wasn't eaten, and his coffee cup was only half drunk. It seemed to take a long time for Clay to take his chair, and when he did, he didn't pick up his fork. He put his head in his hands, and he suddenly looked like he had just crawled twenty miles through a desert wilderness. I had never seen anyone look so tired so quickly.

"And then he said something I will never forget. He said, 'I loved my wife. I didn't kill her. God is my witness. I didn't kill her.'

"I was still trying to figure out what was going on, but Mama had put two and two together too, and she and Papa were looking at each other, speaking without saying a word. And then my papa put his hand on Clay's shoulder and told him he believed him. He and Mama both did, and did he need a place to stay?"

Bonnie had been looking off toward a stack of books as she was telling me this, but now she turned her head to face me.

"And that's how Clay came to be here. First he was our houseguest, and then one of the elders let him use a little studio apartment above his garage. Then, when one of our older members passed away, she left her house to her son, who in turn offered to rent it to Clay for next to nothing, for as long as he needed it. The place is small—and it's become more than he can handle by himself these days—but that house was an answer to prayer, especially because it has a detached garage, where Clay was able to set up a workshop for making clocks and doing other odd repairs on the side.

"All along the way, my father and mother treated Clay like he was one of the family. He came to all our gatherings, every wedding, every funeral. And it didn't take very long for the others in the church to follow suit. No one ever pressed him about what happened back in Lancaster County. It was enough that he told my parents he loved his wife and that they believed him wholeheartedly.

"He was such a gentle soul. I had a hard time believing he once had a temper. That's what he told us anyway. Everyone grew to love him. He was like a brother to me, and all fourteen of my grandchildren think of Clay as their great-uncle."

"That's…that's wonderful," I said, so grateful to know Clayton's life had been filled with measures of happiness. "I can't tell you how glad I am to hear this. All of this."

"I think God wanted Clay to wind up on our doorstep sixty years ago. Not just for himself because he needed us, but for us too. He was more open with my family and me about what had happened to him, and I have always been in awe of his unwavering devotion to Miriam. Even when some of the young single women in the church were interested in him, he stayed loyal to his late wife in every way. He never stopped loving her. He loved her like God loves all of us—with every fiber of his being, even without having that love returned. Her death, followed by the rejection of the very community that was supposed to surround him at such a difficult time, nearly broke the man for good. Instead, God brought Clay here to us. And now, for some reason, God has brought you to him."

I realized with sudden surprise that it was true. All the false leads, all the problems and frustrations, all the doors closed in my face—I'd learned lessons from all of it. And now here I was at last in a position to reconnect brother and sister in the final years of their lives in a meaningful way. Whether Clayton signed the deed or not, I realized, I had already accomplished my most important task of all.

"Shall I draw you a map to his house?" she asked. "Or do you need me to give you a lift out there myself?"

"A map would be great, ma'am. That and a phone, so I can call my driver."

As I watched her sketch the series of roads that would take me to Clayton at last, it finally struck me full force what my problem had been this past week. I'd had trouble trusting my heavenly Father because I'd learned the hard way that I couldn't always trust my earthly father. But just as *Daed* always had our best interests at heart, God always knew what we really needed, even if sometimes it wasn't at all what we thought it would be.

THIRTY-SEVEN

The house where Clayton Raber lived stood a couple hundred yards off the road, nestled among a thick grove of oaks and poplars such that I couldn't see the front door from where I stood. A lawn ready for mowing wrapped around the front of the house, and a leaf-strewn brick walkway led to the small detached garage and the unfenced backyard, where I could see the tail end of a clothesline and two pairs of pants snapping in the breeze. It had been a while since either building had been painted, and cobwebs had gathered in the weathered window frames.

A walking path led to the porch, which needed sweeping and sported a single rocking chair. I stepped up to the door, the felt-wrapped clock still safely nestled in the canvas bag that was now slung over my shoulder. I had told the driver to drop me off and that I'd probably be about an hour. I wasn't sure if I'd need that much time—or if Clayton was even going to let me in at all—so I'd pointed out a little ice-cream stand on the main road less than a mile away and said he should check there first before coming back here, because that's where I'd go to meet up with him if I finished sooner than expected.

I was keenly aware, even in the midst of the peace and quiet of Clayton's simple home, that I was about to hugely alter his day—possibly even his life. On my side, this was a simple matter of needing his help to settle a property dispute. But on his side, my having tracked him down had the potential to reconnect him with an entire world he'd left behind. I didn't know if that was something he wanted. Perhaps he'd said good riddance to all things Amish—including his own family—the day he shook the dust off his feet and walked away. Judging by the letters he'd written to Joan over the years, however, it sounded as if he was open to hearing from her. I hoped the fact she was finally ready to respond would get me in the door even if nothing else could.

I rapped four gentle knocks on the weathered wood and then waited. Birdsong filled the silence. I was about to raise my hand again when the doorknob gave a turn and the door began to open.

I stepped back a little as the form of a bearded, silver-haired man filled the open space in front of me. Clayton Raber, in the flesh, at last. His features held such a scowl that for a moment I feared he was about to yell at me or slam the door in my face. But then I realized he wasn't angry at all. As Ben Sauder had told me, a scar ran along Clayton's brow line, causing him to look angry even when he was not.

"Can I help you?" he said, his tone doubtful but pleasant. The words were in *Englisch*, but I heard the slight inflection of Pennsylvania Dutch still lingering there.

"My name is Matthew Zook. I'm looking for Clayton Raber."

"Guess you found him, then," he said with a guarded half smile, one that contrasted strangely with the still-scowling eyebrows.

He wore a simple plaid shirt and navy blue work pants held up by suspenders, and on his nose perched a pair of wire-rim glasses that had to be decades old. And even though his clothing wasn't Amish, his beard still was, long and bushy and with no mustache. The grayness of the beard and the wrinkles on his face made Clayton look every bit of his eighty-seven years, and yet there was an odd, almost youthful hunger in his eyes. It was as if—even at his advanced age—he was still looking for something.

Surprise at seeing an Amish man on his doorstep may have had something to do with that. I had a feeling that not only had he not run across many Amish people around here over the years, he'd definitely not ever had one appear at his door.

"I'd like to speak with you if I may," I added, suddenly feeling tongue-tied. "I've come from Lancaster County."

"You're a ways from home," he said with just a twinge of sadness. I couldn't help but wonder if he used to tell those words to himself, a long time ago.

"It's actually not that far," I replied gently. When he said nothing in response, I explained that I'd had a bit of trouble tracking him down, but I'd finally gotten as far as Mountain Gap, where the folks at his church had been kind enough to direct me from there. "If it isn't too much trouble, Mr. Raber, I'd really like to talk to you. I need your help with something."

His eyes traveled down to the bundle in my arm. "Is that for me to fix? Because I'm retired, son. Have been for a decade. Didn't they tell you that at the church?"

"They did. I know you're retired now, and what I have in the bag isn't why I've come. It's just something I brought…" I hesitated, not wanting to get ahead of myself. My goal was to cover all of the property stuff first, just so we didn't get sidetracked, and then go into everything else after that. "Really, if we could sit down and chat briefly, I'll explain everything."

He stared at the bundle for a moment longer and then raised his gaze to meet mine. "But I don't fix things any more, my eyes aren't good enough. Sorry about that Mister…what did you say your name was?"

"Matthew. My name's Matthew Zook."

"And what part of Lancaster County are you from?"

I hesitated only a second. "Your part, Mr. Raber."

He cocked his head and his silver brows crinkled over questioning eyes.

"My grandfather was Isaac Zook. He bought your family homestead from your mother sixty years ago. I grew up in the same room in the same house as you."

He seemed to falter for just a moment. He teetered slightly as if I had just thrown open a window and a gust of wind had hit him in the face.

"I'm not from there anymore, Matthew," he said a second later. "I haven't been for a very long time. And I no longer fix things. Sorry I can't help you." He started to back away so that he could close the door. I put my hand out to stop him.

"Please, Mr. Raber. Please. I need your help to solve a problem—a *big* problem—one that was caused unknowingly by your mother when she sold the place to my grandfather. Now I've run into a complication, and you're the only person on earth who can help me."

He stared at me for a long moment. "Do you know who I am, young man?" he demanded, his tone an instant challenge.

"*Ya*, I know exactly who you are," I replied confidently, trying to match his belligerence with equal—if more respectful—intensity. "You're the man who was blamed for his wife's death even though it was an accident."

His eyes narrowed in anger. "What do you know about any of that?"

"I know you are innocent. I know you were declared guilty in the court of Amish opinion, excommunicated, and rejected even by your own family. I know you eventually left town and found a new place to start life over. And from what I've learned today, I know you have continued to love your late wife with fidelity and devotion all the years since."

His eyes grew wide, though I couldn't read the variety of emotions that were surely pinging around inside his head. Surprise. Vindication. Suspicion. Confusion. For a moment it looked as if it was all too much for him and he might just end up shutting the door in my face anyway.

"How in the world would *you* know that I am innocent?" he said, every word out of his mouth sounding as if they weighed ten pounds each. "You're just a kid. You weren't even alive back then."

"If you'll let me in, I'll tell you, I promise," I said quickly. "But I'm actually here for three reasons. The first is what I said before. It's something I need you to do for me, a legal matter involving a property dispute. I can explain things fully, and all I need is your signature on a document to clear everything up."

He seemed to consider that. "And the second?"

I looked down at the bag and then up again. "Well, sir, it has to do with something I found, something I think you'll want to see."

His lips pursed for a long moment. "And the third?"

"Your sister Joan. I came here with a message from her, that she is so very sorry for not having believed you all those years ago."

At the mention of his sister's name, the man at last moved aside and slowly swung the door open wide. Thanking him, I stepped into his living room, an unfussy but dusty space devoid of any fancy decorations or furnishings. The walls were a familiar Amish pastel green, and the couch—at least forty years old with threadbare arms—was upholstered in a darker version of the same color. The coffee table in front of it was of similar vintage and wear, as was a camel-colored armchair nearby. A Bible lay open on the table, along with a crossword puzzle magazine and a tattered Zane Grey Western. From the entry I could see his simple kitchen and eating area. A hallway to my right led to the back of the house.

Though he had electric lights, no television was in the room, nor were any telephones hanging from the walls that I could see. The whole place felt Amish with one major exception: It needed some serious tending to. It wasn't dirty, exactly. It just looked tired and neglected. Bonnie had been right about this place being too much for Clayton now.

The door closed behind us, and he motioned me toward the sofa, hobbling forward himself with the aid of a wooden cane I hadn't noticed before. I took my seat and Clayton eased himself into the armchair. As he settled, I could see that his hands were gnarled with arthritis earned through six decades of making and repairing clocks and other things. For some reason, however, I saw and heard no clocks in here at all.

He was quiet, his eyes on me as I gently set the bag onto the couch beside me and dug into it for the file I had brought. Though I needed to get to the point, I also wanted him to understand the gravity of my request, so I started with a little background.

"Like I said, I grew up in your old house, and I work in your old shop—though of course it hasn't been a clock shop since…since you left. My grandfather turned it into Zook's Tack and Feed after he bought it, as it still is to this day. I manage the store now, and I'm married with my first little one on the way. The whole place—your old place—is very special to me. It's going to be the homestead where I raise my own family."

I could see that he was imagining his former home as a haven of happiness for me as once upon a time it may have been for him. I explained the situation as clearly as I could, laying the conflicting maps on the table in his direction, followed by the quitclaim deed that would solve the entire problem if he would be willing to sign it.

"You do need to know," I added, "that the resort company wants the property pretty badly, and it sounds like they're willing to pay you handsomely for it. I can pay you too, if you feel like that's fair, but nowhere near as much as they can offer. I just want you to understand that up front. If you've been counting on using that property for yourself or selling it as a nest egg, I would understand if you want to deal with them rather than with me."

"I haven't been counting on anything," he said, his eyes on the papers. "I figured when my *mamm* sold the place, she sold my piece too and kept the money for both. As I would have told her to do if she'd asked." Looking up at me, he added, "But the fact that it got left out wasn't her fault, you understand. She didn't even know about this. It was a private matter between my *daed* and me."

I nodded, trying to remember what I'd learned from my conversation with Starbrite's lawyer, Mr. Purcell, and through the various reading I'd done at the library later. These sorts of issues were usually rooted out by title companies, but there wouldn't have been a need for a title company because my grandfather bought the place from Mrs. Raber in full, with no mortgage involved. And because she didn't know about the separate piece that belonged to Clayton, the whole incident had been a simple oversight by unaware parties and ultimately no one's fault. I explained as much to him now, but he surprised me with his response.

"Well, except perhaps mine, seeing as how I was the only person who even knew about that land, and I didn't say anything before I left. It didn't cross my mind at the time." Meeting my eyes, he added, "I can't take any money for something I thought was long gone sixty years ago. Where's a pen? If my name on that line can take care if this for you, I'm happy to sign."

Relief coursed through my veins, but I needed to be fair.

"Are you aware of the value of land in Lancaster County these days?" I asked him. "'Cause we're not just talking about a few hundred dollars here. I feel sure Starbrite would offer you at least a hundred *thousand* dollars, maybe even a hundred and fifty or more."

He looked startled for a moment, but then he smiled, an odd effect when combined with his scowling brow. "Are you aware of the value of setting up treasures in heaven?" he asked with a smile. "Because right is right, son. Now give me a pen."

I grinned in return. "I'm deeply grateful," I said, the understatement of the year. "But for the deed to be legal, you'll need to do the signing in the presence of a notary."

"All right. That's fine, as long as you can get one here or get me over to one. There's a lady in town who is probably open today. You got a driver out there, or did you get yourself all the way up here with your thumb, like I did?"

"My thumb?"

The old man held up a hand, fist clenched and thumb high, the universal signal of the hitchhiker. I laughed.

"No, sir. I have a driver. He dropped me off out front, and I told him to come back in about an hour."

"Well, then. That should give us enough time to cover the second and third reasons for your visit. The part that has something to do with my sister Joan and, I assume, whatever it is you have in that bag there with you."

He sat back in his chair, clasped his hands in his lap, and waited. I hesitated, deciding to explain about the Joan element first. After sixty years of estrangement, I felt sure that would matter even more to Clayton than the old clock we'd discovered in the coal bin.

I'd already told him that I'd had to do a little digging to track him down, so I started there, explaining that I'd gone to see Joan hoping she would have information about his whereabouts. I didn't mention the difficulty I'd had trying to get past his niece, fearing it might be hurtful to him. I figured he didn't need to know the extent of the bitterness which up until yesterday they'd still had toward him.

Instead, I explained how, after several visits to their house, Becky had finally decided to show me the letters Joan had received from him over the years.

"The very first letter mentioned the name of the church here, so that's what I decided to try next. I figured that even if you weren't still connected with that church, someone could tell me how to find you or at least where you'd gone next."

"Where I'd gone next? Where else would I go? This church has been my family." His expression grew distant, as if he were looking past me all the way to that first pastor and his wife who had taken him in—not to mention their daughter, who had become a loyal friend; to the man who had given him this inexpensive place to live; and to all the members of the congregation who had chosen to trust him rather than the sensationalized newspaper headlines of the day. He had spent sixty Christmases in their homes, and sixty birthday parties had been thrown for him. Love had been bestowed on him throughout the years long after the older generation who knew why he left Lancaster County had passed on. "They have been very good to me. They still are, even though I know I have become a tremendous burden to them these days."

"I don't think they see it like that," I offered. "It came across to me as concern."

He huffed. "That's just a nice way of saying I am starting to be a real pain. I'm far too much trouble, the way they keep having to come get me every Sunday, and to help me with the grocery shopping and the housekeeping and everything. They worry about me being out here all by myself in an old house with an overgrown yard and all that. The homeowner handles repairs and such, but the little stuff is still up to me, even if *I'm* not up to *it*." He shook his head slowly. "Not sure what'll happen from here, but I figure the good Lord knows, and that's all that matters."

I hesitated, thinking of Detective De Lucca yesterday and the facility where he would be spending the rest of his days. As an Amish man, I'd never quite understood the need for nursing homes, but as I looked at Clayton now, it made sense. Where else was an *Englischer* to go when he could no longer live alone but had no family around to live with?

The church people here had been a huge help to Clayton over the years, yes, but they were not Amish. They had not been raised as he and I had, to take the biblical command of caring for the elderly literally. They might help him out, but they weren't going to step up to the extent he now needed.

With a surge of guilt, I thought of the money he was giving up by signing over his land to me at no charge. If he sold the place to Starbrite instead, I realized, he would have enough to put himself in one of those kinds of places that De Lucca was in, where he could live comfortably for the rest of his life.

Somehow, though, just the thought of it made me feel sick inside. Old people belonged in families, not shoved off together in some institution. I decided not to say anything about it yet, though I would bring it up later before he signed on the bottom line and ended up signing away the one solution currently available to him.

"Anyway," I continued, "when I talked to Joan yesterday, she was pretty upset, saying how bad she feels for the way she'd treated you back then and for not believing you when you said you were innocent. She asked me to tell you that she is sorry and to see if there was any way you could bring yourself to forgive her."

Clayton's eyes filled with tears, but he blinked them away. "I forgave her and the rest of my family long ago. I had to. I couldn't live with the poison of bitterness toward them. It is not how God would have had me live. Joan was no different from anyone else. Everyone thought I killed Miriam. They thought I was an angry, violent man whose wife didn't love him, so he killed her. The police just couldn't prove it."

"You never thought of returning?"

I could tell by the way he looked at me that he had, maybe early on, but in the end he couldn't bring himself to do it.

"Return to what? There was nothing there for me but blame and unforgiveness for something I hadn't done. What kind of life would that have been? Am I not still spoken of as the clockmaker who killed his wife?"

Even as he said this, I bristled. "Not in my house," I said, with conviction. "You are *not* spoken of that way in my house." As an afterthought, I added, "But *ya*, that's pretty much what people say."

He shook his head sadly. "At least Joan and some of the family members gave me the benefit of the doubt somewhat. They said they knew I hadn't *wanted* to kill Miriam, but that it just happened in a moment of jealous rage. Like everyone else, they thought she was in love with another man and that's why I pushed her."

A storm cloud was gathering behind his eyes as he continued. "I saw it in their faces once I came home from jail. The charges had been dropped, but that made no difference. People still thought I'd done it. Even my own mother, who knew how much I loved Miriam, thought that I'd been angry, got caught up in the moment, and pushed her." He cleared his throat. "Everyone thought I was guilty—everyone."

We were both quiet for a few moments, and I could feel righteous indignation pulsing in my veins for this wronged man.

"I did not push her," he said, enunciating each syllable. "I reached out for her as she tried to run past me, and she whirled away and fell. She was…I don't know what she was. After she lost the child, she started acting strangely, like something was inside her head whispering lies to her. She was not herself that day, and she hadn't been since she lost the baby. I knew something was wrong, but everyone else thought there was an issue with our marriage, that we both wanted out because there was no longer any need for it once the baby was gone. But that wasn't it! I loved Miriam! I *wanted* to be married to her. I always had. I wanted the child too. I wanted a big family and a long and happy life together. Even if she had stayed sick that way, like she was, I would have taken care of her. I loved her, whether something was the matter with her mind or not."

I sat up straight, my heart pounding at the thought that I'd forgotten to tell him that part. Becky still had the brochure, but I remembered most of what it said.

"Miriam *was* sick, Clayton. Have you ever heard of something called postpartum psychosis?"

His sad eyes widened. "What did you say?"

"It's a medical condition. It's very rare but it can happen to a woman who's had a baby—or lost a baby, for that matter. Someone who has the condition will perceive things differently from the way they really are. A woman who has it will act out in ways that aren't like her at all. She might get aggressive or hear things that aren't there or even see things that don't exist. I just learned about it the other day, but as soon as I did, I realized it was probably what was wrong with Miriam back then. That's why she was acting the way she was. She probably developed postpartum psychosis after she lost the baby."

Clayton seemed to need a minute to process this.

"I can't believe I didn't know."

"I don't think that's anything you can blame yourself for. People didn't understand that sort of thing back then like they do now."

"She really was sick," he said in a whisper, to himself. "I knew that. I *knew* it. I knew it all along."

Thirty-Eight

Clayton was so rattled by all by all he'd learned that I offered to make him a cup of tea. He accepted gratefully, probably more because he wanted some time to himself than because he needed something hot to drink. That was fine with me. I could use a moment too.

Poking around in the small kitchen, I started some water to boil and managed to find what I needed in the cabinets. Five minutes later, I carried the steaming cup of tea back into the living room and set it on the coffee table in front of my host. As I resumed my seat on the couch, I saw that he still looked somewhat dazed, but after a few sips, he seemed to focus back in on me. Obviously wishing to change the subject, he asked what I had in the bag, so I pulled out the clock and unwrapped it.

"Oh my!" he murmured, almost as if he were seeing a ghost.

"This is your handiwork, isn't it?" I leaned forward and carefully placed the beautiful timepiece in his lap. "It has your initials on it, along with a reference to a Bible verse about time. I've seen these initials before, carved into the cover of the window seat in your old bedroom."

He nodded. "'To everything there is a season, and a time to every purpose under the heaven.' Ecclesiastes 3:1," he said. "I put that verse on all my clocks."

Clayton ran his hand along the inlaid wood design on the front panel, an incredulous expression on his face.

"I remember making this," he said in wonderment, his eyes taking in the gleaming reddish-brown wood of the case. "It took something like eleven or twelve different woods to create this design. The woman who ordered it couldn't make up her mind about anything. Took her three days just to pick which chimes she wanted."

His eyes were closed, and he was smiling as if he were listening to the music of the chimes now. In that moment, it wasn't hard at all to picture the man in his element, building stunning creations like this one and selling them to folks who would treasure them for generations to come.

"This was one of Miriam's very favorite clocks I ever made," he said when he opened his eyes again. "She would sit and watch me work on it for hours. That made me feel kind of self-conscious at first, but after a while I'd get so caught up in what I was doing that I'd forget she was there. Then some movement or noise would remind me, and I'd come back to the moment. And then I'd glance her way, and for just an instant I might see a look on her face, one that almost felt like love to me." Clayton's smile faded. "That's what I told myself anyway."

When he spoke again, his voice held such melancholy and his old eyes glistened with emotion. "She was fond of me, quite fond, but she really didn't love me, you know," he said, not meeting my eyes. "That much of what people said about us was true. I believe she respected my work, and she enjoyed being with me, and my opinions mattered to her. She treasured our friendship, and I always felt like she would learn to love me over time. But if not, that was okay. I figured I loved her enough for the both of us."

I was surprised by his admission—not just that it might be true, but that he was still willing to admit it all these years later. How painful it must have been to love a woman so much and know your love was not returned.

He dabbed at his eyes, cleared his throat, and seemed to come back to the present. His gaze returned to the clock. "The lady who ordered this was from out of state. Somewhere down south—Georgia or Florida, I think. How in the world did you come by it?"

Now I was the one completely taken aback. All along, I'd been thinking Clayton was the one who had hidden the clock in the coal bin. He'd made it, after all, and it was his clock shop. But I could see now by the look on his face that this was not the case.

"I found it hidden in the back room of the clock shop."

"You *what*?"

"It was buried in the old coal bin in the wall of the back room. I assumed you'd put it there yourself."

"That can't be…" he murmured.

Was he doubting my word?

"I assure you, Mr. Raber, that's where I found it. The day we began the expansion, we were taking down a wall and uncovered the old coal bin. I didn't think anything of it, but a few days later my wife noticed it and was curious, and when she opened the door of the bin to look inside, this clock was down in there."

His already frowning brows shifted even lower. "I just don't see how that can be possible."

"You weren't the one who put it there?"

"Why would I put such a finely crafted timepiece inside a filthy metal bin full of coal dust?"

"Actually, someone had cleaned out all of the coal dust. The clock was wrapped up in a blanket and put down in there."

Clayton shook his head. "This doesn't make any sense at all. The woman who bought this clock was staying at a nearby hotel, and she would slip over to the clock shop while her husband was playing golf." His voice grew almost defensive, as if he wanted to make sure I knew he wasn't crazy. "I spent quite a lot of time with her, designing it. Look, she even wanted this drawer with a recessed latch for hiding away her husband's tobacco."

Lifting the piece with his gnarled old hands, Clayton ran a finger along the side, where the design featured a series of rectangles within rectangles, all inlaid with various colors of wood. But when he got to one rectangle, he pushed it with his thumb and it slid out sideways, revealing a small latch underneath. One push of the latch, and with a gentle sound of a tiny spring, the entire lower front panel popped forward, opening like a drawer. I gasped at the cleverness of the design and the fact that neither Amanda nor I had spotted it ourselves. I was about to say just that when I realized that something was inside the drawer. Clayton saw it too.

"What on earth?" he mumbled as he pulled out what looked like a letter. After studying the envelope for a moment, he thrust it toward me, saying his eyes weren't so good anymore and would I please take a look and tell him what it said.

"I can see enough to know that the letter is addressed to me," he told me. "But what's the name in the return address?"

"Mrs. Homer Upton, Two River Road, Coral Gables, Florida."

"Upton! That's it! That's the name of the woman who ordered the clock! Pull it out, son. Is it a letter? What does it say?"

I reached inside the envelope and pulled out a single folded sheet of paper. Opening it up, I saw that it was dated October 9, 1955, and had been written out in a tight, feminine script. Holding it toward the light, I squinted my eyes and tried to make out the words.

Dear Mr. Raber,

I regret to inform you that my beloved husband, Homer, passed away five days ago, just three weeks before our fortieth anniversary. Because of this, I am sure you will understand that I am canceling the order for the clock. I have no doubt it is quite beautiful, but I fear it would only bring me great pain to see it now, especially as he is no longer here for me to give it to.

I realize you have already gone to a lot of trouble to make it, so I am not expecting a full refund. Please return to me by check whatever amount you think is fair. I will not think poorly of you if you decide you are unable to offer even a partial refund. I know you are an honest businessman and will handle the matter as you see fit. Thank you for all of your help, and again, I apologize.

Sincerely yours,
Florence Upton

I looked over at Clayton, but he seemed as confused as I was. Why would a letter canceling an order for a clock be inside that very clock? It just didn't make sense.

We were both quiet for a minute, our minds racing, but then he spoke, and I realized he may have figured something out.

"Of course. Miriam. She was the one who processed the mail. She was the one who adored this clock. She was the one who drove into town the day after it was finished and had it shipped off to the Uptons." His eyes met mine, but I could not read the emotions there. "Miriam had…she had a fascination for fancy things. She struggled greatly with her desire to own stuff an Amish woman should not have. She had hidden items from me in the past so I wouldn't take them away from her. Not long after we were married, I caught her with trinkets her *Englisch* employer had given her. She'd been hiding them away in a trunk up in the…in the hayloft. I insisted she get rid of them—and she did. But I'm thinking that all those months later, when this letter came in from Mrs. Upton, the temptation was simply too great. Miriam never said a word to me about the order being canceled, probably because she realized she could keep the clock for herself if she said nothing. She was probably waiting until I was finished with it and then just pretended to send it off. In truth, she must have hidden it away in the coal bin instead."

"But it's a mantel clock. It belongs displayed on a shelf or mantel. How could she enjoy having it if was shoved in the bottom of an old, unused coal bin?"

Clayton shook his head sadly from side to side. "You would have to have known her to understand. She couldn't resist beautiful things. She needed to *possess* them. And though it was a great spiritual struggle for her, I have to admit…" He shook his head again, only this time I realized that he was smiling. "Shame on me for saying it, but I have to admit that it almost feels good, knowing that the fancy item she chose to hang on to that way was something that had been made by me."

His words made perfect sense. Glad that he had figured it out, I returned the letter to its envelope and handed it back over to him. It wasn't until he was about to place it back inside the little hidden drawer that he realized something else was there. Clayton set aside Mrs. Upton's note and carefully removed a second envelope from the drawer.

It was a pale lavender color and seemed to have no address or postmark or stamp on the front. Instead, only one word was written there in a flowing script: *Clayton.*

The old clockmaker looked so shocked that I feared he might drop the clock. I jumped up from my seat to set it on the coffee table. Then I sat back down and watched as with shaking hands, Clayton opened the envelope and pulled out three matching lavender pages from inside.

"Mr. Raber, are you okay? What is it?" His face had gone completely white and his hands were trembling violently.

Without a word, he held out the pages to me.

"Miriam wrote this to me," he whispered. "Read it to me."

"Are you sure you don't—"

"Read it!" he commanded in a voice so loud and hoarse that it almost made me jump. "I'm sorry," he added a second later, his tone somewhat softer and his eyes brimming with tears. "I can't see to read it. *Please.*"

On his face I could see both fear and excitement, dread and anticipation. Who knew what these pages might hold? Part of me couldn't wait to find out, though another part wished the man's eyesight were better so that he could do this alone, without me having to be any part of it.

My own hands were shaking a bit as I looked down at the pages that had been scribed on both sides with delicate handwriting. The weathered stationery felt soft to my fingers, as though the years in hiding had turned its fibers into flannel.

I began to read.

Dearest Clayton,

I can't seem to find the words to tell you to your face what I want you to know, so I am writing them in a letter. I'm not sure when I will show this to you, or even if I will. Sometimes it just helps to put my thoughts down on paper, and this is one of those times.

For many weeks now I've been thinking that I should never have let my parents talk you into marrying me. You are sweet and kind and the best friend I have ever had, and you deserve better than me.

Somehow, even if it takes me years to figure it out, I will find a way to be the wife you deserve.

I don't know how to tell you that in the past month or so, my mind had been working on a terrible plan. The plan was that I was going to wait until the baby was born—which is still a few months away as I write this—and then I was going to leave you, and in fact leave Lancaster County. If I weren't so afraid of bringing this baby into the world all on my own, I would have already left before now. I have no idea where I thought I would go, only that I was taking my child in the hopes of the two of us starting life anew elsewhere.

But then this morning I overheard you and your mamm arguing in the mudroom, when she told you to go to the bishop and tell him I was being unfaithful. To my shock, you defended not only my honor but my broken, wounded heart. I was on the stairs, and all I could do was run back to our room with my hand on my mouth to cover my sobs so neither one of you would hear. Your love for me, despite all I have done and all that I am, absolutely astonishes me. In that moment, I realized that the very last thing on earth I wanted to do was to leave you or to leave this marriage.

I want so much to love you the way you love me, Clayton. And it's the wanting to that has me struggling to find the words to tell you this to your face. For the first time in my life, I think I am beginning to understand what real love is. I see you choosing to love me, every day, even when no one else around us can fathom why. Your love for me is deeper, purer, and stronger than anything I have ever known, and you have lavished it on me when I've least deserved it. How can I not respond in love back to you? I am learning to love you like that, Clayton. I can already sense the change in my feelings toward you.

I've been very sad about having to get rid of the Englisch treasures you saw in the hayloft, and I can't promise such a thing won't happen again. If other beautiful items come my way in the future, I know I'll be tempted to hang on to them. But I also know that it's wrong of me, especially because then I'm forced to hide them from you. I promise I am working to conquer this longing to have what is not mine to have. I pray for strength, and though God has not delivered me from my love of worldly possessions, He has blessed me in other ways tenfold.

You are my biggest blessing.

You are the best man I know.

You always have been.

It is because you are this good man that I must ask something very hard of you. If anything should happen to me during childbirth, would you please raise up the infant yourself to be the kind of person you are? If God takes me, my parents will think you will not want this baby, but I know that if I ask this of

you, you will do it out of that love for me that has me
speechless before you.

   Just a little while ago you caught me with this letter,
and even though I have given you reasons not to trust
me in the past, you have given me your trust anyway.
Every time you do something such as that, my heart
grows closer to yours and my soul understands more
than ever before what true love really looks like.

   I am trying, Clayton. Someday, I will be the wife
you deserve, I promise.

   Miriam

When I was finished reading, I looked over at Clayton and saw that he was leaning forward, his eyes closed, his elbows on his knees. Gnarled hands cradled his ancient face. It seemed such a private moment that I was witnessing and yet I could not bring myself to step away and leave the old man alone.

For the last sixty years, Clayton Raber had quietly maintained his integrity, his identity, and the love he had for his wife in the only way he thought he could. In near solitude. For the last sixty years, he had thought he alone had been the one to love. Now he knew the truth.

Miriam had loved him in return.

Clayton was quiet for most of the drive into town and back again, though he managed to put on a friendly enough face for the notary public. After a week of my running around like crazy, all it had taken in the end to settle the entire property dispute was the quick signing of a name followed by the notary's signature and seal. As I paid the woman and she handed the now-official quitclaim deed back to me, I put my hand on Clayton's shoulder and gave it a squeeze. There were no adequate words to describe my gratitude for what he had just done.

We didn't say a lot on the ride back, but it wasn't an awkward silence. He and I had already shared so much in this day that in a sense we'd gone from strangers to the closest of friends in the space of just a few hours. That thought shouldn't have surprised me, I supposed, as I had felt a bond with him ever since I was a young boy.

Maybe it was because of this bond—or because of all I had seen and heard today, or because I just really liked him as a person—but the closer we got to his house, the heavier my heart began to grow. It sounded odd, but now that I had found him, I wasn't ready to let him go.

The driver must have sensed my reluctance, because just before he turned onto the road that would lead us to Clayton's house, he gestured toward the ice-cream stand, which was still open, and asked if we'd like to make a stop first.

"Can I buy you a scoop of rocky road, Clayton?" I asked.

"Actually, pistachio is my favorite," he replied, a bit wearily but with a tiny grin.

I bought one for the driver as well, and the three of us sat at one of several picnic tables under a nearby tree. The birds were singing, the sun was shining and the cold, sweet treat was refreshing on this hot summer day.

Once we were finished, I helped Clayton back to the car. As I was holding the door open for him, easing him inside, it struck me how much he reminded me of my grandfather. Somehow, being with Clayton Raber made me miss *Grossdaadi* just a little bit less. And that was a good thing.

When we arrived at the house, I told the driver I wouldn't be long. As I walked Clayton down the path to the door, I thanked him again for what he had done for me in signing over the property. He assured me that what I had done for him was worth infinitely more. Seeing the deep look of peace in his eyes, I knew that must be true.

Despite my satisfaction over all that had taken place during our time together today, as the older man unlocked the door and fumbled for the light, I found myself feeling overwhelmed with a sense of loss and despair.

Something in me did not want to go. The thought of leaving him here in a house that was slowly coming apart, to live out his days all alone, so far from where he had begun, cut me to the core. I wouldn't be able to pop in and visit him anytime I wanted. To the *Englisch*, eighty miles was a perfectly reasonable distance to travel, but to the Amish, it was logistically a world way.

Clayton finally found the light and flipped it on, and then he turned and stood in the doorway facing me, the two of us in the exact same spots where we'd met just a few hours before. We shared a smile, one that went far beyond words, and then I knew beyond a shadow of a doubt what God would have me do for Clayton Raber.

In a flash I understood why I had been so desperate in my search for him—a desperation that went beyond the scope of a critical property issue. I also knew why I'd been destined to expand the tack shop, so that I would find the old clock and Miriam's letter *now*, and not five or ten years from now when it might have been too late. I knew with complete certainty that God had led me to Clayton so that the man could be restored to his Amish faith, and so that he could have what every devoted husband desired and deserved—to be buried next to the wife he loved in life. I had arrived at just the right time. And if there was anything that a clockmaker could be made to understand, it was time.

He thanked me again for coming, adding, "I know why the good Lord led you here, Matthew. So you could bring peace to an old man in his final days."

Shaking my head, I couldn't help but grin. "This may sound strange, but I think there's another reason God sent me here."

His eyes met mine and he smiled with curiosity. "Oh? And what might that be?"

My smile grew even wider as I pictured Clayton and his sister reuniting at last, Clayton going before the deacons and hearing them welcome him back and asking for his forgiveness. And if there was no place for him at the Helmuths or among other family members, I could easily see him with us instead. I imagined sharing him with Amanda and my parents, building him a *daadi haus* out behind the cottage, taking him to worship and watching him meet his dozens of nieces and nephews, and hearing him sing the old hymns in German. I pictured placing my newborn child in his arms, and, Lord willing, in a year or two another one. Then watching—as the years might roll on—my children climbing onto his lap for a bedtime story. And then on some future day, laying his body next to Miriam's, in the cemetery over the rise from the place where he grew up.

I held his gaze tight on mine. "He sent me to bring you home."

DISCUSSION QUESTIONS

1. This book features two related story lines, one set in the present day and one set back in the 1950s. By seeing what really happened through Clayton's eyes rather than secondhand, through Matthew only, did the story come more alive for you?

2. Why do you think Matthew always felt such a bond of kinship with the infamous clockmaker? What elements of the story end up strengthening that bond?

3. Do you think Clayton would have become a different person had he not been in the buggy accident when he was young? How much are people shaped by what they experience as children?

4. As a clockmaker, Clayton tends to view many things in his life in terms of clocks and how they function. Did any of his various clock-related metaphors resonate with you personally? Which was your favorite?

5. How would you describe Clayton's love for his wife? Did she deserve that love? Was Clayton's love blind or did he see the

reality of the situation but somehow love her anyway? Have you known love like that, or have you seen it in practice?

6. Clayton's community was ready to believe he had murdered his wife. Why do you think that was so? Why do old legends regarding someone's downfall or supposed crime tend to linger?

7. Do you think Clayton and his wife would have ended up having a happy, fulfilling marriage had circumstances played out differently? Why or why not?

8. Soon after leaving Lancaster County, Clayton encounters a kind pastor who is aware of the man's alleged crime but chooses to believe in his innocence anyway. Was this a reflection of the pastor's faith, or was it simply because he was a good judge of character? How much did his gift of discernment play into his decision to take Clayton in? Would you have acted similarly in such a situation?

9. Matthew struggles to trust his heavenly Father because he has learned the hard way that he cannot always trust his earthly father. How much of our relationship with our fathers plays into how we feel about and approach God? How would you compare your relationship with your dad to your relationship with the Lord?

10. Near the end of the story, Matthew imagines Clayton moving back to Lancaster County, getting reconnected with his community, cuddling Matthew's soon-to-be-born child, and later, being laid to rest next to the woman he loved. Do you think this would be a possible scenario for Clayton's life? Why or why not?

Mindy Starns Clark is the bestselling author of numerous books, both fiction and nonfiction, including *The Amish Midwife* (cowritten with Leslie Gould), *The Amish Groom* and *The Amish Blacksmith* (cowritten with Susan Meissner), *Whispers of the Bayou, Under the Cajun Moon,* and *Shadows of Lancaster County,* as well as the popular Million Dollar Mysteries. An *RT Book Club Magazine's* 2011 Career Achievement Award winner, Mindy's numerous honors also include a Christy Award and an Inspirational Reader's Choice Award. She lives with her husband, John, and two daughters near Valley Forge, Pennsylvania. You can connect with Mindy at her website: www.mindystarnsclark.com.

Susan Meissner is a multipublished author, speaker, and writing workshop leader with a background in community journalism. Her novels include *The Shape of Mercy,* named by *Publishers Weekly* as one of the 100 Best Novels of 2008 and a Carol Award winner. She is a pastor's wife and the mother of four young adults. When she's not writing novels, Susan writes small group curriculum for her San Diego church. Visit Susan at her website: www.susanmeissner.com, on Twitter at @SusanMeissner, or at www.facebook.com/susan.meissner.